THE MANUSCRIPTS
OF
PAULINE ARCHANGE

Marie-Claire Blais

THE MANUSCRIPTS
OF
PAULINE ARCHANGE

Translated by
DEREK COLTMAN AND DAVID LOBDELL

Introduction by
BARRY CALLAGHAN

Exile Editions

Ɛ

Publishers of singular
Fiction, Poetry, Translation, Drama, Nonfiction and Graphic Books

2009

Library and Archives Canada Cataloguing in Publication

Blais, Marie-Claire, 1939-
[Manuscrits de Pauline Archange. English]
    The manuscripts of Pauline Archange / Marie-Claire Blais ; translated
by Derek Coltman and David Lobdell ; introduction by Barry Callaghan.

(Exile classics series ; 15)
Includes a translation of: Manuscrits de Pauline Archange, and also a
translation of Les apparences, under the title Dürer's angel.

ISBN 978-1-55096-131-7

    I. Coltman, Derek II. Lobdell, David III. Title. IV. Title: Durer's
angel. V. Series: Exile classics no. 15

PS8503.L33M313 2009   C843'.54   C2009-905677-1

Design and Composition by Digital ReproSet
Cover Photograph by permission of Robert Kohlhuber / iStockphoto
Typeset in Garamond and Bembo at the Moons of Jupiter Studios
Printed in Canada by Gauvin Imprimerie

The publisher would like to acknowledge the financial assistance of
The Canada Council for the Arts and the Ontario Arts Council.

Conseil des Arts   Canada Council
du Canada   for the Arts

ONTARIO ARTS COUNCIL
CONSEIL DES ARTS DE L'ONTARIO

Published in Canada in 2009 by Exile Editions Ltd.
144483 Southgate Road 14
General Delivery
Holstein, Ontario, N0G 2A0
info@exileeditions.com
www.ExileEditions.com

Canadian Sales Distribution: U.S. Sales Distribution:
McArthur & Company   Independent Publishers Group
c/o Harper Collins   814 North Franklin Street
1995 Markham Road   Chicago, IL 60610
Toronto, ON M1B 5M8   www.ipgbook.com
toll free: 1 800 387 0117   toll free: 1 800 888 4741

INTRODUCTION

Marie-Claire Blais: Beside an Empty Ladder

In Montreal, I sat down with Marie-Claire Blais for a light lunch at the Ritz Hotel. She had just published *Dürer's Angel*, the final book of *The Manuscripts of Pauline Archange*, and we had agreed to meet in the elegant outdoor garden café, tables arranged around a small pond, an easeful gaiety in the air, not just because there were so many fine ladies and their men all in sunlight but because of the dozen or so yellow ducklings pedalling around the pond.

Marie-Claire, my old friend, was wearing a nicely tailored maroon jacket with black trousers and a pale blue silk scarf at her throat. She was without makeup except for a smoky black line around her eyes. The line set off the paleness of her skin. She seemed, in her body, almost passive, waiting in an unassuming stillness to talk about her book, but there was an attentive intensity to her shadowed eye.

She laughed as she took another drink. "But Barry, you must take care – to drink so much, we are a danger to ourselves."

I laughed and said, "Of course we are."

She wagged her small hand at me, not in judgment, but out of her concern for a frailty she sees in those around her.

"Take care. We are too passionate. Because of course it is our fate to be separate, it is who we must be."

"You know, after reading your Pauline book, I was thinking about us, and what probably happens to us as writers is that as children we are persecuted by words and our dreams, and like your Pauline, we grow up with our family and we are forced to lead a double life. Look at Pauline: she realizes that by feeding her dreams, her own fantasies, her own stories, that she is betraying her family. She's engaged in an act of treachery."

"I do think," she said, the rhythm of her very good English just a little stilted, "that this is the condition of the artist."

"And about Pauline" – and I felt a little awkward saying this – "there's a lot of Pauline in you, right, your younger self – as Pauline tells the lies we love to read, the dark lies that are her novels, she is also engaged in lying to those who are closest to her."

"Yes, yes. Today, to write novels, confronted by all the temptations of life, with our own trepidation, for the writer to actually concentrate, to think, to be observant, the writer has to retreat. It is amazing. You are with your friends, you are not with your friends. You always betray . . ."

"Is this what your Jean-Le Maigre, the poet, means when he says he wears a crown of lice?"

"Yes, by nature he was born to retreat into himself."

"He went down into the damn cellar."

"Yes," and she drew her scarf closer to her throat.

"So, if I read you right, the writer's got to go down into the cellar of his own darkness to get his work done. And what Pauline says of herself, working within her own darkness, is that she believes she was actually born into the story she is compelled to write. I mean, she's like those little ducklings there in the pond . . ."

"(. . . ?)"

She stared at me. I'd lost her, so I explained, "See, they can't be anything other than ducklings, she can't be anything other than her story, but realizing that, what she hopes to do, see, by writing about her pain, is to free herself from her own story, to escape the blood-letting by standing knee-deep in the blood . . ."

"But don't you think that this is true of everybody who writes," she said, "writes with the awareness of his own blood and flesh? Dostoievsky wrote with his blood, and without his pain, without that humiliation, his work would not exist."

"That's what Pauline says, too," I said. "That if you hadn't produced your novels, you'd be threatened with the sense of never having existed, for anyone."

"Well, maybe I could not live without the writing."

She said this with stern conviction, but also with a gentleness of tone that belied the sternness in her eye.

"So what is on the page," I said, "is the writer's way out, the public admission of one's pain . . ."

"Yes, it is a freedom, when it is out . . ."

"So, the only possibility if you're not writing is . . . what?"

"Look," she said, throwing her head back, wanting to break for a moment the tenor of our little talk, "life in itself is wonderful. Look at us here. In this garden."

We ordered another drink. She was drinking gin. I was drinking cognac. It was three in the afternoon.

"Just to be alive," she said forcefully, "just to live every day is wonderful enough. But writing gives a value to this life, to my life, a life that would otherwise be, let us say, not full."

"Or, too full of a suffering and a violence that allows for no escape."

"Perhaps," she said.

The yellow ducklings were darting in two's and three's between water lily pads in the pond, feeding.

"Your Pauline says that the sap that feeds her books, it is unjust violence . . ."

"Well," she smiled, as if she had been asked to explain that which needed no explanation, "we feed off each other from the moment we are born. A child feeds off his mother, children are starved of their dreams . . ."

"This voraciousness," I said, playing with one of Pauline's words, "is it something in nature itself? Is it something that comes out of poverty? Is it something that comes out of simply being born? That gives rise to monstrousness?"

"This monstrousness, that was in my earlier books, *La Belle Bête, Tête Blanche*, but not so much recently."

"Not in *Pauline Archange?*"

"The people in this book are people with what I would call weaknesses, people with human vices, but they are not monstrous people. I would not say so."

"Some act savagely."

"Well, the priest maybe . . ."

"The priest, the nuns . . ."

"Yes."

"They're kind of half-demented in their brutality."

"I denounce, yes," she said with sudden great firmness, "I denounce ferociously any violence against innocent human beings, or against animals. That brutality is a shock to me. But then we also have people who are more subtle. They are not monsters, they are people with difficult weaknesses. Even the priest in *The Manuscripts* is a compassionate man. He has carnal desire that may be repellant but he is not a brutal person. He is, as a matter of fact, weak, and extremely sensitive to pain. He's contradictory. You have people who are carnally weak, who are culpable, who are also compassionate, even very generous, all at the same time. That is what is so interesting for me as a novelist. There are so many levels to human nature. So many contradictions. Contradictions are what fascinate me."

"Talk about contradiction," I said. "There's a point where that crazy priest talks about pity. In his world, what we do is hunt each other down, like panting animals in the jungle, but for him there is always something more than the bestial call. There is something weirdly fraternal, lacerating, and it is pity, the capacity for tenderness, and apparently it is this capacity that we must judge in a person if we are to judge at all."

Another cognac.

"Well, I did believe that when I wrote it."

"Not now?"

"Well, I do think that pity can be treacherous, too. Perhaps we are always trapped. To be trapped, that's a terrible thing, but we must risk it . . ."

"Like the boy who wants to be the redeemer in *The Wolf*, but that attempt at redemption . . ."

Another gin.

"He is a potential wolf."

"So, now, in your new work you are dealing with people who have potential, who are acutely aware of their own sensibilities, and they are trying to find the courage to love, but they are thwarted as they try for tenderness because they deceive themselves . . . ?"

"Yes, yes, that's true, but then so many people just don't live at all. They don't try to have any passion. They have no passion. They are just neutral. That's real tragedy."

"But your people are all acting on the urge . . ."

"Of awareness. But that awareness, though it is there for a moment, several moments, it is betrayed by itself. It fails. It is grim. We try to be angels but we are tied to the earth."

"And the urge is toward consolation."

"I am not sure we are very good at it."

"You mean, no matter how hard we try, an empty ladder stands beside us . . ."

She only smiled sadly, and then laughed, and we ordered more drinks and she sat in her stillness, absorbed for a moment

in her own thoughts, and I watched the ducklings dart and circle on the surface of the water, and then she said, " You must be
careful, to drink while feeling such melancholy, and to live such
passion . . ."

⸾⸾⸾

There is an empty ladder that stands in *Dürer's Angel*, the
third book of *The Manuscripts of Pauline Archange*, and that
ladder appears in her description of Dürer's woodcut, *Melancholia*:

"The details of that magnificent *Melancholia* came rising slowly
to the surface of my mind as I stood there beside my mother,
drying the dishes, the sullen, unruly angel lost in contemplation, his big fist pressed against his cheek, his hair crowned
with flowers that resembled thorns... Seated on the rough,
ancient earth, his wings were open but he did not fly... In him,
all was violent and passionate meditation, but this was a violence that would be appeased only in labour... When a simple-
minded nun said, ''Genius verges on madness,' I sensed that...
it was in the face of such misunderstanding that the spirit of
Dürer seemed to me so sad, so vulnerable... An empty ladder
stood near the angel, and beyond, the dawn rose over the sea,
though the angel was not looking in that direction. His gaze
spoke of uncompromising and practical thoughts, and indeed,
his appearance bore a closer resemblance to that of a solitary
labourer than an angel. The place in which he meditated,
moreover, was not a peaceful or a restful one; it was a humble
workshop where the entire fervour of his immense genius
would shortly awaken. But awaiting that moment, he brooded
alone, his only companion a dog whose bones could be seen
through its mangy coat and who seemed to share the anxious

thoughts of its master, though it feigned sleep. At the angel's feet lay a hammer and saw. Several nails glittered in the shadows."

⌘

Nails glittering in the shadows.

Flowers that resemble thorns.

Melancholy.

For some readers, a dankness of the heart.

Yet there is something compelling in Marie-Claire Blais' stories, in her way of looking at things.

What is it that makes her prose compelling?

The answer, I believe, is this: Think of all the great children's stories.

The children in these stories are the supreme realists. They see with an unblinking eye, just as Blais sees with an unblinking eye. To children, a man the size of a thumb is a man the size of a thumb. Hunger is hunger. Violence is violence, and because it is nearly always arbitrary, the violence can be monstrous, but it can also, because it is so arbitrary, be hilarious (BLAM and SPLAT out of NOWHERE).

Children see saints who are at heart whores and whores who are at heart saints, they are loved by grandmothers who are malevolent and prayed for by priests who are pedophiles . . . and sometimes what they see is almost slapstick, as when the winter comes in Pauline's house and the family's washing is hung over the supper table, so that droplets of water land on their noses while they eat and "Monsieur Poire, rising from the table with the tyrannic majesty of a drunkard, suddenly had his head imprisoned in the leg of his pyjamas" . . . but then, and always, no matter the grimness or the slapstick . . . if they are children like Oscar in *The Tin Drum*, they stand apart, separate, wearing their crowns of lice, and they spend the rest of their lives madly beating on their drums . . .

There is all of this in Blais' novels. Each book is her drum. Rat-a-tat-tat . . . she says what she sees. Monsters come. Saints and pedophiles go. But, and this is key, there is no call of any kind for retribution.

Quite the opposite.

Blais sees and names those who are broken, those who are stunted by a depravity of spirit, and she describes it all with an unblinking eye. But she refuses to pass judgment.

As the supreme realist, she offers not scorn, not condemnation, but compassion.

This is disconcerting because it is like being offered compassion by a guileless child who is wise beyond adult years.

And, moreover, it is a compassion conveyed in a very particular style, her own style.

A style that is all her own because – in her eye – in Pauline's narrative eye – Pauline not only sees everything for herself but she sees everything that all the other characters see, too, often in the same sentence. It is as if Huck Finn, while telling his story from his point of view, also became Aunt Polly and told her story and then became Jim and told his story, too, saying what they saw as if he'd seen it for them.

If it is true, and I believe it is, that Huck's voice is so believable because nothing stands between his eye and the reader's eye, then Pauline is believable because nothing stands between her all-inclusive eye – and the reader's eye.

This is not faux-Proust, as some have suggested.

This is pure Blais, and the only thing that has changed over the years is that the Blais eye has ranged further afield, and the sentences, the flow of what the narrative eye is seeing, have grown more assured, longer, braver.

The world has indeed become her intoxication, her oyster.

⋙

In the Bible, the prophet is exhorted to LIVE IN THE BLOOD. In the work of Blais, the blood is in the WORD, and it is in the WORD, in her story that she, like Pauline Archange, lives:

> "I thought of nothing but that typewriter: it was an old, grey, machine, ugly and battered, but I loved it as if it were a person. As dilapidated as it was, that instrument was a perpetual source of inspiration to me: in its company, I never felt alone, and the moment I touched its shaky keys, my thoughts became mysteriously clear... A sublime peace settled over me the moment I closed the door of my room... the voice of my mother who was calling me to come and wash the dishes, no longer penetrated the quiet world of my meditation; and even if I did nothing but type out long rows of words, without at all comprehending their significance, forsaking all form as I arranged them on the page for my own pleasure, each word glittered beneath my eyes... my intoxication was complete."

Words glittering, nails in the shadows.
Beside an empty ladder.

Barry Callaghan
September 2009

BOOK ONE

THE MANUSCRIPTS
OF
PAULINE ARCHANGE

To Réjean Ducharme

Translated by Derek Coltman

❧ Chapter One ❧

Like the chorus of my distant miseries, ancient ironies clothed
by time with a smile of pity (though a pity that faintly stinks of
death), the old nuns, who once cradled my life in their cruel
kindness, still keep their eyes on me through the shadowy grilles
of a cloister buried in the colourless countryside, under a sullen
sky, at the fringe of a storm, but perpetually receiving, like a
sickly incense, the lamentation of their prayers, of their hymns
to the Blessed Sacrament. Cheeks sallow from nightly vigils,
their little yes wandering like marbles across the meditative
moons of their faces, each forehead betraying like some secret
frivolity its dark lock of thick hair, quivering proudly beneath
the edge of the coif, they display at their convent's mysterious
windowpanes (through which I can still see ranks of great white
backs majestically bowed toward the altar, slim brown boots
glimmering like furtive breaches of propriety, and a shoelace,
its knot neglected upon awaking, apparently snapping beneath
the gaze of the Mother Superior, whose eyes embrace every
detail of her chapel, the entire discipline of her house in a single glance) that expression of contempt so familiar to the bad
pupils among whom I was numbered: "Pauline Archange has
been disobedient, she must be deprived of the leftovers from
our altar bread . . ."

Hands blue with cold, hair imprisoned by its icy comb, fur cap
so hastily thrown on that it only covers one ear and subjects the

other to the full rigour of the wind, but heart bounding with a mad gaiety, with timidity, with melancholy too, inspired by the mystic thrill of the organ moaning out the *Tantum Ergo* so close by, taking up the heart-piercing melody again and again till one could faint with it, or sometimes till one feels nauseated by it – a beggar with others of my own sort, all of us having hurtled out of our classrooms at the first stroke of the bell, I wait there, beneath the austere gaze of the bars that stand between us and the little Jesus hidden in the golden folds of the chalice, far far away in his warm haven of perfumes and embroidered stuffs that will be raised aloft during the first Mass by a tired priest whose hand, lacking all mystery, densely hairy, will open up the secrets of God quite matter-of-factly, as though he were concerned with no more than a little private money box, in the intimacy of his own room.

"Come back next week, there is no more altar bread today."

It is said that they live solely on prayers and lettuce leaves, that they never sleep or wash; and the evidence is there, wafting between the bars, an honest smell of cabbage, of poverty, of stinginess. Their petrified ecstasy pursues you for a long while through the corridors, under the gray vaulting, and even outside, in the wind that suddenly strikes at your temples with its compact burden of snow, that seems to lacerate your shoulders and your back with its vast, cold, unrelenting draft.

Pressed against my chest, the packet of leftover altar bread is clutched fast in one numbed hand, while the other is clenched around the naked hand of Séraphine Lehout, who had lost her woolly glove and is weeping, her cheeks and nose running with tears that drip onto her coat like dew. Along the mist of roads, cars wander lost, casting dazzling yet blind glances all around them that evoke, though I could not say why, a vast herd of strange animals, lurking in the shadows and opening baleful, flaming eyes into the night. It is snowing, Séraphine Lehout cannot recognize either her street or her house any more. She sobs even more loudly as she feels the wind tugging at the back of her dismally flapping coat, a garment far too large for her, passed on to her by an elder sister, and already worn for several years before Séraphine inherited it.

"Let's eat some of the holy bread. That will put us back on the right path. Mother Sainte-Scholastique said so."

Squatting on the sidewalk, huddled together, we were afraid of flying up into the sky, of being suddenly sucked up by the insistent snowstorm, the bitter enemy of human frailty. "You're only five and I'm five and a half, and I know how to read, and you don't know anything." It is sometimes from a first bond thus insignificant in its circumstances and its promise that all the others are born. Next day, in the classroom, kneeling to stammer out her morning prayer with the rest of the class, Séraphine Lehout bent down before my delighted eyes a neck, a martyred head devoured by lice, whose two slender braids, not having been untied for two months, kept scrupulously intact by their two pieces of string, seemed to encircle her narrow, vulnerable face with a mist of dirty yet beautiful hair, from which her dark and fevered glances could be seen mounting heavenwards, despite the even thicker mist of grime surrounding each thick eyebrow.

"Pauline Archange, pray to the Holy Ghost, like everyone else."

It was Mother Sainte-Scholastique who spoke, from her dais near the window, scarcely any taller than we, her delicate face the captive of a pleated corolla that seemed to fit in perfectly with a whole landscape of flowers in pots that stood in front of the blackboard. The pink of her cheeks was such as to inspire obedience, feelings of goodness. One loved her. But with a love that tended to be decreased by the subtlety of her punishments: kneeling in the corridor, or kneeling in a corner, for instance. And, in addition, she was very nimble-fingered with the cane. Mother Sainte-Scholastique was young, besieged every day by so many pupils that in order to remember our correct names she had to pin them to the necks of our dresses.

"Who is that little girl, there at the back, with pigtails? Tell her to mop up that stream under her chair with her pinafore . . . If you wish to leave the room, girls, it's simple enough, just ask permission. I'll let you have it."

Hands shot up immediately, supplicating in the suffocating air, and Mother Sainte-Scholastique exclaimed, in high dudgeon: "You're just a lot of babies. I shall tell the Mother Superior."

Séraphine Lehout, humiliated, her mouth twisted by shyness on the verge of shame, more sacrificial even than the little saints in our picture books, hooking up with one wavering finger the thick elastic of a stocking hanging around her knee, Séraphine Lehout whose pride was bleeding like the bouquet of lilies, like the cool but deceitful virginity of the little girls torn to pieces at such an early age by God's wild beasts in imaginary arenas, "little girls whose souls were so pure," Mother Sainte-Scholastique used to tell us, "that the angels caught them up in their arms before they had even breathed their last," Séraphine would perhaps be expecting me to provide her, at the end of the day, in the convent yard – where the setting sun traced out strange forms on the ice-polished walls – with a consolation proportionate to the torture she had undergone? Huddled in one another's arms against the wall, we watched the silence spread all around us: the roller-skating square had a huge soul that slept on its back, its arms forming a cross. A tree, the only one, gaped at the sky with a ghostly mouth forever unable to utter its lament. If the branches shook too much, then we went away, feeling shivers suddenly beginning inside us . . . But then we grew calm again as we heard the horns of the streetcars crossing the town, scattering a muttering crowd of workmen in the middle of the street, a crowd of women either too plump or too frail, their pointed heels slithering on the sidewalks' glittering, icy slopes, their sudden fall provoking a cascade of ill-restrained laughs that spurted from between the onlookers' teeth like happy cries. There was the comforting certainty that the town was lighting up like that in order to protect people against thieves, against murderers, in order that they should be able to walk in peace through the streets with a light-hearted step, leaving their children alone at home in their bedrooms, with their homework to finish, with their dreams buzzing pleasantly around their ears. "Do not offend Jesus," Mother Sainte-Scholastique had told us, "either in your games or in your thoughts." But Jesus himself, compassionate as he was, would have loved this trustful hour of the day, when no one was dying of hunger on earth, when, in the poorhouse yard, Séraphine Lehout and Pauline Archange were building their snow forts in all innocence, so as to hide in them if war, or the plague, were to invade the town. Even Séraphine seemed to have forgotten the injustices she had suffered a few hours earlier. Safe behind her snowy rampart, so high, so strong, from which, she claimed, Mother Sainte-Scholastique appeared to her "as tiny as a match and like an ugly little fly," nothing frightened her now. For even if the cold did suddenly shudder through her bones like a disagreeable memory, she could always bury herself, quick as a flash, in the arms of Pauline, and both, hugged together, would roll over and over in the snow, which they thought of now as a warm accomplice, for not only did it cover them up but it concealed all the dirt of the yard (a rat sped by, swift and anxious in its hunger) with its generous, though ephemeral reign of whiteness, a health-giving beauty that whipped up a flaming red in cheeks that had been born as pale as unripe fruit.

But at the assault of the piercing six o'clock siren, those games came suddenly to an end; the streetcar wheels screeched in their rails, a cold orange moon rose up into the sky, like a blown-up version of the catechism picture on the school blackboard, a single scornful eyelid beneath which, safely withdrawn inside its authority, the eye of God glittered with asperity and spite. "That eye sees you everywhere and is watching you," Mother Sainte-Scholastique told us, hanging her barbaric handiwork up on the board with an air of satisfaction. And that eye, it was quite true, never left us in peace; it hung there like a sullen clock, filling each hour of that classroom eternity with a placid contempla-tion of all the sins committed there, all the sins we had the intention of committing in years to come. At six o'clock, Séraphine Lehout fled from the yard as fast as she could run, already crying at the thought of the daily punishment awaiting her at home: an hour standing in the corner of her room to teach her not to be late for dinner. But, in the town, there were still a few people wandering by, drunks with absent smiles who pulled flasks of rum out from their tattered coats and drank down the harsh delights inside as though they were somehow absorbing courage in a liquid state, miraculously poured into their little bottles, so that they could later be beaten by their wives without even noticing. One of these revellers whom I had been envying with my eyes, seeing me trailing the strap of my satchel behind me, carrying the burden of books that I was once more not going to have time to open that evening, asked me to take a short walk with him over the bridge.

"You an orphan?"

"No."

"Well, if it isn't a sin to see kids out on their own like this so late! Where do you live?"

"I don't know."

We were about to disappear into a darkness with no light beyond. My companion was old and kind, he asked me a great many questions in his drunkenness. Occasionally, in the way his voice shook a little, I could detect an accent of anger that I didn't like. Where were we going? How were you supposed to recognize your street in the dark, or the house where your mother was waiting for you with that worried expression: "Where *have* you been, you bad girl?" I could already see the bowl of hot soup on the end of the table, the spoon lying on the tablecloth like some friendly presence . . . "Do you want to kill your poor mother when she's so ill already? Do you *want* to kill me, is that it?" But beside the alien oddness of this man who was taking me away to strange places, my mother's words were losing all their menace.

"I want to go now. I really want to go."

After putting up a slightly weary resistance, the man let me go, then went on laughing for a long while in the darkness, like one of those abstract monsters that inhabit nightmares, without mouths, without faces, so that it would have been impossible to define the astonishment of those features left behind in the dark, and soon I found myself back on the iron bridge I had crossed that afternoon with Séraphine, with a Séraphine laughing as she stopped at every step to be kissed, to insist on being loved forever, more than the sky, more than the earth, eternally, in this world and then in heaven, where we would always be side by side if were lucky enough to die on the same day, in a state of grace, and preferably on the day of our first communion. On one side of the bridge, if you did not avert your eyes, you could see the hospital, and on the other the church, stretching out its cheerful limbs, smiling with every tooth in its windows beneath the tranquil trees that clustered all around it, like the wise men in adoration. It would have been so much nicer to live always with Séraphine beside me, because no sooner had she left me than I began torturing myself about her: without her I'd never be able to eat, I'd never earn a gold star to stick in my exercise book. We didn't need anyone in the world, apart from one another. Always go on playing in the snow, never to go to school, never to go home, to have nothing else to do but to love Séraphine to infinity, since without her the world always became hostile again, nature treacherous, the absurdity of life suddenly gaping into empty black holes underfoot, voids packed with whirling circles of grownups like greedy insects drawn by the guttering light of their own disgust, drinking, eating, uttering strange-sounding words, and endlessly reproducing themselves and their own miseries.

Occasionally, one of these adults would emerge from her hole, suspicious-nosed, like a hesitant mole, and call her child to her as though it were something that belonged to her, calling to boy or girl as though to a bathtub or an armchair: "Darling, come in now, it's dinnertime, you've played enough for today . . ." and the child, disdaining her sweet words, would move toward its mother, suppressing the first hints of hatred in its breast. But Séraphine Lehout and I had only contempt for such endearments, the fly-blown old cookies that some women always inflicted on their children's dreaming appetites as soon as they emerged from school, in the parks, where they sat knitting on their green wooden benches like worried nannies, incubating the shawl, the scarf that was soon to spend the winter strangling the frail quarry docilely playing in the sand beneath that maternal gaze brimming with nervous solicitude. "Are you cold, my angel? Did I hear you cough, my love? Are you hungry, my treasure?" To such insipid language we preferred even Mother Saint-Scholastique's asperity, or the impatient furies of our own mothers, whom we had not chosen, but who were there on our path, lovable without ever experiencing our love, for in our savage independence we had cast off the ties of blood in order to be reborn in our own way, out of a secret dream, a spiritualized birth in which our parents, this time, were to play no role, leaving our numberless desires with virgin existences to fill, an empty landscape to people. Occasionally, from afar and with a disturbed respect, we did look at our parents, much as we gave ourselves up, on summer evenings, to a timorous contemplation of the policemen walking their beats beneath the streetlights, our fascinated eyes riveted on the white truncheons with which they always played, one hand behind their backs. Such beings were an alien way of life, their habits mysterious and incomprehensible; it would have been futile to seek to understand them. Even when you were still tiny, wholly in the power of these inquisitors, washed and tended by them, surviving your childhood illnesses thanks to their vigilant attentions, a small, rebellious object waving its hands and feet about in its barred cot, howling and whimpering over its lack of freedom, even then no one seemed to notice your selfish sorrow, your wish to live alone, without being touched by incestuous hands. But as you grew up, you became aware that these strangers were always there, that it was your duty to live in their house, to share in the difficulties of their existence, and to dream your dreams of escape in silence. For the day would come when you would finally give their proprietary solicitude the slip. But, meanwhile, that closed court represented by the family, summoning into its circle all those uncles, those cousins, those miserly and cruel, carefree or careworn characters that family conversations so often assemble in slanderous convocation, all these relatives said of me, in chorus, that I was not like the others, that decidedly, "Pauline hasn't any heart . . ." And how right they were, because for them that heart was immutably closed. However much it brimmed with generosity and gifts for Séraphine Lehout, it always remained for them a steel door against which I huddled weeping while they hammered clumsily on the other side.

At six in the evening, when I left Séraphine Lehout, my total inability to love anyone else but her in the world used to fill me with despair, since I knew there were beings waiting for me, at home, whose very existence I never recalled until it was time to go back to them, and to whom I was sure of being a source of still further distress, without wishing it. To put off that moment, in order to avoid still another undeserved meal in the company of people who wished me nothing but good and to whom I would do nothing but harm, I used to wander around for a long time in the streets, until cold and hunger had tempered my soul to the requisite hardness. I knew exactly how distressed my mother was by my lateness; I knew that school was scarcely over before she was telephoning all my friends' mothers, telling them of my failure to return home in plaintive tones: "She'd hardly learned to walk, that Pauline of mine, before she was off every-where, wandering all over the place. Oh, it really makes you give up hope, Madame Poire!"

But I still went my own way, defying an authority that I condemned as monstrous, experiencing as an error, a misunder-standing on the part of fate, this burden of suffering that I represented for those who loved me "without reward," as my mother used to say to Madame Poire: "We do everything we can for that child of ours, and never any reward for it." To which the unmovable Madame Poire would reply, as she munched at her fudge, "Well, that's life, isn't it, Madame Archange, girls never do have anything in their heads but leaving home and getting married, my Huguette's no better, heaven knows, always off fooling around in the gulley with her Jacquou, but youth's soon over, that's a fact, and I'm not one for seeing sins wherever I look . . ." This last remark, accompanied by a sensual laugh, was doubtless received by my mother, at the other end of the line, with a cold silence, for Madame Poire would continue almost immediately, in soberer tones: "But the fact remains, Madame Archange, that your little girl, with those intelligent eyes of hers, she's going to go further in life than you and me, that's for sure, and I'll lead her home by her ear when she drops in for her visit, I promise you that, Madame Archange." When I did arrive, at that opportune moment when the entire Poire family was seated around the table making short work of platefuls of pancakes as thin and yellow as their own faces, soaked in a thick brown syrup that ran down from the corners of their mouths, Madame Poire, still in her robe and curlers, would remind me gently about my mother, telling me how she had already telephoned four times, "but as I said to your mother, Huguette's no better, you're sly pusses the both of you, ah well, since you're here don't stand there like a gatepost, take off your hat and have a pancake with us, come on!" And so, time and time again, such friendly invitations proved impossible to refuse, with the result that I only went home "just for somewhere to sleep," as my mother said, "like a drunk." It was a well-known fact in our alley, a denuded passageway inhabited by garbage bins and rats and named "Bellevue Alley," that my friend Huguette Poire spent most of her time with the neighbourhood bad boys, and that, according to her mother's indulgent attitude, "lying was much more serious than liking boys." At the late hour I paid my visits, Huguette was already in her nightclothes – like her mother, who wore the costume of her dreams from morning till night – her hair screwed up so tight in strips of linen that when these improvised curlers were removed in the morning ("but if you want to be beautiful you must make sacrifices," Madame Poire would say as her daughter wailed in protest beneath the ruthless comb), the imprisoned locks opened out into a stiff harmony of accordion pleats, offering to the air and to men's eyes an extraordinary mass of hair waving outwards in all directions, "in order to provoke the gaze," as Mother Sainte Scholastique put it. Sitting next to me, her cheeks running with syrup, she whispered things in my ear, then bounced up and down with laughter, her head hunched down between her shoulders, until her father, who was always particularly bad-tempered whenever he'd had too much to drink, tapped his daughter on the elbow with his fork to make her keep quiet.

"Shut that big mouth of yours," he would order. "You talk as much as your mother."

And that would be the end of our little conspiracy. Huguette swallowed down the rest of her pancake with a melancholy air. I loved Séraphine, Huguette loved Jacquou. He was a handsome young profligate who lived near us – the first man we had shared. That fall he'd had his seventh birthday, which was in itself a source of wonderful superiority to us. But since my meeting with Séraphine I had no choice but to be unfaithful to Jacquou; the memory of his fragile and naked chest still glimmered in my mind, other details of his body too were still magnanimously victorious over the more mystical character of my Séraphine, whose soul was all I had acquaintance with, but, to tell the truth, I was beginning to love him less, which was a source of great pleasure to Huguette.

Jacquou's charm had been further dimmed by the severe chastisement I had received from my father and by the flames of humiliation still so easily fanned back to life in every vein of my burning buttocks. To the despair of Madame Poire – who tended to smooth the velvet of forgiveness over any kind of error that provided delectation for the senses ("After all, Madame Archange, life is so short, no one can be expected to go without their pleasures") – my mother had dragged me in front of a priest to tell the whole sombre truth of the affair; but since I wasn't old enough to be confessed officially, I had been dismissed with the words: "Remember that such things make poor little Jesus cry . . ." My penance was then concluded with "a week of seven-o'clock bedtimes," a delicious torture during which, my mind now at rest, lying in my seven-o'clock bed – my mother came herself to collect me from school, the better to share my penance with me – I would meet Jacquou again, as he was that day when he appeared to us among the raspberry canes, a young savage, naked as a shining star, and crying: "Off with your clothes then girls, and quick about it! I'm in a hurry," that day when we found our way so easily to the accomplishment of his desires, astonished by an enchantment of caresses so easily within our reach. Ever faithful to his nature, arrogantly forthright in his demands, Jacquou hurled himself onward, head held high, into the life that had been fated for him from that day when he first threw himself avidly upon his mother's breast; a life of conquests and fatigue was already beginning for him, and how could he have rejected it when the girls were already proving so eager, so energetic in the quest for discovery, so very curious that his own curiosity even flagged sometimes at its task. "Oh God, girls!" he seemed sometimes to be thinking with a shrug, and then he would spit to one side, exercising his versatility in scorn. One could already see in him the grownup bachelor, ringmaster to a troupe of mistresses, casting a replete, slightly sad, slightly bored eye over his domain. In his presence, for the first time, I had the bright and blinding impression that all those landscapes so carefully kept secret from me since my birth were suddenly emerging, one after another, into the same bright day. Pleasure for the senses did exist. In Huguette Poire's eyes, Jacquou not only was a prince of initiation, he was also a tough guy, a source of titillation, an instructor in vice: "If you knew all the things we do together . . ." she whispered in my ear, sitting at the family meal table, and a second time her father roared: "Are you going to shut that cellar-door mouth of yours!"

The pancakes all devoured, Huguette would start on her homework at one corner of the table beside her empty plate. Empty of food, that is, but still full of the wavering patterns left by the vestiges of her meal, dark splotches, paths through deeply sunken valleys along which she wandered with one pensive eye while at the same time scrawling out the first letters of the alphabet in her exercise book. Meanwhile, her sister Julia, with an almost unhealthy slowness, was clearing away the milk, the butter, the plates, then violently shaking the cloth onto the dog's head. "You ought to concentrate on what you're doing, you ought," Julia told Huguette, and at her words the radio suddenly grunted, while their father gave himself up to the delights of an impromptu concert, the sounds welling up effortlessly from his stomach into his throat as with one hand he supported his hanging belly, like some large and precious object whose full gamut of sonorities, of lamentations, was yet to be revealed. The radio set had an eye, and a voice; it inhabited the room like an unprepossessing lodger, taking up far too much room, talking far too much, yet possessed of a certain mystery.

Huguette turned toward it as though to ask its advice. In the end, she began to weep onto her exercise book and was sent to bed, along with Julia, three of her other sisters, and a brother who also shared the same windowless room.

"Oh, good gracious, Pauline, I'd forgotten you there," Madame Poire exclaimed suddenly. "I'd invite you to spend the night with Huguette, my pet, but there it is, there's just no room, not even for the dog. Wait a second, I'll just slip on my boots and walk you home."

We set off together through the white, empty town, her face candid and friendly beneath its helmet of curlers. She was still eating fudge. Jealous of Madame Poire's influence, my mother received me with a little slap on the side of my head – thereby sparing me the nosebleed she was keeping in reserve for more serious misdemeanours – and said in a choked voice: "Oh, what a trial you are to me, Pauline, spending more time with the neighbours than you do at home. Open your satchel, I'll have to help you with your homework now." One hand pressed against her forehead, worn out by the treatment she was being given daily at the hospital for an illness whose origins I was wholly ignorant, my mother guided my hand across my exercise book; but she was so depressed by the sight of me that she seemed unable to concentrate on the task, and if our eyes happened to meet she lowered hers with the words: "Oh, Pauline, what am I to do with you?" At such moments I felt a rebellious pity for this young woman, already failing in health and worn out by work, and was forced to drive away such thoughts with some cold and invulnerable daydream in which she could play no part, for I was afraid to let myself be moved by that pale brow bent over my ink-splotched page, afraid, above all, of snapping our fragile bond of reticence and silence by making the consolatory gesture that she was expecting of me, and thus proving that we did not belong to the same martyred tribe. Now and then, when one of her blond hairs fell onto my exercise book, I would gaze at it for a long while in the lamplight, thinking vaguely that somewhere inside my mother there existed, perhaps, a sister I did not understand, but so distant, so lost in the austere mists of her life that as time went by we were to become ever more cut off from one another.

"Why are you here on earth?"

"To love God and to serve Him."

She seemed to be repeating the answers with me, captive of a tormented faith she no longer questioned. She broke off, raised my pale chin toward her, and touched one hollow cheek. "You'll die if you go on not eating like this. Is that what you want, to die? You're as green as grass. Mother Sainte-Scholastique says you faint during school. What's the matter with you, for heaven's sake, not wanting to eat when there are so many little children in the world dying of hunger? Aren't you ashamed of yourself, Pauline?"

But it wasn't about my death that my mother was thinking really, it was about hers, the image of which seemed already to be reflected in the extreme poverty of her energies, in the smudges under her eyes, in the savage attacks of vomiting that left her drained of consciousness on her bed; she was doubtless thinking to herself, in her anxiety, that she couldn't go on wasting away as she was, not without some grave reason, and that an end must come to those suffocating pains. But, courageously, she pushed that thought aside, and if it was fine on Sunday she would take us, my little brother and myself, to play in the park, where she would abruptly leave me with a fragile baby in my arms, spraying its laughter and saliva into my face, and tell me to be good while she went off to be sick under a tree. She returned as white as snow, the hand she rested on the bench transparent in the bright sunlight, crisscrossed with blue veins that seemed to quiver with a singular and disturbing life of their own, while the sweat ran slowly down her unresisting neck, then inside the neck of her dress, where she had replaced the missing button with an inelegant safety pin. If we all three sat together on the same bench, sharing our lunch of bread and jam, waiting for the municipal bottle of milk that the park authorities issued free every day at noon, I had the feeling that other families were stopping to stare at us, at this trio apparently halfway into the grave, as Madame Poire so inconsiderately put it, and that we were being written off, because of our emaciated pallor, as dying creatures it would really be best to bury right away, so as to avoid contaminating all those others still in full enjoyment of their health. And this was why my mother, too proud to resign herself to that shameful image, reproached me so bitterly for the signs of her own illness that she recognized in me, even waking me up during the night to make me eat cereals that I ended by throwing up on the bedclothes. "Have you been going around with those consumptives? Tell the truth now, is that it?"

All the people living in our alley suffered from consumption, but my mother, moderate in all things, had limited the disease in her mind to the Carré family, three members of which had already died in the sanatorium. "You've been playing with little Lucienne Carré again, haven't you? How many times have I told you? Do you *want* them to infect you?" Of the Poire family, Julia alone was to be carried off by the disease before her twenty-fifth year, but all through her adolescence she was to be seen banging her great bony, slow body against the table and the walls of the cellar that her family called home, so emaciated that one had the impression that her lungs were moving about outside her body, visible, like a map in a geography book on which the many dark blotches represented countries, or towns, deci-mated by famine. Never sad, never gay, Julia simply waited patiently for her end, playing cards with her father, who was to survive her only too easily, or smoking cigarettes out on the stoop while she read love stories as light and as bland as the nau-seous smoke that curled up from her lips. On very hot days, a cigarette burning between the tips of her fingers, her dark head slumped to one side, she could be seen dozing over her unfin-ished book, a thin line of blood running from her mouth, dead already, it seemed; but the noise of a child striking its shoe against a cobblestone would abruptly wake her, and she would return to her reading, swiftly wiping her mouth with the back of one hand.

As for the other Poires, they all managed to remain in more or less good health, hemmed in by their disease as though it were just one more condition of life that had come into exis-tence with them, impregnated with death, coughing, spitting, but by some miracle of endurance walking over the abyss, or along its edge, as though tuberculosis were no more really than some sort of cold or sick headache, so that in the end it began to take on an appearance of being no more.

My mother pushed me toward my bed, forgetting my books still lying open on the table, adding that for my own good she ought to punish me for always being late, and that I was there-fore to be deprived of my Sunday morning visit to the movies. This punishment, in the hierarchy of griefs, seemed the cruellest of all, for my mother, without knowing it, was robbing me of the only sweetness in my week; that morning of visions – even though the pious selection of our chaplains ensured that the inspiration it offered was of the very lowest quality – at least provided some illumination, however brief, for an imagination constantly in chains. And besides, bound up with the delight of drinking in that screen with my eyes, contemplating the mediocrity of each image as though it were a stained-glass window radiant with celestial and childish ecstasies, there was also the presence of Séraphine beside me, fidgeting on her chair, sucking interminable caramels while persistently crackling their wrappers in her hand, as though to exacerbate my love for her even further, but a presence that I cherished nevertheless, despite my impatient scoldings: "Goodness, Séraphine, have you got worms or something? Why don't you watch the film? Stop looking at me as though I was something in a store window; anybody would think it's the first time in your life you'd ever seen me. I shan't bring you next time . . ." All of which did not prevent her from kneeling up on her chair to chatter to the children in the row behind, while at the same time slyly encircling my neck with her little arm, cold where it was left bare by the sleeve of her shrunken pullover . . . "Yes, I am looking at you, Pauline, and anyway what's it to you if I like looking at you . . ." In short, to miss one of these meetings with Séraphine meant loving Séraphine one day less, suffering the pain of separation from her before the ordained hour, a thing that was unacceptable. As I got into bed, I decided to disobey my mother yet again, and felt forming in my mind for the first time the intoxicating idea of stealing a ten-cent piece: my hand was already making its trembling descent into the granite bowl where my mother's meagre savings glimmered like faded gold. In order to see Séraphine, in order to hold her in my unattentive power for a few short hours, was it not my duty to risk my eternal salvation, to say nothing of my reputation, already so tarnished, among my aunts and cousins? And had I not already leaped over the fire of hell, in one audacious bound, that day when Jacquou had made his abrupt and smiling appearance among the raspberry canes, waving with one hand, like a banner of victory, his red, patched breeches in the wind?

"You see how much I love you, Séraphine," I murmured into my pillow with its stuffing of prickly feathers that sometimes, after creeping out of their threadbare envelope, used to sink to rest in my mouth, "Oh, Séraphine, I shall go to hell because of you."

A few inches from my bed, my baby brother was punctuating my thoughts with his animal sighs, mouth gaping in the moonlight that floated down from the motionless curtains, his sparse hair damp with a warm sweat of sleep that I sometimes reached out to touch with my finger, so as to keep any repugnance alive. A crucifix kept watch in the shadows, calm and desolate, weary of our nighttime snufflings, and made desolate too by the dismally insipid colour of the walls upon which it had to rest its lacerated body, in the company of other, profaner images, a little boy going fishing in a springtime-green landscape, a calendar depicting the laughing satisfaction of a bald, toothless baby, its nose as flat as a dried prune, a barbarous sort of creature just like my brother Jeannot, whom I avoided by turning over on my side. On the days of melancholy fatigue when I couldn't go to school, unless it was to faint as soon as morning prayers were over, my mother would imprison me next to her on her invalid's bed and we would talk without looking at one another, each preserving her secrecy by turning her back.

"We ought to have help in the house, but it costs too much . . . I can't do the washing anymore, or get your father's dinner, we ought to have someone in . . . We ought to have someone to look after you when I go to the hospital for my treatment, you can't follow me around everywhere like a little monkey. And besides it's no fun for a kid your age . . . Maybe I ought to send you to the country to stay with your uncle Jérôme . . . What do you think?"

But my mother had scarcely finished speaking before I was tiptoeing out of her room, making my way cautiously toward the kitchen, then opening the door into the street outside, black with dust and even more oppressed than myself by the hot air. I ran aimlessly along the silent sidewalks, all through those long June afternoons when the children in school were falling into a discouraged sleep over their exams, when mankind, hardly able to breathe, seemed to have simply given up existing . . .

Those Sundays when I had stolen more than the usual two dimes – one for me and one for Séraphine – were spent in a sacrilegious liberty that appeared even more beautiful for that very reason, taking privileged walks after the movies were over, eating ices, reading down on our knees beneath the counters of restaurants, half concealed by the legs of noisy bands of youngsters who, instead of going to church with their parents, used to congregate at Laurel, Candies & Cigars in order to smoke cigarettes and chatter to one another with an air of triumph, while also casting fleeting glances at the comic papers we were reading, pages sprinkled with naked silhouettes, sirens, snake women, stories of serious and superhuman races, the winged potency of a young man in a mask, flying through the air, scantily clad in a blue cape that enabled him to land calmly in the kitchens of his consenting victims and clutch them to him without being observed, his ridiculous cloak depriving us, alas, of so many fascinating details.

"You're too young to understand that stuff, and besides, you can't even read . . ."

The coarse laughter ricocheted above our heads. Laurel, Candies & Cigars – all contained in a single person, albeit one who represented by virtue of his name both of the two most sought-after commodities in his restaurant – came over to us, a white apron around his imposing waist, his black, tweedy knee planted rocklike in front of our eyes: "Come on, you dirty-minded kids, you're too young for that. Go on home now."

And we took our leave, outraged and muttering dire insults beneath our breath . . .

If I saw my mother standing on the kitchen step as I came home, I realized immediately that inside, behind her, there was a whole secret tribunal waiting to emerge from the shadows and pass judgement on my morning thefts. I carried my sin defiantly toward her, preparing to justify myself, but always needlessly, for time after time my mother greeted me with the same lost, drained gaze, uttering the words of my deliverance: "I don't feel well, Pauline, but we'll go over and have dinner with your grandmother, perhaps that'll take your mind off the streets for a moment." Occasionally, in a sharper tone, she would add: "And go and wash up, you little bum. I'm ashamed of you in that filthy dress." In order to economize, we often made the journey to my grandmother's on foot, my mother's eyes fixed on the horizon in a glazed, unhappy stare as she pushed the baby's stroller in front of her, or, on winter evenings, a sled in which I had also been deposited. I sat there dreaming as I watched the flakes of snow settling on Jeannot's reddened nose, forgetting the effort it was costing my mother to push us both across the town. Grand-mère Josette would come down to meet us, clutching the stair rail with one feverishly quivering hand, shod in a pair of old slippers borrowed from her husband, each with a little hole in the toe like an eye, and taking Jeannot in her arms she immediately inquired about my father's absence. "Well, daughter, and where's that Jos? I never see him now."

"Oh, he has to work nights as well as days now," my mother answered sadly. "He even works Sundays. These are bad times to bring up kids, we can never make ends meet . . ."

"Yes, it's no joke these days," my grandmother answered. "It's almost as though the good Lord was out to punish us for something."

"Oh, Mama, you mustn't say things like that. You mustn't talk like that about the Lord . . . not in front of the children . . ."

As my mother uttered this discreet reproach, I was already racing up the stairs, determined to be first, to see my grandfather alone; but he, whether from indifference or because he felt like being conspiratorial, pretended not to see me, merely continuing to eat his mush of carrots, with an expression of sulky fury that I even found a little frightening.

"Are you cross, are you cross again, Onézimon?"

He remained silent, his big nose, covered with gray and gold hairs, bent toward his dish.

"I bet you don't like having to eat mushy things, do you? Neither do I . . . If I tell you your nose is like a caterpillar's garden, will you get even madder?"

Finally my grandfather replied "that he was black with anger," that he did indeed loathe mushy things, but that since he only had one tooth left he was doomed never to eat anything else, and that the women of the house, my grandmother and her "damned daughters," were torturing him, "like cats playing with a mouse."

"Onézimon, eat your carrots," Grand-mère Josette said, pointing at her husband with one finger. "And don't encourage him to show off, Pauline, that's all he's waiting for, the obstinate old creature."

"Come on then, Pauline, we'll leave the women together."

But before following my grandfather into his workshop, I made my way over to the side of the house that was forbidden me. "That side belongs to our courting couple and poor Uncle Sébastien," my grandmother would say. "Courting couples are like invalids, they have to be left alone. Come and play with your bricks, Pauline, and stop nosing around everywhere" – a wavering exhortation that I listened to with one ear while at the same time dragging myself over on my knees to the glazed door into the sitting room, where beneath a lamentable bunch of flowers printed on the surface of the glass, framing the scene with a misty halo as though one were peering through a key-hole, Aunt Alice, skulking behind a veil of modesty, was kissing her earthly fiancé Boniface, who, when he was not contemplating the rigid beauty of his Alice, already seated high on that throne of dominion from which she would never again descend, was gazing with melancholy eyes at his large, flat, wholly un-imaginative feet, lying on the carpet like chastened dogs, but faithful according to him, slightly stupid, but capable of carrying his timid soul over the threshold of matrimony . . . "Oh, Alice," he sighed. "let's be married soon . . ."

"Wait, Boniface, my feelings toward you are still what one might call . . . hesitant. Love will come . . . Love always comes . . ."

Alice had always "talked like a queen," my mother observed with an edge of envious disapproval. "She was the only one who stayed on at school till the end, while the others were all out at work selling hats." And though it was true that my aunt did display a certain wan eloquence in her speech, this was partly in the hope of resembling her brother, Sébastien, whose eccentricity of character she admired, and also because she had spent a great deal of her time reading *A Thousand and One Hints for Marri-*

age, Marriage: That Sacred Door, The Virtuous Approach to Love, savouring the veiled vocabulary with which they urged her to take up a vocation that she believed sublime and unique, worthy of her ideal of integrity and high dreams. Alas, at the first close embrace, at the first caress of a black-haired hand laid upon that hard, dry bosom of hers, and above all at the sight of those dull, dumb feet of her fiancé's lumbering around the bedroom, all her dreams of passion would evaporate, and the frigid fiancée would become a bitter and domineering wife.

"Hey there, sly puss, what are you up to? Trying to get a peek at the courting couple? Come in and see me instead, I'm as dull as a toad all alone . . ."

If I hesitated to visit Uncle Sébastien, it was because I felt that the fate of this young man, whom I loved, not only was threatened in itself but also was in some way bound up with the tragedy that might one day separate me from Séraphine: vague fragments of a catastrophe making up part of a being dear to me, but that I did not wish to identify, believing perhaps, in the superstition of a nightmare, that Uncle Sébastien, afflicted as he was by a misfortune personal to himself, might without knowing it inspire misfortune in general to swoop down on Séraphine and me.

"Why don't you come in? You're my only friend in the world, Pauline!"

In the end, Sébastien drew me in by pity. "What would you like me to tell you today? The story of the gray fox who went skating in the church? The story of the candle-stealing camel? Look under the bed, that's where all my stories are, I write three of them a day . . . You can read them when you're older. You'll see all the things we'll do together. A glass of water, Pauline, don't say anything to anyone, just give me a glass of water . . . It's not their fault, they just forgot me. I'm thirsty . . ."

But when I tried to help him drink it, tactfully, he pushed my hand away. "I can drink without any help, little slyboots. I feel perfectly well, you know. Couldn't you just open the window a little? I'm afraid you'll suffocate in here. And besides, we have to let the monsters get out. Can you see them? I'm not afraid of them, they're my friends. I talk to them and they stop roaring then. You must never get in a temper, Pauline, the monsters don't like that?"

"Where are they?" I asked.

"On my desk, in my inkwell. Everywhere. Can you see the little flame coming out of their mouths? There now. It's gone out. Perhaps my fever's beginning to ease off. I'll be up tomorrow, that's a promise."

A smell of medicines tingled in my nostrils as I went nearer to Uncle Sébastien, trying to see his face more clearly, to feel the angry delirium of his gaze, like a smile of pain, more vividly. Then I halted, as though at the entrance to some unknown path on the fringe of a forest.

"Are you afraid of me then, Pauline?" he asked gently, then closed his eyes as though abandoning himself to sleep.

It was as he slid into one of these abrupt dozes, still shaken with delirium, that poor Sébastien was to die, quite simply, one spring morning, his pain-racked face imprinted with an expression of irony, and also of hope (for hadn't he told Grand-mère Josette that very morning, first thing, that he felt much better?), as though he had succumbed to his pneumonia by mistake, confused by the giddying flames that flickered in his brain. It was then, looking at the white sheet that covered Sébastien's absence, in the empty room, that an agonizing concern tightened around my heart. Was this how every object worthy of love was condemned to perish? All around, only silence to be heard. Did that mean that everyone was surrounded by this tight, black ring of agony that was there wherever you went? In so cruel a world, the immensity of whose cruelty seemed suddenly to well up in the mind, in this single image of murderous destruction, it seemed absurd to love Séraphine, and above all to want to protect her, when so many men were dying every moment in the world, as we were informed daily, not only by the radio, by the papers, but also by the bleeding visions of all our dreams, those dreams in which we were already submerged and floating at the hour of our birth, since the world was forever burning, forever bleeding, how, yes how, in this world that seemed to be gestating a future even more hostile, even more bloody for us to suffer, how could love possess the gift of survival?

"Hey, Pauline, come with me. I've got some new toys to show you . . ."

A little ashamed at still loving life too much, when Uncle Sébastien was rotting alone under the ground, I followed my frivolous grandfather into his workshop, where we both stood gazing at the miraculous toys he had carved – "to sell for peanuts to those rich kids' parents, who are just as stingy as poor people," he added scornfully. "Hey, Pauline, what do you think of this red and blue train? Can't you just see yourself riding off up to the mountains in a train like that, early one morning, without any women, quiet as you please, smoking your pipe – ah, that's real happiness for you where a man's concerned. And this doll here, what do you say to that? Red hair just like your grandmother's, just like Josette's when she was still young and full of the joys of life. You ought to have seen her in those days. She wasn't always at church then, and . . ."

But what had drawn my eyes above all was a white sled, so perfectly graceful, so enchantingly shaped that you could already envisage the delicate union of such a possession with its future owner, an owner whom I imagined as exquisite as our

Jacquou – though never to be found playing in any gully – flashing like a carefree arrow, stomach flattened against his precious sled, down the solitary slope of a hill that was his and his alone to play on.

"Hey there, Pauline, what are you thinking about like that, with your mouth hanging open like a donkey?"

But suddenly the sadness had come back, the piercing feeling that not merely Sébastien's early death, not only that, but the death of everything breathing all around you was a terrible outrage. To have lived five years already, five years on this cold and contradictory earth, and now the sixth year coming toward you out of the darkness, like a beggar, fixing its eyes upon you so humbly, but demanding your charity, your trust.

"Hey there, Pauline, you're getting older fast. You'll soon be as old as me."

And yet, all thoughts of death, of the incomprehensible passage of time, seemed to vanish sometimes for day on end, and I found myself climbing that ladder of anguish, those steps, those hours that yesterday had seemed in their passive unendingness eternal, with a light step: my sixth year just arrived, like all the other years before it, without producing any further upheaval in the dramatic order of things. Séraphine did not change because it had come, the days accumulated around her as they did around me, and though the hour of our separation was coming nearer, we were both too happy together to be deeply aware of the moment when our shared world would no longer exist.

Since she was too sick to look after me at home after school, my mother had followed the advice pressed upon her by Madame Poire, who, as soon as they had reached their sixth year, entrusted all her daughters to the patriotic tutelage of the Girl Guide movement, so that, after graduating first from the Brownies and then from the Guides, at the respectable age of fourteen they were all able to profess the true scouting faith, duly initiated, nurtured, and firm to the very roots.

"You must realize, Madame Archange," Madame Poire told my mother, as the latter hesitated slightly before entrusting me to what seemed an army of scout mistresses and their seconds-in-command, the tie-wearing directors of my future group, the Blue Ribbons. "You must realize that these children need fresh air, they can't go on playing in the alley forever, and besides, the Brownies are classy, they have their meetings, they learn their semaphoring – well, it doesn't help them catch any husbands, I know, but the main thing is, they get to go camping in the summer, up in the mountains, yes, Madame Archange, and what's more, on the weekends they get to go out into the woods, they study botany, the birds, the plants, not that that's any help catching a husband either, of course . . ." And so I had dragged Séraphine into the Brownies with me, and the hope of camping out one day in the mountains, under a clear and kindly night sky, with a crescent moon planted at the apex of our tent, had driven away some of my sombre forebodings. At the very first meeting of the Blue Ribbons we attended, in a dusty cellar that I furnished with all possible qualities of mystery, as though in that lightless space, hired specifically for our pitiable little meetings, the fate of the world had been debated by those little girls who afterwards, on their way home in the evening dark, kept getting lost in the snow, and in many cases did not get to bed without a thrashing – at that very first meeting Séraphine and I were both deeply affected by a tall counsellor, possessor of a virile step but a gentle voice, and also by her second-in-command, who resembled her like a sister, so disturbingly indeed that whenever we talked about the one the other would appear as well, smiling the same generous smile as the first. Agnès and Berthe: scarcely had they glanced at us when Séraphine hung her head and savagely squeezed my hand to communicate the violence of her passion, whereupon I did the same in my turn, so that the counsellor, Agnès, was obliged to shout out in her big voice: "Left, right, a Brownie is a free and independent individual, you must each take a different team, one left, one right, a Brownie is committed in the first place to the service of her country . . ."

But in the severity displayed by Agnès, or by Berthe, I caught no hint of that harsh, curt tone that made me quiver on my bench in school, when Mother Sainte-Scholastique was giving us a lecture: on the contrary, the consoling energy these women deployed – rigorously masculine in their flat-heeled shoes, in their narrowly cut suits beneath which pointed buttocks provided further expression of their will power and daring, yet rigorously maternal too, even though they cloaked that vulnerable quality beneath a soldierly appearance itself extremely fragile – on the contrary, their energy, their restless vigour seemed to contain for us the very element of sturdy tenderness of which we had hitherto been deprived.

As I turned my gaze each day toward fresh faces, becoming greedy for the pale honours of scouting life, so each day I forgot Séraphine a little more, beginning, perhaps, to cherish my former habit of loving Séraphine more than I did Séraphine herself. If I suddenly lost Séraphine's hand during one of our games in the mountains, I no longer succumbed to panic; I was too quickly reassured by the comradely vision of our counsellors and their aides galloping like crazed goats toward the summits of the snowy hills, shouting in those abrupt tones of theirs: "First team to the top wins the pennant. Keep up, Brownies, keep up!" And comforted by the tinkling, as of distant bells, made by all the mess tins and knives that hung in glittering ranks from their black leather belts, I told myself that I would find Séraphine again around the fire, that evening, in the brightly lit chalet where the exhausted teams were to rest from their race.

It is true that I did find Séraphine again, along with all the others, but my indifference detected in those thin little features an expression of wounded dependency that I preferred not to acknowledge, because I knew myself to be its cruel cause; that face with its sickly tints, its burning eyes, far from drawing my gaze, as it had so often done in the past, deflected it instead toward other faces, pinker and gayer, revealing an experience, a solicitude of a grownup kind that Séraphine, now so little in my eyes, could no longer comprehend. My ungrateful friendship left habit to perform the chore of assuring it that Séraphine was still there, in all the places where my eyes had loved to find her, in the school corridors, or sharing my desk during classes, using her thumbnail to squash the brown lice as they fell on her open exercise book, among the inkblots. On Sundays, if I scolded her on the way to the movies, my eyes no longer darted to seek hers: I spoke to her now without seeing her. It was only natural, therefore, I thought to myself, to love someone else, since Séraphine bored me. The Séraphine who sobbed now at my ever more frequent and unjust criticisms, asking me in suppliant tones as she wiped her nose on the sleeve of her coat: "Why do you keep picking on me all the time, Pauline? Why are you so mean to me?" – that first Séraphine, in the weariness of my feelings toward her, I could suddenly do nothing but torture.

It took the cry of a Séraphine crushed beneath the wheels of one of those blind buses from which, in earlier days, we had so often rescued one another, during those evenings of fog and storm, it took the sight of her death just beside me to make me comprehend that I had quite deliberately lost her, in a series of inattentive moments now suddenly revealed to me in a frozen, implacable light. This sin of neglect – as life was to prove to me in every way – far from damming the stream of my future infidelities, to others and myself, was merely the starting point of a thousand other shifty betrayals: the inexplicable fatigue of a worship, a love that suddenly tramples on the chosen being, the chosen object, for the sake of a passing preference, a new source of curiosity for the heart or senses that one is unable to resist. In a hot madness of promises, Séraphine and I had vowed never to part, ephemeral promises flitted from our lips every day after school, and the death of all those happy moments having occurred, I resigned myself to it little by little, without ever achieving a sufficient awareness of how shocking it was, this disappearance of Séraphine into a world wholly unknown, forever impenetrable, like that tiny coffin that had borne away from me, into the distance of the misty graveyard under the trees, the fallen, sleeping form of a little girl whose features I had not been able to recognize.

"Have you no heart, Pauline?" my mother sighed, observing the hard expression on my face with contempt. "And there was a time when I thought Séraphine was the only person in the world you loved. More than your own mother, I used to think. And now there you are, with your face all yellow with meanness."

"She was the one who was mean. Going away like that."

I had abandoned Séraphine, had abandoned her several months before, but it seemed to me that in death she had found an eternal vengeance, a punishment far too severe for all the instants I still had to live without her. "You weren't kind enough to Séraphine," my mother repeated. "Ah, Pauline, you've never been kind."

Listening to the voice of a dry and lonely repentance within myself, I thought of Séraphine, blaming myself for not having been able, during those last weeks of her life, to feel as I once had, in school, all the blows that Mother Sainte-Scholastique had inflicted upon her, smiling inwardly perhaps beneath the rain of slaps that reddened my friend's ears, loving in Séraphine – rather like Mother Sainte-Scholastique herself, who gauged affection by the degree of torture one could bear – the sacrificial victim with whom my egoism draped itself as with some tragic mantle, since it is rarely, if one is suffering oneself, that the suffering of others does not provide some form of tormented diversion. In inverse proportion to the need I felt for a liberty away from Séraphine, in a miserly paradise she would have no claim to share, no Séraphine herself had experienced an ever greater longing to be close to me, and nothing, it now seemed certain, could have so cruelly lacerated her affection as that conflict between our two solitudes, once they had ceased to meet.

Her ghost was henceforth to haunt my games, to blow across the surface of my forgetfulness, of my pastimes with Jacquou or Huguette Poire, in an icy and sombre current. The daring of those pleasures shared in the gully had lost its freshness. Each of us was alone, capable at every instant of a monstrous forgetfulness with regard to our fellow beings, intoxicated with self to the point of crime. This sensual intoxication vibrated throughout the whole of nature, and if one so willed it, the earth could become the realm of oblivion, an appalling haunt of delights from which charity could be excluded. On certain summer days, so sumptuous were they in the colour of their skies, the quality of the air, it was as though we were being swathed in a mantle of warmth, exquisite in its airy nonchalance, a white beatitude within which it seemed impossible, forbidden even, to think of anyone other than oneself. Huguette Poire, pressing her lips against Jacquou's golden neck, was only too quick to reveal those first lascivious thoughts, those already expert caresses of which tomorrow she would be the perfect mistress. Each was hungry and thirsty for riches belonging to another. Jacquou gave and received, obedient only to the dictates of his wild, capricious spirit, unaware of being, already, woman's slave; and once his thirst had been assuaged, there would pass fleetingly at times across his eyes, as fatigue sometimes can, that quiet innocence of which the whole world dreams.

Human avidity penetrated everywhere, and no compassion equal to its needs ever came to its relief. Every evening, as a punishment imposed by Mother Sainte-Scholastique to cure my arrogance, I was obliged to stay behind and clean the blackboards, and it was thus, on one occasion, through the half-open door, that I came to surprise a trembling confession of that avidity being made by a nun, in the next classroom, to a little girl whose knees she was fondling. With what a profusion of revelatory gestures, of fleeting and guilty actions, each of us was forced to live, struggling to reduce that soul-shattering chaos to order, and to understand it in the light of our swift and swiftly exhausted pities!

It was much easier, for example, to forgive the clumsiness of a Mother Saint-Bernard de la Croix, selecting for her accomplice a stupid but pretty child whose dull gaze held so very little in the way of promise, than to erase the image of that cruel sovereignty which Mother Sainte-Scholastique and a whole chorus of her bitter-clawed companions maintained so ruthlessly over their defenceless pupils.

Along the whole length of our path through childhood, until we reached those lucid shadows that mark its end, two powers held continual sway: the first, disciplinary and destructive, that of the whip; and the other resulting from it, in a remorse-soaked sweetness, the power of pursuit, of seduction, of the rape of bodies – and souls, perhaps – against which judgment is powerless, for which it can have only pity. Wounds inflicted, wounds closing up alone in silence, or too deep to heal at all, or too shameful to be admitted, all the laws of terror cloaked each individual being so utterly as to make him invisible to his fellow creatures. By living too much in the company of misted mirrors that lie as they reflect you, you can become a stranger to your own image. My mother, who because of her illness used to be visited once a week by a young Franciscan to whom she made her scrupulous confession, was involuntarily to close her eyes later on, when I was almost twelve, to the unfortunate frailties this priest exhibited when alone with me – against my will, but a will there was no one to defend. "What's all that blood on your legs? You've gone and scratched yourself again, climbing trees like a boy as usual, I suppose. When will you start to be sensible like other people" my mother scolded, in that simplicity of hers that would never had ventured to formulate even the idea of such evil, let alone dare to attack "religion in person," of which the mystical Franciscan with his wandering eyes, of whose strange behaviour once outside her room she remained wholly unaware, was a representative. If I wept or moaned while in his grip, my mother, as she lay vomiting on the other side of the wall, was in too much pain herself to hear me. Nor did this interplay of sufferings include any corresponding consolation in its pattern: my mother always tried to clean up all traces of her sickness behind her, so as not to drive my father to despair, and I on my side used to bury my bloodied clothing deep in earth. Was this long silence to become one day the redemption of mankind? So my mother believed, as her eyes avoided mine during the daily recitation of my catechism lesson beside her bed: "Purity, hope, charity . . ."

That word "purity" conjured up nothing for me but corruption, putrefaction lying in ambush, and my whole being fought against it as though against some unhealthy power.

"What is it you've got in that head of yours, Pauline? Don't you want to learn your catechism? Don't you love the Good Lord either, then? Is there nothing in the world you love?"

Not only had Séraphine's death killed all innocence in my world, but that innocence like a diaphanous dream that burst at last in the air, had never existed, would never exist, and that fiery certainty was the only faith, the only hope of our lightless times. Since man was not good, what could he long to perform other than the evil that filled him with joy and spleen?

With the approach of summer, a procession of illnesses was once again prowling around us. Great green flies alighted everywhere, on the bars outside the windows, on the congealed, tasteless food, on the faces of babies, whose smooth, damp temples seemed to have a particular attraction for the creatures. Pale urchins were always fainting all over the place, in streetcars, in public parks, sliding slowly down between their mothers' arms, pieced without doubt by the arrow tipped with poisoned languor that hovered in the filthy town air, whose arid pressure one could feel perpetually in one's chest, until the autumn came. The poor families sought refuge in the sanatoriums, one after another; all the Carré children, with whom I spent a lot of my time despite my mother's embargo, vanished into these mysterious haunts of healing, about which my mother forbade me to speak, adding that "talking about sanatoriums was enough to make you start spitting blood . . ." I had only to run a temperature for more than a day or two for my mother to put her hand on my forehead and say: "It's there, it's the illness. The bigger you get, Pauline, the less you eat. I shall have to send you out to the country, as quick as possible, tomorrow morning, as soon as you're up."

And so it was that one morning my Uncle Victorin stepped triumphantly out of his tiny black automobile, the roundness of whose roof made a perfect marriage with the roundness of the hat he wore on the top of a bald head, round as well, like an apple, announcing to my mother that I was about to leave with him "for the mountain air, where you will eat like a pig, my girl, because in Saintonge du Délire, anyone who doesn't eat, we beat them." Waiting for me, in this village lost in the country, I had "thirty girl cousins as fat as barrels," my uncle assured me, "six aunts as big as that table, and a grandmother as stubborn as a mule."

"You won't be alone in the world," my mother added. "Here with your father and me, it's as though you're all alone in the world."

"Hey there, kids who don't smile, my wife she wallops them . . . Come on, sourpuss, give me a smile, can't you."

Vast landscapes were unwinding flaccidly past my eyes. Turning my head whenever poor Uncle Victorin decided to address me, invariably in terms of some wild animal – "Hey, come out of your bushes, you sly little fox, you wait and see the larruping my wife'll give your behind this evening!" – I felt welling up inside me a mixture of contempt and condemnation for this fat stranger who sat smoking cigars beside me, boasting in a flood of coarse words about his job as "cook at the lumber camp where you can stuff your belly day and night," never imagining that I would one day be enchanted by this image of the furiously energetic Victorin, dressed all in white among his sweating lumberjacks, tossing his pancakes over the fire at sunset, and surrounded by a mist of insects attracted from the scented forest. No, such a thought did not cross my mind: I loved no one, I thought to myself, and would never be capable of loving again.

"Town kids, they're worse than boats from hell, take my word for it! You eat nothing but that white bread, whereas we out here eat black bread, black grapes, which is why we've got some religion in us, and good hearts besides . . ."

We arrived that evening, along a little road out at the world's end. You somehow knew that the line of the sky couldn't possibly continue on the other side of the mountains. Unending sandy tracks, all so alike that for a long while, as night fell, we drove around and around inside this imprisoned landscape saying: "Saintonge du Délire may be this way, or perhaps it's that way," but never reaching anything but the same fence on one side of the road, the same sheep on the other, the same cross at

the end of the village, all so alike that for a long while those tortured tracks, those dusty trails wavered on the fringe of memory like something disturbingly unfinished, some task or other
left behind one only half completed.

"I can see a little patch of light, that must be it. There's a
kerosene lamp . . ."

And so, at last, the house belonging to my grandmother and my
uncles did appear, thanks to that almost imperceptible red glow
behind the tiny window in its door, and thrust abruptly into the
sooty limbo inhabited by all these relations of mine now suddenly created by the Good Lord to my great surprise, for I had
never until that evening suspected that they really existed, and
existed in a condition of life so different from my own – as I
gazed at all those faces advancing toward me, all those rugged
chins quarried in accordance with some ancestral model that
must have been fearful indeed, I sought in vain for some sign of
an austere but nevertheless welcoming emotion that seemed, in
fact, to be wholly lacking in those rough-hewn faces, as well as
in those cold blue eyes, happily softened by the remarkable
thickness of their brows and lashes.

"You're just in time for soup," said a strongly built woman
standing with one hand on her hip. "If it isn't a sin to see these
kids from the town, all as pale as corpses . . ."

"Pale as wax, but their sins as black as coal!" a crippled-look-
ing little boy said, then immediately went off into bursts of mad
laughter between his hunched-up, skeleton shoulders. "Is it true
you're my cousin?"

"Jacob!" a voice roared; but the fist that followed it, re-
bounding off the child's cheek, merely caused him to redouble
his laughter.

Jacob was never to cross the threshold of his deliverance. He was already a member, within the family group itself, of the despised caste of "invalids," dismally flanked by a young brother with epilepsy, a deaf and dumb sister, and an aunt suffering, like himself, from paralysis of one hand and a touching contraction of the back that bent them both down toward the ground, as well as causing them to clutch their chests with those malformed hands, cruelly crushed by nature, and yet able to accomplish so many things. And lastly – the perverse gift of a Providence exhausted by all the gifts she had bestowed elsewhere – Jacob also counted among the list of his brothers and sisters handicapped since birth "a little blue brother," as they all called him, not daring to give a graceful name to an unformed grub that was all ugliness, grief, and guilt of the world, perhaps. This baby was the last born, but Jacob's mother, quick to find consolation, was already carrying, in that flaccid belly beneath the coarse linen smock she wore year in and year out, the fourteenth embryonic horror that it would have been better, in the justice of pity, to throw out onto the garbage heap; but since pity did not exist except in Jacob's dreams, another cripple would come into the world, carrying on the innocent lineage of misfortune. There was also an army of men, of healthy children, that rose every morning in this house, not only to trample upon the weak but also to cultivate the earth, to provide food for men and beasts. As for Jacob, working all day among the pigs as he did, he appeared to share his meals with them. The infirmities of his Aunt Attala and the epileptic's fits did at least seem to inspire a degree of respect, but Jacob, never having submitted to anyone, sometimes wandering alone in the woods for nights on end, existed so low down on the family scale that he had come little by little to hear the whip whistling down on his bones as no more, he said, "than the little noise a sharp wind makes in the trees."

Jacob and I shared a bug-infested mattress; in another corner of the room, stretching out their long, giraffe necks in the darkness, the twins Evelyn and Ruth kept nightly watch, scratching themselves with slow deliberation, exchanging obscene little giggles when the pitiable Aunt Attala made her usual cascading, fervent use of the chamber pot that lurked beneath her bed. Jacob used to sing softly in his sleep, as others weep: I listened to him, deep in a hopeless melancholy, counting the hours with panic. Jacob's inward deliriums disturbed me; he often talked of cruel battles that took place in the mountains between the pigs, who had risen in rebellion, and their former masters, men of the same tribe as his father, "giants with black teeth and blue eyes full of spit, one day the pigs devoured them, ate them up, the skulls, then the hearts, leaving bits of bloody skin for the eagle who came in the night . . ." He quivered with pleasure as he recounted these banquets, and the vast panorama of violence he conjured up seemed to appease long-past humiliations. But he inspired fear, this ten-year-old boy, apparently so gentle, but whose heart was filled with a fusion of pity and absolute revenge. At night, with his cold, twisted hand, he used to touch my hair . . .

"If you don't eat tomorrow, my father will whip you the way he whips me. And he'll make your blood run all around under the table . . . Bang, bang! Oh, he'll really whip the daylights out of you, little cousin."

Jacob's father often used to make me eat by force, while his wife and Aunt Attala held my mouth open with fingers like quivering pincers. He threw anything there was around into my mouth, as though it were a well – balls of bread, molasses, spoonfuls of fly-blown milk – and in the presence of so rare a spectacle, Jacob, who was deliberately deprived of food as a punishment for his frequent insults to the village priest, and indeed to everything that represented for him a religion he condemned as spiritless and monstrous, the murderer of the poor "spitting in the soup bowl of the crippled and sick" – Jacob, so prompt to defend me in other circumstances, full of solicitude if I was cold beside him at night, when faced with my indifference to my daily bread could only silently share his father's fury, and suddenly even resembled him for a moment, his wild, wide pupils glittering with that same tiny, fixed flame, that gleam of cruelty and savage unease that sometimes made me think that the men in that house were all lost, damned.

Once these painful meals were over, Jacob returned to his usual delicate and ferocious humour, his tender stratagems, and the exercise of what was his most precious possession, in that vale of toil where no one ever smiled: a sense of the absurd that enabled him to pierce through appearances and pass judgment upon others, a judgment that he delivered with gay and honest mockery, as though he had grasped that men's hypocrisy could be made to yield by laughter. "Blasphemer, you will burn in hellfire," he was told again and again as he did his miraculous imitation of their vain old curé, standing up on the table, one hand on his belly, his frail body shaken by a vast series of those laughs, bitter laughs perhaps, that he had selected from all the hoard of barbarous things he had experienced and observed as his instrument of vengeance, nothing of childhood left in him but a melancholy and dreamy expression, only just perceptible, in the corners of his mouth. "He has hair as fine as a chick's down and no brain underneath it. He's crazy, completely crazy, a sinner, and apart from that a blasphemer, a blasphemer against the priests and the Lord above!"

"The Lord above's crazy too, and you just don't know how he laughs!"

Jacob was more afraid of the asylum than of death. He saw himself already a captive in those haunts abandoned to misfortune, a prisoner "until the end of time and the demons," living on forever, simply by mistake, in a bottomless and lightless abyss. And Jacob was right, since he was to spend his life going from one institution to another, rebellious at first and constantly inventing fresh blasphemies, then gradually resigning himself to a disease from which he had never suffered, other than in his family's primitive imaginations, until he became simply a boy inert with unhappiness, no longer dreaming, no longer thinking of anything but the immensity of the void surrounding him, wandering aimlessly through the fetid soul of a children's home. But meanwhile, blood was the daily colour of his life, and the woods his escape. One Sunday, when Jacob was exercising his skill by "spitting into the holy-water font so as to poison Saint Margaret," his father dragged him back by his ear to the house, where he was whipped with dry, thorny branches in the presence of his mother and aunt.

"Ha, pegleg, show us your wooden leg then, Pa!"

(During a nocturnal exchange of confidences Jacob had once told me how he had seen his father, "that big pig without a heart, take off his wooden leg to go to bed, yes, Cousin Pauline, as true as I'm talking to you, he's got a wooden leg, after he cut his real leg off in the threshing machine. Hey, ain't that a big laugh, him beating me 'cause I'm twisted up like a rattler, and him so ashamed he has to go and hide that pegleg of his under his damned mattress at night!")

"If I did have a wooden leg, you devil, I'd have squashed you flat with it a long time ago, believe me."

"Squash me flat with it then, so I can spit on it!"

"Viper!"

"Pig!"

"Aren't you ashamed, Jacob? Aren't you ashamed, husband," Jacob's mother finally cried, "fighting like that, trying to kill one another? What would m'sieur le curé say if he saw you! Aren't you ashamed Jacob, with your face all bleeding, aren't you ashamed, husband, torturing him like you was wringing the neck of some cock? Jacob, say your prayers and go to bed. Such shameful goings on. What would poor m'sieur le curé say?"

"He'd say we're a family of pigs. And he'd be right at that, because that's what we are. And so's the curé."

His mother washed Jacob's wounds under the pump. "You'll end up in the asylum, Jacob, if you keep on with your wickedness. Aren't you ashamed, haven't you any brain in your head, just teeth to bite with?"

On "the nights of the big whippings," as Jacob called them, the father whipped all the children who happened to be in the room, going from one to another in a crazed, waltzing stupor while the women chorused their protests:
"Are you mad, husband? You've put out Pauline's eyes . . . You can beat our kids, they're ours, the Good Lord gave them to us, but not other people's children, husband . . . You can hit them on the legs, not on the face . . . husband!"

"It's on their faces that the pride is written," the father answered, and slashed more violently than ever. The fragility of our eyelids was of no interest to him: who sees the victim he is torturing? "Do you hear me, Jacob, I'm going to tear those filthy eyes of yours out of your face as sure as any bird . . ." But it was I who received the blow, and my eyes were bleeding. I could just make out Jacob and his father leaning over me, both maliciously smiling. "Hey, little cousin, you caught it that time, didn't you. Come on, up on your feet, don't play the invalid."

"He's made you bleed, just like me," Jacob said with that air of suffering satisfaction that was usual with him in the presence of others' misfortunes. "He twisted my hand like a bit of old rag, that old bugger. Watch, cousin, look how I spit at him!"

"What would m'sieur le curé say if he saw you," the mother said. "You husband, harness the horse, you'll have to take Cousin Pauline to the hospital. What would m'sieur le curé say?"

Night was falling over the fields. A hostile mist was impregnating that already vile and humiliated landscape. His arms crossed on his chest, Jacob blasphemed as he spat into the dust of the road.

"Hai, hai, gallop, you damned old nag," Jacob's father roared, clutching the reins, for this was the end of what my Uncle Victorin had poetically called "the season of full stomachs, of happy holidays in the sun."

৯ Chapter Two ৪

"Still not dead, Pauline, still there making your mother weep, will you never change? Oh! if only the Good Lord had punished you enough to make you understand!"

Once more my mother was right. I trailed my existence from one end of the house to the other, interminably jumping rope. Séraphine had been dead a year already. Jacob was wasting away in a home. My own injured eyes, the source of so much concern to me during my two months in the clinic, but now almost cured, opened with indifference upon a world slightly hazed with mist, stripped of all the sickly charms with which it can so long be clothed by convalescence. I was still living in the company of those silent patients I had become so accustomed to: a chair, a table still carried the anaemic child with blue temples who was wheeled from one room to another; even my mother, as she cut up the red meat — "precious calf's liver too, it would save the lives of all the starving little children in the world" — that she had such difficulty paying for each Saturday, even my mother reminded me of the butcher-doctor in his blood-spattered smock who had opened the door to us that night in Saintonge du Délire, breathing his drunkard's breath over us as he exclaimed: "Just as I've got to bed and switched off the light you come knocking with a pair of bleeding eyes . . . Make her lie down on the floor so her eyes don't come running down her nose. I'll go and see if my old bus has any gas in it, then I'll run you to the hospital, where they can stick your eyes back in with mustard, heaven help us." My mother was moving in an orbit far away from me, somewhere in a realm of anguish full of vainly fluttering memories. "Why don't you go out into the sun and play, it'll do you good to breathe the fresh air. You're always there under my feet, round and round, day and night, as though you're in a cage." No longer having any reasons for living or loving, I had hoped to become blind, to follow the opaque trajectory of a wholly inward vision; but here I was, without having deserved it, not only beginning to see again but also, alas, beginning to suffer the persecution of being seen: my parents' eyes were once again mounting their watch, and there was no peace any more, either within, where my soul was evaporating away with boredom, or without, for never had I felt the sun's rays to be so brutal or the air so diseased.

"You ought to do a little work, you ought to be going back to school."

I left Mother Sainte-Scholastique for Mother Saint-Théophile, more covert in her tortures, swift to scent the odour of sin wherever she moved, and unable to live without the winged genius of our Holy Mother, the Principal, "Yes, children, you must always realize to what extent our Reverend Mother was weaned by the Lord . . . She has been granted all the graces, all the virtues, ah! if you only knew the gratification I feel at having a saint so near to us, at the very door of our classroom," for Mother Saint-Théophile's secret taste for sin, her dreams of it, her obsession with it were expressed in her every sentence, whether guilty or innocent, through which she enjoyed forbidden pleasures, and let fall at every step, without being aware of it, these germinating seeds of lubricity that we all recognized for what they were with interest or malice. For my part, taking advantage of Mother Saint-Théophile's delight in talking of her visits to the Reverend Mother Principal, or of the Principal's invitations to visit us, I simply slumped on my desk and slept, "as tired as a thousand men and as shattered as a whole army," as my mother put it, unable to meet the gaze of the dazzling sun that slanted through the classroom, sleeping all the time, and everywhere, the same heavy, motionless sleep.

"To your misfortune, my good Mother Saint-Théophile, I must now entrust this unsheared black sheep to your care. Do with her what you will, for she has already been expelled from three schools for her behaviour. But we have the reputation of being a charitable house, so let us give her one last chance, Good Mother, this poor child . . ."

"We shall receive much gratification from the task, Reverend Mother," Mother Saint-Théophile replied, pinching the newcomer's arm. Whereupon the girl herself, whose name was Louisette Denis, reacted immediately with a viperfish grimace, then ran over and sat down next to me.

"They're worse than two magpies, those two old crackpots," Louisette Denis hissed in my ear. "They do nothing but yammer all day. I'm getting out of here."

But she stayed, and brought such a breath of fresh air into the classroom that it no longer occurred to me to slump on my desk. Mother Saint-Théophile was forced, despite everything, to pay homage to the gifts of a naturally first-rate mind. "The Lord has endowed you with a generous share indeed of His divine intelligence, and person, but He has not separated the wheat from the tares . . . Reverend Mother tells me that you were so impolite in the corridor this morning that she was unable to believe her saintly ears. You will go and make your apologies to her, Louisette Denis, this very instant."

That was how Louisette Denis spent her days, perpetually on the way somewhere with apologies she never made; and stirred by the electric rhythm of her feet racing down the corridor, I sensed the sleeping demons reawakening in me. In Séraphine I had loved a child: in Louisette I loved a sister more fully alive than myself, and though I had been unable in the past to protect Séraphine from injustices and cruelty, now, with Louisette as an ally ready armed for the fray, I felt empowered to rend the veil of an authority for which I felt so little love. Ah, I thought, how we will be able to make fun of Mother Saint-Théophile now, of the Principal, of Mother Sainte-Scholastique, and even of Uncle Victorin and Jacob's father. "All doomed to burn in hell for their wickedness," Lousiette said, "and we, we shall watch them burn."

Louisette Denis knew how to defend herself like a tiger, how to "shriek like a devil having its tail burned if Mother Saint-Théophile ever tries to touch me with her cane . . ." She had already broken several plates over the head of her adoptive mother, against whom she had sworn perpetual enmity, and she would wring her sisters' necks, she claimed. In short, she no longer had any fear of anything neither of God nor of man.

"Let's imagine that you're my brother and I'm your brother too, and that we swear an eternal oath, with me pricking you till you bleed with my knife, and then if you break the oath, I kill you."

But already conscious of my unfaithful nature, I no longer dared to make such promises. "I can't promise that, because I'm such a liar."

"You lie like a trumpet," my mother said. "I've never known anyone who lied the way you do. You lie as naturally as you breathe, and I can see that nose of yours twitching, so you know the Good Lord is listening . . . You must confess all those lies to the priest, you must make a really full confession, Pauline."

And so we arrived, hundreds of milling children flooding the gloom of the church, eager to spill out our confessions into the bottomless urn of repentance held in the blessing-laden hands of our poor confessors, prisoners of their duties year in and year out, stretching toward our secrets a long, indiscreet ear sometimes bristling with hairs, seated in their cells, head against the grille, repeating in a sleepwalker's voice: "And how many times? Was it in act or in thought? Did you consent or not? My child, that is what is called 'sinful contacts.' Were you alone or with others? Ah! heaven defend us! You mustn't ever do it again, you'll go straight to hell. Quickly, your act of contrition . . ." The slavery of sin, and the confusion of it, reddened our cheeks; we raced quickly back to our seats in order to throw ourselves at God's feet and implore his clemency, heads between our hands, praying beneath the arid protection of the statues, peeping with one eye at our neighbours, inviting the row of boys with a hint of a smile to share their examinations of conscience with us. We emerged from the crypt of the church as we had arrived, twittering, coughing, in a restless rustling of shoe leather and voices. "Behave yourselves," Mother Saint-Théophile called from the front of her flock, "behave yourselves, girls. Remember that you are still in enjoyment of grace."

But once we were outside the church, a whirl of black-clad legs scattered in all directions, and without the aid of the Reverend Mother Principal, Mother Saint-Théophile was powerless to keep us following in the wake of her skirts. "Ah, what would become of me without our Reverend Mother, wretched children that you are, deserting your mother's bosom." Louis-ette nudged me with her elbow: "They're nuts, those two old magpies, always complimenting one another like that, Reverend Mother this, Mother Saint-Théophile that, perhaps they sleep in the same jacket at night, in the same pair of pajama trousers. Anyway, I know nuns don't go to the lavatory; I tried to watch to see if they did, well they don't. They're too much afraid of upsetting Our Lord above."

Long after our confessions had been made, the savour of repentance already faded, the confessor's words still buzzed in our ears. "Sinful contacts, what *are* they?" Louisette Denis asked. "Do you know what they are?"

"Yes, it's what we do in the gully with Jacquou."

"No, not those sinful contacts, I know all about those. My kid brother teaches me those in bed at night. I mean the others, the ones that are really big sins, like Father Carmen said in con-fession . . . Perhaps we can have a try at them, just to see . . ."

"No, no, I can't. My conscience is worse than that camel. One more sin would break its back."

Everyone seemed to throw the word "conscience" about all the time, as though it were a sort of ball. "Haven't you a single grain of conscience then?" my mother would ask. "Keep a pure conscience," the Reverend Mother Principal told us. "Be as pure as lilies." "I'm going to scrub it for you now, that filthy con-science of yours," Jacob's father used to say to him; and if some-one was particularly beautiful, that was above all because he or she had "a beautiful conscience."

"Come home with me after school. I'll lock the door of my room, then we'll see what we shall see. We'll find out if they're as horrible as they say, these sinful contacts."

Stripping off her black dress and hurling it in a ball into one corner – "hideous old hand-me-down, how I hate you. Come on then, Pauline Archange, let's see what there is to see" – Louisette set about exploring the various parts of her body with nimble fingers: "That there, that's the haunt of sin, according to Father Carmen. He says if you touch it you can get your fingers burned. Look, the harder I press, the less it burns . . . Talk about a rotten old liar. Hey look, your navel's smaller than mine, Pauline Archange. I've got knees like a boy's, I don't want to be a girl, I hate dolls, and babies and all that muck. They cry and they smell, boy do they! What I want to be is a man who walks about on the snow with snowshoes. Here, hand me my little brother's ski pants hanging over there. What I want to be is a beggar selling rags in the street, or else a little old man with glasses who mends umbrellas at a nickel apiece . . . Come on, Pauline Archange, help me cross the suspenders properly, in front like Papa. Oh heavens, how I hate my old Sisters' dress, and the Sisters too, and the black stockings and the black shoes, as though my real mother was dying every day of the week, as if wherever you walked there's a coffin waiting, as if Papa were marrying that old frump of a Céleste who wants me to call her Mama . . . The Sisters, they're like a lot of black spiders, with little yellow feet. If there was a Good Lord up in heaven the way they say, he'd never have made creatures like them. If he did create them and all, then he's got no conscience . . . Hey, show me your haunt of sin again to see if it's the same as mine . . . Pah, I hate girls, they're all exactly the same with their haunts of sin, whereas boys . . ."

But soon Louisette Denis was talking with great simplicity about "the sex of butterflies, and ants, and crocodiles," arousing a haunted watchfulness in Mother Saint-Théophile and the Reverend Mother Principal, her twin in obsession, by asking in class: "What sex would the Holy Ghost be then?" with that delightful air of hers that made her friendship so lively, evasive, and fleet-footed as the years that were dropping from our lives.

Séraphine was already ahead of me on the path of time, and in a few years, perhaps, I should be peering back to scrutinize the already faded days I was now in such a hurry to live through beside Lousiette Denis. Sometimes still, in memory, I went back to Séraphine: wild and joyful, the murmuring voices rang through our tent. "A Brownie is always prepared!" came the voice of our counsellors, barefooted in the morning dew, and on our toes, in front of the tents, we shivered our way through morning exercise.

"What's that, are you yawning, Brownies? That's not allowed here. One, two, three, four, one, on your feet, on your hands, faster now, left, right, there's the bell in the chaplain's tent. Time for Mass, on with your clothes . . ."

We arrived at the chaplain's tent, panting, still clutching one shoe, our ties knotted under our ears – "Beret on there, quickly! You can't take communion without a hat . . . Dignity, we must keep our dignity" – believing more than ever in the existence of grace among the scent of flowers, the aroma of the melancholy incense wafted into our faces by acolyte-Brownie Huguette Poire, jangling the gold mess tins that glittered at our badly buckled belts with the pressure of an authoritative finger. "A little silence there," the chaplain ordered with an irritated gesture, for he alone was impatient for the end of these two weeks "surrounded by too many women."

"I shall have done my duty, but it's no joke, all these little wildcats."

"More than your duty, monsieur l'Abbé," our counsellor corrected him. "You will have accomplished your mission. For us, duty does not exist, the scout movement has only missions. It serves God and the homeland."

It was in the exaltation of such petty duties that I had neglected Séraphine.

You who can climb the highest trees, Pauline Archange, who always carry off the pennant of honour for your team in the races, I appoint you 'champion of the sick'; it will be your task to help those who faint and have to be picked up before communion . . ."

With energetic step, the assistant counsellor Berthe and I carried those who had fallen back to their tents, then poured carafes of water over their heads. "What do you expect, it's the only thing that will bring them round, and a Brownie is not afraid to suffer . . ."

Our farewell to the camp ended in tears. In a plaintive circle, beneath the trees, our joined hands with their ragged nails rose and fell to the rhythm of the long goodbye: "Goodbye, my friends, we'll meet again, my friends, in this world, my friends, or in the next, we'll meet again, my friends, we'll meet again one day . . ." while the captain smiled till his face almost split, thinking – as he had already assured us in morose tones and on several occasions that he so often did – "of his good old pipe, of his good old curé expecting him in town, of his proper man's business," of saying goodbye until the following summer to "all those women swarming around him like flies."

One day, from her distant and foreign shore, the grande dame of the Girl-Guide movement descended upon us, provoking fresh activities in the town's agitated companies.

"The flag of pride must fly above our company, girls, for never have humble Brownies like yourselves received such an honour as to behold, in person, in flesh and blood, our remarkable founder, Lady Baron Topwell. Ah, girls! it is something that all your lives you'll never forget . . ."

In every parish, hundreds of little girls, members of each and every company, the Leaping Deer, the Golden Lion, the Fleeting Hare, the Fearless Bear, the Valiant Stag, were weaving garlands of flowers and praises, training their raucous little voices to produce the vast, military rumble that was to acclaim Lady Baron Topwell, at the summit of her glory, capped, booted, bosom held high beneath her thick velvet tie, the will power expressed by her shoulders undeterred by the mass of decorations that fluttered around them like so many tiny, angry wings, frankly mannish, her lips darkened by a summary moustache, waving to us from her dais of splendour, and immediately drawing from our numerous and serried ranks an "Always Prepared!" of supreme decisiveness that was the pure product of our breathless admiration, of our unlimited veneration for a personage of state so eagerly awaited. The roses, scattered in profusion, languished at her big feet, suffocated no doubt by the fouled air in the vast reception room; the Leaping Deer and the Golden Lions laid before her, among other honorific gifts, assurances of homage and fidelity, poems written in red ink symbolizing our common blood.

> *The Leaping Deer will serve you until death.*
> *He is your warrior, your faith.*
> *The Golden Lions have hearts of bronze,*
> *Their courage knows no bounds.*

Being unable to speak our language, Lady Baron could only lean out sentimentally over this farmyard of little animals so eager to serve her and exclaim in a moved, deep voice full of emotion:

"W…e…l…l…Go…od…Ah! W…e…ll, w…ell…"
Left arms raised in the solemn ritual salute, chanting the hymn
of our homeland, our cup of ecstasy was brimming over. The
idea of death, of our childhood sacrificed in the light of a noble
setting sun, our bodies pierced with arrows, our heads falling
under the axe, should Lady Baron ask it of us some day not far
hence, a myriad such images fluttered mechanically against our
fevered temples…Ah! We are yours, do with us what you will,
you have such a lovely uniform, such pretty leather boots, and
your name sounds a little different from ours when we hear it,
you've come from so far away, we want to go away with you on
your ship, Mother Saint-Théophile will beat us again . . . ah!

But Lady Baron departed toward further triumphs, shed-
ding a tear, blowing her nose noisily into her checkered handkerchief: "Fare…we…ll…Fare…we…ll." And so our great
adventure ended: the great captain left without us.

With November upon us, Mother Saint-Théophile set about
exhuming all the dead and departed from purgatory; in each
flake of snow that fell we were urged to see "one more soul in
the hands of God." The earth lay thick with these white souls,
soaking our feet. The petrified washing on its lines of ice rocked
in the cold blast: stiff souls still wearing their nightdresses, or a
pair of torn pants, its legs waving with anger … "It's a pack of
lies all that," Louisette Denis said. "There'd be too many people
in purgatory, and in hell; no wonder I loathe all those batty old
sisters . . ."

"Our annual retreat will do you good, Louisette Denis. The
Reverend Mother Principal and I pray for your conversion: the

month of the dead is also the month of repentance, don't forget that."

The chaplain in charge of our retreat had served his apprenticeship in a jail: he opened the door of his monastery to us "like the gates of His most beauteous prison." "Come in, my children," he continued, "the hour of your trial is at hand, and God is here as your judge beneath my roof," then saw us to our rooms, which he described as "our cells gilded with the divine light of heaven," and forthwith left us alone "to consider the verdict of our own conscience." Terrified by this eccentric jailer-like attitude, I spent my nights in Louisette's room, hiding under her bed if I heard Mother Saint-Théophile's step in the corridor.

"Well, she may have left her Reverend Mother Principal behind in the convent to come to this retreat, but now she's getting just as soppy over Father Gustave as she is over the Reverend Mother; what she likes, that one, is skirts, cassocks, anything that drags about on the ground all black and snaky. Look at the way she stares at Father Gustave during his sermons with her mouth hanging open, dripping with love, the old fool. What she likes, believe me, is superiors, superiority, yes, that's what she's mad for, so that she can spy on us and get us punished. This is the first time I've ever been in a monastery, and I'm here to tell you it's the last, they're not catching me twice with their retreats, they're not going to convert yours truly . . . Honestly, have you ever seen such a dismal place, and anyway it stinks of the Sisters or something or other anyway, and you can't even go outside to play, you just have to pray all the time, a week of just praying, I mean just imagine! No, they're certainly not going to catch me a second time . . . Do you know what Father Gustave did yesterday? I told him I hadn't got any sins to confess, and he said he'd put me all alone in a little 'cell full of rats.'

He's mad that one, just plain mad, believe me. If he tries putting me in a cell I'll bite him till he bleeds . . ."

"The Reverend Mother Principal said you're possessed by the devil, and they ought to clean the evil spirits out of you with holy water. You have all the bad luck, Louisette Denis. And so do I."

"I'll clean her evil spirits out for her, you bet, that crazy old hag with her blue lips and her fingers made of candle wax, I'll scrub her face for her in the dishwater . . ."

We were still at the joyful task of slandering our teachers, hands crossed under our necks, one leg in the moon-dappled air, when Mother Saint-Théophile opened the door, like one of those November ghosts I was so afraid of, eye-blasting in her ugliness, her eyes starting out of her head under her white percale bonnet, banging her fist on her chest as she cried: "Ah! I knew it, I knew it. The Reverend Mother Principal herself put me on my guard against this peril."

"What's the matter?" Louisette Denis asked. "Are you jealous or something? What's it got to do with you if we want to talk? We can't pray all night, we're not monks yet, are we, Pauline Archange? I want to go home with Pauline Archange, I've had enough of this retreat. So have you, Pauline Archange, so come on, let's go home."

Standing up on her bed, Louisette Denis began tearing at her hair while Mother Saint-Théophile looked on in a dull stupor.

"It's too bad my hair's cut short, I can tell you that, because if it was long I'd pull it out in handfuls, I'm so fed up with you Sisters and the Fathers and the whole thing . . . Come on, Pauline Archange, what are we doing anyway in this dump?"

"What are you doing?" Mother Saint-Théophile demanded, recovering her breath. "You dare to ask me that? You have the effrontery? Heaven help me, I must call Father Gustave. Help, help!"

"Talk about an old fool," Louisette Denis said, following Mother Saint-Théophile's hysterical retreat along the corridor out of the corner of one eye. "Perhaps we ought to put on our coats, pack our suitcases, and get out of here before Father Gustave gets hold of us by our skirts. Come on, Pauline Archange, hurry up, it's a matter of life and death when you've got people as nuts as that after you."

We were about to slink out when a hand descended upon us. "Such delinquents must be dealt with by force," Father Gustave said as he marched us along the corridor. "But remember, my good Mother Saint-Théophile, that souls possessed by demons can be cured by gentleness alone." In the chapel, Louisette Denis refused to kneel. "No and no and no. I've had enough. I want to go home. I shall tell my father, if my father were around, this wouldn't have happened."

"We are awaiting your complete confession. The court will show you all possible clemency if you confess everything."

"What ever does that mean? I don't understand a word of all that jargon."

"Confess, my child, confess or I shall put you in the cell for prisoners, the cell full of rats."

The judges finally decided that I was innocent. "The poor little thing has been bewitched, yes, it's clearly a case of possession; they do still occur from time to time even today. Louisette Denis, the devil resides in you, in his most pernicious form. He must be driven out, and I take the task upon me gladly, my child, have no fear."

"It's true, I'm stuffed with devils, they're called Barababble, Contactus, Baraguggle, and all my heaps of devils hate you like the fires of hell! Aren't you afraid? Aren't you ashamed?"

"You are right, dear Father Gustave," Mother Saint-Théophile said in a grief-stricken voice.

And next day Louisette Denis was shut up in a dark little room that contained a *prie-dieu*, a crucifix, but no trace of any rats. When Father Gustave went to bring her out, a day later, she bit his hand so hard that he yelled. "It wasn't me, it was the rats..." That was the end of our retreat for that year.

When my mother saw me coming back from the monastery three days before the others, when she perceived my evasive air as I handed her the note from Mother Saint-Théophile about the sinful activities I had been seduced into, she avoided my glance, withdrawn completely into a contemplation of the unpleasant duties I had forced upon her.

"Remember, parents and educators," our priest used to say in his sermons, "the child that is punished does not suffer. We alone suffer when we fulfill our duty and punish them for the good of their souls. We alone experience pains worthy of Abraham sacrificing his son."

"Oh Pauline, how wicked of you, doing this to your mother ... I feel too sick inside today to face the idea of beating you, but you wait till your father gets home. He'll drop your pants and give your thin bottom a tanning you won't forget in a long time."

My father, when he did come home, tired and hungry after still another day in the factory, warming his icy fingers on his bowl of steaming soup, pretended for a long while not to understand what my mother wanted of him.

"Now, Jos, don't drink your soup like that, you'll scald your insides. We can't just let our kids do anything they get into their heads, they must learn right and wrong."

"I'm dying of cold," my father answered. "Let me at least get warm first ... The boss has three automobiles, four houses, and yet he's too poor to heat his factory."

But when the meal was over, when the table had been cleared, my father still hesitated. "Don't be so impatient, wife, let me roll a cigarette first at least . . . A man has a right to his pleasures . . . Where is that Pauline of ours?" he said finally, getting up from his chair, his thumbs stuck inside his suspenders. "Pauline Archange, where are you hiding?"

He hit me hard, so as to get it over with quicker, and as soon as my nose began to bleed he considered his work was over. "Now get off to bed. The Good Lord will punish you himself on Judgment Day."

But that judgment was already here among us and we were not free.

"You have to get angry," Louisette Denis said. "You have to show the Sisters you're not sheep, you have to let them know you're lobsters, you have to bite them . . ."

I suddenly thought of Jacob in his institution. My mother and I visited him once a year. I could see him, a prisoner with a shaved head walking toward us in a gray garment like a sack, tied around his waist with a piece of string. Jacob no longer had a name. His number was indistinguishable in the crowd. The nuns of the Institute of the Saviour of the Poor had to embrace too many miseries at once to pay attention to any individual grief: Jacob's cheated intelligence wandered like a ghost among other ghosts more fragile still. "It's as though they'd softened up his brain, that little kid who used to be as alert as a wolf." And it is true that in this limbo of weariness Jacob's spirit, tenacious though it was, would one day melt into that human wax that a naked spirit is without any protective envelope against the world. Yet the nuns laboured constantly to give them form, these abstract lives: by day, by night, despite their mask of asperity they continued to deploy a saintly heroism in the struggle against a massive, distant grief. But in vain, for all that energy of theirs seems to spill over into mere nothingness, offered up to God with their prayers at dawn, their flagellations by night, while the inmates wept with cold and hunger. The Institute of the Saviour rose up from the midst of a splendid landscape, on the edge of a stream, surrounded by hills; but the pure air coursing past outside never reached the slave accomplishing his humiliating task within. During our visits, Jacob never left off scrubbing the floor of the big room, down on his knees. "He spends all his time scrubbing the floor, it's a mania of his, we let him do it, we let them do anything they like, unless it's wrong."

"We can't leave that child here," my mother announced. "I'll take him back home with me and bring him up with my own children. Come on, Jacob, get dressed, you're coming back to town with us."

"You make me spit," Jacob said, but very calmly, as one talks in dreams.

Jacob had been given permission to come and live with us for a while, "long enough to set his head to rights," my mother said; but as soon as he arrived, his strange behaviour startled us again. Accustomed to living amid yells, Jacob yelled himself, or else remained totally silent for hours on end, kneeling on the tiled kitchen floor which he was always wanting to scrub, despite my mother's protestations. "But, Jacob, you've already done it three times today. Don't you think that's enough?" That was how Jacob came to attack my mother with a penknife, with the result that my father began talking about his nephew's departure.

"For once, wife, this idea of yours wasn't a good one. Why don't you write to Jacob's father and tell him to fetch the boy, take him back to the country. All you've succeeded in doing for that kid is to feed him up a bit and give him somewhere to sleep, but his manners are so bad it's not believable. I saw him yesterday licking the butter on the butter dish, and the other day he snatched all Pauline's calf liver off her plate and gulped it down like a real wild beast. We can't keep him, we can't afford it!"

When Jacob saw his father in the doorway, he began trembling and hid under the table. "You're not to touch that kid of yours in my house," my father said. "Don't you dare lay a finger on him in front of me!" But Jacob's father grasped his son in one great hand, brandished him briefly aloft like a writhing serpent, and then, enfolding him brutally in his arms, slyly expressing his intention of exercising the right to torture what was his the moment he had left us, he flung open the door with a laugh as Jacob shrieked through his tears: "I'm going to hell, Cousin Pauline. You don't love me after all, because you didn't keep me, I'm going . . ."

⚘ Chapter Three ⚘

When the month of the dead was over at last, the classrooms were lit up by preparations for Christmas. Mother Sainte-Alma's white coif fluttered above the blackboards with their burden of numbers. "Quickly now, we must be joyful, children, the Lord is about to be born. Rub all those horrors off the blackboard, do we need numbers when the Lord is about to be born? Don't you agree, Mother Saint-Théophile?"

"No," Mother Saint-Théophile replied, "we don't approve of such an attitude, the Reverend Mother Principal and I. We believe that our students should prepare themselves for the birth of Jesus, not in joy but in penitence."

"A month of penitence is enough. Now then, children, I need some angels' voices for my carols. Louisette Denis, Huguette Poire, Pauline Archange, Julie, Victoria Poulain, I count on you all to act in my play: 'Let there be more rejoicing on Earth than in Heaven.' Be in my music room at three o'clock!"

"There they are, my Christmas angels," Mother Sainte-Alma cried as she saw us entering the music room. "Tch, tch . . . Now then, girls, you at the pianos over there, stop your practicing for today, it's time for our carols . . ." But Mother Sainte-Alma spoke in vain, for the thirty girls practiced their scales, each at her piano, deafer than posts to the wavering din that rose from their long-suffering instruments, some simply allowing their fingers to glide over the ivory keys in a dream of almost sulky sonorities, the others making their pianos reverberate like drums beneath their frail fingers, all with flaming cheeks, undoubtedly proud of themselves, straight-backed on their too mobile stools, imprisoned in their dignity as though in iron corsets.

"Whatever can they be playing, I wonder," Mother Sainte-Alma said. "The tone doesn't sound quite right to me. Louisette Denis, do go over and tap them on the shoulder for me, and ask them if they'll be good enough to leave off deafening us like that."

"Now, my little voices, away we go . . ."

Mother Sainte-Alma consulted her piano, listening with emotion to the lonely quiver of the selected note. "Doh . . . doh . . . Now then, girls, away we go. It's as easy as breathing, sing.

> *"The Holy Child is born to us.*
> *Glory to the Holy Child . . ."*

We sang: a hundred, two hundred girls dazzled by the wonder of their own voices, eyes fixed on the indulgent baton of Mother Sainte-Alma, who had certainly lost a few notes but was no longer looking for them, so confounded was she by the bronchial wheezings and the coughs that were mingled with our song's sincerity, obliged to smile, her ears ringing with the pain of it, but nevertheless obliged to smile more and more widely so as to encourage us to further efforts, for what she wanted for her chapel was, above all, angels. The voices would come on Christmas Eve, with the grace of the Lord to whom all was possible, but the ephemeral beauty of the angels, that was something she herself could concoct for us: "Paper dresses made of white crepe paper, magnificent cardboard wings, ah! I can already see you making the real angels jealous!" Completely out of breath, we abandoned the carol for Mother Sainte-Alma's play. "Louisette Denis, you will be Saint Lacrimonius, you, Pauline Archange, the gladiator and the lion, that means changing roles four times, and you, Victoria Poulain, you will be the mountain." Louisette Denis, clothed in her thin martyr's tunic, her knees and shoulders bare, a spray of palm in one hand, her boy's head garlanded with flowers, walked haughtily around the stage – "Indecently is the word," Mother Saint-Théophile said. "Bare knees! If the Reverend Mother Principal were to see you" – visibly in seventh heaven at having survived both fire and flood, eyeing her tormentors with scorn as she repeated her valiant refrain:

"To none of your deaths shall I yield,
for God is my faith and my shield . . ."

"Try to be less indifferent," Mother Sainte-Alma urged, her panic-struck eyes seeing the beaked profile of the real Saint Lacrimonius in the flames. "The fire is bound to burn you a bit, after all."

"The more it burns, the better I like it. I'm not Saint Lacrimonius for nothing."

Surrounded by the golden whirlwind of her spiky beams, Julie Poulain hurled herself too soon onto the mountain, leaping up onto the back of her sister Victoria, who impatiently shook her off again. "Listen, Julie, the sun doesn't come up in the middle of the night . . ."

"Ssh, ssh," Mother Sainte-Alma said. "Saint Lacrimonius is still deep in his prayers. It's still night, you can sit down again, sun!" All our rehearsals were "one more opportunity not to study," my mother said, "and the best way of catching a cold," for we ran straight out of school, burning with excitement and gaiety, gulping down the December cold like some bitter beverage, coughing and coughing, but too preoccupied to be aware of the fever that consumed us. Regretfully, I allowed myself to slide down between the cold sheets, threatening my mother that I would get even sicker if she didn't let me go to school the next day.

"In the meantime, I'll go and make you a mustard plaster, Pauline Archange. Though I wonder why I bother to look after you at all, you're a real little monster." The napkin full of hot, strong mustard, pressed against a chest still shivering with cold, had the same effect as the burning martyrdom that Louisette Denis, in our play, had accepted like a dream, a dream that had now become both concrete and monotonous for me, since this was at least the fifth time in a year that my mother had thrown me into this burning bush.

My mother's austerity, her wordless melancholy, reminded me suddenly that winter was the hardest, the longest season of all. Lost in her own thoughts, my mother forgot me for whole days together: I washed less and less, and then found myself saddened at the sight of my grimy hands spread out on the white table-cloth, or else, at other times, by a gray line around my neck, making me realize that the time had now come to accept sole mastery over my own body, this flesh that some mysterious incident had caused to clothe my bones, and that each one of us, after all, had perhaps lost his mother in his cradle, and that this duty of learning cleanliness in my own solitude was as nothing compared to all the other duties still ahead. Such as that of earning my living, which I was already considering, so as to be better prepared when the moment came, which always appeared to me in all its fatality during the harsh nudity of winter.

I would be having other brothers and sisters one day: I would have to forswear the luxury of going to school, give up my laziness, and my friendships, which were only an extension of the former in my mother's eyes. Wasn't she always saying to me: "Instead of fooling around with Louisette Denis, you should be putting your little brother to bed and doing the dishes," which immediately fanned Louisette's feelings for me into renewed warmth, for she felt a great pity for these future responsibilities about which I talked unendingly.

"Papa says that when she gets to the sixth grade a girl should go out and earn her living."

"If you leave school, Pauline Archange, I'll go too. We'll sweep the streets together."

Winter was also the time when indoors, over our heads, in the Poire and Carré households as well as our own, there hung lines of sparse washing that hit you on the nose with their ironic droplets during meals . . . plop, plop in your bowl of coffee; and Monsieur Poire, rising from the table with the tyrannical majesty of a drunkard, suddenly had his head imprisoned in the legs of his pajamas, his great hands abruptly fending off this unprepossessing woolly character who had languished all day beside the coal-less stove and seemed still to be running with water like a drowned corpse.

Washdays plunged my mother into a state of humble dissatisfaction which she tried to redeem with hopes: "Why don't we move, Jos? It's a terrible neighbourhood here for children. Why don't we go and live in Saint-Thomas des Rois? That's a much nicer parish, there are trees, and they speak better than around here."

"Oh, we're happy enough here. More than happy."

With a disillusioned smile whose subtlety was usually lost on my father, my mother reproached her husband for this simplicity of his in his expectation of happiness. She didn't know how to express what it was she wanted for us, what she had once desired for herself, an existence one could be proud of, and the thought that I too would give up my schooling later on, as she had before she was fifteen, widened even further the abyss between herself and others.

"We're not in real want, we're not too badly off. Have you already forgotten what it was like when I was a kid? Seventeen of us there were, and everyone had to learn to work. My pa did not let anyone get around him, he was a real tough nut! I promise we'll move one day . . . You'll have it, that house of yours!"

My father worked all day at the factory, studied in the evenings, worked at night mending roads, and was nevertheless astonished to "feel like a man who's had it before he's forty." He was losing weight, losing his hair, but he never stopped comparing his present comfortable life with the insecurity he had lived through in the past, as a labourer in his father's fields. "He was a fair man, my father. At Christmas, if all he had to give his children was four oranges, then he cut them up into seventeen portions, and everyone thanked him." The only pleasure he allowed himself at that time was his bike rides, which he took on Sundays with me in the basket, proudly waving at the neighbours under a stormy sky while I watched him ungratefully from between my clenched fists. I wasn't thinking about my father, there in his basket, but of Louisette Denis. The two of us had now reached that stage of friendship where we were both waiting for some happy event capable of suddenly transforming us for one another. We were so excessively well-behaved in school after our stay at the monastery that we scarcely recognized one another, and Mother Saint-Théophile herself seemed to be pained by a good behaviour that was nothing but numbness of mind, an indifference to good marks, so that in her feeling of regret at no longer being able to punish us she said to the Reverend Mother Principal: "I had always thought as much, Reverend Mother, those two girls have too much intelligence and not enough heart."

During classes, we gazed into one another's eyes with sighs of boredom: what were we going to become, that was our mindless, yawning question. And we went on gazing at one another for hours on end, as a pool gazes up at the sky, void of all emotions, but with tiny ripples of unease occasionally ruffling those not very profound waters.

Germaine Léonard's arrival was to transform our lives. For the first time, a doctor entered the portals of our disease-infested buildings, a firm voice insisted on our behalf upon "profound changes, Mother Superior, radical changes; otherwise, you will lose a great many more of your students."

"Since your charity is inspired by faith," the Mother Superior replied, "we are grateful to you for your activities here. But there's no possibility of our finding any money to pay you for them: we live only for the glory of God."

Germaine Léonard interrupted the Superior with a demand for the immediate institution of an infirmary, adding with an air of distaste: "That disused chapel would do."

Never having experienced such a thing as a cure for our ills, we raced as one child to the infirmary to present our rotting teeth, our sore throats, our racking coughs rasping up from the abyss like appeals for love and kindness. And surrounded by this sea of feverish abandon, by forty jostling, coughing little girls, pulled at by too many hands, poisoned by too many breaths, Mlle Léonard seemed suddenly overwhelmed and appalled at her own magnanimous inspiration in offering to look after us.

"Leave me alone," she cried. "Or rather stand in line. I can't examine you all at the same time."

The wave of little girls gradually receded toward its usual shore; one by one they made their way downstairs again toward the dark classrooms lit by the feeble glimmer of bare electric bulbs: outside, darkness was already falling, snow-laden and slow. Yet it was still only three in the afternoon, and Mlle Léonard was working at her desk, biting the end of her pencil, turning the pages of her files, while Louisette Denis and I lurked in a corner, unseen, and continued to drink her in with our eyes. For us, that high and noble mind hummed like a thousand bees, for besides giving her services free to our school, Germaine Léonard not only worked at the hospital but was also writing a thesis on atheism, a project that was later to earn her dismissal from our school. An ugly expression of anger occasionally quivered on our friend's lips, her mouth betrayed the presence of a slightly brutal sensuality, but always in her eyes there was the same unfailing expression of intelligent, sensitive pity, and it was the harmonizing influence of this indomitable pity that alone enabled the two forever irreconcilable halves of her face to form a complete and single person. We loved her selfishly, hoping to continue existing for many years in the wake of her dignity. We each aspired, now that she was there, to the liberation of delights we as yet had no right to. Certainly the joys of intelligence aroused our emotion; but the thought that there also existed delights equally attractive and less chaste, and that Mlle Léonard was in enjoyment of both kinds – for despite the curt discretion with which she cloaked her life, she had been unable to conceal completely her passion for a man – this thought incited us to even greater efforts to understand Mlle Léonard and the life she represented in our eyes.

"Oh, how I'd like to be thirty like her!"

"You said it, Pauline! How free we'd be, how happy! In the daytime we could look after the sick people, and at night . . ." But Louisette Denis stopped there, able to comprehend certain things with a clarity still half in shadow, yet still unable to absorb them fully; for though Germaine Léonard had proudly resisted the medical colleague who opened his arms to her one evening as she came out of the hospital – despite the contrary desire apparent in her eyes and lips, a desire to offer themselves to him – Louisette Denis was able to sense, as I was, that we were witnesses to an inner storm on the verge of abandon, and that this woman who gave herself up exclusively during the day to our sufferings kept in reserve for her nights a passionate explosion of radiance in which we were completely forgotten.

"You're not being discreet, come back this evening. Not now . . . Someone might see us."

But the young man suddenly kissed Mlle Léonard on the back of her neck, on that spot where our gazes had lingered all day in their possessive innocence.

How many days, how many hours would we have to wait at each other's side for life's great realities to unfold! There was hardly a moment when we were not together, Louisette Denis and I. This feverish state of expectation made us inseparable, and seeing us everywhere and forever hanging around her, hand in hand, "like two happy, affectionate monkeys," began to irritate Mlle Léonard. She said to me one day, among other observations of a medical nature – "A throat that's been sore for a whole year and you haven't mentioned it to your mother, and why won't you eat like other people!" – that there was, without any doubt, "a certain excessiveness in the attachment you and Louisette Denis have for one another.

"A certain exaggeration, God be thanked, you're only eight still, and it's obvious you haven't met any boys yet."

But falling into the trap of a confidential moment, I told Mlle Léonard my life story. How sweet it was to pour out that murmuring flood into the ears of a being dear to the heart when one had been accustomed, since the cradle, to reveal one's secrets only in scrupulous confession at the feet of a priest; the pleasure of a confession without shame and without repentance was so delightful, now the opportunity for it had at last occurred, that I was quite unable to stop.

"That's enough now," Mlle Léonard broke in. "You can go on another day!"

"Séraphine is dead! Ah, my poor little Séraphine, I loved her so much. She can never come back and play with me now."

"Your attachment for her was too important to you," Mlle Léonard cut in, deciding that her working day was now over and that it was time I went home. "You must beware of the excesses in your nature." She attacked her hair vigorously with her comb. "It's five o'clock. What are you waiting for?"

"We can go together, Mlle Léonard. I can easily go past the hospital on the way to my street."

"I'm in a hurry. Good night."

Our conversations often ended in that way.

"It's intolerable," she would add in a brutal tone. "What will people think if you're always at my heels, you and Louisette Denis?"

Despite herself, Mlle Léonard was still steeped in the ancient, hellfire-fearing prejudices that had constituted her parents' principles of life, even though they served in her case only as the most transparent of armours against her own passionate and generous nature. So that she tended to put herself on the side of those who might condemn her, striving to resemble them in their blindness, their harshness. I loved the simplicity of her heart, which she had revealed on several occasions in our presence, displaying her pity at the fate of one of our classmates doomed by leukemia, ashamed of her tears but unable to control them, overwhelmed every time by a fresh outburst of pity and revolt. She had hugged me in her arms one day when she thought I was dying, though in fact I had simply gone into a long faint, as often happened, so often indeed that I myself no longer paid any attention; if we were out in the recreation yard Louisette would simply run over to the drinking fountain and come back with water to sprinkle on my cheeks – having soaked it up in the dirty handkerchief that only left its place among the orange peels stuffing her pocket on the day of the big spring wash – whereupon I would quietly get up again, my heart still quivering with a rich ecstasy of colours and lightheadedness, while Mlle Léonard cried "Ah, my God, my God," thereby endowing my fainting spell with a particular human quality . . . It meant that I carried with me, down into the heavy silence of my beating blood, the plaintive reverberations of a lament that was letting me know, for the very first time, that there was someone there.

Unfortunately, Germaine Léonard soon reached the stage of accusing me of fainting on purpose, to attract attention. This was but one example of the way in which she often yielded to the unreasonable impulse of mistrust that made up the less sensitive part of her character, a mistrust of people in general that always asserted itself with the same harshness. But in order to understand how Mlle Léonard had acquired these obsessions it would doubtless have been necessary to possess an insight into her past, a thing quite impossible in my case, since she had already traversed so many alien stretches of life, all completely closed to me, before entering our lives. I had perhaps encountered her at a moment when she had been deeply wounded in her pride by a town she could not love, a town whose material poverty was associated for her with the hardness of men's hearts and minds, at a moment when she believed that her professional duties were our only possible path of salvation. Perhaps she was afraid above all, in a little town where slander could so easily fall like heavy, bruising hail from every tongue, that the revelation of her relationships might prevent her from helping us? We had already witnessed the dismissal of several teachers for usually undefined moral reasons, among them the abrupt departure of Mother Saint-Bernard de la Croix, leaving behind her that "sad little darling Solange," as we called her, with a spiteful delight that was also a kind of budding social condemnation. Germaine Léonard therefore made every effort to live her life in accordance with the strict image we had imposed upon her. "A very strange woman," the Mother Superior said, "but not without her saintliness." For our Superior thanked God in her prayers for having sent her this unworldly messenger whose only thought was to reduce the mortality rate in her convent. Germaine Léonard doubtless scorned this false image of herself; but this mantle of virtue that others had thrown over her true nature, in order not to see it, also served her as protection against us.

The month of May intoxicated us. We were at last emerging from winter's aridity into the scented warmth of spring, running up the aisle to the Virgin Mary, all white in the chapel gloom, with bunches of flowers to lay at her uncovered feet, charming bare feet that seemed to be inviting us outside to run in the grass with them. We murmured our *Aves* with an intensity never before attained, no longer gazing up at the Virgin Mary as the royal Mother of our misfortunes on this earth, but as the divinity of all joys and pleasures. One and all, we emerged from school at a run, hair streaming in the wind, pushing aside the young Abbé who was on his way, in that fine weather, to administer Extreme Unction to sick parishioners, eyes lowered to the deathly pardon he was clutching against his chest, seeing already, beyond our sunlit faces, the arms of distress stretching up to him from an immaculate bed, the Angel of Death passing his invisible torch over the cheeks of a dying man. But we, as we jostled him, had no thought in our heads but to hurl ourselves as quickly as we could into the hot street already thrumming with our cries. The cheeky urchins scarcely bothered to stop their ball games, the girls to halt their rope jumping, to allow the herds of cars to get by. Just try running over me, you old junkheap!" And the steel-throated horn vanished at last in a cloud of smoke, breaking our ranks and our chains. "Can't you play somewhere else, for the love of Christ?" a voice roared, and as though in answer my mother emerged on the stoop, calling to me and making signs which I pretended not to understand. "Ro-sa-ry, Pauline Archange, Ro-sa-ry!" her strained face and voice were saying, and I was waiting for her to begin telling her own rosary only so that I could rush into the kitchen and sneak one, two, three glasses of water, a bonfire of coolness I was already imagining as I jumped rope with Huguette Poire and Victoria Poulain, whose backs, like mine, were also wet with sweat beneath their convent uniforms. A few steps away from the street noises, Julia Poire watched us playing with a smile, peeping through her bedroom shutters. She seemed to find the sun too much for her of late. She smoked, she read in the shade of our games, and occasionally I caught her sad, avid gaze resting upon us.

On Sundays, after Mass, our hair braided beneath the wrinkled felt hats that were with us from baptism to funeral – it was beneath the sunshade mourning of these featureless hats that the newly born child, from under his feline, still half asleep eyelids, recognized the uncle, the godfather, the father who were his reception party into the world – we went out to take the air on the green slopes of Père Isaac Park, Louisette Denis and I. The bus struggled upward, on the verge of collapse beneath its burden of working-class families. On arrival, we all trampled on each other's feet, digging elbows into our neighbour's vulnerable stomach, and soon found ourselves out on the pavement, trembling and weak from the journey, our lunchtime apple pies crushed in our pockets. Happiness lay beyond the park gates, for inside there were real trees, and flowers everywhere to delight the eye – though only the eye, for it was forbidden to pick them. The grass of the slopes where we went to play was as fine as the sand on a beach, and the sky, all blue kindness, suddenly made my heart less hard, for I found myself suddenly thinking of my mother with a fleeting tenderness, telling myself that a walk in this park would have done her good, while at the same time assuring myself that I would lie to her if she asked me why I hadn't been home for lunch.

Still victims of our curiosity, Louisette and I went around catching the couples making love in the bushes, alerted to their presence by the tip of a naked foot peeping out from a hiding place beneath the willows. Mlle Léonard was never to forgive us for the indiscretion of chance that led us, once again, to stumble across her private path. Though they were but the flimsiest shreds of her secrecy that we succeeded in stripping from her, for she was still conscious, in a public park as much as in the street, of the dignity she owed it both to herself and to others to maintain, and as she sat straight-backed on her yellow wooden bench, beside the man who was whispering something in her ear, we had scarcely time to glimpse more than the joy at last written unconcealed upon her face before she had suddenly sensed our presence nearby, gazing sadly, one finger to her mouth, at these two alien figures making little holes, as in a dream, in that broad tapestry of shrubs and lilacs. "Heavens, there's someone there!" she exclaimed; but we were already tearing down toward the river.

Oh, the dissatisfaction of those days when nothing one did was ever noble or good, but according to grownups, passing judgment, always senseless or cruel. "Yes, very cruel," Mlle Léonard repeated as we listened to her humbly in her office. "You behave sometimes like monsters." But there was a gulf between us: the different social conditions of our lives. She had never committed the sins of which she accused us, but wasn't it simply because she'd never had the opportunities? What is the good of loving a being so far away from me, I thought. There was already a misunderstanding between us over the meaning of dignity, for if Mlle Léonard was apprehensive of revealing her secrets it was because she enjoyed a reputation of moral superiority in all men's eyes, something that bore no resemblance at all to the strange pride I experienced in disobeying orders or lying. Mlle Léonard repeated what my mother had already told me, that I lived "in pride and self-satisfaction," and for self-satisfaction there was no pardon.

When we talked with pride about "those who are going away to the sanatorium and the sea," Mlle Léonard looked at us with hardness in her gaze, without pity for the ignorance we had been simple-minded enough to reveal once again, an ignorance that was her greatest enemy, she said, forgetting that it was above all ours.

It sometimes seemed to me that I would meet nothing but death at the end of my weary struggles, like Séraphine and so many others. The Reverend Mother Principal announced to us one day during the fever of the June exams, concealing beneath the crucifix that dangled against her burning habit a tiny hand like the claw of a bird of prey, that "an epidemic of infantile paralysis has broken out in town: how many of you will return here in September, God alone knows!" And once more, a grave-lined avenue, the vacations yawned before us! Then, without wavering, we answered in unison the questions: "What is the love of God? What is hope?"

"The love of God is infinite goodness, infinite pity, and infinity itself."

But the Reverend Mother Principal was not listening. "We knew perfectly well that it will be the same this summer: instead of praying for your souls, you will still prefer to live in vices and idleness."

Mlle Léonard had the same terror "of all those vices hatched by poverty," though she never named them, and lowered a chaste gaze at the thought of certain actions for which she was already severely condemning me, even though I had not yet performed them. But how to survive this long summer so exactly like so many others? Jeannot's big, suppliant eyes followed me everywhere in the street. My mother often entrusted him to my care during vacation, but I forgot him for hours on end on the outside steps, where he remained sucking his thumb and dreaming bitter dreams. Sometimes I went over to watch the older children who lit bonfires in the sunken lane opposite. They tortured insects and small animals over the flames or fought and hit one another till they bled, wholly engrossed in themselves and their violence. And so the summer passed, very slowly, in eating all the rotting fruits that idleness proffered to our senses . . .

In August, my father abruptly decided "that a girl of eight and a half" ought to be of some use in society, and he took me over on his bicycle to stay with my Uncle Roméo and his four daughters, where I spent my days, like them, earning twenty cents a day selling "toffee applies, five cents each," "french fries crisply as velvet," and "ice cream as soft as soap." Under the rigid protection of Uncle Roméo, constantly knocking us against the wall with his naked torso, my cousins and I gazed down at our slave's fingers as they dipped green apples – which were full of white maggots – in a majestic red syrup that it was forbidden to taste. "Eating during working hours is not allowed," my uncle said; but work once over, quick as a flash he was packing up his apples and his sticks. Whereupon, keeping our backs to him, we as quickly devoured his french fries and refreshed ourselves with chocolate ice cream, then finished off our working day with a "swing contest" to see who could "get up highest in the sky," only to fall low indeed when we returned to earth, since we all promptly threw up all our stolen riches on the gravel.

"That'll teach you, you little pests, that'll teach you to devour a poor man's substance!"

Uncle Roméo then shut himself up in the bathroom for what seemed an eternity. To our huge impatience, he remained in there trimming his beard, doing his accounts, and shouting orders for the following day – "All those who aren't up by six will get ten cents docked from their pay, so it'll be too bad for the lazy ones!" – and we yelled in vain to make him come out for prayers. In the end, dropping with sleep over our rosaries, my Cousin Cécile and I were ordered off to bed by my aunt. But I lay awake for ages thinking about my cousin's savings, which lay wrapped in a spotted handkerchief beneath her pillow. Although I admired her enormously because "her talents were better suited to a store counter than a school desk," as my father put it, I envied her above all for the three dollar bills that she unfolded and folded up again all day in front of my nose, when I myself was still at that inferior age when one has nothing but dolls' faces to fondle.

But since Séraphine's death I no longer had anyone to make happy, other than myself, and the uneasy generosity I experienced when handing out gifts of fans to far too many surprised little girls in my street, that same generosity overwhelmed me with shame when I saw my Cousin Cécile's tears. Soon the whole family was inundating me with tears and reproaches, and my theft burned in my conscience like the memory of a great crime. I went up to my room before dessert, when the others were still playing out in the yard, and it was in vain that they called up to me, for I no longer had the courage even to approach the window and look at my friends. I was to be sent to boarding school in September. In that black asylum, peopled with thieves like myself, how was I ever to see Germaine Léonard and Louisette Denis again? Louisette Denis had promised never to leave me, to come and share my prison with me, but I had been too unfaithful to Séraphine myself to put any faith in Louisette's tender protestations. And besides, I deserved my father's cruelty. In my solitude, who could say, I might perhaps be converted? "I am very pleased with your conduct," Mlle Léonard said. "You are at last behaving like a normal human being!" Ah, to realize that dream of goodness, to accomplish that sudden self-metamorphosis!

And little by little, each evening in my solitary confinement, I gathered together the fragments of my life; my imagination wrote wild and passionate stories while my body feigned sleep. I remembered my first visions, during those days of penance after my mother had forbidden me to meet Jacquou in the gully. There were no longer enormous horses flashing across the sky, but other objects, other beings seemed to take birth from me in that room. Jacob came back to life, the minuscule image of a wretchedness I had no wish to see again. And my mother, who had always had so little existence in her own eyes, never having lived except for others, my mother emerged from the shadows like an unfinished portrait, and the void where her frightened features should have been seemed to be saying: "Finish this brief sketch of me." But neither Jacob nor my mother awakened my love for creation. I had read too few books and no one ever thought to buy me any. I had never known the gift of words except with Séraphine, and since her death it seemed to me that I had lost them all, the words that had lived for me then, through her. And it must doubtless have been in dreams that I was writing then, for I saw images only, without knowing the words.

September was approaching. My big suitcase lay in the shadows, packed with black things, like my past.

✺ Chapter Four ✺

It is night at the end of the long tunnel retraced by memory: Mother Sainte-Gabrielle d'Egypte is dozing on her feet at the end of the dormitory, her face wholly drained of lice, her sinewy chin strangled by the ribbon of her nightcap, so calm, so denuded suddenly of any concealing hatred that we might almost believe our torturer had at last left us forever, with the daylight. But a single quiver from one of the beds would suffice to wake her from that false sleep. All the windows have been closed against temptations, but still, from the street outside, there rise the crude, singsong blasphemies of the vagabonds being driven out, probably with cruel kicks, from the dark, smoke-filled taverns: "Ah Jesus, throwin' me out like that . . . Ah, Holy Mother o' God, what'll become of me now?" Perhaps they have already lost their souls, perhaps they somehow let them escape on their drunken, blasphemy-laden breaths. Suddenly, nothing seems so terrible as having a soul to save! And yet, as I gaze without fear at Mother Sainte-Gabrielle d'Egypte's face, I let myself yield a little to the night's melting pity: who knows, perhaps this woman will have become kindly when she wakes? But when the bell rings, much too soon, just when I am beginning to feel sleepy, Sainte-Gabrielle d'Egypte comes patrolling between the beds with her cane while we pray, voicelessly and hopelessly, oh my God, bless this day, preserve us from evil. And as we wash, as we dress beneath our bedclothes to respect the laws of modesty, hunger writhes in our insides, the same old unsatisfied hunger of yesterday.

"Your white veil, it's the first Friday of the month!"

The scents of breakfast come wafting from the refectory; but the breakfast is not for us, not yet. It is for the novices, who have been at prayer all night. Lips glued against my white veil, I eat off tiny scraps of lace as I walk along the corridors, passing beggars slouched against the steps, waiting for the remains of our yesterday's stew. They watch us humbly as we disappear toward the chapel. At the first stroke of the clapper, all our knees drop onto the cold flagstones; at the second, I rush to my seat and open a missal brimming with funereal or saintly pictures, little photographs of dead people smiling amid the flowers of a frozen spring: here is Uncle Sébastien disguised as a handsome, immortal young man, and nearer to me still, Séraphine in her first-communion dress, her face half hidden by a bunch of roses held in one hand. I envy Séraphine, who will never make sacrilegious communions and who is already in paradise. As for me, my sin is too heinous to be admitted to any priest. I shall go to hell with my fellow sinners. But what is hell? Is it that wild thrumming of fear in my ears when I think I hear the souls of the damned howling in the dormitory silence, or the fear of a more mysterious punishment on earth? Who knows, God may well revenge himself by punishing someone other than me; Jeannot for example, who still possesses the innocence that I have lost. Or my mother, who is already too sick to visit me. Mlle Léonard doesn't forget me, though: every Sunday, in the visiting room, she deposits in my lap a stock of dry biscuits and codliver-oil capsules, she asks me if I am coughing and if I am eating properly and I answer all these questions with lies. Then she says curtly: "It's not for your sake I come, it's for your poor mother's . . ." Sometimes she gives me a book, which I caress with my fingers, even though I don't much like the resigned title – *The Adventures of a Prisoner* or *The Story of an Underground Captive*: I feel that my fingers are brushing freedom with every line.

We emerge from the chapel, two by two, taking care not to let our elbows touch, because that is a sin. Mother Sainte-Gabrielle announces that "we must clean out the classrooms before filling our stomachs." We scrub the blackboards, we scrape the ink stains off the floorboards with a razor blade, and Mother Sainte-Gabrielle stands over us, wearing an ironic, weary expression. Oh, what a dismal task a tyrant's is! How dreary never to receive any homage but the animal supplication of those thin faces, without hated, without love! To look down at all those bowed heads inside which so much hypocrisy is furtively concealed! But there is the second bell for breakfast, at last! The big bowl of gruel is carried in past our noses, its reek made bearable by familiarity. Bless us, O Lord, and that which we are about to eat; there is no knowing if one is quivering with nausea or hunger, but one must eat. The tall Mother in charge of the refectory, a bearded Argus, dips her spoon parsimoniously into the boiled garbage before her: at the sound of her tongue smacking behind her black lips – "Hmmm, what delicious gruel" – we gulp down the contents of our bowls with a feeling of deliverance, for an initial void recedes, leaving its place to another, and this well-digested inward absence already feels a little less like the hunger of the evening before. We have eaten, prayed, done the novices' dishes, ah, Mother Sainte-Gabrielle, can we have permission now to leave the room?

"You can go at twelve, after classes."

"I want to go now, Mother."

"No."

All morning Mother Sainte-Gabrielle will continue to eye her victims with tenderness. She pretends to forget the torture she is inflicting on those lower bowels that God has so unfortunately created, she even forces herself to suffer with us, refusing to leave the room herself until midday. (Hence the almost winged urgency with which we see her vanishing up toward the second floor, her face red, her lips tightly pinched over her inner mystery.) She comforts us by telling us "that the body is nothing, a mere appearance of vanity, nothing more." It would be nice to believe her, oh how nice!

But one acquires the habit of living with a body thus slighted and humiliated. As we walk through the big girls' dormitory, in the morning, we are sometimes witnesses to strange scenes. "Quicker, walk quicker," Mother Sainte-Gabrielle cries, but the eye of memory flicks avidly open, capturing forever the image of a young girl sobbing on her knees beside her bloodstained bed, while the nun standing near her seems to be hiding in her round, magnanimous eyes the murderer, the incurable monster whose thoughts one can read.

"Give me something, Mother, it's running all down my legs . . ."

"It's a punishment from God, do as best you can with toilet paper."

"You must flatten your chest with a wide band of elastic so as not to tempt the devil." "You must wear a corset and pull your stomach in against your spine." That's the life the big girls lead, and we feel pity for their bodies subjected to those hard regulations. In the meantime, Mother Saint-Gabrielle d'Egypte keeps her jealous eye on us too. One by one, she takes away from me the books that Mlle Léonard brings.

"That's not the sort of book for you. You'd far better read the *Imitation of Jesus Christ.*"

Later, she was to wait until night to seize our secret diaries, our exercise books full of poems. Why should we have the right to make our inner landscapes fruitful, the right to think and even to live, when she, from the moment of her entry into the convent, had renounced all hope, all vanity? And it was not the fear of God alone that haunted her compulsive brain – in which the waves had nevertheless now ceased to flow, leaving only a tempest of obsessions, a paralyzed impulsion toward the shore of life; there was also the terror of man. She was to say one day, during class, with a snort of disgust, that "all men are pigs," and then, astonished by this outburst, become suddenly silent, one hand up to her mouth. The smallest girls listen to her. They consent perhaps to her disgust. But I escape, I fly toward Jacquou and our gully, toward the explosive dazzle of that day in the trees. That summer will never come again, or that summer and miraculous autumn when Séraphine was beside me in our games. And now I see no one to love. I find that one of my classmates has slipped me a note during school: "Pauline Archange, wate for me in the recriation yard, we can skip roap together, signed, Augustine Gendron who loves you," but cruelly I draw away from Augustine and the poverty she exhales. During recreation I stand in the hole made by the courtyard and gaze up at the sky. I am bored.

One Sunday, a Sunday just like all the others, Mlle Léonard informed me of the birth of a little brother. He had been christened. His name was Emile. I listened to Mlle Léonard with only half an ear, watching the rain fall outside.

"Do you understand what I'm trying to tell you," she asked suddenly, "that there are beings born sometimes to bring others grief?"

And as sometimes happened with her, when she was suffering from the impact of intense pity, I saw that she was trembling as she walked toward the door. My existence seemed to me even more dismal when I thought of Emile. I was already comparing him with Jeannot, crying, soiling his diapers. But Emile didn't cry, a fact that disturbed my mother. Until he was two months old he was looked upon as growing normally, but then, quite suddenly, the child that my mother had fed seemed to be finding his nourishment within himself like some form of growth entirely alien to us. Emile had rejected our human appearances: even though he displayed features both recognizable and akin to ours, the same smile, the same eyes, he was nevertheless living deep in some more vegetable, slower sphere. I played with his feet and hands, but no echo of warmth responded in him. He gazed into a distant emptiness.

"What is he looking at like that?"

My mother hid her head in her hands. "Oh, my God! Oh, my God!" she moaned very softly. My father went over and tried to comfort her, but that seemed to increase her despair. They knew nothing of the irresistible curiosity that bound me to this small being, all calm, all hidden harmony, all gentleness. It must be very strange to be shut up in that little body and to be seeing all those far-off things that my eyes couldn't see. To be so fragile and so soft at the same time, so that no one dared touch you. Life is no more than a slight breath that might leave you at any moment, and that is why you have to be lifted up very delicately, for fear your bones will break. But I was often forbidden to go near Emile; they used to lock the door of his room. I thought of him as being like a mysterious plant in the house. On certain days, his eyes could be seen to light up with a sterile, impotent compassion, the compassion of the wandering soul he had embodied perhaps, and bending down close to his face I searched for a glimpse of Séraphine's soul beneath his eyelids. Each time I left to go back to boarding school, I tried to foster the hope of finding myself growing better through Emile. Who could tell, if someone could find a way of drawing him out, might he not one day emerge from the flowery sleep that lived inside him? But none of us seemed to have the key to his real language. The months passed. Emile was no longer silent. He cried all day, my mother wrote to me. "Before, he slept, now he is in pain," and thus she never had the strength to finish her letters.

My father, however, never stopped believing in "the miracles of Providence." He decided one morning that we ought to go on a pilgrimage, convinced that if we bathed Emile in the holy waters at the chapel of Sainte-Justice our prayers for his recovery would be answered. He even talked of making the journey on foot, but Grand-mère Josette went into a panic over "her legs all covered in ulcers," and my father had to resign himself to taking the train. Transplanted out of his fragile shell, exiled in our arms, which were unable to hold him without causing him distress – for a pain all our tender care remained wholly ignorant of was even then beginning to put down roots in him – Emile cried, choking with his sobs. "Oh, what is it, what is the matter with you?" my mother said, touching his brow. And then, unable to bear the burden of it any longer, she slowly lowered Emile into the arms of Grand-mère Josette, who rocked him in turn to the rhythm of the train. "The only consolation, daughter, is that Emile's tears are washing away the sins of the world," my grandmother said, and at this involuntary blasphemy in which she felt involved, my mother could only reply in a dead voice: "It would be better if he died!"

And while my grandparents knelt to beg for Emile's recovery, my mother, standing stiffly in the gloom, remained aloof. She was asking for her child's death, without noticing, above her head, a picture of one of the Stations of the Cross that depicted, in a purple violence devoid of beauty, the crowning of

Jesus surrounded by the men he had tried to save. Drained of all colour in her gray clothes, she seemed to provide the picture with a necessary hint of mourning that it lacked. Outside, in the radiant autumnal sunlight, there was already a crowd of pilgrims moving toward the chapel path, pushing the wheelchair or the bed from whose summit there would suddenly appear a fleshless arm, or else a face, abruptly protruding from its corolla of white sheets, in which it seemed impossible to recognize anything other than the toothless gaping of the foam-covered mouths. Moans were rising from each of these sitting or lying bodies, and beside each sufferer there stood a dry-eyed mother, looking straight ahead of her at nothing.

Inside the chapel, and in the garden where the miraculous spring rose, everywhere you looked there were the walls of crutches discarded by all the cripples at the moment of their recovery. As I filled my bottle with water, I wondered how those sufferers had reacted to the shock of their cure, and if they then remembered the void in which they had slept. With what high excitement, for example, would all those Mongoloid children sitting dribbling and whimpering on the grass react to the sudden sensation of intelligence as it began flowing beneath their thick skulls like a stream of fire, to the freshness of a new imagination strengthened by that long rest? Perhaps, quite simply, they would experience a great unhappiness at seeing with what wretched garments their bodies had been clothed, and an even greater unhappiness at recognizing in the spring's clear pool the defective masks, the faces, from which they could nevermore escape. But I plagued my father to let me bathe Emile in the spring itself, so that his contact with the miracle would be closer still. Piteously, Emile resisted: unable to move his arms and hands, he cried even louder. Made insensitive by faith, we watched him striking his head feebly against the water. The sole

– and ironic – miracle we were vouchsafed consisted in a subtle change of colour in Emile's delicate complexion. A few little blue patches, of the palest sky blue, seemed to appear around his temples, on his delicate white cheeks. He was choking.

"But there's medicine too," my father said, "that can sometimes work miracles."

But Mlle Léonard told us quite simply that there was no hope, and that it was time my mother said goodbye to her baby. "Tomorrow it will be too late. You won't have the heart to do it anymore . . ." My mother listened to this advice in a profound absence. The expression on her face, the fixed gaze she directed ahead of her, her whole being, seemed to be denying the existence of the child being discussed. At the end of his tether, my father began looking for "faith-healing advertisements" in the newspapers when he got home from work in the evening. Madame Flanche warmed up "her healing creams" in the bottom of the oven where her "honey and raisin cookies" were baking, she saw "babies like this one every day, with legs and arms deader than dead wood – just the same"; and without any respect for my mother's grief, she tore Emile from her arms and laid him down naked on the table.

"I shall use my best ointment on him," she said as she rolled up her sleeves. "He needs it well rubbed into his spine."

Madame Flanche looked me right in the eyes, saying that she could "read all the secrets in the depths of people's hearts that way . . ." Perhaps she knew that I was the cause of Emile's ills, that he was expiating on my behalf all those crimes I could not confess to anyone, my abandonment of Séraphine, my neglect of Jacob, and now the theft of my Cousin Cécile's savings? In my shame, I quickly closed my eyes. But at the same time Emile's fragility, his exiled existence, made me understand that there perhaps existed a mysterious race of men, not subject to our ordinary laws, but living according to the dictates of their hearts, beings marked by mystery at birth, surrounded by an infinite solitude, and often, too, the possessors of an infinite pity.

I thought Mlle Léonard, who tried to so hard to be like us in order to conceal the difference that she sensed within her: despite myself, I was hungry to meet a being who was capable of following the call of his desires and his truth to their conclusion. But the days passed, and I still said my rosary with the others, out in the corridor, in the evening, unable to see anything on my horizon but the pimply faces of my classmates and the banner of harshness brandished every morning by Mother Sainte-Gabrielle as she told us during catechism lessons about "the vile impurity that lay in wait for us everywhere in the world"; and that harshness seemed to triumph over our love of life, so that the breath of grace that had brushed me for an instant, through Emile, died and vanished as soon as I heard Mother Sainte-Gabrielle's voice again.

And yet, when the convent gate was pulled aside for us to take our daily walk, I noticed that there were some of us who seemed less stunted, less colourless in the light of day. I had never noticed that some of the nuns among us were kindly creatures, so crushed was I by the cruelty of the others. When the nun who supervised our walks turned to look at us, her face was beautiful and desolate; she would raise her eyes to heaven with resignation. "Oh God," she seemed to be saying, "my place was never in this convent, give me the courage to leave it." And if a girl from the older students' hotel suddenly broke from the ranks, pretending to stop and lace up her shoe, letting the others pass, then ran into the door of a shop only to emerge a little later and wander alone where she pleased for an hour, until the noon bell, then Mother Sainte-Adèle would close her eyes to it, allowing a little of her own imprisoned soul to take wing with the beloved pupil. I dreamed of joining the truant girl, but I never dared. Geneviève Després was a vision in the distance, lit by bright sunbeams; I could not see her face, but I was aware of her bare, serious brow, and the two blond braids that sped behind her, down her back.

As I sat in the private study room, still doing penance, copying out the pages of my dictionary or scrawling out the hundredth *Egypte*

Egypte

of my imposition – "You will write our five hundred times 'I will be respectful to Mother Saint-Gabrielle d'Egypte'" – Geneviève was roller skating out in the yard with the big girls of her own class, and the sweetness of her laughter made my punishment crueller still. Another evening, because I'd been talking to Augustine Gendron during study time, I was sent out into the corridor for an hour. I immediately rushed down to the yard, but Geneviève had already tired of skating: she was sitting under a tree, and Mother Sainte-Adèle was talking to her in a low voice. Geneviève suddenly jumped up and ran off toward a group of friends who were waiting for her near the gate. Mother Sainte-Adèle smiled sadly after her, her hand seeming to sketch a protective gesture in the air. Then the hand fell back wearily on her lap.

She was to leave the convent in a few months, had already made her official request to the Superior, and one day she would perhaps have a husband, children of her own, but never, she thought to herself, would she forget Geneviève and the fervour of this friendship. But how was she to know that tomorrow she might become the slave of that future husband, of those children, and in the lustreless clarity of that new life perhaps forget Geneviève, forget her deliberately, so that if some former pupil tried to awaken the memory of her she would perhaps only answer, bitterly: "Geneviève Després, but who was she? Ah yes, that one . . . What ever happened to her?"

Since Séraphine's death I could no longer approach anyone in the present without in some way imagining the metamorphosis of his or her future. Who could say, perhaps Geneviève seemed wholly charming to me today simply because her defects were all invisible to me still, or rather because she hadn't had the time to reveal all the beauty and ugliness her heart must contain, for she too, like myself, must doubtless be guilty of crimes she knew nothing about, since she too was human.

Every being I encountered at that time inspired me with the same anxiety. What was she hiding? What would he become? My mother had always seemed to me wholly good and kind, but now, since the birth of Emile, murderous thoughts that she could no longer keep secret would sometimes flicker across her eyes, or make their presence felt in her gestures. How could one make Emile die without killing him? Perhaps one could forget him after his bath, leave him alone on a table or a chair? Even my father seemed to be in some degree an accomplice to these smoldering crimes of the mind. He always saved Emile from my mother's negligence, but in my eyes the crime had already been committed, and Emile's existence kept alive inside me a deep-rooted mourning that was invisible to all scrutiny but my own. My mother scarcely ate any more, refusing to provide her guilty thoughts with nourishment; and when she did eat, she immediately became prey, despite herself, to a nausea whose origin lay in the murder she had failed to perform. My father came home early from work to continue nursing my mother through this long revulsion from life. If I came home from boarding school for a few days, I would find my father holding my mother's head over a bowl, a painful *tableau vivant* that I escaped by going out to play in the street.

I waited for Louisette Denis, but she never seemed to come out any more. When I knocked at her parents' door, I was told that "Louisette has gone a long way away, but she will come back when she's better." I thought of Séraphine, and Louisette suddenly seemed to me in grave danger, a Louisette who was neither healthy nor gay any more, whom I would perhaps never see again, I thought. I wrote her letters in my solitude: "You're just like the others, you're like Sébastien and Séraphine, you want to go away too, but I don't want you to go, you can't be sick, you're the strongest in the class, Mlle Léonard said, and you're the one who understands everything quickest, Mlle Léonard said, you can run as fast as a kite, I love you, so that's why you can't be sick like Julia Poire and go away."

I imagined Louisette's return; but it was a return devoid of joy, each of us gazing at the other without recognition. She would have lost her health and I my hope. If we had already killed Emile several times, in thought or in words, how many other crimes were we not capable of committing? The eyes of the body must be blind indeed never to see anything but the innocence in men's faces, to be dazzled immediately by a mirage of goodness. The real gaze must doubtless come from some further, higher place, like that cold sun keeping vigil so far off from me in Emile's soul. He could see nothing, so they said, and yet I sensed that if Emile did see, then he saw without pity. It was in vain that my own gaze had sought for repose in freshness and innocence. It seemed to me now that innocence was death and that the cruel glimmer I could see in my mother's eyes was evil, perhaps destruction, and yet life at the same time. I could no longer go back, seeking to forget this revelation; the violence was there, everywhere, concealed in the flesh, or else revealed by it. The frontier of appearances once crossed, one could put very small trust indeed in the dignity of this body so long allied to the beast: was it going to kill, violate, or simply love, take pleasure in, protect its fellow creature, that being alien to itself yet the source of such great comfort?

It must be terrible indeed to love people, since my parents were so ashamed of it! Mother Sainte-Gabrielle d'Egypte herself would quiver with disgust as she spoke of "that forbidden fruit that leaves a taste of ashes after it." And then she would bite her lips, conscious, for a moment, of the cold ashes piled over her own heart, a heart that had never loved. She was right perhaps, I thought, where Uncle Marius was concerned. "He often falls into the abyss of drink," my mother said of him. "A real pig, your uncle, there is no gainsaying it, he drinks all day long." He had sold his furniture to keep himself afloat in an ocean of beer on whose waves he lay chanting melancholy ditties:

> *"Oh, take a glass of beer, my pretty,*
> *Take a glass with me, my kitty,*
> *One quick glass and then some pussy,*
> *Pussy!"*

What is more, it was already too late "to tear him from the arms of lust!" He occasionally emerged from his inner fog to make little obscene gestures, invitations that led him into jail. On occasion, my mother would ask me "to run an errand for him, to buy him a crust of bread so he doesn't starve, poor degraded man!" And I would tremble as I saw him coming toward me, standing in his doorway, not him alone, Uncle Marius, the pitiful man who had drunk too much beer, but the beast that emerged in front of him from a blind thicket of sensuality and whose great head I could already see, snorting its way toward me. A little girl of nine could have been an object of desire to him, but in that solitude of his, utterly abandoned by all except his vice, doubtless a lamp, a table, an object of any kind wavering in the light of drunkenness could equally have become a target for that desire. According to my mother, he was "a very sick man and a great sinner"; but my family was too fertile in misfortunes, I thought to myself, and if I was destined to survive it one day, then it would perhaps be simply in order to go down into that depth of mud and dried leaves to take a last look at all the living and the degenerate dead from whom, more than my birth, more than my life, I had to extract my resurrection.

The adults kept from us a carnal mystery that they judged devoid of beauty; but for us there was no real mystery except in the violence of their words and their suggestions, and this shadow of sin they cast over acts so simple and naked was something we thought of with sadness. How fiercely we aspired to live freely, in the harmony of happy minds and bodies! During Vespers on Sundays, the big girls went up into the loft and danced, all dressed up, beneath a cloud of feathers which they stuck all around their faces and tucked in their necks, thereby revealing, far from our imposed, imprisoned life, that they were already in possession of those imaginary men for whom they danced, even though they had not yet had either the time or the freedom to conquer them. They too seemed to know that love has no mystery. But as soon as Vespers was over, they would perhaps forget that knowledge again, and with forgetfulness how many devious scruples would once more stir back to life in their souls?

While all these young girls were peeping out at the boys in the street, nudging one another over by the window, Geneviève Després kept aloof in a corner, her head buried in her hands. For some days now I had no longer been hearing that dazzling laugh of hers. It was almost time for Mother Sainte-Adèle's departure.

Geneviève's silence reminded me suddenly how unhappy I was myself. A child of sorrow seemed to be born every instant in my thoughts – Jacob, Séraphine, or Louisette, each with a burning arm tight around my waist – and I no longer dared to walk alone in the yard, for fear of suddenly shivering into fragments at the contact of my own pity. Sometimes I compared Emile's body to a white chalice in which all the agonies were held imprisoned: he alone was unable to melt or be shattered by grief, because he was suffering itself, but I who thought of nothing but my own amusement, who was redeeming no one, I felt that there was a perpetual danger of the pain suddenly pouring out, like a liquid, through all the fissures in my body, that at some moment, under a sky already heavy with rain, I was going to begin weeping without end, weeping until my whole being had been wept away. Mother Sainte-Gabrielle d'Egypte, who had stopped scolding me, because, she said, "it's useless, you haven't a single tear inside you anywhere, you're not like other people!", was amazed at these tears, running without reason down the obduracy of a face that had never shown emotion on her account. These tears shocked her even more when she handed me my end-of-month report, and the vision of my high and futile marks filled me with disgust rather than pride. If I was first in my class that day, it was not on account of my intelligence, which was at a low ebb indeed, but simply because I was less mediocre than the others; I could never hope to become like

Mlle Léonard one day – "You weren't born for that," my father said, and he was doubtless right.

While the others were seeing their parents in the visiting room, I danced with idle steps on Geneviève's shadow as she moved ahead of me, retreating toward a river of shade under the trees, at the far end of the yard. I was alone, and unworthy of being loved in my tattered dress. I could have mended it, admittedly, but any transformation of myself seemed futile.

I got up each morning hoping to live, but very often it was only in order to make my way toward violent nightmares, from the moment I woke. I got up and dressed, still trembling from the terrors of the night, but in the day just beginning, other bad dreams began to claim their right to live as well, inside me. When Mother Sainte-Gabrielle d'Egypte rang the morning bell, I awoke to find my anguish exactly as I had left it the evening before, in the brown shadow of a forest that I visited so often in my dreams. The dormitory corridors seemed to open up, one after the other, into the vast rooms of my nightmares, where I met Jacob weeping as his father beat him, Séraphine running alone among the tall grass of a black field . . . And yet it was daylight, we were walking toward the chapel, the sun was rising in the depths of my interminable forest; soon I would be less afraid of my memories, they would all find their rightful places in the distant fresco. Oh, to live always inside oneself as though in a jail! Mother Sainte-Gabrielle shook her insanely jangling keys in our ears, but without ever finding the secret of our deliverance . . .

I observed in myself the imprint of those monsters I judged so severely in others. When Augustine Gendron's hand confided itself to mine, during the midday walk, I dreamed of crushing those frail fingers between mine to stifle my despair at living. I understood the executioner's decision in the presence of his victim: one tortured others in order to avoid those same tortures for oneself. But how fruitless to make Augustine Gendron suffer: if I did inflict any violence upon her, then I felt that I was undergoing it myself, through her. I hadn't even the courage to love the harm I did to others. Yet there were so many men who did rend that veil of conscience, and killed their brothers. On Saturdays I used to read accounts of such murders out loud to Uncle Marius from *Night Beat* and *The Dawn of Crime*, illustrated newspapers whose details continued to haunt me long afterwards. "Holy Mary, that puts terrible black thoughts in your heads," Uncle Marius groaned, leaning over my shoulder as he followed the confession of yesterday's murderer:

I'm just a poor man and I ask the Lord's forgiveness if I lost my patience, but I hadn't a cent left in my pocket and there they were looking at me, all seven of them, like little birds dying of hunger and their heads sticking out of the nest, those kids, they just looked at me with their dirty grimy mouths all open and their mother there on all fours under the table with a bottle of gin under her nose. I've always been quite a patient man but suddenly I knew I'd had my bellyful. And there was that blamed winter wind coming in the door, it's a fact, in summer you don't feel like killing everyone so much, it's funny how crime is more of a winter thing, but in winter I just don't have the patience, I just feel so mad, not ugly with it, but just mad, like I said. So it was Friday evening and I was going home of course, mister officer, sir, and those kids just looked at me like I just can't tell you with those hungry eyes, I can't stand that, they was so thin you could see the bones through the gray skin

on them, and not only that but everything in that house is gray,
walls like a prison, gray paper curtains, God in heaven, I
thought there's gotta be some pity, they oughta be in heaven
instead of here, the lot of them. I ain't got no patience left but
you'd of done the same, mister, you'd of killed them all the seven
of them, but as for the blood there was blood all right, a real
river of it.

"Yes, that's really put some very black thoughts in my head," Uncle Marius went on, blowing his nose. "That sort of thing really makes me cry, more than the curé's sermons at Mass. There's days when I'd like to drown your aunt, but I'm too afraid. Too afraid of being hung like a chicken!"

Uncle Marius cried even more over "the lovely shexual cases"; he felt great sympathy for "that kind-hearted fellow Gaston Soreil, 48, of Mont-Caprice, accused of having shexual relations with a woman of sixty-seven, a mental defective," and for "Raymond Girard, 65, accused of assault with immodest intent upon the person of a nine-year-old boy." "All that, you see," he informed me, swatting with one hand at a cloud of grasshoppers invading us from the road, "all that is the good life. I don't see why people have to be put in prison just because they lead the good life."

"It's not allowed, Uncle Marius. You will go to hell. When you look at me like that with those nasty thoughts in your eyes, I'm quite sure you're committing sins. God doesn't like it."

But it was vain to hope for conversion from Uncle Marius.

"Every week you must do your GD," our scout counsellor told us. "A GD is a good deed that makes you feel sick . . ." And so it was that I visited Uncle Marius on Saturdays and bought his obscene newspapers for him. But I preferred the GDs during vacations, when we set out at dawn in groups, wearing our

Brownie uniforms, to distribute pots of jam to the old people in various homes. These old people, who no longer slept and scarcely breathed any more, seemed to have been reduced to no more than avid mouths set in white bones: a sleepy tongue would emerge lazily from its cavern, lick the drops of jam off the spoon, then retire into hiding once more. "Eat, grandma, eat," a nun standing next to us said, and the wrinkled animal of death, death itself, emerged from among all the old lady's white hairs to taste the jam. The old lady fell back on her bed, exhausted, her mouth open.

"Grandma is very old. She isn't very hungry any more at her age," the nun said. "You won't believe me, but do you know, she's only ninety-eight?"

The long fingers of the dying brushed us with caresses as we passed. "It's my little Dorothée come back to me . . . It's my little girl . . . I thought I'd lost her . . ." Some of them, pink and transparent in the morning light, were rocking dolls in their arms, like old dreams; others were pulling themselves up a little in their beds to look at the garden, outside the window, then their eyes would suddenly set into a beatitude without mind or memory. A big-bosomed nurse passed by between the beds with reeking pails to whose contents she seemed oblivious, since for her the enduring stench of all this wretchedness had an aroma of goodness. "I told him, old Grandpa Barreau, if you eat that meat you'll be as sick as a dog, and who'll have to clean you up again? Me, always me, as we all know. Four times a night I've been up for that old man, a real baby without a bit of gratitude, not a word of thanks. He has me scurrying about for him from morning till night, and in the middle of the night too. But when he's not there any more I'll feel really bad inside, I know I will. He's my favourite of the old men. When he's not here any more, there'll be no one who needs me as much as he does."

I imagined the long night in the ward and the nurse bending over each bed, speaking the language of agony and necessity to every occupant. "Water, you old fox you, water again, is it? Don't you ever do anything but drink then? Here I am, slaving away till cockcrow . . . Don't move around on your pillow, I'm bringing you some . . . But this is the last time." Even before night had fallen, those who were going to die before dawn had begun to call to her. "What is it then, my pretty? You're in pain? Ah, where is it then? You must sleep, don't cry like that, no, no, don't cry, it's too tiring. And besides, it hurts my ears to listen to you!"

"Nurse, I'm sinking, I can feel it, I'm beginning to go . . ."

"No, no, my pet, wait, I'll give you a little air. Now don't make those noises in your throat, you're just tiring yourself out for nothing."

The painful mutterings of these decomposing bodies grew even louder when they seemed to be streaming out of the sufferer, through his nose and mouth, through the glass tubes that imprisoned his face.

"What was it you said, my old darling, say it again, I can't hear very well."

"R . . . r . . . rrr . . . rrr . . ."

"Yes, oh yes, it's true, they ought to have come to visit you, those children of yours."

"Wrrrr . . . ong . . . die . . . I . . . ll . . . one . . ."

"What about me? Am I a piece of furniture? A bed table or something? You're all the same, all ungrateful, not a single word of thanks before you go!"

When the dying man's children did arrive, it was frequently too late.

"Ah, here you are, now he doesn't need you any more, now he's in heaven, with the angels! Here you are, with your shoes all polished and your stiff collars, like a lot of pallbearers! Aren't you ashamed? Aren't you ashamed to arrive just in time for the funeral?"

We left the old people's home deep in thought, imagining, at the end of the brown arm that was now stretching in the summer sunshine, the fleshless hand of old age, and its shakiness. But if we suddenly glimpsed a ribbon of water flowing under the trees, our uniforms were all torn off in a trice, and at the first blast of our counsellor's whistle a wall of blue woolly bloomers collapsed into the water. The counsellor sat on a stone, waiting for the bathing to end. If Huguette Poire invited her to join us, she replied curtly that "children's joys are often grownups' misfortunes." A few minutes later, after prudently removing her tie and hat, she would execute a few swift semaphore signals in the wind. In the distance, we could hear the bleating of goats. Yes, I thought to myself, our GD day is often a lovely day. But then, not having thought about her for so long, I suddenly remembered Grand-mère Josette. "Her heart is getting weaker and weaker, she's dying of old age," my mother said. But she's only sixty-eight, I thought, and here she is slowing down like some worn-out old machine.

"But it's so unjust . . ."

"Everything is just," my mother replied. "Each of us must die, like all the rest. It's the other life that counts."

I had neglected Grand-mère Josette a great deal. I was told to keep an eye on her while she sat rocking in the yard, but quite often I left her there alone, while I went to play with other children in the street. Sometimes she would stop her gentle rocking suddenly, then look at me tenderly before falling into a strange sleep that made me frightened. "Grand-mère, do you sleep in the middle of the day now?" She didn't answer. Then she would wake again, murmuring apologies. "Ah, Pauline, it's very strange, what happens to old people. One shouldn't ever get old . . ." A day that was over was another day taken by death. My mother had once talked about "rising in the world, changing our neigh-bourhood and our way of life . . ." but since the birth of Emile she seemed to have given up such ideas. "That child has got to go, I can't stand to see him any more, they must take him away."

And on the hot July days when Huguette Poire and Jacquou came pinging stones from his slingshot against my window, inviting me "to come and have a bicycle ride in Isaac Park," I thought about Emile as though about my own life, unable to separate myself from him for fear I might die of it. But the Rev-erend Mother who was in charge of the Children's Home under-stood my parents' strange desire. She had a slightly hunchbacked body, humble eyes, and I felt that she took Emile to her with her whole being "as a true grace." It was comforting to think that Emile's life, once absorbed into this woman's soul, would dis-cover its usefulness, its happiness.

"If you love them, these little creatures, they live for years. They're like lambs that the Good Lord has forgotten on the earth. Seeing him like that, it's as though he's determined never to more his arms and legs, as though his eyes are blind, but if you go on loving them for a long time, they do learn things. Later on, he'll be able to sit up. We'll teach him how to move about, very gradually, in the swimming bath, and then, when he's big-ger, we'll give him an appliance to help him walk . . ."

Nearby, out in the corridor, we heard a young boy's foot-steps, and the squeaking of a heavy iron appliance he was push-ing in front of him.

"André, come and see. This is Emile, a friend for you . . ." The boy smiled without comprehension. The nun went over to him, took his hand, then laid the opened fingers on Emile's forehead. "Love," she said, stroking the boy's hand. "Love." In the sick boy's silence, formless words seemed to bubble up; there was language there, and the nun understood it, for she turned with shining eyes and said: "He's happy too, you see! All you have to do is love them!"

I had lost Emile, perhaps; but when I thought of him, I imagined that nun to myself, with all the others who shared her labour, toiling to prevent a single tiny life from dissolving into nothing. Doubtless, their devotion to their patients was such that they did not stop to contemplate the misery they were nursing. It was their task, a patient labour, to make sure that each of those small creatures continued to breathe, never to let them be blown out in a moment of forgetfulness! Emile was no longer afraid of water. A touch of the Reverend Mother's hand on his head, and he cried no longer. Other mute and gentle beings floated with him on the green ripples of the big tank. Wading in the water herself, immersed up to her belt, the Reverend Mother helped a half-formed hand or foot to move with her aid, offering thanks to God for the slightest movement, or even the shadow of one. "It's beautiful, that. I've been trying to get that little hand to move for months . . . Once more . . . and again . . . very good, that's the way . . . They understand everything, true angels!" I thought with joy that the Reverend Mother was right to love Emile: he at least would never do harm to those who gave him their simple love, whereas I who loved Séraphine had caused her so much pain.

In the evenings, once seven o'clock was past, I sat in the empty house and let Emile's absence take possession of me. The light from the sky came slanting in at the open window, and I played with its dusty beams as though they were my thoughts. When my mother called to me from outside, I didn't answer.

"Whatever are you doing, for heaven's sake, all alone up there when everyone else is out on the sidewalk in the nice fresh air?" But for three weeks now I had not spoken to anyone.

"A real monster you can't help thinking, Madame Poire, that child of mine. She won't even talk to her own mother any more."

"Pooh! Madame Archange, I'd be only too pleased, I would, if that Huguette of mine would stop talking for a while! She chatters non-stop like a magpie. She doesn't even stop jabbering while her father's beating her!"

By leaning out of the window I could look down on all the women's gossiping heads, huddled together for the evening chorus. "Ah, who would ever have believed it, but it was certainly no Christian marriage. Have you ever known anything like it, have you, a child being born a month after its mother's wedding?" "Have I? Never!" "It's a scandal! But these days the young people just have no religion!" "Oh, Madame Whatsit, you're so right, so horribly right!" As the evening advanced, the men brought out their chairs onto the already crowded sidewalks, the women began washing their children, and in the greasy August heat they all sat out there sweating, suffocating, but never for a moment interrupting that passionate stream of slander against their neighbours.

"I have to tell you, Madame Poire, it's no good pretending: I don't much like seeing your Huguette with that wicked little Jacquou. He's always shooting stones with that catapult of his, and Huguette follows him about everywhere . . ."

"It's not my fault, I'm not in favour of separating the sexes, Madame Archange. Fine weather's soon over, you know. Just think of my Julia with her lungs all eaten away . . . yes, already . . ."

One evening I saw Mlle Léonard waling past our door. My mother went over to her and whispered something in her ear. Obviously she was telling Mlle Léonard that I was a monster and that I refused to come down and be with the others on the sidewalk. Mlle Léonard herself, as she stood listening to my mother, had a conspiratorial air I didn't much care for.

"Go up and see her," my mother said out loud. "Perhaps she'll talk to you." As soon as I heard Mlle Léonard's step on the stairs, I felt that I wouldn't have the heart to speak to her. Hidden behind the armchair, I watched her walking about in the gloom, calling out to me: "Pauline, are you there?" But I didn't speak.

"Very well, hide then, since you don't want to see me this evening. I just wanted to tell you . . ." She hesitated, then went on with weariness in her voice. "I've got into some slight difficulties, like everyone else. I shan't be able to go on giving my services in the public schools next semester. I'll still be working at the hospital. So . . . good night. Perhaps I'll see you again."

I heard her going back down the stairs. So many things seemed to be disappearing with Emile. The house was even emptier, the silence more frightening.

"Here come the firemen! They're having a parade! Come down, Pauline Archange!"

First of all, emerging from the darkening horizon, we saw five red puppets lifting first one leg, then the other in front of them to the sound of an invisible fanfare. The fire chief, of whom it was said that "he has read too many books and has ideas too big for his head," was himself beating the drum with a funereal fist, for he had lost "seven men at a blow in the hotel fire." "But it's a really lovely funeral," Huguette Poire said. "It's such a pity Julia isn't here!" And soon, around the corner of the street, there appeared another twenty, thirty, forty firemen. They passed in procession in their hundreds along the front of the Palace of Justice, pulling behind them, as though in a dream, the caskets of the seven heroes snuffed out with the flames on the roof. "A real man's death," my father said admiringly, for those seven firemen between them had just had time to save one woman. "Except that she died several hours later from her injuries." They went on marching endlessly past us, implacable and proud, their big blue eyes glittering beneath their helmets in the heat. "We need a storm. This heat is killing!" A drop of rain against one's forehead. It was a hope.

The fire chief mounted the platform and began his speech: "We are proud, in this town, to have firemen who are heroes, heroes who are not afraid to stamp out the flames wherever they burn and consume, wherever they ravage and kill. Hell is here in this very place, in this neighbourhood where a single match can set the torch to these ruins that are our homes. People are burned, hotels burn down, but the Palace of Justice, that does not burn. I shall take advantage of this occasion, which brings us all together here, to assure you that the Firemen's Association is against fires, unhappy childhoods, and the death penalty. On this day of mourning, let us all join in singing the Firemen's Hymn, thereby asserting our brotherhood in humanity."

"It's such a pity Julia's home in bed," Huguette Poire said in my ear. "She does to like things like this – speeches, and funerals. She always has a good cry at the firemen . . . Come on, let's go and get her. You too, Jacquou . . ."

Stretched out on the sofa, in the kitchen, Julia Poire turned away her head, as though to avoid seeing us. She coughed soundlessly into a handkerchief already soaked with blood.

"Not today, I'm not feeling . . . It's not one of my good days."

"But you'll never see the firemen looking so fine again, like kings they are, with the red fire engines, lovely music, and coffins in the street, everywhere you look, it's so lovely it makes you shiver . . . Come on, Julia, we'll take your hands, Pauline and me, and Jacquou can push from behind . . ."

"All right, kids, I'll go, but it's only to give you pleasure, because it's not one of my good days." But never had Julia Poire seen "a sight as beautiful as this, except in love stories." She clung to my shoulder with her damp hand so as not to fall, and her breath grazed my cheek. "Traitor fire, rebel fire, we shall stamp you out," the fire chief was chanting, and Julia Poire's fevered gaze, as she raised it toward him, was all expectancy.

The rain fell slowly, and side by side in our immobility we watched the last shadows of the procession vanish into the distance. A delicious coolness suddenly flooded over us, and I thought that the time had come for me to end my silence with my mother. I would still carry it to bed with me at night, the anguish from which I felt I had been liberated at that moment. It was even possible that it was going to continue growing with me, like the memory of the violence I had witnessed toward those I loved. If I had been given my being in some other form, perhaps I could have felt a pang of pity as I leaned down to observe a person such as myself, in order to tell her story; but born into the very story I wanted to write, I aspired only to find a way out of it. What made me feel most desolate was the thought that it was such a long, such a hard business for me to live, and that in a book it would take only a few pages; yet without those few pages I was in danger of never having existed for anyone.

BOOK TWO

VIVRE! VIVRE!

To Jacques Vallée

Translated by Derek Coltman

❧ Chapter One ❧

There all our possession are, standing or lying in the chaos of an open truck as it carries us off toward the neighbouring parish; my mother, head bowed between stove and washboard, herself resembling one of those worn and heavy objects among which she sits, one hand in her lap, laying bare to our neighbours' eyes, though without knowing it, all the naked vulnerability of her own body and that of the child she is clasping to her, doubly clothed by the imprisoning folds of her voluminous cloak. The air is pure, but all around us floats the presence of a concealed oppression that moves with us wherever we go; for although we are emerging, as in a dream, from a tunnel of gray houses in whose backward depths I can still make out the waving hands and shadowy faces of my friends, the distance separating us from our new parish is still too short to mist over my memories and my sins, so that I have the impression of another and equally familiar landscape rising for us only a little way ahead, scarcely producing any transformation at all in a human family now stripped of all its mystery for me . . . And yet, as we pass the Poires' house, I pretend not to recognize Julia when she smiles at me from her bed, her thin arms hooked around the bars of her window. But though my heart has suddenly closed against the misfortunes of others, it is in vain, for my eyes can forget nothing. As we move forward under the stripped autumn trees, I see again people I thought I had forgotten. Many I have seen only once, pressing their faces, crushing their lips against the steamy square of a windowpane, a glazed door – on winter evenings when even poverty believes itself invisible as it huddles down against unheated walls – and suddenly, through a snow-dusted square of glass, opening into the night magnificent eyes that shine in solitude above a line of whiteness, leaving the sketchy angle of an emaciated cheek in shadow, so that I felt, pausing before some underground passageway through which my gaze plunged to encounter a woman throwing down bread for her children onto the beaten earth floor, that it was its duty immediately to struggle upwards again, toward the consolation of those beautiful eyes, floating at the window. How could I part from the eyes, the eyelids, the hands of these beings my gaze had rested on so many times, melting into them in order to seize their secret thoughts, how could I separate myself from them now that they were becoming for me the eyes, the hands of beings I had secretly stolen in order to nourish my own life?

It was with the same ardour that I listened to my father's stories, thinking that I myself, once I could transmute it into my own language, would one day inherit that vast tempest blowing through his words as he told me for the hundredth time, in the same simple words, about "the terrible blizzard on Christmas Day when you were still a baby in your mother's womb," a story that seemed to reflect, in a distant past, something of the desolate fury I was feeling in the present.

"It was a lovely night, calm as calm. We were all coming back from your grandfather's in the cart, and the Midnight Mass had been so beautiful, it was as though nothing in the world was moving, not a tree, not a flake of snow, it was so cold and so calm that we held our breaths, even your Uncle Marius didn't dare drink any more, he squeezed his bottle between his knees so as not to give way, your mother was wrapped up in her quilt like a mummy, and then, you may not believe me but all of a sudden, in the middle of that starry night, the wind got up, like a man

all alone suddenly bursting with his bottled-up energy, no one
had seen a wind like it in thirty years, the trees all twisted, snow
splattering everywhere, our faces all wet with it. I hung onto the
reins, the horse was scared out of its wits, the snow kept falling
in great sheets on the road, hour after hour, it came at us from
every side, a cruel, wicked snow, full of vengeance, and maybe
that's why you're such a wicked girl, Pauline, it's as though the
cruelty in that snow got into your mother's womb that night,
because she groaned and groaned. We went swinging from one
side of the road to the other like a ship in a storm, and we knew
it was a matter of life and death, we said our prayers then and
that was when your Uncle Marius gave way to his temptation,
that was when I saw him standing up like a demon in his catskin
coat and downing every last drop of fire in his bottle. All our
hearts were breaking with the sadness of it all, but your Uncle
Marius, there he was, laughing and singing, happy as a sea captain, and after four hours of litanies to the Holy Virgin the snow
was still falling and we were getting in deeper and deeper, there
wasn't even a road any more, just a white sheet of damnation
everywhere, lost, we were lost, there was nothing left but to give
up, to let go, the horse was choking and we were too. Then the
cart began to move with a din out of hell and the horse tried to
gallop, then stopped dead, two of its legs broken in the snow as
we tipped over into the ditch, the whole lot of us, your drunken
uncle as well, still laughing, damned soul as he was. There was a
moment's silence, we thought we were dead, but no, oh it's not
going to be born normal this child of ours your mother sobbed,
so she was right, it was because of the blizzard that you're so
wicked. We stayed like that in the snow, right up to our bellies,
calling for help like the poor wretches we were, but no one
went by, not a soul, nothing but the black night all around. We
couldn't move a leg, the blood seemed to be freezing in our

veins, as though death was upon us, then your Uncle Marius and your mother were able to pull themselves out suddenly, like a gift from heaven, so they tried to help me out, but the more they tried, the deeper I sank, it was more like glue than snow, and as I tried harder and harder to move, my heart began dragging inside me, it was a dead weight dragging inside me like a great cart. There was a little crack, then suddenly silence, it was as though I was dead at the end of my tether, then God in his goodness permitted the mayor of the village to go by suddenly, big, strong, strapping fellow that he was, he helped me out of that hole, digging the snow out in great shovelfuls, but ever since that day it's as though my heart is dragging inside me, it's like when a heart's worn out, like an old horse that ought to be sent to the slaughterhouse . . ."

At the end of the story, as my father's hand flattened against his chest, I felt the same painful quivering in my own heart. But my pain, now, came from the desire for happiness to which I was so afraid of giving way. To myself, I told the story of a storm in which I parted from my parents without sadness. "It was a long time since I'd left my mother's womb, I walked along all alone in the darkness, it was snowing so hard the flakes were big as saucers, there was no one holding my hand, the snow was deep but I wasn't afraid of anything, as I passed my friends' houses I could see everyone feasting on Christmas turkey and the Christmas trees glittering against the far walls of the rooms. Julia Poire was eating with a healthy appetite, Séraphine was there too, eating beside her little brother, and you could hear the church organ and the bells on the carriages along the road, it was as though my heart was beating out happy music at the end of its tether . . ." And yet I had the feeling I was betraying my father by writing that story. When my father looked me in the eyes and told me I "led a double life," could there be any doubt that he was referring to these infinite variations I was always playing upon a secret world to which the only path was that of treachery? Every gesture I made seemed to create a widening rift between my parents and myself, a cruel rift that I felt was under my control. If my mother spoke to me more gently, in an attempt to touch my heart, I responded with a shrug, a curt flick of the head that was as good as an absence. Even thus devoured with pride, I nevertheless realized all the hurt I was inflicting on others; but once a rupture has occurred, how can one contain the pain of it? I had already known affection with Séraphine, with Sébastien, with Jacob, but when confronted with obligations to love I had not chosen, then I retreated at once. My father never understood that a caress cannot be asked for, that one either receives it or does not receive it, unexpectedly, one day no different from the rest, from a discreet hand that brushes for a moment against your skin and makes a gift of that unhoped-for moment of proximity. As I observed my father and his perpetually disappointed expectation, my irritation steadily increased, for in the avidity of his embrace, which often encircled no more than the shadows of those near him (since my mother, like myself, could turn an austere eye upon demands for affection), I recognized the existence of a suppliant race of beings, in his image, whom no love would ever satisfy, since their demands spring up forever anew, never permitting one the rest, the silence that are also necessary when one loves. I also felt how much I pitied my father, and that slightly sad pity, capable of love in secret, was perhaps a bond of loyalty between us, so cut off from one another otherwise.

"Don't waste time, don't sit there daydreaming like that, Pauline Archange, get on with your homework. If you think I'm going to go on sending you to school all your life, then you've another thing coming . . ."

But with my head bent over my exercise book I continued to think of that storm, of the evenings in those days gone by when it snowed so heavily on Séraphine and me that we were forced to take refuge at the ceremonial vigils for the city's recently dead: "At the end of the white street, under the big net of snow wetting our noses, the sudden glimpse of a wreath of flowers on a door, surrounded by a red glow, told us that a corpse was living there behind that door, with its relations all around it, and that the room would smell good and be nice and warm." But if we were there officially, the whole class with a Sister in attendance, if we were ordered into rows to say our beads, then the fragile spell that had rescued us from the snow-storm, inviting us in for an instant to share a dead person's sleep, that magic was rudely interrupted by the clatter of a church clapper, right in our ears, by the noise of our knees falling onto their *prie-dieus*, while the dead man himself seemed to sink with ever increasing hostility still further down into his lacy pillow, thrusting nearer and nearer to our fascinated eyes, panic-struck by the guttering candlelight, a waxen profile that had already ceased to belong to him, a bitter mouth whose green lips seemed to have been outlined with a knife, so that we could sense, behind those transparent and motionless lips, a smile that predated his death and still refused to fade. "Well one thing, the embalming was well done," Séraphine commented, her eyes ashine. "Did you notice how he was praying with his hands pressed together like that? And what a nice suit that was they put on him, though it didn't look as if he appreciated it."

"For goodness' sake be quiet, Séraphine Lehout, you do nothing but chatter. You're not supposed to talk when you're viewing dead people. You look at them, but you don't talk."

Families of total strangers greeted us with kindness, a father or a daughter would emerge piously from the shadows to shake our hands. "Another soul that God in his goodness has called back to Him. Ah! how sad it is . . ." they murmured in muffled voices, sniffing back their tears, or simply letting them stream down glistening cheeks and trickle, unchecked, onto the black material of their clothes, while in both our hearts there welled up an identical contagion of grief and an identical jealousy because we were not the person being mourned with such abandon! Others received our condolences like congratulations, crushing our proffered fingers with an abstracted air, thinking of their imminent deliverance, keeping watch on the corpse out of the corners of their eyes; for although tyranny had at last been vanquished and was lying there in its coffin, that being who had made them suffer the whole length of their lives still seemed an object to be feared, even when frozen in eternal rest. In this way, accompanying these unknown kith and kin, we would follow on from Mass to cemetery, spectators of an explosion of emotions, of secrets abruptly confided amid sobs to the corpse being laid in the earth, surprising the grief of separation wherever it appeared, on naked faces, in the hollows of necks heavily bowed, and suddenly aware within our own fragile bodies of the spur of a great dread that teetered on the verge of disgust. "There was a hole and a man inside it, when the earth began raining down on top of him it was too sad, Séraphine and I always wanted to leave . . ."

When my father became impatient at seeing me writing away at the end of the table, he reproached me for "filling up exercise books so quickly when they cost ten cents each, as if that's all I've got to do in this life, paying for ink and paper for you . . ."

Then he would push me toward my bedroom and hand me a broom, "to clean out that sty in there."

"And don't just stroke the floor either, with your eyes turned up to the ceiling like Saint Cecilia playing her piano. At your age I was already working, I was cutting cabbages and digging potatoes, and then my father said to me: 'It's time you were off to the town to work,' so I went, and us farming people then, when we went to work in the city we were no more than muck, the bosses just walked all over us, they told us we stank, they said we were lousy. A man's honour, a man's pride, that was something no one had ever heard of in those days, when you went into a factory it was like going down into the mines, you came out every evening shivering, with your belly empty, and what they paid us at the end of the week, well it was almost pennies, and to think we were so dumb we were glad to get it, we let the whole world use us like stepping stones."

No, I thought, as my broom sent the layers of dust billowing up through the sunbeams in gilded clouds, no one is ever going to work the clothes off my back, no one is going to humiliate me like that . . . But I worked when my turn came, nevertheless, during vacations and holidays. In the morning, as the iceman with his "ice for your iceboxes" yelled his way along our street, my father came in and sat by my bed waiting for me to wake up, and eventually, seeing that I was deliberately refusing to open my eyes, hurled my clothes into my face. Then we ate our breakfast side by side in silence (sometimes with my mother there too, on the occasions when she got up "to untangle that cotton hair of yours"), walked one behind the other downstairs to the street, still sodden with sleep, and often parted to go our separate ways without having addressed a single word to one another.

As in a dream, I followed the tinkling bell on the milkman's cart. The clumsy silhouette of a gray horse with black patches suddenly parted a wall of mist at the end of the alley, and I watched the sun slowly rise from behind the black mass of the tenements. But it wasn't until I heard the noise of the first trolley grinding along the tracks that I woke up completely. The newsboys came to meet me with their singsong insults.

"Hey, girlie, you're white as a sheet today. Are you here to sell papers or to sleep, make up your mind, for Chrissake!"

All you could see of them was dripping noses protruding from beneath blue cloth caps.

"Come on, you'd better get your regular dozen unloaded on the boulevard quick, cos' there's your door-to-door deliveries after that, and, Jesus, but it's cold this morning!"

There was scarcely time even to catch a glimpse of them before they were away "to do their elevator stints in the big stores all day"; occasionally we exchanged "digs in the ribs like a lot of louts," the language of elbows and fists, as my mother called it with stupefaction, a language that became my language too in the newsboys' world, so that when I got home in the evening it was as much as I could do to stifle the flowery blasphemies that rose to my lips, for I was unable to glance down at Jeannot clutching my skirt without thinking: "Get the hell away from me, you Christ-forsaken brat."

Our raucous voices battered at the passers-by in the morning stillness: "Read the *Moon*, five cents, the *Moon*, m'sieu, no books for you, deputy says, picks on shoulders and back to the land, men, five persons blow out their brains in a single night, the *Moon*, m'sieu, five cents . . ." I admired the newsboys as I watched them scuttling around the railroad stations in the early dawn, their tins of polish around their necks, at the ready to leap upon the feet of the first passenger to emerge, with an air of triumph, through the arch of smoke that hovered, momentarily, over the exit barrier from the newly arrived night trains. Quick as a flash, the newsboy had slapped his blacking on the man's boots and spat on top of it, while the passenger, from his corpulent height, pulled loose hairs out of his fox coat, or stared in front of him at the thick mist of his breath in the cold morning air. "It's enough to make you sick, he didn't even pay me!" But the noble flame of pride was quickly extinguished, and the newsboy remembered how much he needed the rich man: the gaze that followed the departing passenger's back looked, in the end, very like a smile of consent, a bond of servitude the newsboy was unable to root out in himself, since it was necessary to him if he was to live. Begging without shame, he held out his pale hand everywhere, artfully catering to the ladies, carefully assuming the profile of a graceful but brutal jawbone whose expression he had just been studying in the window of the butcher's on the corner.

When Mlle Léonard left the hospital, late in the evening, she would suddenly perceive them through her tiredness, these precocious beggars who never failed to offend her sight: "Spare a penny, m'dame, it's for my mom who's deaf and dumb, deaf as a post, mam'zelle!"

"Aren't you ashamed to beg," Mlle Léonard exclaimed, then added in a gentler tone: "You don't look very well, my friend. I'm a doctor at the hospital across, come up and see me in my office tomorrow morning. Germaine Léonard, third floor . . ." And she moved off again with her rapid steps, shoulders slightly bowed, leaving the newsboy astonished and humiliated. "Sick, me, for Chrissake, never! Strong as a lion, that's me, muscles like iron I've got, I'm gonna be a boxer, don't she know that. Telling me a thing like that, talk about a kind old dame. Them packages I lift every morning in the store basement, they weigh a ton."

Then, his attention caught by the shadow of a cat on the prowl among the banks of snow, the newsboy rushed off in pursuit, and was soon swallowed up by the night.

My bag of papers hanging in front of me as I walked, hat pulled down over my eyes "so I can chew my gum in peace," I too spat on the sidewalk as I walked along, and if Germaine Léonard's eyes happened to light on me I knew immediately that in her eyes I was "one of that gang of guttersnipes," and that she had condemned me.

"So this is what you've come to, Pauline Archange?"

"That's right."

"A bad-mannered little girl who is rude to people?"

"That's right. And I chew gum too. And I swear."

Yet I had dreamed of a quite different meeting with Mlle Léonard. Fired by the ardour her presence had once inspired in me, during her time at the convent school, I envisaged myself confessing to her "my longing to stay at school for a long time, because one day I want to write the book of Pauline Archange"; but that dream was vanishing into thin air now, for Mlle Léonard responded to my cheeky air with a grimace of her lower lip in which, as in the days when I had first known her, she seemed to concentrate all that cruel sulkiness that made her suddenly a total stranger to me. When she decided you were unworthy of her friendship she immediately took back all she had given, and exacted retribution too, with hurt, unhappy words of which she herself never really became aware until several days later, just when you had begun to cease smarting from them. Whereupon she would apologize clumsily and invite me to "come and spend a moment in her office," where I thought I would be able to see her alone, though it was a wonder she even recognized me among her crowd of patients as she busily distributed prescriptions to all comers, or went around plunging an aggressive thermometer beneath all the upcurled tongues, and since I did not dare to move up with the line to be examined in turn, I was forced to follow her progress around that white room with my eyes alone, seeking to uncover what it was that Mlle Léonard continually concealed from us beneath the surface of her kindness. But in the hospital Mlle Léonard displayed merely what she was in that place: "a creature crazed with charity," our Mother Superior had said, "but that is not enough; atheists are sources of scandal wherever they exist, and they must be rooted out." And it was no doubt in order to confront that punishment, meted out by ignorance, that Mlle Léonard continued her headlong course along the path of an involuntary saintliness, saying to herself every day what she had said to our Superior as she took her final leave: "You can save the souls . . . I'll save the bodies."

She was no longer to be seen abandoning herself to a man's arms as she had once, at the end of the day, when Louisette Denis and I waited for her after school. Her feelings seemed too filled with sadness to allow her to love. Austere and cold, she had found a way of assuming the masculine authority she needed in her work, and the colleagues who had loved her in earlier days now had too much respect for the virile aspect of her intelligence to think of her body. Head tilted to one side, she waxed indignant during their Saturday medical conferences, at which all the others were men, over "the profound injustice of our social system, which must be changed," provoking those who listened to vague interrogations, to flickers of concern that came to nothing. And it was at this time too that there began for Mlle Léonard the era of besieging hostility that was to age her so quickly. In a city where no comprehension was possible for a being possessed of different moral qualities from ours, for a mind capable of embracing a wider horizon, how was Mlle Léonard ever to succeed in breaking through the dense layers of our mediocrity, the heavy slumber of our prejudices? Not that she herself was entirely free from the prejudices she was fighting, but when a rare illumination touched her heart she was able to understand, and to love, with a real and deep intelligence. I was too young myself to value her rightly, and very often, as I crossed the sidewalk to avoid saying good day to her, I was aware that it was to myself I was doing the harm, rather than to Germaine Léonard, who had no need of me. But since Séraphines' death, though I still desired to love and to be loved, it was never in the way that others loved me, bending down to pity my humble fate as Mlle Léonard did. No, I wanted above all else to impose myself upon others by means of some irresistible inner worth that I did not possess, since my mother would say, as she looked up when I returned home in the evening: "So there you are, Pauline Archange, filthy of course, you're a worse guttersnipe to look at than your Cousin Jacob."

I often stared my mother down, eyes blazing with the violence she so much disliked, forgetting that she too, with her tiredness and her fits of nerves, needed indulgence as much as I did. For since the birth of my sister our new home seemed to have become too confined, and my mother's only remaining consolation for that useless move was the cleanliness of the walls, whose whiteness she would sit contemplating in the evening, as she sewed, punctuating that occupation with melancholy sighs, while Jeannot whispered in his sleep that he was "afraid of falling," though always averting that fate all the same by hooking one foot around my ankle, or suddenly clutching the tail of my pajama top, the icy embraces of his imperilled sleep from which I could only rescue myself by sliding over to the very edge of the bed, where I lay endlessly tracing the path of the ray of light along the passage, the line of shadow across the wooden floor. And there was my mother's face too, approaching and receding in my field of vision, in that fluid space that was bringing me nearer all the time to the tick-tock of the big clock and also, already, I thought to myself, to the time to get up.

Ah, to go back to our old neighbourhood, to Madame Poire, Huguette, Jacquou! I was so afraid of "Madame E.E. Boisvert, the madwoman next door, and her poor daughters! A sadist, that woman, Pauline Archange – mark my words . . ." my mother said, her voice drained of all charity at the thought of encountering "madness itself, madness that goes beyond all bounds . . ." in the person of that neighbour of ours, in appearance as easygoing as the nun she had once been, fat and overflowing with kindness if you paid attention only to the collapsing carapace of a body slung between her legs (for though with time I forgave that woman many things, I always blamed her, unjustly perhaps, for the monstrous sight of her body); I continued for a long while, when I thought of her, to see those short, demented legs carrying the great belly like a sack of worm-eaten meat, that chest whose vastness was so entirely lacking in majesty, panting with pleasure at the sight of pain inflicted on others, even though the same body, clothing the less insensitive soul of some other person, would have inspired me with great pity), but beneath the appearance a torturer born, exercising all her gifts for wide-eyed treachery upon the person of her daughter Clara – "Clara, my child from the second bed," as she called her, though of Clara's father we never saw the slightest sign, he being the only quarry in that family intelligent enough to have found a refuge.

If we were jumping rope in the street, in the evening, one of us would suddenly stop and look around with uneasy eyes: "I feel as though someone's watching me," and we would suddenly realize, seeing Clara's reddening cheeks, the way she shook her long hair back over her shoulders, that her mother, a great owl in the orderly thicket of their shutters, was staring at her from a distance, and we knew that her struggles as she forced herself to jump back into the circling rope were in vain, for her mother's relentless glare was bound to lasso her again in the end. This gleeful exercise of an omnipotent cruelty upon so weak a creature appeared to those who witnessed it to be a mystery whose secret rites it would be better not to uncover. It is in the same way, perhaps, that we lack the courage to investigate what does on beyond prison walls, inside the places of torture among which we live. Having discovered one day that Madame E.E. Boisvert had left Clara alone in their house for a week "with two crusts of bread and a piece of cheese," my mother invited her to come every day to us for her midday meal. With ink-stained fingernails, Clara swooped voraciously upon the food that was placed in front of her, so intent on her hunger that she did not seem to hear the baby crying in its high chair. She wiped her bread round and round in the gravy, endlessly cleaning up her already clean plate, then let her begging eyes, with their encir-cled olive shadows, wander across to our still-unemptied plates.

"You promise to say nothing to my mother, Pauline Ar-change, you promise on the head of Jesus Christ? Coming to eat at your house doesn't mean I'm a beggar, I only come to please you, you know that."

What a temptation, with one curt word of truth to break that marriage of torturer and victim! A few days later, following the advice of my mother, who was "shocked to the core by that heart harder than rock," I told Madame E.E. Boisvert what we thought of her: "My mother said it herself, the way you treat Clara it's like the story of Aurora the child-martyr who ate the soap, she's so starved she has to come and eat with us."

At that, the horse took the bit between its teeth. Back pressed to their kitchen wall, I watched as her imperious arm was raised to strike her daughter, as it seized the terrified and cowering child in its downward flight, then pinned her to the table.

"You're not going to forget this, Clara Boisvert, you're not going to forget this for a long time."

"Stop, Mama, stop, stop!"

It was in vain that I joined my cries to Clara's and begged with her for mercy. The accursed arm struck and struck again, perpetuating the inhumanity of all those other acts I had already seen or felt, repeating without scruple the gestures of Jacob's father crippling his son, and as I looked at my clenched fists trembling with impotence and rage I told myself that there could never be forgiveness for such actions, never any hope on this earth where every day thousands of people, wounded or killed by their fellow beings, crumpled at the foot of the torturer's stake as Clara was crumpling from that table, before my eyes, and offered to our impotence their bruised and swollen backs, like Clara's, from which my eyes, in their shame, could no longer tear themselves away. The words I wrote in my exercise book that evening – "Pauline Archange, it's as though the older you get, the deeper you sink into hell, you are always making Séraphine suffer, over and over again, it's as though you can't stop yourself" – those words did not console me for the immense pain I felt as I thought of Clara, whom I had betrayed, thinking to help her, delivering her up myself to her mother's terrible hands.

I even found a kind of justice in the fact that I was hounded by Clara's mother myself, in my turn, and I said nothing about it to my own mother. During the year I spent as a day girl at the convent boarding school, I used to leave the private study room before night fell, but even so I was quite often unable to avoid the silhouetted figure of Madame E.E. standing alone under a lighted sign and mumbling to herself ("Pray, pray, say your rosary, pray without rest, says the Blessed Virgin") in the convent forecourt, peering at each emerging girl as she waited for me. I ran toward the bus, seeking refuge among the unshaven work- men, all reading their newspapers with a preoccupied air as they stood or sat, only to turn round suddenly and find her beside me, pinching my side through my coat, that poor madwoman for whom I felt not the slightest pity, reciting her interior mono- logue out loud, foaming with jealousy: "Ah, Pauline Archange, we think we're so intelligent because we're always at the top of the class, don't we, Pauline, little muck heap, little gutter filth!"

After a while, since these scenes were repeated almost daily, in church even, or in the street, my mother, seeing me come home one evening in tears, flew over to the telephone with a look of sudden rage: "Madame Boisvert, that's enough, if you don't leave these kids alone I'll get the police after you." My mother went off the deep end like this every five years or so, and I thought to myself, watching her crush the absent dragon Madame E.E. beneath her feet, that if she didn't give way to these impulses of her nature more often, it was solely because her delicate health did not permit it. Five years before, had we not run to and fro together across the newly polished bedroom floor, simply as a gesture of defiance against our landlord's ultimatum: "I'll have no children running about in my house!"

"Oh, I'd like to smash a chair over that man's head! Quick, hand me a chair, Pauline Archange, while your father's not here to see me in a state . . ."

Within the family circle my mother displayed this rebellious side of her character more often. "Just because your so-called French aunt comes to see us once a year, tiptoeing around like a

queen, doesn't mean we have to get down on our knees to her!"
Though, even as she protested, my mother was energetically
scouring the house, hiding away in the closet the odd remnants
of her ironing or her washing ("Your aunt has a sharp nose on
her, go round all the legs of the beds with a duster"), and when
the much-travelled aunt arrived we were all washed and combed,
sitting in a row on the mauve sofa. Her forehead, wide and bare
beneath a mountain of hair dressed in sausage curls, seemed
already to be projecting it inner thoughts toward some far horizon, where they wandered through unknown countries without
even seeing us. Her nose alone, long and stern, remained with
us, observing us with kindness.

"Ah, France!" she sighed. "France!"

And Uncle Gaspart gave an approving nod of the head, well
aware, in his modesty, that he was the true begetter of his wife's
great love affair "with the land of our ancestors," immuring himself late into the evening in his shoe store so that he could afford
to make her a present of it. "He'll work himself to death out of
love for his wife, it's a disgrace," my father said. But despite his
lugubrious air and the drooping moustache that covered his lips,
Uncle Gaspart seemed freer and happier with things as they
were, and if he was asked why he didn't accompany his wife, he
smiled mysteriously, for he alone knew what a heavy shadow his
presence would have cast upon his wife's embraces with *la
France*. And when you thought about it, it would have been as
insane as following her to meetings with real lovers, watching her
as she deceived him before his very eyes, as she melted into
ecstasy over "every French hill, over the air in France, the purest
in the world, the sky in France, the bluest in the world . . ."

"How very right you are, Catherine," my uncle therefore
replied, listening with only half an ear as his wife went on to tell,
with touching affection, how "as soon as I stepped off the boat

I knelt down on the soil of France and kissed it passionately," for Gaspart's thoughts were entirely on his January sale, "which is going to lose me money again," his eyes deciphering on our ceiling the painful sums his generosity was costing him. If my aunt scarcely glanced at us, it was because she did not care for children: "I love France alone, and little French children . . ." Whereupon she produced from her muff a photograph of a "dear little daughter of France with her mother," the latter's face turned toward the daughter with an air of familiar dissatisfaction that immediately conjured up a resemblance to my mother and myself; but moved as I was by the gulf of distance that separated me from those two sad creatures, standing figures against a background of gray courtyard that was only too similar to the back of our own tenement, I ignored that resemblance in my search for two seemingly inaccessible beings, living so far away, when those beings, with whom I shared such strong moral similarities, were living in fact so near at hand, within the walls of our own home.

"Poor things, how unhappy they look! Ah, how lucky we are to be so happy, over here," my mother commented, observing me with eyes full of reproach, for she was only too well aware that whenever our aunt came to visit us I always "had my head turned by her tales of France." And later, jealous of a love that seemed, by widening our frontiers, to strengthen my need to write, my mother said with disdain: "France, poetry – you'll soon forget all that when you've got children of your own!"

Nor did she like to see me cutting the poems of Romaine Petit-Page out of the Saturday newspaper; perhaps, quite simply, because my admiration for that poetess seemed to her absurd.

O France, here I stand before you
Like a bitter pilgrim . . .

I imagined Romaine Petit-Page as someone my own age, a young girl endowed with sparkling genius, her life a perpetual blossoming beneath the lace and golden curls with which she decked her works ("the delicate lace of your smile," "the snow that falls like lace upon my heart"), perhaps growing up, very slowly, in the bland company of the heroes in her three novels *(Childhood's Cradle, The Adolescent Prince, The Flower of Youth)*, heroes endowed with a blond and slender beauty who never actually dared kiss young girls, oh no!, but who gazed on them, from behind a screen of rosebushes, as they played the piano, ardent perhaps, but chaste, so "paralyzed with love" in their haggard contemplation, "rosier than the roses that tumbled down on their pure necks in the westering sunlight," that in a sublime distraction of all their senses "their fingers, bloodied by the thorns, sprinkled luminous red drops upon the grass," an outcome that seemed to satisfy the author's desires entirely, but stirred up more troubled emotion in me that if I had seen Jacquou, as in days gone by, erupt with his spellbinding pirouettes into that garden of wearisome virginity from which there was no escape in these books, from one volume to the next. Romaine Petit-Page never answered my letters, until, one day, thanks to a three-page flight on the subject of the mourning vigils I used to attend with Séraphine, she invited me to join her group:

> *What a tender age is yours,*
> *Little bird lost in the mist,*
> *the age of all our noblest dreams,*
> *ah, what freshness, I welcome you*
> *with happiness into my enchanted kingdom,*
> *meet me after five o'clock Mass,*
> *on Wednesday, in the Place des Jannes,*
> *my friends will be there . . . so come . . .*

What joy to wait, my newspapers under my arm, my head wandering in the cold air, for the appearance of Romaine the Catholic and her band of acolytes, emerging from the church in a bemused wonderment of mutual adoration, a pious and dreamy band of Narcissuses exclaiming one after the other at "the lovely snow it's snowing now." It had been snowing for three days, and the sidewalks were lined on either side by mountain ranges of less than pristine whiteness, but they did not seem to notice that; sinking into the deep snow, they fell and got up again, exchanging wild, artificial laughter, scattering around the shoulders of their poetess – who was sinking to the top of one boot in the snow while making great gestures toward me with one hand – a rosary of caresses, the tributes of their passionate comradeship, which she received with a dazzling display of vitality, disclosing those white and regular teeth of hers to one and all in the moonlight, laying her lips with conscious deliberation on the cheeks being offered her, touching the bodies of the boys ("on their calm and innocent breasts"), their necks, their brows, ("which expressed a vague nostalgia for purity"), but never giving herself to them, reserving for her fiancé Georges, a delicate young man who sometimes fainted during Mass, the treasures of expectation.

Later, Georges gave up his place to Pierre, who in turn stepped down for Louis, the whole group continuing to languish and swarm around these eternally succeeding courtships while Romaine Petit-Page, with honeyed affection, went on consummating her marriages of true minds. All, at the contact of her many-sided gifts, abruptly began producing poems or acting in plays, and each of them, spurred on by the adoration Romaine Petit-Page felt for them all, became absorbed in his or her own adorable uniqueness, aware of the same bland virtuosity flowing through every vein, anxious to master everything, to play the piano, to sing, to paint, all embracing as a body the same lack of skill, all partaking without any sense of disillusion in the same harmonious absence of talent. As for me, I seemed to be something of a disappointment to the poetess and her clan, a creature possessing none of their qualities, not even as old as the youngest among them, a boy named Julien Laforêt, who, at twelve, as he crushed your fingers in a soldierly handshake, bragged with his nose in the air of being "an overeducated monster." The night before, my mother had poured a whole bottle of oil over my head to kill the lice, and the stink of it wafted up into my nostrils as I gazed at Romaine Petit-Page's beautiful hair, the beautiful curls that encroached on her pink-powdered cheeks so as to offer some protection to a very slight aging face, to the hard features of whose plain-speaking she felt ashamed, for she had contrived to disguise her body and her mind as what they no longer were: the face of the little girl she had once been – the face that had perhaps melted the hearts of a grownup audience when she read out her poems at the age of nine – and the body of the dancer she dreamed of being; for it was in such ways, in a frantic struggle to prolong the idyll of childhood within and around herself, that she who loved beauty so much was unendingly committing sins of taste against it.

Romaine Petit-Page probably thought of me as too young to become a regular member of her group, so during the next three years she never invited me to visit her except in the intimacy of her family circle, surrounded by all the nephews and nieces who climbed up to lean on her shoulder on those Sunday afternoons, sharing the joyous effusions that sprang from Romaine whenever she touched a piano, playing with her, writing with her, and all the while galloping around the room to "the song of the wild colt speeding o'er the plain." Yet never had I felt so dispirited before when I thought of my own life, and the impulsive kindness and affection with which that family always surrounded me on those visits seemed only to increase the inner pain when I finally returned home, to my parents who never read and were complete strangers to music. This social barrier, so subtle and so cruel, seemed familiar: wasn't it the same barrier that I had felt insinuating itself between myself and Mlle Léonard, when she confused me with all those other urchins on the street, prevented by her severity from distinguishing the being I truly was from that caricature of me so visibly acting the hooligan along with all the others? Unhappily, this barrier became wider still when Romaine Petit-Page attempted to find in me some reflection of what she herself had been, marvelling at the presence of an innocence, a freshness I no longer possessed, vestiges of her own dreams that she always yearned to share with those she loved; and if some of her friends allowed themselves to be replaced little by little by these creatures born of her illusions, perhaps it was solely to keep their true inner beings intact. But the unmannerly, untamed creature that had always been me seemed perpetually about to burst out of its newly imposed envelope; shying at sudden pitfalls, it managed to choke back its blasphemies, yet even as it struggled to keep its language chaste, it was shaken abruptly by sudden tremors of anguish, for I would hear myself saying: "Ah, if only I was a writer too, the books I'd write then! It's easy, all you do is just say what you feel . . ." Romaine Petit-Page closed her eyes and forgave me, but for a long time, on my way home, as I walked down the steps that led back to the subterranean part of the city, my ignorance continued to oppress me; I sped past the newsboys at a run, fearing that I might begin to speak like them again if I so much as stopped to say hello.

When Romaine lent me books "of powerful religious and literary inspiration," the intoxication of words and images with which they filled me was somehow no longer quite so satisfying, for now I had become jealous of those books, depressed because I was not writing books myself. And it seemed to me that this curse of ignorance was not only something inside me, placed there to prevent me from writing, but that it inhabited a whole insular world all around me, its sway extending even to the higher regions of society, a dictatorial incompetence whose voice could be heard mumbling away everywhere, over the radio as well as in the pulpit, borrowing our own familiar accent, our crippled language, in order to exhort us perpetually to the same old slavery ("Cit'zens, respect your bosses, God, and the fam'ly, go back to the land"), and sighing such funereal refrains across our school textbooks as:

> *"Conjugate the following in the past tense:*
> *To deck this cemetery with lilacs.*
> *To watch the descent into the grave . . ."*

Those who held dominion over us seemed all-powerful in the power that we had given them, and to shake off the yoke we would have had to love it less. A clerical or political despot congratulating himself in public upon "never having read a book in all his God-fearing life" strengthened the communal ignorance and even made it dismally bearable. Faced with so many people participating in the sleep of a passive solidarity, each individual contracting his frontiers to include only himself, I told myself that there were others keeping their vehemence intact for later, appeasing their irreconcilable ardour with the present while they waited, and rose every morning, perhaps, with the thought of a future that held more hope.

Nevertheless, the days passed, and now it was my turn to see Jeannot come sobbing home from school; as I bent down to console him, it was suddenly Séraphine's face that was confronting me again, and the memory of that long-past humiliation, that face, still so fearful, cowering behind bent arms to evade the imagined blows that we had no intention of inflicting. "Oh, why have the Brothers punished him again? Why does he find it so difficult to learn things, that child? Is he retarded, like Emile?" Sometimes my mother did not even use Emile's name, referring to him as "the Other" with a sigh of resignation, inwardly disturbed by a suggestion from Mlle Léonard that "there was a danger of Emile's illness reappearing somewhere else."

My mother was too modest a woman to contradict these grave errors, now frequently upon Germaine Léonard's lips, and though she herself had come round to thinking the disease from which Jeannot suffered was no more than sheer laziness, still the ghost of Emile was always there in her tortured conscience, and if a false prophetess, speaking from her high seat of medical judgment, was prepared to give concrete existence to such errors, referring to them as "difficult truths," my mother, still punishing herself inwardly for a crime she had never committed, tended to accept those errors as truths. Jeannot did of course grow up, graduating to the status of being called Jean, and my mother was to comment to my father later on, in a plaintive voice: "They have too much talent, those children of ours, they all want to keep on with their studies as if we were millionaires!" But Mlle Léonard persisted in clinging to the image of "your little brother Jeannot who had such difficulty learning like the others," as if all her power over others, or her secret shield against us, depended upon the reiteration of that prejudice.

During her years of solitude, which were still punctuated by brief affairs (such as the sensual alliances she entered into during her periods of study abroad), Mlle Léonard continued to mutilate her own spiritual urge toward reform in this way, by pronouncing judgments that had still lost nothing of their archaic distrust toward the class to which I belonged. I could not tell her about Jacquou playing with little girls in the ravine, in our childhood, without inspiring intense disgust in her. "What a shocking upbringing that child must have had!" she seemed to be saying with that twist of the mouth, that quivering of the nostrils, as irrevocable disdain once more took possession of her face. Yet this was the selfsame woman who loved men too much to be faithful to any one of them, and who, too noble and too lucid to allow the intensity of love to make inroads upon her work, was still striving to reconcile the two, a course that seemed more likely to make solitude, rather than any man, her companion as she grew older. How beautiful they were, those mornings when as she set foot inside the hospital, or the infirmary at school, we saw her radiating that strange happiness in which her yesterday's smile, so twisted and sullen, was dissolved into an expression of tenderness and reverie, so that all her movements lost their customary abruptness and she came toward us with softened steps, walking close to the sun-drenched walls, her short-sighted head tilted to one side!

But Mlle Léonard despised affairs that went on too long, and very soon she would revert to her former liberty and hardworking habits: in that life in which she believed she gave so little of herself it sometimes happened that she gave herself completely, for it was always beside a man she had decided to break things off with as soon as the sun rose, in the trust of their very carnal friendship, that she would astonish herself by suddenly revealing things she had never uttered to anyone, only to reproach herself later for betraying gratitude for a purely physical happiness with words from so deep in her soul. At that early hour, when she was already dressed and about to leave for the hospital, preparing to close behind her the door of the room where her companion still slept, the sky seemed so dark out there, the day so icy cold! In the bitterness of such days, days when she had brought an affair to an end, Mlle Léonard wrote virulent articles for *The Workers' Journal* in which she fearlessly attacked all that she herself stood for, her own parents even, as though, thanks to some noble and spiritual metamorphosis working upon that disappointed love, she had acquired, over and above the pity she always possessed, another kind of humility less brutal than her own, a miraculous perception of the unhappiness and injustice that she now denounced in a style of austere inspiration, so that from that irreligious pen there flowed a force, a lyricism whose despairing demand for justice was fed by an ecstasy sprung from the sincerest faith.

Germaine Léonard also went through periods of inward fog when she saw nothing, understood nothing, her soul invaded by bad dreams, emerging from her mute indignation only in order to make savage attempts at affirming her own superiority, and one knew that at such times, in her desire to keep up appearances, she would have slandered a friend, sacrificed whatever she loved most in the world – for in the face of all the persecutions imposed on her she had difficulty maintaining her self-control, and to make herself understood by those who condemned her writings she would borrow their own reactionary opinions, or lose herself in blind moralistic denunciations.

It was futile to attempt to convince Mlle Léonard that it was possible for me to escape from the conditions of my existence: she had so little faith in my family, and the mysterious emancipation she dreamed of for us was before all else, perhaps, her own. When I confided to her that I intended to write, but that my father objected to "my exercise books full of scribbles and crazy ideas when exercise books are so expensive," she was nevertheless moved by an immediate impulse of generosity, and while she felt about in her leather briefcase for some small change "with which to buy some clean notebooks and a good grammar," I stood wondering whether the smile she was giving me was one of kindness or of irony . . .

I still wake up in the night full of dread: my chest heaves with my heavy, irregular breathing, the lightning-shattered horses that once spun round and round, up in the whirling clouds, speeding endlessly across the summer sky, all the creatures that once terrified me, with their movements, with their beauty, or with the strangeness they had acquired from a delirious imagination, all of them close in upon me still, trample my sleep, turn everything into violence. And how often that violence in my dreams has been given flesh in real life, in distant places and all around me. I feel it in my chest, like the memory of the storm that makes my father's heart beat so wildly; the most savage of visions have been made reality: I see Clara again, the bleeding weals across her back. "Why, Pauline, tell me why you allowed all that?" "Come on then," Séraphine chimes in, "come and get warm at the funeral home until the snow has stopped," and she runs over to me, I see her red cheeks under her fur hat, she tells me to wait for her outside a store "while I go in and buy all the lamps," but the light still fails, Séraphine does not come back. I would so much like to meet Jacob again too, "the real Jacob who lives only in my heart," but abruptly I am awake, and beside my bed my mother is standing, watching me.

"You've been coughing away for two hours now, keeping the baby from going to sleep. She's still wide awake and kicking about as though it's the middle of the day. Try not to breathe so loud, try to think of others," she said as she closed the bedroom door behind her.

The night begins again. It is the day of the move. We are travelling through a black tunnel, then another. But suddenly, out on the other side, the light dazzles us. My mother lifts her head, and without looking at me she says: "It's as though we can begin to breathe at last, eh, our Pauline?"

❧ Chapter Two ❧

The Mother Superior's whispers into the microphone, her words of welcome to the new girls, provoke an anxious tingling in the nerves of all those present that extends, in ever widening circles, out along the galleries and into the yard: Sisters and boarders bustle off toward the corridors, a rebellious coif fluttering at the head of every file, its wearer already ringing the bell, announcing the beginning of the first morning class, a return to habits that my companions have forgotten but will quickly remember as a pair of prying eyes catches them changing out of their black stockings into transparent ones, beneath the sheltering curve of the stairs . . . Mother Saint-Georges scrutinizes our marks, scorning the "excellents" in our reports, searching our faces for telltale traces of pride, and as she goes down the list, ascertaining our fathers' professions ("Lavatory attendant, Mother Saint-Georges." "Funeral florist, Mother Saint-Georges . . ."), she gives a tiny cough or two of awestruck confusion when Marthe Dubos, whose ambition is to be "a lieutenant in the navy, or else an airplane pilot," announces through the gum she is chewing that her father is "a big lawyer, heartless as anything, all he thinks of is getting his hands on other people's money," for that note from the social scale has struck an answering chord in Mother Saint-Georges's heart, and she replies with a quiver: "We're always happy to see lawyers in our convent," and then, turning her attention to the upper juniors, she orders us curtly "to go and sit at the back to learn humility."

Cut off from me by a curtain of ferns, Louisette Denis hides her forehead behind a pale, trembling hand; if she dared to glance at me for an instant, perhaps she would understand that I am ashamed at having written to her so little during her two years at the sanatorium, but she keeps her eyes humbly lowered, as though she wanted to ask forgiveness for that long absence and the illness that has transformed her in my eyes; she seems to be feeling, as I am, that the being I am meeting again today, in this classroom, is no longer the sprightly and healthy friend who once shared my inner impulse toward life . . . Séraphine, if you came back onto the earth I would really be kind to you, I'd never make you cry and I'd never scold you again, ever" – those words I wrote yesterday in my exercise book are no longer sincere now, this morning, as I refuse my affection to this Louisette who had been brushed by death.

A girl lazily stretching her arm in a ray of sunshine across her desk, the buzzing of the flies from the ceiling overhead (on the inside of the lampshades, where their shadows dart wildly and in vain), the autumn wind blowing in through the half-open window, this whole familiar existence in which each of us feels the melancholy of the jailed captive is my existence too, I keep telling myself. "Yes, Pauline Archange, it's not your fault that Louisette Denis was ill with her fever for so long, you're alive, so just look somewhere else, that's all, look at Marthe Dubos, there is someone really bouncing with health at least, all plump curves and built like a giantess, whereas Louisette Denis is a matchstick, she's lucky she's not in the same grave as Séraphine!" And in order to defend this free, unsociable existence, to shield it against the inroads of pity, I yield once more to the same old thought: "The only thing is to behave as if you're the only person in the world!" During the summer, when I really was "the only person in the world," when I deliberately forgot the existence of others, who could possibly tell after all?

The determination to live for myself, to wrest moments of happiness from a being incapable of feeling happy, was a crime perhaps, but a crime savoured in solitude, one that no one had the right to make me expiate . . . My mother was delighted to see us setting off for Isaac Park on those warm July mornings, unaware that as soon as we were inside the gate I sat down under a tree alone to read, scarcely recognizing the silhouettes of Jeannot and my sister busily playing in the distance, wielding their red spades on a pale heap of sand. Their quavering voices, raised to summon me, no longer seemed to reach my ears, for over and above the intoxication of reading in the open air, away from everyone, I was also feeling a sudden and inexplicable intoxication with my own being, with self; I had to touch my forehead several times in order to feel all the warmth of that self's existence, crouched inside there, and at that moment of absolute gratitude toward life, when I myself existed more than ever before, my brother and sister on the other hand no longer existed at all . . . They existed even less, I thought, than the sunlight falling pitilessly on my worn sandals, and by closing my eyes I was able to forget them completely.

How could they feel the same ardour at living as I did? For whereas I spent my evenings wandering around the streets, Jean's had been spent in his pajamas, sitting beside my mother while she rocked the baby to sleep, and as I slipped away on my bicycle I would see him stretching out a hand between the bars of the iron balcony, toward the still rosy sky, a captive hand that waved at me in friendship each time I passed in front of our house. But seeing in that gesture still another reason for feeling guilty about my liberty, I never answered Jean's wave, only coming to realize too late that on those summer evenings, when my brother sat stretching out his hand to me, it was the same rebellion I had once felt that he was seeking to express now in his turn; but because he had expressed it without anger, I had not recognized it.

My mother saw little of my father, since he studied late into the night (in the same bedroom where she herself slept while he worked), and the trusting presence of a child sitting on her lap, or playing beside her, filled the void that had been left by Emile, that absence from which she hoped still to recover; she fought off her memories by gathering about her the children that remained, perpetually increasing her family to keep solitude at bay, and when I saw her abandoning herself in that way to her thoughts, allowing her usual severity to wander at rest around her, did she know, I wonder, that she had lost, not one child, but two? The flame of rebellion that had, after all, been engendered in her womb would flare up one day in the hearts of those children too, those beings she kept there beside her on the balcony, during those evenings, to protect herself, and they too would doubtless escape from her in time, as I myself had done.

She had nourished violent, unfulfilled desires, and there was no way for her to realize them now except through us, for it is often the role of children to uproot the secret dreams in their parents' hearts, to kill those dreams inside a mother or a father so that they can live them in his or her stead. Meanwhile, my mother liked to hold my sister's head in the palm of her hand, that fragile skull whose wall seemed almost transparent beneath the silky covering of hair (if you caressed that skull with your fingertips you could feel that it was still not closed, and that death as well as life could seep out through the deep, sinuous line beneath the tight-stretched skin), such was the sweetness in feeling that presence so close to her, that being she had made, sleeping, opening its eyes for an instant, a being whose utter obedience, whose tender affection without taint of servility she could still love . . .

But the mother love that had been disappointed, humiliated, seemed to be saying to me: "You, Pauline Archange, you've never given your parents anything good, you think of no one but yourself, it's all you can do to bring yourself to wash your brothers and sisters in the morning, you won't peel the potatoes properly, go off on your bicycle, do, I don't want to set eyes on you, thank goodness I've got other children besides you, otherwise it would be no joke . . . You've got a heart harder than a stone, only worse, because some stones can be split, as we know . . . I saw you this afternoon, you cruel girl, when your Aunt Judith was saying goodbye to us in the Immaculate Sisters' courtyard before she went to Africa, an aunt who's a missionary and going away for ten years into the bush, just to save souls and nurse lepers, and you couldn't even weep a single tear! I didn't ask you to sob like Grand-mère Josette, just one tear, so that your cousins could see you have a heart, but no, I saw you with that nasty smile of yours on your face, a real monster, what is it that goes on inside that head of yours, Pauline Archange? And worse still, when everyone else was wearing a black hat on their head, you had to wear that shameful red hat, there are times when I just can't understand you! You may never see her again, your Aunt Judith, but it was as clear as daylight, you just didn't care, one way or the other. Ten years, that's a long time, all that sacrifice for the love of God above! You think you're the only person in the world, don't you, Pauline Archange, writing your stories and reading books just like the priests say you mustn't, but your Aunt Judith, she always had her nose stuck in those forbidden books too, she was just like that at your age, an outrage monsieur le curé thought it was, she went skating with the boys in the parish too, yes, she was a bad lot like you, but she was converted suddenly one day, whereas you're never going to be converted, never, you'll never go to Africa the way your aunt has, I just wonder what you think life is all about!"

It was true that I had expressed no sadness when Mother Judith de la Bonté, as she laid her face against mine through the snowy material of her veil, had brushed my cheek with her burning breath, for as they bent toward us one by one in their veils, their feet crushing the flowers in the flower beds, all those nuns whose faith was about to send them away from us into exile, it had suddenly seemed to me that they were entrusting us that afternoon with the last dying flickers of their joy in living, all the keen-eyed contemplation of this world of which they were all capable but which they had never exercised till then, except in their cloistered chapel, yes, it seemed to me that in spite of everything, as they leaned toward us to say their goodbyes, it was the summer, the sensual ecstasy of the summer that they were pouring into us, with its scent of roses and peonies, and there was the thought that though each of them was weeping as she embraced her friends and her relations, she must also be smiling a little too, beneath her tears; for tomorrow at dawn my Aunt Judith, who had been dreaming of this departure for so long, would be departing at last, quitting the pacific contemplation of her convent for "the real world, ah! real men, at last!", and that real humanity was already waiting to meet her on their ship, to which her intrepid imagination was bearing her as she exchanged that inner smile with me, that smile with which my mother was later to reproach me because I had had the temerity to express it . . .

What wanderlust drove Judith and her companions to flee so far! God, Judith said, was drawing her to those far places; she had recognized "the divine beggar avid for pity, all covered with wounds, his face devoured by leprosy," but she lost the power to pray, all the same, confronted with a forehead scorched to the bone by the disease, a forehead to which she could offer only baptism "like the ironic caress of water on a brazier, ah! my dear sister, if you knew all that we see here, it's very hard sometimes, but I am happy here and never wish to leave, I am recovering slowly from my malaria, you know how it is, the exile, the difference in climate . . ." My mother was thrown into sudden gloom by the absence of heroism in her own life and wrote bitterly in reply to Judith, her uneven writing overflowing with passion and vehemence: "You for your part, dear sister, don't know what it means to be the mother of a family and wash diapers all day long, to have a Pauline who doesn't listen to a word you say, you've always had Africa in your blood you see, I hear that poor Sébastien died devouring those African sunsets of yours with his eyes, you remember those pictures you had that are still all over the place at Grand-mère Josette's, but he died all the same, without ever leaving his room, poor unhappy boy, sometimes I think it's not enough, the vocation of a wife and mother, there's not much to it, I don't know what I'd do if the good Franciscan didn't come and see me once a week when I'm sick, there are days, you can't imagine, when one is just too tired to go on living . . ."

My mother did not dare to delve beneath the outward appearances that others presented to her, and Father Benjamin Robert had, for her, all the appearances of sanctity, of a blind virtue that she accepted as a source of comfort without ever trying to find chinks in it, perhaps for fear of losing her illusions, but also because, in his presence – confronted by that noble and illumined brow always suddenly uncovered in his moments of indignation against any trammelling authority, by the flood of burning, passionately convinced words that unfailingly welled up in him as he bent his long head over you, beating the air with fevered hand, whether addressing children in the street or a man alone on his deathbed, as soon as he began one of those simple, yet profound sermons of his in which the words "live, love, and I repeat again, live" excited all our hearts and scourged our senses – yes, in his presence my mother sensed confusedly, she whom we loved so badly, that this man was drunk with love and that with him near her she would find, like so many others before her, the means to calm her moral distress.

When she said to this man: "I confess it, Father, I have already killed Emile more than once in my heart," he replied with a shrug of that bowed back: "We all kill without cease in our hearts, we kill all day long. Don't dwell on it too much, my daughter"; and perhaps he was thinking at that moment of his superiors, of "all those who condemn charity, noble and diseased charity," for he had already been sent several times to expiate the dissipations of his secret life in "the prisons for bad priests," even though he had known in those places the happiness of no longer being alone, as well as "the despair of human compassion" among his banished brothers.

It was never his wish to hurt others, but the grave sins he committed against his own merit, his stubborn and often puerile mendacity, combined to drown him despite himself in a forgetfulness of the pure laws of his heart . . . When he begged with such crazed avidity, on behalf of all mankind, for your pity and your tenderness, he was begging for them on his own behalf as well, and when he rested his fixed and tortured gaze upon you, that gaze of an inquisitor that was never anything but kind, tolerant, and grave, it was as though someone had come and seated himself beside you, as though that great despairing body of his, looking so wise in its armchair, all its life in its eyes, was throwing all its expectations, all its desires at your feet. The sound of my mother's breathing could be heard from her bedroom, clusters of flies blackened the translucency of the flypaper coiling down from the ceiling, and everywhere I went, that gaze still followed me, its keen weight never leaving me as I stood facing the window with its glazed curtains, doing the dishes.

"A pity, my dear child, a man is unhappy when he needs others too much. It is wrong of me to talk to you like this, I know that, you can't possibly understand me, you even seem to be afraid of me when I look at you. But I sometimes find myself thinking that I might be able to awaken your heart to pity. Pity is a very beautiful thing, one that is often cloaked in many impurities, madnesses, weaknesses, but a beautiful thing all the same! It is the fascination of human beings for other human beings, that is all. One cannot resist the vileness of men, one simply finds them worthy and good despite themselves. We hunt each other down like panting animals in the jungle, but there is more between us, between all of us, than simply that bestial call. There is something else, something so lacerating, so fraternal! I pity you for still feeling the fear of living that your parents, your teachers have inspired in you: one feels so filled with joy when there is nothing left with the power to extinguish the flame of love in one's breast, not injustice, not misfortune, not even shame, for what is shame, and is it, in the end, worth the trouble? People will tell you terrible things about me one day, perhaps. And perhaps you will believe them. But we must not always judge a man by his outward aspects; there can be so many of them, and even then they hide others, underneath, that no one ever reaches.

"It is the person's capacity for tenderness that we must judge. But perhaps you don't understand me: you are so young. Well, it's not important, I have already told you that I no longer feel any shame! In earlier days, when I was no more than a proud priest, greedy for privileges, my superiors sent me as chaplain to a prison. It was there that I understood it all: I had never thought about other human beings before that day. Living among those criminals, as I spoke to them about God, so I discovered that my innocence was false, that my heart was a never-ending lie. The true murderer of others was myself, the man indifferent to others, the pious priest. And that realization was a sudden light exploding inside me. It is true that it almost made me mad, that it seriously disturbed my mind, but this dizzying power that still shakes my being is the hand of God, you understand: the divine will is still striving to stir all that is carnal and compassionate within me into action, and it seems to me now that I was born for the holy mission of disgrace, the disgrace of unreasonable charity, which is often punished . . ."

He spoke in a low voice, as though to himself, confiding in those who did not understand him or who did not even wish to listen to him, and on rainy days, when people began running for their streetcars the moment they emerged from their factories, Benjamin Robert, undeterred, bareheaded beneath the downpour, was still holding up a wildly gesturing hand as he argued with a friend, his gray coat flapping around his legs, his feet comfortably apart, each in its puddle of water, and even in the moments of silence, when he paused for breath, you felt that he was still talking away behind his half-open lips, despite the fact that he was also capable of listening to you, bending his sober, meditative head down toward you . . .

"Don't go yet . . . Another three minutes!"

He also liked to encounter his adversaries: Mlle Léonard always fled when she saw him walking toward her, "that spiritual tub-thumper, that unhappy fanatic," but he would seize her joyfully by the arm. "You're just the person I was looking for, Mlle Léonard, I've got a prisoner for you at two o'clock . . . An infection of the knee, I'm counting on you to see to this brave lad of mine!"

"No," Mlle Léonard replied with an offended air. "I've already got quite enough patients, I refuse to spend my time treating every malefactor in the city. Goodbye."

"It was you yourself that said it, Doctor, your profession is the salvation of bodies! And think of all the despised, scourged, battered bodies among those prisoners I once had in my charge! In the rehabilitation centers we have for priests the scourge is never used, but in ordinary prisons, for the condemned man without defense, stripped of all power, rape is punished with a set number of strokes with a whip! What injustice! But the man I wish to become must one day kill the priest in me, even if only in order to set right such terrifying injustices!" ("Poor crazed creature," Mlle Léonard thought. "If only I could get rid of him!") "You are in a hurry, I'm sorry. Let me walk with you as far as the hospital, then I'll leave you. You must get used to me, even if you don't like me; are we not both working for the same cause? It is still the divine will! This prisoner who will be visiting you at two o'clock, I will not conceal from you that in the eyes of men he has a criminal record, but let us not talk of his crimes, if you don't mind, our dark and narrow justice will do that for us. I spoke of an infection of the knee, but there is something much more serious involved, something very mysterious that I don't understand. It is as though this young man has suddenly decided to defy his judges and their punishments, to take upon himself the task of imposing on his body all the labour of redemption that others wished to inflict on him. You understand me, perhaps: out of pride he prefers to crucify himself . . ." ("I understand," Mlle Léonard thought with a disgusted contraction of the lips. "He has had physical relations with this prisoner, which explains everything . . .") "I see that you do not understand me," Benjamin Robert went on, lowering his eyes. "One achieves very little understanding of others by judging them always as you are judging me at this moment. But what you judge so severely, and what I have betrayed in what I have just told you, is a secret that does not perhaps belong to you. It is sometimes necessary to show a murderer that his is loved, that he too is loved, to burst one's way through the toughened husk of our prejudices at a single blow, to reach him at whatever cost, for what prevents us from understanding him is our distance from him, the superiority that keeps our pride aloof from his humiliation. One has to become one with him if one is to cease judging him, and when he becomes a fragment of your own soul, your own body, you can awaken love in him, and very often scruples too."

"What foul weather, what really filthy weather we're having," Mlle Léonard said, no longer daring to look at the priest. "I'm going to be late because of you."

"When it is raining as it is today I think of those interminable moments, of that persecution by time that flourishes in every prison cell. At night I do not sleep, for any distraction, just a few hours of sleep, is enough to make one lose contact with that thought . . . And when you want to change things, that thought quickly becomes a hallucination, a vision of death on earth. I have already explained it all in lectures, but no one listens to me. I have written articles that no one reads. And when I talk too much, they silence me by force, they send me packing to a monastery to stifle this rebellion I feel, but it's quite useless, isn't it? A man is always free when he wishes to be: the liberty of hearts and minds is not like wisdom or calmness of mind, for those are virtues we cannot always acquire when we have already lost our reason. When I am with simple people, I sometimes find that calmness of mind again. And I also find, in those families I visit every day, the same silence as in our prisons. There is so much slumbering violence, so many unspoken murders beneath everyday routines! It is futile, wanting to bring beings together when they are all such strangers to each other! But did you know that these worn-out, wordless beings, these mothers with their aches and pains who need a priest only as a friend, a brother capable of understanding their stifled secrets, these beings also have a voice when you listen for it. I even feel sometimes that they share my own rebellion against the vast authority, visible and invisible, that has always trampled on the weak of this world . . . You must understand all that only too well, Doctor, and I not right?"

"I don't know what you're talking about. I just do my work. That's all I know about," Mlle Léonard said.

"You do your work, but never in vain. You do succeed in conquering physical ills, in curing men. But for us, for those who have been consecrated to God, it seems that we are forbidden to do our work in life itself. To love life, for us, is a blasphemy. We work in the desert. How can we pray when all around us the punishment of innocence goes on and on? From the letter of the law to the very architecture of the prisons, our whole social system is a great marble edifice of self-styled truth heaped on the condemned man's head, and very often on the head of the man who has been condemned unjustly. The immaculate way in which the judges acquit themselves of even their cruellest functions, the rite in the Palace of Justice, those words dipped in venomous irony, the uniform of the police, the

jangling of the iron keys, the smell of the mattresses, the cama-
raderie of the wardens, the periods of solitary confinement,
everything urges the victim to postpone his revolt, to contemplate his former and genuine crimes, to associate himself with
the destiny of the guilty!

"That is something of what this young man has written to
me, Philippe, Philippe l'Heureux, who at the age of eighteen –
as he will perhaps tell you himself, with pride, later today – has
already known seven prisons, and how many murderers, how
many suicides! The same prisoner also wrote to me a year ago"
– he drew from his pocket a volume of Baudelaire between
whose pages he kept some of the letters he received, letters that
he read and reread at night, "like a Bible of misfortune," he used
to say – "and I hope you will let me read you a passage from this
letter. 'The justice that a prisoner imposes on himself,' he wrote
to me, 'is implacable and gray. It is the sister of repentance. One
begins suddenly to think of suicide as the last stage of one's
inner rebellion; it suddenly seems more worthy to die than to
live: as for me, when I escape, I shall never be found crouching
in a thicket, ringed on all sides by brutish creatures yelling at me
to give myself up, no, if I am ever trapped and found I shall be
dead, the revolver still pressed against my shattered skull.' You
see what I mean: our self-satisfied judges, those pillars of society, that is what they inspire in our children!"

"I have to leave you here," Mlle Léonard said, starting to
cross the street. "The hospital is just there. Goodbye . . . Father
. . . goodbye . . ."

She was already moving away from him. Benjamin Robert
smiled sadly, his arms folded on his chest. "A pity!" he murmured as he looked at the falling rain.

Germaine Léonard recovered a little of life's kindness in the arms of a man, and very often those whom she had despised, during the day, seemed to melt with her into the tender passion of her nights, so that her heart, momentarily assuaged and conquered, judged no one and forgave those she had offended, so that she thought to herself, cradled in a dream of fond indulgence and domination, "I understand that wretched priest," though even then, even as she believed she understood him, it was only because she felt liberated from him, because he wasn't there. But later she would feel the same hostility again, the same terror at "a troubled and alien life" imposing itself upon her through the priest's agency, she would feel it all again as soon as she set foot again in the hospital, for it was there, it seemed to her, that she was most in danger of yielding "to degrading pity. That man is diseased with pity . . . It's a poison! A vice!" (Had she herself not acquired her compassion through the coldness, no, she thought, the austerity of her natural temperament?) And was it not her duty to resist the attractions of any kind of suffering? But now she was liable to find herself trembling as she noted the day's medical events in her notebook: "Lucie Beauchemin, aged 9, room 220, leukemia. Death occurred at 1600 hours." Before, the notebook would then have been swiftly replaced in her pocket, but today she hesitated before letting that face vanish, striving to capture something of it before it went. "They had shaved her head. Little by little all response ceased, except for occasional weak smiles. Futile efforts to replace her blood. At the end of the day, her empty room, not even a sheet on the bed. I . . ."

No sooner was it written than she was erasing it, this admission of sensibility from that other inner being that was suddenly rebelling like this against all her customs, daring to speak of itself, of life, "that useless and torturing service one cannot escape," of the profound disgust for God that filled her when she thought of

Lucie Beauchemin – "What pitiless being could have consented in secret to the agony of that child?" – but then, abruptly, she pulled herself up short, fearful of the agitation in her mind for "there is a great danger in talking about oneself," and as she struck out the words she had just written, crushing them beneath her plump fist, one by one, she experienced a strange pride at overcoming in herself the need to write, at killing "the loathsome pity" that Benjamin Robert had left in his wake, for now, without that pity, she could live once more . . .

Confession brought my mother calm. When the priest left the house I searched her forehead for signs of a new peace there, and it seemed to me that her deliverance from Emile was approaching. "I think I'll get up, Pauline, I feel better off all of a sudden. Look after the baby for me, she's still in her carriage, down in the yard . . ."

"I haven't the time. I'm writing."

"Oh yes, Pauline Archange, we all know you've never got time when it comes to helping your mother."

As I listened to Benjamin Robert, his love of life had seized hold of me, carried me away. I was trembling with the happiness of telling about it, in my exercise book. But I found myself faced as always with the same lack of skill, repeating the same poverty-stricken things: "You remember when you were very hot in the park, the other day, you looked at your old sandals and when you put a finger in front of your eye you couldn't see Jeannot or your sister any more, the wide blue sky was crushing you with is heat, the sun was burning you, that day you were alive and that's all that matters. When Benjamin Robert looks at me my heart beats very hard, it's just like in the park, with the heat and the sun, I'm alive and that's all that matters. But when he goes away again it's sad and empty in the kitchen, the flies struggle in a black layer on the flypaper, and that makes me feel sick. My mother sends me to see if my sister is still asleep out in the courtyard and sometimes I arrive just in time to frighten off the big rat who's walking round and round the baby's carriage. There's no danger, because my mother has put a piece of wire netting against flies over it, but I think that the boys from next door who are worse than wild beasts and love killing animals so much, they ought to kill our big rat with bricks the way they do when they kill cats and birds. Once I saw one who had caught a cat and then smashed it against the wall, all night we could hear it moaning under the steps. Benjamin Robert couldn't say that Christians have hearts if he saw that, he'd say that some people are born like wild beasts and they can never change, sometimes they are even so wicked they keep the cats alive so they can torture them a long time and when they pull off the bits of the cat's skin and it screams they don't feel the hurt that it is doing under the animal's bones, they laugh all around it the poor martyr, no, if Benjamin Robert saw that he'd say that we Christian people we're worse than savage lions and he would be very hurt by it, he'd say that the suffering of the cat is worse than the suffering of Jesus on his cross . . ."

But how many times had Benjamin Robert not lost hope of rehabilitating this cruel fury, whose cause, for all that, seemed to him entirely human?

"It is true, my child, that those who openly practice cruelty are often avenging themselves on the unfortunate conditions of their existence, but there are some cruel and barbaric games to which we must refuse our commiseration. A priest has no right, perhaps, to speak in such terms, for our role has always been that of tacit complicity, of murderous accommodation, and hell is filled with those bad angels of resignation who have left their slaves the task of killing for them in their absence . . . And when Jesus was crucified, we, I am afraid, were not there . . . If we had the courage to plunge our hands in blood like the great criminals – I am not speaking of that unconscious and blind form of crime that we find everywhere, or of the sadism of mobs – if we had the strength to condemn life, to love it with a devastating and pitiless love, like the love that damns and consumes the soul of the true murderer, a love that may even seduce his heart to the point of sanctity, we would then be able to understand everything, we would hold the secret of another life whose absolute severity, whose absolute truth would dazzle us.

"But the race of rebels is above all a proud and at the same time pitiable tribe, for it is hard to suffer the scorn of men! For a long while I was aware that my own weakness in this respect prevented me from cutting myself loose from them. We love respect. Veneration and a noble image of ourselves always flatter our vanity, even when that image is a false one. It is no longer discipline, perhaps, that keeps the religious in his convent, but that vanity of his, the fear of his true image being unveiled, fear! . . .

"A priest who wishes to embrace life and all its errors is nevertheless aware that there is always an army of virtuous priests behind him, ready to rise and protect him, to forgive him his sins; he knows that the punishments of society will always be spared him. You never read in the papers, do you, that some priest has committed rape? No, the priest loves lies too much to tolerate such accusations, his privileged position always turns his head. He has his regrets, yes, that goes without saying; he may also fall into an excessive piety; but he never knows the torture of the conscience, the lacerating inner crisis that is the pariah's daily fate. No, on the contrary, his conscience is bolted and barred in on itself for all eternity, asleep! And the tragedy is, he doesn't know it! That is why I had this insane idea one day, while I was reading through some letters from a friend, yes, it occurred to me that it was time for priests to risk their souls utterly, but it is an insane idea and I must still think about it a great deal.

"It was the will of God that woke me up, one night, when I was sleeping in my comfortable chaplain's cell – ah! the good priest's room with its chaste curtains, its lifeless crucifix – it was the divine will that tore me from my bed, drove me up against the wall, and there, pressed against that wall, I heard the lamentations of a prisoner condemned to death, a boy so young that when I saw him next morning, smiling as he walked to the dining hall, I fell to trembling with terror for him. But had I dreamed it? In my sleeplessness, anything can happen . . . Was it this boy with the impudent smile on his face who had wept all night?

"The following night I had a dream: it was dawn, and I was getting up to prepare for Mass when suddenly I noticed that my bed was all covered with blood . . . 'You have nothing to fear,' an invisible voice told me. 'You are not hurt, you are lying in the bed of another who has shed his blood.' At that, I left my bed and ran out into the corridor, where the door of Philippe's cell was opened for me. 'Come,' he said to me. He was dressed all in white, and was so pale that he seemed to have no more than a few instants to live. He opened his arms to me, and I went up to him and kissed him on the cheek. 'That is the first time that,' he began, but was visibly too weakened to finish his sentence, and closed his eyes. On his face there was a vague and cruel smile as a sign to me that he was still alive . . ."

Mlle Léonard's disdainful expression, condemning "the weaknesses of this sick priest . . . yes, very sick . . ." (she emphasized this last word with spiteful obstinacy: Benjamin Robert was evading universally recognized laws, and therefore her personal moral laws), the whole way in which she looked at him had irritated the priest, for he knew the true nature of his friendship for Philippe and scorned "any judgment of men by their appearances, which even when they are true conceal other actions beneath, complex, unknown . . ."

For him, life was nothing but an illicit quest for love and humility, and he employed his body to this end "like an instrument for attaining knowledge, fleeing all mystical inclinations, all the traps laid by illusion or sleep that have often turned priests away from their true vocations on this earth." He confessed openly to "daring to live the life of each individual, the life of all, deliberately assuming the incoherence of love," and it was lucidly, without a troubled mind, that he sometimes exchanged his cassock for a workman's clothes, leaving his "frock of hypocrisy and lies" in a hired locker in one of the city's railroad stations, to go out in search of what Mlle Léonard called "haunts of fornication," blushing with shame for the priest, though he, scorning her evasive terms, would have said: "That evening I had the desire to hold a man in my arms" (adding in his heart: "A man forgotten by the rest of the world").

But these moments of passing tenderness could not be compared to the painful and kindly feeling that bound him to Philippe, for whom he was filled with "an extreme compassion without hope . . ." He had chosen Philippe, as he himself explained in his letters to him in prison, "because there is in you, not only the obscure matter of which crime is made, but something more serious that we will search for together. Have no fear, I shall not speak of grace, I am more inclined to say that there is in you an understanding, a deep awareness of the evil for which you are responsible . . . This power to kill, to torment others seems to lacerate your own being before it attains your victim." Philippe protested in a preoccupied way, speaking of other things; "Isn't your generosity a bad thing for me, since you believe me to be good? Though in fact I am neither good nor vile, I want above all else to leave this world, I've had enough of it!" His tone varied as abruptly as the young man's mood: "I beg you, Father, don't send any more of your books for a while, I have enough to last me a month as it is. Even when you are tired of sending me books you will continue, perhaps, to heap your kindness upon me, which makes me unhappy, for I am afraid of gratitude. In my cage, I turn the pages of a book as one follows the spoor of a wandering animal, step by step. I have been rescued from the death penalty, so now I must make use of my life and dissect it in front of my own eyes like a corpse! Thank you for the Spinoza, which has helped me to understand some of my paradoxical intuitions. So don't feel it's your duty to write to me: my real friends understand that I have no need of comfort."

What Benjamin Robert required of Philippe was "the truth, a return to the unconfessed violence of your being. You know only too well, Philippe, even though without wishing it you have obtained a pardon from your judges – for that is their idea of pardon, you see – even if you are now imprisoned for life, it is futile to seek escape from the eternal inward trial, since you will never be able to escape the cold-eyed analysis of that judge who lives inside you . . . There has been talk of your 'tragic precocity, of the delirium of a brain on fire,' but it was with the firmest deliberation that you killed your father, without delirium and perhaps even, who knows, armed with that same cold insolence that you censure in those who are judging you today. If I speak to you in this way, Philippe, it is because you had the courage to face down my hypocrisy that morning, in the prison dining hall: for you, I was nothing but 'a despicable prison chaplain, that's all, you are here to bless us, here in this black and grimy city of ours, and the smell of vice and misery doesn't even reach your nostrils! Ah! You are comic, you prophets and high priests, I am ashamed for you all, as I was ashamed for my father when he was alive!' I did not believe I had deserved those words, true, but now I understand them better. More gently then, you spoke about yourself, about your father: 'I decided he hadn't the right to live.'

"But is that a sufficient reason, Philippe?"

"All reasons are good reasons, in books as well as in life . . . Take a look at the world, it is awash with blood, we are all so cynical, you see. Oh, yes, we are indeed! The leaders we choose, aren't they thieves and murderers? We are all too ravenous for human flesh to have the right to live! Think of my father. He had a sincere love of justice, so he said, he had told my mother over and over again that he would never pronounce an ultimate sentence, and it is true that thanks to him, to his power above all, certain executions never took place. But in that impure profession he could not stay pure, he betrayed all his principles . . . A single error, a single moment of weakness, the taste for blood perhaps, the temptation of death . . . How is one to explain his attitude? And whom did he condemn? A man of his own class? No. A poor man who came home one evening drunk, discouraged, and burned down the house where his wife and his nine children were asleep! Think of that, in the night: my father, that perfect man, that man so respected by his friends and family, had legally killed someone . . . Imagine the terror of the incendiary they were going to hang . . . And why? For a pitiful crime committed from fatigue, from weariness . . . I am ashamed, if only you knew how ashamed, I wake up in the morning sweating with shame!

"But you are listening to me very quietly, very wisely, like a confessor, your head bent forward. What is it you expect of me? That I should ask forgiveness of God? I have no regrets, I would do it all again, you understand, it is the soul of that hanged man that howls through me! It is his shame that shrieks, and there is nothing I can do now to stop it. In fact, Father, do you know, as I look at you like that, you and your air of innocence, you who so love to bend down toward us in our distress and edge us gently toward repentance, the nausea of repentance rather, even as I look at you a revolutionary idea flashes across my mind, yes, have you already guessed it perhaps, I should like to conquer all the pride in you, erase every trace of God inside you . . . pervert your heart . . ."

"You must have pity, my child. We have deceived men's souls, often and often, I confess it . . . but if such a thing exists . . . a lying sincerity, then many priests have lived according to it, and you who have torn from another the power, the shame of judging others, I beg you not to abuse that power in your turn . . ."

"Ah!" Philippe cried in disgust. "You defend their weakness!"

"Perhaps, I am not yet ready for an emancipation from lies. It will be a long struggle, I sense that. I was overwhelmed last night by a dream, a strange vision . . . That dream seems to confirm what you are now asking of me, a complete metamorphosis of my whole being, an identification with the despair of conscience, with your evil fortune! Your intention is perverted, perhaps, but it represents for me an admirable challenge, a wild fury of daring, and if I had not dreamed that dream I would not understand you. But last night my soul began to bleed for you. What you require of me is an inhuman pity, you are asking me to carry your cross, to become a reprobate like yourself, but you forget how fragile and timorous my conscience is . . . Do not smile, it is the truth. But what is the damnation of a priest on earth . . . For you, as for me, it is perhaps the only courageous act of redemption!"

"I hadn't thought of it like that," Philippe said with a smile. "When I spoke of perverting your heart it was only out of a thirst for vengeance. But if you are mad enough to take the provocations of a juvenile delinquent seriously, then I confess it makes me afraid for you. The poisoned air of this prison turned your head last night! There are so many things prowling in the air here . . . so many vices, so many guilty thoughts and regrets! And here you are, sick with a repentance that doesn't belong to you! You will be wretched! You will be greedy for recognition, for gratitude, like all men, and I hate gratitude and benefactors! I shall be like a beggar turned away from the door . . . No, I assure you, you are mad. Be reasonable, go back to your chapel, everyone likes your sermons, your Masses and all that, because no one will understand you if you suddenly decide to change your spots . . . The prisoners here will be full of contempt for you, because society is no better in here after all! You will lose your soul in vain, and for me the thing just isn't worth the trouble . . . I no longer believe in my own life . . . Yes, it would be a grave error . . . And don't be afraid, I can manage it all on my own, my little labour of redemption, I don't need you. I get tired very quickly, you know . . . I understand all the forms of weariness there are . . . It amused me for a while, the idea of pushing you down into the darkness, of imprisoning you in this night of mine, but now the game has begun to bore me!

"You are too simple, Father, and also you said it yourself, you're not ready. Crime is not noble, though it is the duty of all those who have committed it to glorify it without end, and you will hear me say: 'Crime is a cry, a revolution. The path of crime is the most difficult path there is in life, an act of rebellion, an incandescence of suffering.' But don't listen to me: I like the sound of my own voice, that's all. In solitude, especially, I talk a great deal to myself. When you are making death the whole of your life's work, how else can you speak of it except with triumph? What do you think, my poor parish priest? But you don't know what I'm talking about, I can tell that from the uneasy look in your eyes, from the way your hands are trembling. I was wrong to tempt you, simply in order to gain your compassion and then destroy it without gratitude. No, don't tell me I can still be saved, it isn't true. In killing, I did perhaps desire the good of another, good, if you like, in its pure state; but an evil deed is still abhorrent, so that doesn't mean anything any more . . ."

In a surge of pity, Benjamin Robert felt at this point that he "wanted to lose his life, for the teaching of Christ drives us irresistibly toward the profanation of appearances: Philippe's honesty, the cruelty of his wish to destroy the false priest in me, these seemed to awaken a new man within me, a man who repudiated all lies at last. But that man still shrank away from the light, striving to stay hidden inside me, desperate for my protection. What did he fear? What I myself still fear . . . the scorn of men!"

He often spoke to me about this scorn: "It is strange, my dear child, I sometimes think that this nail we drive into the criminal's astonished flesh, this hate that scars him forever, I sometimes think that this scorn on the part of men is the wretched man's greatest ordeal . . . Very often he will use it as a garment of pride to cover his sin, but it is a garment that soils him even more than the memory of that sin . . ."

Benjamin Robert's words still felt little mark upon me, however, for after having written those few lines in which I spoke of nothing but myself I was already thinking of going out to meet my friends again. My mother touched me on the shoulder and stood looking at me angrily.

"You haven't the time to help your mother, but you've got time to go out heaven knows where all the time. Where do you think you're going like that?"

"Why do you always want to know everything?"

"It is written in the Fourth Commandment, you mustn't answer back to your mother. Honour they father and thy mother. That's what it says as sure as I'm speaking to you now."

"I'm going to the big arena to the meeting of all the monsignors. Romaine Petit-Page is acting in *The Angels on the Hill*."

"I hope it's a Catholic play at least?"

"The priests never write anything but Catholic plays, apparently."

"You have no respect for religion, Pauline Archange, you have no respect for anything any more, that's all we needed . . . At least go and wash your face before you go out . . ."

On the stage of the "big arena" (which served in winter as a rink for ice-hockey players, blue and red teams speeding with bent knees across the smooth ice, head sunk between their high shoulders, pursuing as though it were and inner meditation that black disk in fact so fugitive and brutal – for even as the crowd howled, even as the stands quivered with a vexed mist of hands and faces, one of the players abruptly fell, his forehead scored by the intrepid roundel's searing speed), on this stage there now fluttered a crowd of angels without grace whose simpering smiles were seemingly intended as a greeting to the row of bishops who stood at the back of the arena, all waiting in majestic impatience for their turn in the ceremony of "The Tricentenary of Monseigneur Fontaine Mercier," until, one by one, they were named, and the violet undulations of their robes swam toward us with an unfurling of colours and courtly bows "worthy of the most beautiful birds in the whole world!" Julien Laforêt sighed on the bench where he stood beside me.

"What a spectacle, my little Pauline, it reminds me of the sixteenth century! What dignity, what superb vanity there is in the princes of our Church! It always moves me like this, it is what I shall be when I am older! Our bishops are great actors, it is wonderful to watch. If only I could have a cassock of that savage red, in velvet, I should be so happy. I can see Romaine giving us a little wave . . . She is impressed too by all this pomp, I can see. She is very fond of you, you know. She says you are gifted. Are you looking at my medal? It's nothing, I always win medals for my Latin versions. All this wealth of history before our very eyes! I shall never forget it. This is Monseigneur Céleste now, a purple and solitary figure lit with the sun of his own power. How noble he looks! If the others are princes, then he is a king. I should do the same thing if I were in his place. I should wait and come forward only at the end, so as to excite an even greater admiration. I should bow just like that before the deeply moved spectators.

"Now the angels are beginning to waltz on the hills again. I prefer the bishops, though they're not so pure it's true. 'To be pure is to be without admixture,' as Plato says. I'm not like that. Nor are they. Almost every human being is each more impure than the next in that sense. With the exception of our friend Romaine Petit-Page. With her, it's different. They say that children are capable of purity. That's an illusion. It is true that I shall soon be thirteen, so that I am in fact no longer a child. Vanity is a vice, but is it a vice in the priesthood? Look at the birds, they are vain. All nature is vain.

"Oh, look . . . Romaine is smiling among the angels . . . I prefer her when she's writing or playing the piano. I still wonder when I read Plato whether he really loves poets. He looked upon the poet as a sacred being of course, but didn't he also think of him perhaps as someone who made him smile. In *The Republic* he displays a genuine deference toward him, he has him crowned with the sacred bay and pours oil on his head. But careful! That means nothing. In *Phaedrus*, in his hierarchy of souls, the poet is only in the sixth rank, between the soothsayer on one side and the artisan, the peasant on the other. Romaine wouldn't like hearing me say that. She believes in the sacral aspect of the poet, you understand? In all her poems, she says, she 'gives of her flesh and her blood.'

"And I tell her it's just so much flesh and blood wasted. She says I'm 'a frantic intellectual, with a Utopian imagination.' And it's true: I like fairy stories, I like the bishops in all their splendour, I appreciate order and unity, like a political leader. Ah, the unity in the works of Plato, what an admirable virtue! Plato's thought is eminently exacting, but above all in the sphere of intelligence, it is even more aesthetic, though perhaps I am wrong . . .

"If you go on selling newspapers and calendars after school, my little Pauline, you will never be able to cultivate your mind, and you will go on for a long time making mistakes when you speak. I will be your teacher, just like with my sisters. Six sisters, that's a lot. They never read anything but books of devotion, don't even want to hear Plato talked about. Yet when people speak to me about him I find it such a joy. Though the fact remains that Plato is too ready to sacrifice the good of the individual to the good of the whole. After all, the idea of the individual didn't have the absolute value for him that it has acquired with us through Christianity.

"It's over, everyone's leaving . . . A pity! I really think I'm going to be a cardinal, or else a deputy in Parliament. Romaine is waiting for us in the arena. Come on, we must go down to her. Are you writing, Pauline? Good, you must go on . . . You'll never be able to write as well as Romaine, that's impossible. You talk too much about dead people and vigils in your poems, always gloomy things. Whereas Romaine only talks about the clouds that wander noiselessly above the sea, about 'the sunlight that lights up his hair as it does his soul,' though I have to admit that I find clouds particularly tiresome. Everyone is applauding . . . It's a life I dream of living: if I could only have a great red cape and live always in the piety and elegance of a convent, completely swathed in velvet . . ."

But Julien Laforêt seemed to inspire more irritation than respect in me when I wrote about him in my exercise book: With his crew cut and his nose like an eagle's beak he looks just as nice as pie and you feel you'd like to eat him up like a piece of pink sugar candy, but if Romaine Petit-Page only knew what a slinky hypocrite he is under it all, that little boy of hers! He's a tiger waiting to pounce. But me, I'm not afraid of him, he's nothing but a mud-farter. Talk about a lucky devil! Romaine Petit-Page calls him "my blond angel, my golden prince." You'd never find anyone calling me anything like that. It's just because he has a big head and talks properly. After the ceremony with the bishops, we all went to the Restaurant de la Boule for cakes and ice cream. Julien Laforêt was still talking on and on in an irritable voice, but I never say anything with Romaine's gang. I'm too afraid of not saying the right thing . . . Julien was proving that he too could exasperate Romaine Petit-Page, hammering his words home with stubborn nods of the head as he expressed "a great admiration for our politicians" . . . Relinquishing her fiancé's hand, which she had been stroking on the table as though it were an apple she had been making melancholy efforts to coax into shape, Romaine sat up in her chair with indignation.

"Ah, be quiet," she said. "You are only a child . . . I might even say a babe-in-arms! You still hadn't come into the world in the days when poets, we unhappy poets, weren't even permitted to read Balzac. You say you can love such ignorance on the part of our politicians? No, it isn't possible. I know you. You are intelligent and pure, you too. Do not change. Do not leave our world." (With the tips of her fingers she brushed the neck of her smiling and impassive fiancé.) "Ah, how disturbing it is, the thought of hearts beating together outside of time, parallel in an eternity of beauty and hope . . ."

"When a man is there to govern," Julien said curtly (though he had lowered his eyes, somewhat alarmed by his friend's reaction), "it is his duty to dominate, to crush his people beneath him. He is a being bursting with life, with mobility, with quicksilver motion, like the ocean, like the sea! He smashes all that stands in his way. Moreover, Plato, who is a philosopher of life . . ."

"Eat your cake, my darling . . ."

"The political leader is not, after all, a shepherd charged with the task of merely keeping watch over his people. No, he is the man who knows, the man who can, the master of a supreme power!"

Romaine gazed at Julien without listening to him, thinking nostalgically back to those past days when Julien, still submissive and adoring, had acted in her Mobile Theatre for Youth, those days when she herself wrote the plays she acted in, touring the parish halls of remote villages, bringing to life for an audience that often could not read or write that dream of virtue and innocence in which Julien, together with other schoolboys of his age, embodied for her that perpetual and faintly ludicrous passion of hers for purity.

Confronted by any young, cherubic face, she always yielded despite herself to the mythology of her own work, and thus victimized by her own imagination she loved in Julien what she idolized in herself, even though the love of self, forever threatened by life, still seemed to her the most painful of all the forms that love can take, as she herself wrote in her letters to Julien: "You are the bearer of my childhood soul. Never snap its gossamer thread. You are for me the necessary rose and its necessary thorn."

She went travelling in the company of her taciturn and graceful fiancé, and both spent their time in other countries writing novels whose theme they never ceased to live out in daily life, their eyes and hands forever meeting in the same ecstasy, and untroubled happiness of which they alone could know the exquisite delight. But Julien, the accomplice of this exiled love, continued to receive letters from Romaine.

"Don't forget me," she begged. "Pray for me, my darling little Julien that I love so much, that I shall love for always. I can still see your face bathed in tears when the time came for us to leave, and this absence will be hard for you, I know that! How can you dare write to me that my love for my fiancé is against you! You know you are a part of Louis and myself. Haven't you always loved Louis like the ideal brother, an elder brother here to guide you? We shall always be there to love you, to make up for the loss of your parents. I don't really know you, you also write. But that isn't true. I imagine you, I dream your image: isn't that already what you are for me?

"To imagine a fictitious being is already to touch that being, to live his magic qualities. The person who can give us, without knowing it perhaps, the desire to create, to invent, is he not someone deserving to be loved? And that is the way in which I love you. But in that high region where my affection for your reigns, nothing can ever touch you, we are miraculously friends. One day, when you are grown up, we must go on a beautiful trip together, all three of us. Why deprive ourselves of such a joy, so utterly pure, a sweet dream for your wonderful adolescence that I preserve within me, always intact – for it will be there always, won't it, that part of me that is tender and simple, always moved by the rains of spring . . . Do you remember, my darling, that fairy summer . . ."

Romaine's love for those she invited to share her artificial kingdom was sincere, and Julien, who had admired her in the beginning for her many talents – even though that admiration was now beginning to weaken – would have been very glad to have loved her in his turn with the same devotion, but the decorative exterior of that friendship, the *coquetterie* with which it was embellished, had lost its power of seduction for him. That ethereal veil of a dream of tenderness, "that dream as tenuous as a secret whispered in the ear," as Romaine put it, he now experienced as a sticky web coating his life, a threat to the intellectual rigour he aspired to.

Yet how could he not feel for her, at the same time, the pity that one feels for people who have humiliated themselves in front of you, people whose innocence is no more than a ridiculous cloak of darkness thrown over the real life they will never be able to understand or accept? "Those bygone days will not come back," Romaine Petit-Page thought as she watched Julien devouring his second cake – and that sensual appetite wounded her like a betrayal. "He loves me less, perhaps, with my hair long, yet I haven't changed, and my love for him is immutable . . . The people one loves do not change . . ." Then she turned to me, gazing at me gently, hungry for that image of herself that she sought behind my eyes.

"You know that I wept such floods of tears, yes, like a spring overflowing, when I read your poem on the death of Séraphine. My fiancé was beside me as I read, and we both shed tears as we meditated on your words, vainly I know . . . for it is too late, Séraphine has passed through the portal of the doves, she has followed the angels back to their home . . . Oh, heavens, six o'clock already, and at seven I'm singing for the children on the radio. We must be off, my friends . . . Pauline, don't forget your calendars . . ."

But I was no longer sad when I parted from Romaine Petit-Page and her friends. Julien Laforêt gave my hand a violent shake without looking at me. "Always remember our princes of the Church in all their majesty this afternoon. Never forget the dignity of that spectacle!"

I ran out into the warm, deserted street . . .

That wall, the social barrier that seemed always to have protected the rich from our gaze, it did perhaps fall at moments all the same, as when one of us, for instance, selling calendars from house to house, penetrated the secret core of a family's life, edged furtively toward the drawing room where well-dressed children played – the remains of a richly scented meal still left uncleared on the table – and remained there, troubled and yet calm, on the threshold of this house that was thus yielding up its customs, its comfortable and bustling inner life. That little girl reading, lying beside her brother, the one looking like a long animal with her darting neck and the amazing slimness of her legs, was it really toward the girl poised at her door for such a fleeting moment that she was directing that confident and mocking gaze?

"You'll see. My mother will tell you the story of her life. What's your name?"

"Pauline Archange."

"Well, that's not a name fit for the garbage dump like mine. Bellemort. Michelle Bellemort. We pronounce it 'Bellemar' so as not to bring bad luck, you can see why. Well, for a start I don't like schoolwork. I spent a year lying on a board, because of my back. All I like is looking out the window."

The mother drew a little bag filled with quarters out of her generously cut bodice. "The doctor and I are always glad to encourage the girl-guide movement. The Guides always carry the banner for the Feast of the Blessed Sacrament in May . . ."

"No, madame, it's the Crusaders for Christ who carry the banners. We're different, we die for home and country."

"Oh, good! My husband and I support all the good causes. Without exception."

She turned to her daughter. "Take her into your room and show her your books, you spoiled child. We were most afraid we were going to lose her, you know. That she's not even more of an invalid today is simply a miracle. It's because her father and I loved her to the point of madness. And they say that love and prayers can cure people. Which is true. She just isn't interested in anything any more, though. She goes to school of course, with the Ursuline Sisters of the Divination, but she just won't try to learn. We give her everything she wants, the doctor and I. A bicycle, just imagine! If I'd had a present like that at her age . . . But then, I wasn't loved to the point of madness, I was loved with moderation, which is always so much more sensible. You see how tall she's grown despite it all, even though she was lying there like a poor dead thing for a whole year! She's all legs now!"

"I told her, Mama, I told her you'd tell her the story of your life. Didn't I?"

"And on top of it all, she always has to be right! Haven't you understood yet that God in his mercy – and probably as irritated as I am at seeing you always stuck in front of your bedroom window like that, dreaming of I don't know what – haven't you understood that God up above, worn out with impatience and kindness, has sent you a friend."

"I don't need a friend, Mama. I'm looking out the window."

"Ah! And what do you see out your window? The sky . . . The clouds . . . Nothing very much . . . The carpenter's son sawing wood all day for his father . . ."

Whatever Michelle wanted, her parents gave her: the closets in her bedroom were bursting with dresses and shoes she never wore, since she refused to go out, and that room, which for me was the haunt of all material desire, was nothing to her but "the prison where she had lived like a beetle on its back, feebly waving its legs at the sun," where the only joy she had known in her immobility, indifferent as she was to the presents showered upon her, was "looking out the window . . ."

"I wish I could live forever on my back. You see that boy on the other side of the street? That's my boyfriend, but he doesn't know it. He never saw me when I lay watching him with my head behind the curtains. Now I'm better, and I waste my time studying Latin when I'd be so happy here, with nothing to do, allowed to think as I please! When he sawed wood for his father I sawed with him, as easy as anything, from a distance, just thinking about him. But my body, that didn't move, the way you can just sleep all night and not even budge. It's true my back was as heavy as stone when I breathed. But I just thought about him, night and day, and my back began to hurt less. When he was thirsty and ran to drink a glass of water, how thirsty I was too! The days when I didn't see him I knew he was playing with his ball in the clover field next door, and I couldn't wait to see him again, all out of breath with his red hair falling over his face! I was so happy with him when I lived on my back and no one knew! But look at me now, Mama's right,

I'm as tall and thin as a post. If he were to see me he wouldn't like me. But perhaps he never will see me."

"Do you read, sometimes?"

"No. The ends of love stories, that's all I like. But in any case, I've begun my trousseau. Though I know quite well he'll never want to marry me, I'm too young for him. I've got a drawer filled with Mama's old brassieres. They may come in useful one day. But in the meantime I haven't got even the shadow of a suggestion to fit into them. Mama says "men find girls with budding breasts attractive," but when they're not even budding you can't get very far, believe me! So I must face up to being an old maid with a moustache and a crooked back, like my aunts. When I was lying there I used to like seeing the children walking to school. It seemed to me that I could follow them right into the classroom, right to their desks, that my eyes would carry my body with them like wings, that with just my eyes I would be able to see everything and learn everything. Now I don't even want to open a book any more. When you're living upright on your legs, that's how it is, you don't know what you want any more."

There with Michelle, who still spent long hours stretched out beside her window while I read her books, never speaking to me except to ask frivolous questions: "Tell me quickly if it ends with a wedding. Does he love her just a little, after all? Of course I know she isn't worthy of him, you never are in novels, but tell me all the same whether he has taken pity on her lost virginity and married her in the end. He must, he absolutely must, or I shan't be able to sleep again tonight . . . Read the end bit now, right away, then you'll know for sure" – there with Michelle I became familiar with the inner dream that had haunted her for so long, at her window, and I understood why she had never cast so much as a glance of affection toward all the things she possessed: she didn't want toys or books any more, she wanted human beings, and the distance separating her from the unknown boy whose every gesture she had observed, that distance was now enmeshing her in such a web of susceptibility and shyness that she was no longer able to break out of it and go to him . . .

"It's all such silly nonsense," her mother said one day when I was alone with her. "In the first place, can one be in love at your age, tell me that. No, it's not possible. Or else the love is a neurosis. Michelle has always been precocious, though without being very intelligent, for she has never done at all well with the Ursulines. She has always been preoccupied with marriage, which is not normal. And her father and I both had such dreams of making a career woman of her . . . Marriage isn't a vocation in life. But then I ask you, Pauline, if she loves him, this carpenter's son, all she has to do is walk across the road, then she'd be able to get a good look at him, which would do her good. He has freckles on his nose, just a kid with no future at all. And to think of how I dreamed of her marrying some professional man! But there, as you well know, I'd give her the moon if I could, and if she's still sighing for him in ten years' time, then she shall have him, her carpenter's son! But she might at least wait. I waited till I was mature, you know, mature in every way! Well, the moral of all this is that we have worshipped our daughter more than was right, the doctor and I, and God, who is very jealous as we know, is looking down from heaven and punishing us!"

The hours I spent reading in Michelle's room were often interrupted by the arrival of my mother. Tired of telephoning for me, she would decide to come and fetch me home from Madame Bellemort's herself, though it was with a timidity very like my own that she actually crossed the threshold, hiding Jean's head in her skirt as she asked humbly: "Is Pauline Archange here?"

"Oh, do come in, madame, I'll go and call her. She's a good girl, that Pauline, I'm very fond of her!"

"I always thought she had a heart like a stone," my mother replied, then relapsed into mistrustful silence.

Madame Bellemort bent down toward Jean and stroked his cheek maternally. "How pale he is! Is he quite well?"

"One of his ears is discharging, we don't know why."

"But I must call my husband. The good man has no patients at the moment and he's bored. He's a dreamer, like his daughter. Do you know what he does, madame, all day long? He stares at his pencils and his files and he thinks. You must admit it's unreasonable. When he could be saving the whole human race! What a family! Luckily, however, the doctor has me as his secretary and better half, and I won't let him sit there dreaming from morning till night: I find him patients. So just go through here, along the corridor, then into his office on the right. I'll wake him out of his daydreams for you. Though it sometimes takes quite a while. You must admit, madame, that in this creation of His, although it's so beautiful, so perfect, the good Lord did include some bizarre creatures . . ."

On the way home, my mother scolded us both bitterly as the neighbours watched from their balconies, the rocking of their chairs following us along the street.

"I just don't know what's got into your head, making friends with the daughter of the local doctor. And as for you, my boy," she went on, shaking the gently weeping Jean by one shoulder, "don't you forget you're the cause of my humiliation in front of those people! Couldn't you have told me, couldn't you, that you chewed your bedclothes at night? I couldn't be expected to guess it, could I? I've got other things in the world to worry about besides you! Have you ever heard of such a thing, stuffing your ear full of bits of wool and cloth? Much more of it and you'd have been as deaf as a post. The doctor said so. You've disgraced me. You couldn't be content with sucking your thumb till it was as thin as a matchstick, right up till you were three years old, no! As soon as we cured you of that silly habit with mittens, you begin another! You start making nests in your ears, as if you were a bird! Stop that crying, it won't do you a bit of good."

"It's because he needs some sort of distraction so as to get to sleep, that's what Michelle's mother said."

"And I didn't ask for your opinion, Pauline Archange. When I think of the disgrace of all that coming out of his ear . . . What will they think of us, those people?"

My mother's rebukes, for all their harshness, concealed a nobility so touching in her wish to shield us all from humiliation that her distress filled me with pain on her behalf. I was to continue visiting Michelle; but from that day on, there was always to be "a moment of shame" between us: by penetrating the secret of Jean's waxy ear, they had also penetrated our negligence, our poverty . . .

ꙮ Chapter Three ꙮ

When I told my mother: "We're giving a performance in the big shed, the whole gang of us. Anyone can come who wants to, it's only five cents a head!", she rose up in jealous indignation.

"It's as though you just rack your brains for new ways of being selfish. I tell you, Pauline Archange, your father won't like it at all when he finds out you've taken his beaver hat again for your play acting. Yesterday you stole my sheets to make your stage curtains – there are limits, you know! Your father will send them all packing, all that rabble coming into our yard all the time, bicycles and all, and that will be the end of it, no messing about, just like I'm talking to you now, you and your performances!"

My father kicked down our cardboard scenery, stripped me on the stage of "the hat and cloak of Saint Christopher walking on the waters" – thus expressing, perhaps, the fear of imagination that I inspired in him, an angry urge to destroy in me what was threatening him, too, inwardly.

"That'll teach you not to go thinking the whole world revolves around you! You saw them, buzzing off like a lot of wasps, eh, those friends of yours? So now you know, I don't want any performances in my yard! Have you got that now, once and for all? You've got a head thicker than a mule, but I'm having the last word! My father, he always had the last word. When he said to the right, you went to the right – and no messing about! We went on our knees to him because we respected him. But kids today don't have respect for anything any more, not even your father, who is sacred! You're even too proud to kneel down in front of me at the morning blessing on New Year's Day! It wasn't like that with my father. We threw ourselves at his feet, I tell you, all his sons together, asking for his precious blessing, yes my girl, all sixteen of us! We had gratitude in our hearts in those days! We venerated our parents so much we almost fainted with the adoration we felt, even when we were beaten. Punishment is necessary when the time comes! So learn your lesson and leave off those sulks. My beaver hat, five dollars it cost, I swear to heaven, do you think I'm a millionaire!"

Then he added, fanning my anger still higher:

"Your grandmother, now there was a woman with real talent! She could milk her cows, then go out and do the work of ten men! She was up at five, and she worked, she did, she didn't hang about in the streets, I can tell you! And on top of that, she was a real storyteller. None of your curtains and stages for her, she told it all straight to your face with all her little kids around her, sitting by the fire in the evening, her sewing on her lap, her face all wrinkled by the cold, and when she began to speak, without a word of a lie, the babies stopped yelling in their cradle. And it wasn't made-up things with her either, the stories she told had the water and the trees in them, and there was no end to them; she didn't even know how to read and write, but she could tell things a hundred times better than all those books you read!"

My grandmother's austere figure standing in silhouette "at the edge of her land," covering the horizon with her determined gaze, the heavy and dreamless brain that I imagined beneath her sparse hair, did not conceal for me this mystery my father was telling me about. On her deathbed, her great head sunk in the pillow, she watched her Grandson Jacob as he killed flies by imprisoning them alive in a jar, and she groaned bitterly:

"Look, at those old hands on the sheet, dear God, they'll never do any work in your service again! The scythe is going to cut them like old black roots! You too, wicked Jacob living with the pigs, you will be scythed down too. I'm going up to pray for your soul in paradise and keep you always under my eye the way ghosts do. Trust in the mercy of God in heaven even though you have sinned a thousand times. Twisted, paralyzed hands! Oh indeed, what a misfortune it is to die! You, Jacob, go and bring me some water, I'm choking on my prayers. What is she going to say, the Holy Virgin, when she sees my old hands that have changed so much, when she has such beautiful hands, so they say . . . Go on, out with you, wicked Jacob, it's worse than a curse having you in the room, and now I must think of my repentance. You, you're possessed by the devil, your father himself said it, so now I must go out all alone like a little rosary lamp for praying to the Virgin in May, so be off with you, Jacob, I don't want you there seeing me go out with my face all twisted . . ."

My grandmother carried with her into death a vision of the world bordered by black forests, and the memory of that forsaken landscape, which seemed to her inhabited by the few beings she had brought into the world – for in the silence of death their whisperings near her bed were now only faintly audible still – that memory was for her a happy one.

"Yes, your grandmother sighed four times: 'It's my land that's going! My land that produces nothing good, but it is my earth that's slipping away, it is the scythe that's passing over it!' You can't understand that, feelings like that, Pauline Archange, you're too spoiled!"

"Well anyway, I'm not going to be a dumbbell like Grandma who couldn't even read and signed her name with a cross. That was really a disgrace at seventy years old! Julien Laforêt, he learned to read and write when he was four, and all on his own, what's more. He was no higher than a gnat's knee and he could write his name on a slate all right!"

My father shrugged his shoulders and didn't answer. Suddenly I thought of Julien with envy. He was respected, he was loved. On beautiful summer evenings, out in the country with his family, standing on a rock, he read out his essays on French literature to his sisters, who sat timidly dipping their feet in the stream as they listened. Clad in brief blue shorts, arms raised toward heaven, he discoursed on "Nature that now listens to me . . . Ah, my sisters, let us listen to the countryside in our turn, let us bend our attention to the song of the spring as we do to the melody of the human voice . . . Don't laugh, Gabrielle, nature is serious and I mean what I say. Well then, I was speaking of the sadness in Chateaubriand. Are you with me?"

"Yes," they answered in chorus.

"The most beautiful essays are those done on vacation! I can already imagine the joy my teachers will feel as they read this: To what extents is the melancholy of Chateaubriand a Christian sentiment? (I am a priest-toady, you see.) When Chateaubriand, consciously attempting to summarize his concept of Christianity, declares: 'The Christian always looks upon himself as a traveller who journeys in this world through a vale of tears and finds repose only in the grave,' he is expressing a profoundly Christian sentiment."

"Yes, yes," his sisters cried.

"Be silent! Yes, for us, Christ's faithful, there is but one reality, our salvation! And it is into striving for that eternal salvation that all our efforts should be channelled . . . (Shame on you, liar and sycophant!) All this, needless to say, strikes no chord in your feminine souls, but I shall continue, for the celestial countryside is listening to me. Chateaubriand forgets, however, that though on the one hand our ultimate and necessary end is our happiness in heaven, on the other hand it is our duty to strive with all our strength for happiness here below. According to Saint Thomas Aquinas, our aim should be the progressive construction of that happiness, though in the full knowledge that we can never enjoy it, in this world, other than imperfectly, or perhaps I should say incompletely. And though Christianity requires us to put aside the things of this earth, it does so only when we believe them to be an end in themselves! Indeed, it teaches us that because those things come from God, our Creator, they must inevitably lead us toward Him. One of the greatest saints, Saint Francis of Assisi, was, you will remember, a joyful saint. (My teacher would say here: 'Saint Thomas Aquinas and Saint Francis of Assisi. Well, you're in good company there!') Have you never felt it, my sisters, inferior animals of the Creation, the melancholy of Chateaubriand?"

"Yes, yes, yes."

"Then that is very wrong of you. Remember, that vague feeling of sadness is not Christian in its essence, since the hopes of the fervent Christian exclude sadness from among the passions. And what is passion? It is a noble sentiment and one that requires a great elevation of the soul. That is the definition given by my friend Romaine, who is an admirer of Lamartine. Thus 'the poet of the *Méditations*,' she says, 'in his verses, unfailingly divested of sensuality, never sings to physical descriptions of the beloved, but speaks of her always with discretion, as it were "with the fingertips."' Though you, sisters, you must beware of that 'with the fingertips': it is dangerous. Set your minds rather on the union of two hearts, of two souls:

> *"As two sighs commingle,*
> *So our souls a single*
> *Soul do make . . .*

"Ah, the sun is setting in his papal robes! How beautiful it is! Through and beyond the beloved, Romaine was saying to me yesterday, 'we must look for God, who is our stairway to the light.' There you are! But should the beloved vanish from his sight, what anguish for the poet! 'The sun of the living no longer warms the dead . . .' Look how the sun sinks below the mountains. You will never see it again! As you undress, at night, does that thought sometimes occur to you? That the day just finished will never return! Such is the fleeting duration of our happy days. They fly from us inexorably."

"Yes, yes, yes!"

I sometimes went to Julien's home, with Romaine Petit-Page and her friends, to "picnic on art," as she put it; though they were melancholy hours for me, since I did not feel myself possessed either of the grace of Julien's sisters, whom Romaine instructed in the dance under the trees, or of the ebullience of her Louis, whose thick locks and wildly flashing eyes succeeded in throwing a romantic halo over the platitude of the poems he recited:

> *O muscles, you are asleep.*
> *How to awake you*
> *From this incubation?*
> *You sleep on, like the oyster.*
> *We pierce the oyster for its pearl*
> *But the oyster enriched with a pearl*

Is enriched also with a maker of pearls.
The pearl corresponds to its oyster
As the knife blow
To the pierced belly.
How melancholy that acceptance of the motive
That accepts the blow.
We lop the branch that takes no part
In the mission of the tree.
O tree, do not condemn your branch:
It is the arm of God that's waving there . . ."

"Ah!" Romaine Petit-Page sighed. "What love one must feel to write like that! How many times, my beloved Louis, have I too not felt a poem in gestation, then found that my very desire for it was paralyzing my power of expression. Very humbly, I would set out in quest of it, and I would bring back, poor moonraker that I was, some unexpected relic of it, yes, a true glint of infinity in a shard. But isn't it always so? For to create is to come near to heaven. 'Except ye be converted, and become as little children, ye shall not enter into the kingdom of heaven,' Jesus tells us. One must be a little child to go to heaven after our human life here, isn't that so, Julien?"

"It is a fact that science has not yet confirmed," Julien said. "Moreover . . . all our actions here on earth . . ."

"Yes, yes. That's enough. You must let the grownups talk, my darling. I would even go so far as to say that my fiancé has the genius of childhood. He will be a great poet. Do you remember, Louis, those radiant nights of illumination we had in Paris? Such experiences I lived through . . . miracles! A marriage between poets is so pure a union, the bodies of poets are all perfumes and refinement! I remember your head, Louis, as it rested on my shoulder.

"And there was another young man, almost a boy still, very handsome, very slender, a young writer too, like us, sleeping there on my bed. We had met him in the street perhaps and gathered him to us, for I cannot remember what he was doing there, in my room. But I remember that divine visitation that made our two throats as one, and tore our chests, that wild breath I had always until then accepted all alone, terrified and moved in my unworthiness, that presence of goodness itself, of the divine summons, of certainty, all those things, which make me tremble even as I tell them to you, for I still feel a great strangeness when I talk about myself, a sort of shyness, you understand? Well, this time I was able to share it at last, that suffering, with my two companions. I recognized it there in your wild gazelle's eyes, Louis. Tell me that you felt it too. For I saw you transformed, my angel, there before me, breathing the air of another world, you also, stretching out your hands to grasp a form of beauty so evident that it seemed to be there, so close to us, sculpted in the void like a cloud, and at that moment, entranced, my mouth stopped by a great silence from above, I gazed at you, my love, with the respect that comes over us before the priest's raised hand.

"Oh, Julien, you are too proud and precocious, you cannot understand the innocence in my little Louis, the tenderness in his poems! Isn't it so, Louis, there in Paris, that moment between us was so beautiful, so strange, that we both wept together for our limitations as we thanked God for such approval of the work we have to do with such humble means! How I wish that they could come to know that, all those others, those tormented artists, how I wish I could tell them that for them too, for them above all, 'the Lord is a Shepherd.' How many things must I accomplish now to merit having experienced such an hour?"

"Let's go and pick apples," Julien Laforêt said, stretching his imperious hand toward me. "Come on, my little Pauline!" I walked along beside him without speaking, but he exclaimed:

"Be silent, Pauline. Women should always be silent. When I listen to our friend Romaine, I always get hungry. I want to eat apples. I for one enjoy this earthly life! As for you, Pauline, write bad poems if you wish, but I forbid you to read them aloud: it's too distressing. Are you yawning? Then rest yourself here, under this tree, and I will tell you about Plato. Don't bite your nails, it's a bad habit. It's so warm and pleasant here! A fine day to think about Plato! Look at the sun shining through the branches, such is our life, which passes and never returns! The thought of old age obsesses me a great deal. You too, perhaps. But when it's fine, then I think about Plato. Plato and friendship. That is to be the subject of my thesis, one day. I think about it all the time. I already have three notebooks full of ideas and so far I have never shown them to anyone.

"I have a friend, André Chevreux. He may perhaps be worthy to read them one day. But his sensibility is superior to my own, for he possesses Christian humility, a quality that I, alas, will never be able to acquire. And the great question that we must in fact ask ourselves, my dear Pauline, is this: 'Is what draws two beings together the fact of their being similar or the fact of their being opposite to one another?' Homer, however, has already furnished a reply to this when he implies that it is identity, similitude, that urges individuals toward one another. But will the virtuous man seek out those in whom he recognizes virtue? Not always, I fear. And it is said that the good man, insofar as he is good, is sufficient onto himself, a happy state that I myself have experienced, albeit briefly. Close your eyes, Pauline, I have no need of you: I know that you are listening to me in your sleep.

"As I was saying, I am concerned with grasping the developments of Plato's thought and with seeking out the reason for the existence of love. And love is the search for happiness. And the search for happiness is a bringing to birth in beauty. Socrates explains that all men are procreative, both as to their bodies and as to their minds: a happy discovery. In consequence, when they come of age they desire to procreate. That is our divine task, for by means of this procreation that perpetuates him, Socrates says, man participates in the immortality of the divinity. And you, Pauline, you sleep! This procreation, in order to be realized, demands the presence of beauty and harmony, for 'the ugly can never be in accord with the divine, whereas the beautiful is in accord with it!'

"Love therefore, becomes a search for the good. This desire for the good, which all men have, thus implies by its very nature a wish for immortality. And, we must agree, it is this immortality that man and woman are seeking through their union. But, as I said earlier, man is also procreative as to his mind, and this I hope, Pauline, will be my form of procreativeness and yours. You, unhappily, are still in the limbo of childhood, but harsh maturity lies in wait for us all! To continue: our minds can procreate in their turn wisdom, prudence, justice, and all the other virtues as well as all the works of poets and artists generally. What a wealth of progeny! Such is 'the vocation of love,' but of a love in terms of the mind, needless to say. Our erotic passions must therefore be transformed into mystic emotions, as our friend Romaine has taught me, but I do sometimes wonder whether she's right."

When I fell asleep during Julien's discourses he left me there alone, my head leaning against a tree, then came back to me a few minutes later, his arms laden with apples, which he dropped at my feet with a laugh.

"Don't be afraid, it's me! These apples are delicious, this is my fifth I'm eating now . . . Yes, as I was saying a moment ago, what then is the role of the philosopher in this world? Do we even have a role? We are not, how shall I say, 'culture merchants' – though that would be a noble mission – but perhaps our duty lies in guiding men toward the truth. What one must clearly realize is that the wise man – and for our purposes the wise man is me – when he has attained in solitude to the contemplation of the great mysteries, has a duty to return to his less fortunate brothers – in this case to you, my little Pauline – in order to lead them, despite themselves, toward 'the grasp of Being.' Ah, how I dream of being that man who delivers the humble from their darkness. To deliver others of the truth they bear within them. That truth is buried in you yourself, Pauline. My soul, like the soul of the philosophers, is pregnant, but I am myself at the same time the midwife, the bringer to term of men's minds and he who awakens them to their liberating mission in this world!"

The innocence in love that Romaine and her friends talked about so ceaselessly made me ashamed of my secrets, for in their company, fearing the hardness of their gaze on my life, I said nothing. They could not understand a secret even more troubling than the death of Séraphine. It was nothing but the story of a rape, but I would never have dreamed of telling it to anyone, neither to Julien Laforêt, whose gaze seemed to leap so lightly over the abysses of conscience, nor to Romaine Petit-Page, who smiled at me with an air of penetrating kindness. Benjamin Robert had said that he "would awaken my heart to pity," for to him I was "a secretive, perhaps a wicked child" because of the hurt he felt when his singular presence sometimes inspired me to coldness, though when he obtained proof of a pity he had long been begging for, he was sad. No one had seen him for several months. "Perhaps his superiors are punishing him again for his misdeeds!" Mlle Léonard said in scathing tones. "That man is capable of anything, we all know that!" Germaine Léonard was more suspicious than ever of the priest's behaviour since Philippe had been admitted to her hospital, for unable as she was to take her eyes off "those two escaped prisoners," she had discreetly spied on them, and could still not forget their strange conversation in the room where Philippe was awaiting the results of a medical examination. It was there that Benjamin Robert had told his dream.

"Yes, Philippe, I am very much afraid of a dream . . . Aren't all our dreams prophecies, after all? It was a winter's night. I was still in the monastery, I think. I was kneeling at my bedside in prayer when a man came knocking at my cell door. He was a little man, and there was a malicious smile on his face. He came over to me and whispered in my ear: 'Come home with me, come and bless my daughter!' I followed him. He led me out into the cold night, then into an unlighted hovel where there were emaciated children with hardly any clothes on their backs, begging. At the end of a long passage, through the open door of a room, I saw a little girl of three smiling at me as she sat on a big bed. She was surrounded by men, their eyes fixed on her avidly, yet she seemed quite calm there in the midst of them. 'In my monastery she would be shielded from such shame,' I thought, opening my arms to her. But she had no understood my gesture, for though she opened her arms in answer, it was as an invitation to perform the act of love."

"What misfortune lies in wait for the priest who attempts to debase himself like a man," Philippe said. "Take care, my friend, for you may be a seeker after the greatest love on earth one day, only to find yourself the next a seeker after the greatest misfortune, the greatest catastrophe; and one discovers in misfortune that a host of bonds one was trying to break are suddenly tightening closer about your throat, choking you with an even greater dread than before . . . Out of compassion, and out of pride too, you will be on the brink of a crime . . ."

Benjamin Robert was to say later that he had yielded, not to pride "but above all to lust," a mode of behaviour that after the passage of several years seemed obscure even to him . . . This man resembled no other in his weaknesses, for even when he was provoking disgust by the effrontery of his actions he still managed to ensnare men's hearts with his goodness. For Germaine Léonard, this "goodness in vice itself" was not a virtue, and she remarked coldly: "Chalk is still chalk and cheese is still cheese! A man that misguided cannot be good!"

Benjamin Robert suffered from insomnia, and when he seduced other beings, perhaps that also took place, for him, in that unconscious state of fantasy that was his substitute for sleep, as though in a dream, so that one was made captive by a gaze, by a smile, which then suddenly shed all their innocence and began, disturbingly, magnetically, to insinuate their way inside you. His strange gestures scarcely caused you any surprise: the blind arms closing around you brought respite from the intensity of the gaze that had pursued you for so long . . . Sometimes everything began with the most everyday of incidents, as I had described in my exercise book: "As it was fine and the birds were singing, Benjamin Robert took us on an expedition, Jeannot and me and some other children from the parish, into the woods. We all went swimming and it was a happy time. We all held hands and sang together, Jeannot was tired and Father Benjamin carried him on his shoulders, so he really looked like one of the saints in the pictures with a sheep around his neck. After that, everyone played hide-and-seek, and Father Benjamin told them not to go too far away. But everyone did go far away, down by the water, and Benjamin Robert was worried. I oughtn't to have stayed there, it's true, behind a bush reading my book, because Benjamin Robert was smoking, his eyes looking at me from a long way away.

"'Why aren't you playing with the others, Pauline?'

"'That's my business. If I want to read, I can. I'm not a baby any more, I'm too old for hide-and-seek.'

"'Impudent little girl. Well, at least come over and keep me company . . . You always hide from me.'

"'That's my business.'

"That day he just stroked my cheek and hair. The others came back, yelling and laughing. Then we all went home on the bus, then everyone sang in the bus, though not me because I didn't feel like singing."

While we were recovering from the sickness of our disgust, Benjamin Robert might disappear again into another self-imposed period of confinement; but in that solitude he relived the anguish he had inflicted upon others. How many times would his passions betray the good faith of that heart so in love with Justice? Was there then no peace except in suffering?

Victim or assailant, each was possessed by the bleeding world of his or her dreams. In one of these dreams, still haunted by Benjamin Robert's presence, I put my hand to my chest to discover with terror "that I had lost my heart, that perhaps I had lost it in the gravel like a dropped quarter . . ." Then, in a sunny courtyard beside a church, I saw "my friends the little newsboys, play-ing with my heart and bouncing it like a bright red ball, they were playing with my heart under the branches of a big white lilac, and the blood was running all over its white flowers." And yet it seemed to me, as I awoke, that this blood, spilled in unjust violence, would one day be the sap that fed my books, since no one can erase in us the marks of what we have once lived, and in feeling their presence within me, those marks, I was no longer alone . . .

BOOK THREE

DÜRER'S ANGEL

To Jacques Hébert

Translated by David Lobdell

❧ Chapter One ❧

I had wanted for so long to tell the story of my life that I actually believed at times that it was in my power to do so; but when it came to putting into words the events of my past, they vanished like smoke, leaving before me on the soiled white page of my notebook only the fleeting silhouette of that person I had been and that I still cherished so deeply. I watched her bent back receding down a busy street, swallowed up by the teeming crowds, and when I thought later of this ignoble disappearance, my soul was filled with terror and awe. "But the time for tears has passed," my mother said. I had scarcely noticed the disappearance of Grand-mère Josette, so absorbed was I in my own life. But, suddenly, I wanted to find her again, not only her but all those who had once lived about her, the dead as well as the living (so transformed now in my imagination that they existed already somewhere on the far side of life). But as quickly as I called them back, the voices of all those lost ones were abruptly hushed within me, smothered by the impatient calls of my companions, Elisa Moutonnet, Louisette Denis, and Marthe Dubos, who stood beneath the window of my room, calling my name, or who awaited me in the convent yard before the nine o'clock bell, gripping their exercise books on their knees, eager to recount to me their adventures of the previous evening. The days ran smoothly together, and the hordes of the dead entered the night. Staging plays with my companions in Elisa Moutonnet's basement, imitating the actors in soap-operas on Radio-Province, I quickly forgot Grand-mère Josette, Sébastien, and all

the others from whom time seemed to want to separate me forever.

Those Christmas seasons would never return. On Christmas
Eve, the longest and most delightful night of the year, I would
refuse to go to bed, or even to lie down and close my eyes, until
the hour of midnight mass. With my hands clasped behind my
back, I would tiptoe up to the living room door, which had been
closed to conceal from my curious eyes the decorated tree which
spread its branches in the shadows (and which would not be
illuminated until the family returned from mass). Only its pun-
gent aroma reached me on the farther side of the door, titillat-
ing my senses, like all those aunts and uncles who spoke in whispers as they brushed past me, their arms filled with mysterious
boxes and ribbons . . . I had been forbidden to speak to them,
for they were deeply absorbed in their business of bringing a
little happiness into the house on that one night of the year
and they had eyes only for the gifts they were wrapping, their
thoughts dreamily wrapped up in the joys which their fingers
gently caressed. And if I asked Sébastien, "What are they doing
there, they're acting so strange?" he would reply brusquely:

"When I was a child I used to sleep on Christmas Eve. You'll
never grow up if you don't sleep. Tell Grand-mère Josette to
come and get you off my hands."

Grand-mère Josette and Alice were cleaning the kitchen,
while Judith watched over the baking rolls.

"I don't want her in here," said Grand-mère Josette. "Onézimon, come and look after your grandchild, she's getting under
our feet!"

"I have no time for that," replied my grandfather gruffly.
"I'm smoking my pipe."

"Make yourself useful, Pauline Archange, hop on my broom and we'll pretend it's a horse, we'll sweep the kitchen together."

This broom, which had been wrapped in one of my grandmother's old shawls, bore a slight resemblance to my Aunt Alice, who bent her stern face over me, staring down into my eyes from the top of the long sleeve against which I pressed my face: this broom and my Aunt Alice, carrying me through the house "like an old bundle of rags and dust," left me suddenly very sleepy, and afraid that I might not open my eyes again before midnight, I felt Grandfather Onézimon carry me toward the bed where my mother had already laid Jeannot, who was then only a few weeks old and who had slept almost continuously since the night of his birth, revealing, from the wet corolla of his bedclothes, a puny white fist which trembled a little in the pale rays of the lamp. My grandfather pulled the blanket roughly over my head, and though I slipped toward sleep, a fitful drowsiness broken only by the chiming of the clock and the sounds of nearby voices, I did not entirely lose consciousness, so sensitive was I to those noises, those voices which reached me there in that room, such as the following conversation between Grand-mère Josette and Judith, which I seemed to hear in the depth of my pillow, the words imprinting themselves on my memory through the heavy buzzing of the blood in my brain:

"Sébastien was coughing again last night."

"It's only a cold, Maman, it'll pass."

"Oh, I'm not complaining. On Christmas Eve we have to thank God for his small mercies, but even the Virgin Mary found it hard to watch her son being nailed to a cross. It may be our last Christmas together, you're going away to the convent, and one day to Africa – oh, I know there's no use saying it, but those countries are so far away! And then there's Alice who wants to marry her Boniface, she's so afraid of becoming an old maid she grabbed the first widower who came her way! There's still Marie-Joséphine, but when her fiancé returns from the war, she'll throw herself into his arms. Sébastien is the only one left to me now, and who knows if God won't decide to take him away too!"

"Oh, Maman, the rolls are burning!"

How was I to pull myself from the dull orb of sleep when Grand-mère Josette entered the room, announcing that it was time to leave for mass? Outside, the night was cold and dark. Dressed by those rough hands which had pulled me so rudely from the warmth of my bed, I could no longer recall why she had come for me, and a heavy sadness settled over me as I followed Grandfather Onézimon into the snowy streets . . .

"Wake up, Pauline, you're four years old now, old enough to watch the baby Jesus being born in his crèche in the church, see how nice it is out tonight, everyone's going to mass, the snow's as thick as yarn and it tickles your nose, look, your cousins are running along the sidewalk over there, they're throwing snowballs at each other, they're not daydreaming like you, oh no, they're not sleepy little moles! Your Aunt Alice and your grandmother are trudging along behind us, chattering away as usual, their hands in their muffs. The only thing we're missing tonight are stars in the sky for the wise men. But when you see the little wax Jesus with his little baby blue eyes, when you hear Marie-Joséphine pounding the organ and the choir singing, 'Glory to God on Earth as it is in Heaven,' I tell you, Pauline, you'll wake up! Can you hear the bells on the horses and buggies? They're all going to church. Everyone's here, the rich, the poor, even the beggars, the only one missing is Sébastien, he has a sore throat, poor frail little thing!"

Crossing the threshold of the church, I opened my eyes to the deep red glow of the sanctuary lamp, which spilled its ecclesiastical brilliance upon all those people who, for an hour or more on that festive night, had set aside their social differences, just as a few moments before in the streets of our community a cloud of snow had enveloped them all in its cleansing whiteness: the men, shaking the snow from their hats; the women, blowing their noses and moving toward the altar along the long red velvet carpet (which, in a matter of hours, would be as white as the sidewalks outside); and the families standing huddled together, while the head of the household tried to locate the bench he had rented for his brood on that snowy Christmas Eve. In their robes embroidered in gold, the priest and his curates stood before the altar, their arms raised in our direction. There they would remain until dawn, singing one mass after another, the "*Glo-o-ria, Glo-o-ria in Excelsis Deo*" of the choir, accompanied by the rich melody of the organ played by my Aunt Marie-Joséphine, causing the stained-glass windows to rattle a little and disturbing the sleep of the children (only the very smallest of which would not awaken, curled up on the benches like big balls of wool and sucking their thumbs), and inviting us to join in a sort of ecstasy where the lives of men and their mortal differences no longer existed. In the convent of the Franciscan Sisters adjacent to the church, another mass was being offered, sung by the Choir of the Nuns of Christmas; and throughout the city, the countless parishes, which have reposed all year in a sort of lethargic melancholy, awakened on this one night of the year, as on Easter morning, and trembling with repressed joys, were given up to a few hours of simple rejoicing, to the mystical wonder which the church had afforded us by throwing wide all the doors of its theatres.

Those weeks which preceded Christmas would never return, with all their frantic festivity, as the priests gathered their flocks together in the naves of the churches to conduct "the raffle of benches for the midnight mass," gazing at the submissive people who huddled at their feet and to whom they sold benches "at a fair and reasonable price." The fable which for centuries had inspired men's souls was gradually losing its magical appeal and was being replaced now by something that was little more than a profane feast, no longer consecrated to a child's dream of shepherds and magi but to the fulfillment of more personal and mundane pleasures. That was why, on that Christmas Eve, sitting in the church next to Grandfather Onézimon, I sensed vaguely that I was witnessing events that were almost tragic in their nature, for I knew that they would never return, with the awkwardness of their hymns so badly sung and the simple goodwill of all those familial bonds which gently confined me. When my gaze came to rest upon the face of Marie-Joséphine, all but hidden behind the choir, bewildered by the effusions of music which issued from beneath her fingertips, I sensed a deep anxiety in her which she could not quite conceal but which seemed to hang in the air between us, entangled with the music, for even as we caressed with our voices the cruel innocence of that night, bound up with the image of the smiling babe that lay between the ox and the ass in the stable, we had forgotten the end of that tragic tale of blood and humiliation, something which Marie-Joséphine apparently had not forgotten, for she seemed even then to be thinking of the agonies of her soldier-lover at war in a distant land.

After mass, the families dispersed gaily in the streets, the milkman and the baker climbing onto their horse-drawn carts, which stood side by side in the presbytery yard, a heavy froth hanging from the nostrils of their hungry horses, who had carried bread and milk all week as their masters complained about "these damned chilly mornings, wrap my feet in sheepskin and still my left toe freezes," their beasts seeming a little less weary on this Christmas Eve, as if they had shared in the mildly ecstatic visions of their owners, straightening their backs at their approach, snorting beneath their bell-studded collars, ready to flee into the white night with their little fairy-like sleighs floating soundlessly behind them, the baker no longer calling, "Bread, plain bread, sliced bread, good homemade bread for sale!" but "Merry Christmas, everybody! Merry Christmas, young and old!" the resounding gaiety of his words following us along our return route.

"It's plain to see he has no wife, that one! Grand-mère Josette should have wrung his neck a long time ago, the good-for-nothing!" exclaimed Grandfather Onézimon, tapping the end of his cane against the bouncing shoulder of my cousin, Béran-gère ("she with the big rosy cheeks, like McIntosh apples," as her mother described her), Bérangère, who toddled along beside me, laughing and shouting beneath the hail of snowballs which her brothers rained down upon us from the farther side of the street . . .

"If you children won't walk along the street quietly and decently, there won't be any celebrations when we get home!"

The moment we caught sight of the lighted tree through the living room window, we rushed up the steps and into the house, halting breathlessly on the threshold of the kitchen, for our elders were already gathered about the table, devouring with their eyes, wide and almost liquid in the candlelight, the sumptuous array of food which lay spread out before them. Caught up in the spirit of festive joy which permeated our house that night, the hungry children passed their plates back again and again for "more of the turkey's insides," and my aunts no longer smiled with embarrassment before the scantily-laid table which they beheld on the other three hundred and sixty-four days of the year, when Grand-mère Josette would console them by saying, "We'll eat at Christmas, Judith, but today we must do penance." No, everyone in the family ate that night, shamelessly and with a smiling frenzy (with the exception of Grand-mère Josette, who was too pleased with the sudden appetite of Sébastien to think of herself), and dazzled by the perfection of Grand-mère Josette's masterpiece, by the splendour of this meal which she had so painstakingly prepared, we momentarily forgot the sacrifices and the anxieties which had gone into its making. Until my grandfather exclaimed with recognition, that is:

"We are a lot of potatoes to afford this, eh, Josette?"

Grand-mère Josette was offended. "You're spoiled, Onézimon," she replied. "You talk as if you hadn't had a thing to eat all your life. Now, tuck your napkin in your neck and be still!"

We finally made our way into the living room, where, kneeling beside the tree, we gazed with glittering eyes, not at the crèche and its small waxen figures, which was at any rate only a replica of the one we had already seen at church, but at the snowy landscape which lay father back beneath the branches, behind the silent stable, with its hills and its sheep and its shepherd who stood with his back to us, his hat in one hand . . . back there, on the farther side of the village, our gifts sparkled in the shadows, a thin rain of pine needles falling onto their golden wrappings.

Grandfather Onézimon rose from his chair and declared, "Once again, we are all gathered here together on this occasion to receive the blessing of Our Lord, and I have a few little words I wish to say to you, so be patient, I won't be long . . ."

It was the moment for my grandfather's annual sermon, a speech which my grandmother always had to cut short by pulling on her husband's sleeve, "because when he begins to talk, he'll go on talking till dawn if you let him."

"The gifts, Onézimon!"

"I'll start with the women, since it seems the Good Lord prefers them. Here, I see something peeping out of this box . . . this must be the apron for Alice."

What touched us most about these simple gifts (a jar of jam wrapped in blue paper covered with stars, a doll made from old rags), was the patience, the care that had gone into their making, the loving concern with which Grand-mère Josette had knitted the scarf for Sébastien or the pair of gloves for me, the simple sentiments which she communicated to us in this way in order to warm our hearts for a fleeting moment in the midst of our troubled lives. For during those hours of childhood happiness, the dark lights of the distant storm were already beginning to shine faintly upon our small sheltered world. They suddenly stopped singing, *Bagpipes in the woods, playing, resounding*," on the radio, to bring us news of the bloodshed in another part of the world, a metallic voice slipping, as it were, through some imperceptible fissure in the wall and leaping into the room with its strange message of peace:

"The war atones for the sins of the world!"

Then the singing of Christmas carols was resumed with an increased vigour, the voices of the angels settling like balm upon the bloody massacres of the world.

"Don't cry, Marie-Joséphine, he'll be home soon."

"It's been so long . . . so long . . ."

"Think of the martyrdom of Jesus on the cross."

Marie-Joséphine rushed to her room, her head in her hands. But the ecstatic cries of Bérangère, embracing her doll, exclaiming "Thank you! Thank you!", her mouth filled with chocolates, her long hair flying about her shoulders, quickly distracted Grand-mère Josette from the tearful outburst of her daughter and her own sorrow when her eyes came to rest upon Sébastien, who was singing beside her and whose hand she unconsciously gripped in her own, "to see if he had a fever."

With the gradual disappearance of the people about us, the illness of Sébastien, the departure of Judith for the convent, the marriage of Alice, we were beginning already to witness the painful disintegration of the naïve joys of our childhood, and it would be impossible thereafter to be happy on Christmas Eve. We would still go to Grand-mère Josette's "to receive the New Year's benediction," but in the dark living room that had once sparkled with light, we would no longer see Sébastien standing with his sisters and singing a hymn; there would remain of his presence in that house nothing but a framed photograph on the wall, the student he had once been gazing down upon us with a look that was at once triumphant and mischievous, this photograph transporting us back to a more exalted, spring-like season, to a time when Sébastien had been the recipient of numerous prizes and his healthy laughter had been only the external reflection of a quick and flashing intelligence.

As the years went by, I continued to pass the occasional night at Grand-mère Josette's, sleeping in the living room beneath the silent gaze of Sébastien, who remained awake even as I slipped slowly toward death, though not yet ceasing to breathe. I recall one morning, I awoke at dawn with a toothache, and the shaft of white light which pierced the red window-shutters only intensified the pain of the burning abscess. Rising from my bed, I ran toward the window to see if my cousin Bérangère was play-

ing in the street (she was always up so early, greeting with her little bird-like cries the first shivering women trudging to church),
but she was still asleep, and the morning was even yet several
hours away. Stiff in his framed arrogance, Sébastien seemed once
again to be saying to me:

"Silly little girl, come now, how will you ever endure the
flames of purgatory if you're going to cry over a little toothache?"

"I'm not going to purgatory!"

"Oh? They tell me that even the saints have to take their
turn down there . . ."

Finally, when I could no longer restrain my tears, Grand-
mère Josette, who slept very lightly, awakening every hour in the
belief that she could still hear her son coughing on the farther
side of the wall, came hurrying to my side, her grey hair hanging loosely about her shoulders, and taking me in her arms, she
asked, as she had done on so many occasions with her delirious
son:

"What is it? What is it?"

I didn't confess to her the true nature of my ailment, for she
would only have sent me to the butcher-dentist at the parish
clinic. Instead, I whimpered through my tears, "It isn't my teeth
that hurt, it's my ears!"

"Well, and that's what comes of playing outside with Bérangère in weather like this without your boots on! If you'd listen to
us, Pauline, you wouldn't wake up at night with earache! Don't
cry, now, I'm going to make you feel better . . . I'm going to fix
you a nice heat compress . . ."

These "heat compresses" were often no more than a pair of
my grandfather's old undershorts which had been warmed for a
few minutes on the kitchen stove, but as soon as Grand-mère
Josette applied the balm to my burning head, the pain began to
diminish . . .

Grandfather Onézimon appeared on the threshold, his eyes blinking, his hair dishevelled.

"Go back to bed, Onézimon, we don't need you here."

"What's she crying about? It's nothing serious."

"We all know you have no sympathy for sick people."

"Sickness doesn't exist, it's only a woman's fancy," mumbled my grandfather, returning to his bed. "Me, I'm never sick! And I never complain either."

With the passage of time, I played less and less with Bérangère, for while I dragged my "reader" everywhere with me, she was still too young to go to school. Grandfather Onézimon would still take her on his knee occasionally "to throw her in the air like a balloon," but then to me he would say simply:

"We're going to do our homework together tonight."

I accused him of not knowing how to read, but he concentrated all the same on the page which was clouded with symbols that he could not understand, thrusting an inspired finger at the crude drawing in my book:

"It says: 'It is r-a-i-n-i-n-g!' See, the man is taking out his umbrella and his rubbers! Oh yes . . . *it is raining, I am raining, you are raining*, that's what it says there!"

"Without intending any disrespect, Papa," said Marie-Joséphine, who was seated at the farther end of the table, writing a letter to her fiancé, "the verb *to rain* is not conjugated like the verb *to have*. Oh no, Papa, not at all!"

"You don't know anything about it," grumbled my grandfather. "Whoever said education was for women? Come, Pauline, there are too many women around here, they're always trying to take a man down a peg or two."

As soon as my grandfather had closed the door of his workshop behind us, he took from his pocket two dimes, which he placed in my hand, saying with an air of self-satisfaction, "That's to buy yourself another little Chinese!"

"They cost twenty-five cents this year . . ."

"Eh? The price is going up, I see. Even heaven is becoming expensive these days! How are your little Chinese on the blackboard at school? Are they still climbing toward heaven?"

"Mother Sainte-Scholastique painted the road to heaven in pink. Whenever you give me pennies, my little Chinese climb a little closer to heaven . . ."

"Good! Good! But you're sure they're baptized before they die? I don't want to waste my money on them if they're going to end up in hell just like all the other Chinese!"

"The little Chinese who are baptized go to heaven, Mother Sainte-Scholastique said. But Séraphine likes the little Africans better. Mother Sainte-Scholastique says they lie all along the road in Africa, and sometimes the leopards come and eat them up. That makes Séraphine cry."

"Oh yes, me too! A good thing there's missionaries to save them. Without the missionaries there'd be too many innocent little children in hell, so many poor little chickens burning up in the devil's fire! I tell you, Pauline Archange, sometimes it makes you wonder what the Good Lord is thinking about!"

"You would go to hell too, Grand-Papa, if you weren't baptized. Mother Sainte-Scholastique said so."

"Your Mother has a harsh tongue, like all women! What are you going to call your little Chinese?"

"I'm going to call her Bérangère."

"Good, good. But you're sure a bit of holy water is enough to send them flying straight to heaven? How much does it cost to save them outright, so they don't have to wait in purgatory?"

"It costs a dollar, Mother Sainte-Scholastique said so."

"What? That's highway robbery! In my time, we used to be able to buy the little Chinese and their place in heaven for ten cents. Sometimes, I do think the Good Lord is exaggerating!"

Every month, Mother Sainte-Scholastique drew a new map of the "Holy Redeemed Children," which she attached to the classroom wall, unable to tear her eyes from this fresco which was a living testimony to the racist awe which she had experienced in drawing that long route strewn with quarters, that humiliating road which "the little Chinese" or "the little African" had to follow in order to reach paradise. At the bottom of the map, we could see the damned swimming in their pool of fire, "those who died without the grace of baptism," as Mother Sainte-Scholastique explained, stabbing at them with her pointer. A little higher up, a tall missionary dressed in white led the souls that had been fortunate enough to receive the sacrament of baptism away from the ravine of ignorance. Represented by photographs of actual Chinese children, these souls toddled along behind the priest, smiling with their little white teeth, rising and falling on their swings of redemption to the rhythm of the coins which we so generously offered them.

When an entire week passed during which I had no money for Mother Sainte-Scholastique, she cruelly pinned the photograph of Bérangère closer to the ravine, surrounded by an entire family of writhing black snakes.

"Give her a little more money, and she'll be able to learn her catechism!"

This commerce in Chinese was clearly a profitable one, for periodically Mother Sainte-Scholastique would open her cupboard door and with great respect place "these sacred dollars" in the box in which she also stored the celluloid birds which she awarded to "the best students in the class," the fragile brood with its transparent wings looking distinctly uncomfortable in the box which served as its nest, a large white carton with the word K-O-T-E-X printed in big blue letters across its face. In this way, Mother Sainte-Scholastique candidly glorified our scorn for those foreign races which we had so blatantly adopted, our instinct to condemn those very individuals whom we had embraced with our faith! When this little Chinese, who had long been a symbol of our deplorable desire to possess and control others (because for a few pennies we had bought multitudes of red and yellow souls) – when he suddenly materialized before us, in the guise of an exiled orphan adopted by one of the neighbourhood families and sent to our school to sit on a bench alongside his new brothers and sister, how quick we were to persecute him! The parents of the adopted child, who already had nine children of their own, would often find the orphan in the evening, black and blue from the beating he had received, the blood from his nose running out on the snow, while the cruel laughter of the students echoed in the night: "We beat up Ping-Pong! We beat up Ping-Pong!"

Occasionally, however, these redeemed children would intercede for us in our actual lives: in their company, for example, we often experienced less fear in crossing the bridge after school. "Hold onto the hand of my little Chinese, then you won't fall," Séraphine would say, and if the wind pushed us up against the iron railing, she spoke of "our guardian angel beating its wings against us . . ." But night always fell too quickly and nothing ever seemed more frightening to us than to hear the neighing of horses which passed us invisibly in the dark, their heavy carts skating over the icy bridge, while a surly voice called: "Scrap-iron for sale! Umbrellas, bells, chains!" These sounds were more evocative of the world of nightmares than of the world of reality, and when the seller of scrap-iron lowered before our streaming faces a lamp wrapped in fog and snow, we were much too terrified to speak. Seated beside him, "beneath a furry blanket as warm as a coal furnace," we listened to him sing as he drove his frisky horse through the storm: "*Oh, the good wind . . . Oh, the fine wind . . .*" Séraphine rubbed her eyes with her mittens (which were pinned to the sleeves of her coat), but she could not make out her house in the storm.

"Is it a red brick house or a grey one?"

"I don't remember."

"I'll find it, don't cry, I don't like little girls who snivel like calves . . . '*Oh, the good wind . . . Oh, the fine wind . . .*' By God, it's a fine day, eh?"

When he stopped miraculously before our door, one of us shouted through her tears, "It's here!" but our whimpering must have irritated him, for he would not let us down from the cart until he had had a good laugh at us. Then, in a more melancholy voice, he began once again to sing: "*Oh, the good wind, my love is calling me, my love is waiting for me . . .* Good night, my little mice . . . *Oh, the good wind, my love is waiting for me!*"

I threw myself up against my mother's skirts without even stopping to observe what she was doing.

Holding a spoonful of soup before her mouth, she sighed impatiently: "You and Séraphine have been wandering about the streets again, haven't you?"

But even as I took refuge against my mother's legs, I could still hear the neighing of the horses and the sounds of their heavy hoof beats in the night.

"We've got less than nothing," groaned Uncle Victorin, who sat smoking with my father in the adjoining room. "I don't ask for much, bicycle wheels, rags, torn stockings, I only want to dress my children for the winter, Jacob is worse than a snake with his thirsty tongue, he costs me so much, damn him!"

"Whenever I give you a dollar for Jacob's medicine, you spend it on drink, Victorin. You're nothing but a drunkard, and the Good Lord will punish you!"

"Give me a dollar, and I'll take Jacob to the doctor tomorrow. I promise you that on the head of the Holy Mother!"

"Don't take the name of our Holy Mother in vain with your evil lies! Take the dollar, and look after your sick boy. You've already beaten him enough, wicked father that you are!"

"Victorin is going to end up taking the very clothes off our backs," my mother said, opening the "expense book" on Monday evening. "We're in the red again because of him."

"Help your neighbour, it says in the Scriptures," replied my father.

"Oh, sometimes I think you're too good for this world, Jos!"

I was doing my homework in the bedroom that evening, for my parents had covered the kitchen table with bills and blue food coupons. Then the clock struck eight, and once again I sensed all my hopes springing to life, rising as it were from each object in the room, as if, from this sudden intimacy with myself, from the dust cloths which covered the furniture to the halo of light cast by the lamp upon Jean's brow, a new life was about to blossom for me, one which would end only with the dawn and my departure for school, but to hold onto it, I had to keep my eyes open, staring fixedly at a brown flower-like spot on the ceiling . . . My mother's voice sounded like an echo in the timelessness of the world which lay spread all about me.

"We're behind in the rent, Jos!"

When the house finally lapsed into silence, I could still hear Jean's fitful sighs, so close to me; it would soon be "bottle time," and already he was beginning to awaken. When I stretched my hand in his direction, one of his fingers squirmed into my palm and rested there, as delicate and dreamy as a butterfly, but the moment my hand began to tremble, a shudder passed through his entire body and he suddenly awakened, shaken with irritation. Then, how was I to recapture my dream, for entering the room and taking the baby in her arms, my mother abruptly brought the world of daily affairs back into my secret life.

"Have you done your spelling?" she asked me.

"No."

"Then I'll have to get you up at six o'clock when the milkman arrives."

A life of studies and duties began with the dawn, a life that had to be lived in the present tense, and it was in vain that I tried to race back toward a past that seemed, nonetheless, so near. From that distant world, Sébastien called me with his gentle resigned eyes, and I returned with him to my grandmother's house, where Bérangère was still playing with marbles on the staircase. It was a morning that stood out vividly in my memory, and we could hear the calls of our Aunt Marie-Joséphine (who suffered so much from rheumatism in the legs) as she swept down the long staircase into the arms of her fiancé, embracing him against the door, with never a thought for us, for the one upon whom she gazed at that moment seemed to have returned from a journey to the land of the dead.

❧ Chapter Two ❧

Even as I tried to evoke all those images from my past, seeking words with which to preserve them, the present and the future seemed much more alive to me than the events I had already experienced, for time had not yet touched those days which still lay before me, unpopulated perhaps but filled with the hopes which my capricious imagination had lent them.

My parents scarcely saw me now that I had begun to earn my own living. Every afternoon after school, Louisette Denis, Marthe Dubos, Elisa Moutonnet and I took ourselves downtown to Eloi Gagnon et Frères, where we worked as salesgirls, and henceforth, whenever my father spoke to me, it was merely to demand payment for my room and board, my private salary which I parted with bitterly, for in sharing with my father my pitiful earnings, it seemed to me that I was also sharing the humiliation of the work itself, the fatigue of all those hours spent standing behind a freezing counter ("The doors must be left open, even in winter, to attract customers," the owner said), hours which I willingly sacrificed to this thankless task in the naïve belief that I was thus increasing my freedom to buy books and writing tablets, whereas, in fact, I was actually sacrificing that very freedom by agreeing every evening to work overtime, participating in a form of communal slavery which brought us little more than the grudging appreciation of our employer and his associates.

I envied Elisa Moutonnet, who spent all her money on movies. On payday, Louisette Denis and I would leave her at the entrance to the cinema, applying make-up to her face, while we, who were not allowed to enter, remained in the lot outside the movie house, listening to the muffled sounds that reached us from the dark interior. Later, Elisa would tell us the story of the movie, for though we had tried to participate in her experience by pressing our ears to a broken windowpane, we invariably managed to hear only scraps of dialogue, fragments of love-making which all but blotted out the plot of the film in our minds: "My love! Oh, my love, I want a child, a child of love!"

Elisa Moutonnet never failed to astonish us when she emerged blushing from the cinema only to declare: "You didn't miss a thing, it was a stupid story."

"Tell us about it anyway . . ."

"Oh, why bother, there's nothing to tell. A man, a woman, they loved each other, they had a child, that's life, eh? But you're too young to understand those things, you two!"

After the store had closed for the day, we would rehearse our badly-written plays until midnight, the time elapsing in day-dreams as we sat about a candle, while Marthe Dubos talked of Saint-Ex and the plane she would one day pilot herself. With what grace and agility did she already flash through the midnight sky, and though there was nothing graceful or even agile about her, no one had ever dreamed as she did of space, "of the clean, starless sky," stuffing her mouth with food even as she talked and becoming each day heavier and heavier. Her book held open before her, she could simultaneously devour an enormous plate of food and follow, step by step, her ascetic hero as he struggled, famished and thirsty, across the sun-baked desert, nothing to sustain him in that entire colourless landscape but a shrivelled orange, his eyes filled with supplication as they came to rest upon his unfaithful companion, the airplane with its crippled engine and its sun-scorched wings. When Marthe Dubos finally fell silent, I no longer had the courage to return home, for I had followed her too far into the world of her exiles, where a man achieved a state of purity only in solitude, where he became mystical and charitable only when he was no longer faced with the problem of distinguishing between the senses and the spirit; and the sun, the night, the ocean of which she spoke, in all their rolling strength, crushed my fragility, undermining the obedience which I still owed my parents, who awaited me anxiously at home. My mother didn't believe me when I told her that I had passed the night at Elisa Moutonnet's, in order not to awaken my brothers and sisters.

"You'll end up in the home for delinquent girls, just like Huguette Poire. Playing the tramp at her age! Did you see her with her six months' belly sticking out from under her apron? And showing it off as if it were a Christmas present! That's what happens to little girls who sleep away from home!"

"I only slept on the sofa at Elisa Moutonnet's place. Ask her mother, if you have to know everything."

"Don't talk back to your mother!"

I always felt very sad when they spoke to me of Huguette Poire, for if she had "danced to the end of her cord," as my mother so often said, her fleeting audacity had quickly vanished when, on her miserable bed at the Maria-Goretti-Des Pécheresses Home for Girls, the nuns had refused to look after her, covering the sounds of her anguished cries and supplications with their cruel prayers in the chapel. Why was my mother incapable of envisioning the faceless son that Huguette had left behind her, beneath a cold and dispassionate sky, where not so much as a breath of charity was expelled to gather in this new life? Why couldn't she imagine the pain with which Huguette Poire had quickly escaped that place of expiation and shame, without a backward glance, with not a single thought for the ill-begotten child which she brought into the world?

My mother was even more severe in her judgment of "the pilgrimage of Huguette Poire through the hotels of the harbour, where for twenty-five cents she'll give herself to just any steve-dore who comes her way . . ." But for me, the flight of Huguette Poire and her heedless prostitution in the poor quarters of the city was no more reprehensible than the life she had had to live at home, in the company of her ailing sisters and her alcoholic father. When she admired herself, her eyes limpid with grati-tude, in the lovely crinoline dress and the high-heeled shoes bought by one of her lovers, she was only trying to annul the pains of her former existence, but because her innocent desires had all the appearances of vice, people chose to see in her only a cheap little girl inclined toward lust.

Passing near the rut in which Huguette's soul floundered, perhaps Benjamin Robert was the only one to comprehend the mysterious desire and need for love which lay buried beneath the trappings of that lust, for he alone, of all the people I knew, was in touch with the "criminality" of others. On winter nights, when so many innocent, satiated priests slept in their comfort-able monasteries, protected by their faith (which amounted to little more than a legitimate indifference to virtue), only Benja-min Robert, who openly accused himself of all crimes and who wandered at night through the city streets, allowing his feet to be guided by his extravagant pity, only he confronted with compassion the distress of the children of the streets, leading them drunken and dirty to the refuge which he had personally created for them; for he, too, had suffered, and it seemed to him that each of the creatures he encountered in those streets was worthy of the pure love which he was so desperately in search of himself. His wrath was directed only against individuals like Germaine Léonard, who repulsed any attempt on his part to solicit assistance in his mission, refusing to give him the medicine he requested "for the twelve-year-old drunkards, inflamed with alcohol, their stomachs so ravaged they can no longer eat, they're on the verge of starvation, each and every one of them . . ." The calm expression of defiance with which she responded to "the restless philanthropy of this priest," the smile which he read on her lips even as he spoke of such grave matters, momentarily crushed his love for his fellow man, and waving his arms desperately in the air, he exclaimed:

"But are you a doctor of angels or men? Does your concept of justice stop dead on the doorstep of your hospital? It's a shame, I tell you, a shame!"

But as if to exasperate him even more, Germaine Léonard merely repeated, in a voice choked with hatred, what she had already told him on so many previous occasions: "I live for my patients! My conscience is clear! I have no crimes to repent!"

"Oh, indeed!" he murmured angrily. "And, nothing is more dangerous than these sleepy, self-satisfied consciences! These hard, reasonable consciences from which all life has slowly been drained . . ."

"Hold your tongue, Father, you're becoming delirious."

She sincerely believed that everything the priest told her was tinged with exaggeration and madness, that his tales of alcoholic children were only another of the hallucinations "of a depraved and disturbed mind." Each day at the hospital, she was witness to the same social ills, and she endeavoured in her own way to cope with them; but from behind the protective wall of her profession, it always seemed to her that this sobriety which she demonstrated in her dealings with human depravity was legitimate and just, whereas in real life she found it unhealthy to come in contact with those same germs which she studied so minutely in the laboratory. And thus, even if Germaine Léonard had learned from someone else the story of Huguette Poire, she shared with my mother her implacable judgment of the girl, condemning Huguette for a weakness, a spiritual malaise which she could not even begin to imagine, she who had always been so strong and irreproachable, at least in appearance, she who had grappled with the defiance of men by attacking them with the impertinence of her character and the cold assurance of her intellectual authority.

When I asked Elisa Moutonnet how she came to have so many books (she received the same salary at the store as I), she replied evasively, her head resting in her hands, her heavy-lidded eyes gazing lazily in my direction:

"Because I take them from the bookstores."

"You mean you steal them?"

"No, I slip them into the pocket of my coat when no one is looking."

"But that's stealing!"

"Oh, don't exaggerate so!"

Several moments before the noon bell, Elisa Moutonnet, Marthe Dubos and Louisette Denis rose abruptly from their bench, claiming that they heard the first faint sounds of the bell, but Mother Sainte-Alfréda commanded them at once to be reseated:

"We haven't said our prayer yet, girls!"

If they were so anxious to get out of that classroom, it was because they invariably spent their lunch hours "hunting for books" . . . Each girl entered the bookstore as if she were setting foot in her own private domain, surveying with a possessive and arrogant gaze the rows of books which stretched into the semi-darkness . . . A single employee guarded the shop, his black moustache barely visible from behind a great pile of volumes, in his hand a half-eaten apple which he was dreamily munching . . . but Elisa Moutonnet knew that this man was only playing at being invisible, a game which she played herself with consummate skill. She claimed that an agile spy could easily evade the detection of this clerk, who appeared at once so absent-minded and insignificant, and it was with an extreme caution ("like a cat walking on jars without knocking them over") that her hands moved over the shelves while her eyes remained fixed before her. If the clerk raised his head, she smiled at him in such a friendly fashion that the man was compelled, finally, to lower his eyes in embarrassment. "It's not a question of technique but of charm," said Elisa, but when Louisette Denis reacted to the glance of an employee with a big childish grin, the clerk was more alarmed than seduced, and he approached her suspiciously:

"Are you looking for something, mademoiselle?"

"Yes, a book for my sister. A book on the Index."

"We have only religious works here."

"Oh, but you have some, sir. I saw them hidden beneath the others, down there."

"I had a close call that time," said Louisette Denis to Elisa Moutonnet several minutes later, as we waited for the bus on the sidewalk. "It's your fault too, because you tried to teach me new tricks when I already have too many of my own. I was so nervous I took three copies of the same book!"

"It's just as I said, Louisette Denis, you don't look respectable enough to make a good thief."

Seated or standing in the noisy bus, we read, our heads buried in our books, exchanging absent looks whenever someone jostled us. In a spirit of rivalry, we often glanced over each other's shoulders, for while Louisette Denis and I were still on the letter A in the popular collection, *I've Read All, I've Seen All* ("What is the atmosphere?" . . . "What is arboriculture?"), Elisa Moutonnet and Marthe Dubos were innocently devouring volumes on biology and botany, subjects which they discussed between themselves with a mysterious, doctoral air.

I returned home, a book in my hand. My mother placed a steaming bowl before me, though I scarcely touched it, once again incurring her wrath.

"Books, everywhere books!" she grumbled. "That isn't going to get you through your exams at the convent! You never open your algebra text, but you're always ready to read forbidden books!"

"It's very simple," added my father. "Next year she'll have to go to work full time and sweat a little for the food she's always ready to stuff into her mouth! No more studying! No more fancy dreams! We'll see who's so smart!"

A heavy anguish invaded my thoughts, then, the words I was reading suddenly vanishing in the fog that lay all about me and that constricted my heart. For a moment, I had the impression that Jean and my sister were staring at me, I thought I could see their wistful faces through the film of my angry tears; but no, it was only the steam from the scalding soup rising slowly before my eyes.

"Eat . . . eat . . ." said my mother to Jean. "Stop playing with your food! You're spilling bread all over my clean tablecloth!"

"It's for the birds."

"What birds? Eat or your father will slap you! There's a limit to everything!"

"It's for the sparrows who eat horse turds in the street."

"Oh, listen to him! His language is worse than the neighbours! Anyone would think I'd brought him up to be a foulmouthed little beast, just like the other mothers in the neighbourhood! But I hope I've done better than that!"

"It's written in the Scriptures," said my father, helping Geneviève to drink her milk (she was seated on his knee, gazing about her with her big blue eyes that always seemed a little surprised), "that the Good Lord looks after his own birds and his flowers. Now, listen to your mother and eat."

"It's an obsession of his, he thinks of nothing but birds, it isn't healthy, I tell you!"

When the telephone rang during dessert, the voice of Elisa Moutonnet reassured me a little. We were talking as usual, of our reading, but the tone of our conversation upset my mother, who confided to my father:

"She's talking about boys again. I know it! Pauline Archange thinks I don't understand all those fancy, mixed-up sentences of hers. But I understand, alright. Oh yes, I understand everything!"

For my mother, who heard only such feverish phrases as, "What I seek is the Desert of Love, not Conquerors, but the Desert of Love . . . I'll get it in the bus, yes, at one o'clock, in front of the pharmacy . . ." – for her, these words were the symptoms of "a certain madness," the language of an inaccessible world which was a constant and powerful threat to her.

I remember a Sunday morning, very early, at the hour when my parents usually awoke me for mass: I had already risen from the bed where Geneviève still slept, her face buried beneath the jumble of toys with which she had surrounded herself the night before, and with a small packsack on my back, I stood with my friends awaiting the express train for Sainte-Elisabeth des Près, a train which would carry us through sleepy little villages and over snow-covered hills bathed in the cool blue light of morning, to Sainte-Elisabeth, where we would descend from the train in a great cloud of steam. It was an old train, and the countryside seemed almost to welcome it, breaking as it did the monotony of the early morning stillness: at the sound of its grinding wheels on the rails, other familiar sounds could be heard in the distant farmyards, the crowing of a rooster, the barking of a dog . . . As we descended laughing from the train, the countryside seemed already to be trembling with life. Clear little streams rushed beneath the snow, and the mountain seemed so much more accessible than on other mornings, the fog which hung over it still obscuring from our eyes its silvery peak.

Elisa Moutonnet and Louisette Denis reached the top of Hill Number One (according to the signs which a scout troop had left behind it, this hill was "only a camel's hump, next sign five miles higher, up and on"), while Marthe Dubos and I were still making our way through the pine forest below. A sign nailed to the trunk of a tree bore the following message: *CAUTION; BEARS.*

"In my airplane, I could already have flown around the Sainte's peak three times! I'm hungry. Do you want a piece of honey cake, Pauline Archange?"

"If you spend all your time eating, we'll never get to the top!"

At the foot of Hill Number Two, having wrestled for two hours through dense brush and up muddy slopes, Marthe Dubos once again opened her sack and exclaimed:

"My stomach's empty! I can't go any farther! This is no ordinary mountain, it's as steep as a ladder! What encouraging words do the scouts have for us here?"

"They say: 'Keep straight up, next brook, seven miles.'"

"They're trying to kill me, I know it! And to think that the sky is so beautiful and that I could be as light as a butterfly if I were flying today! Give me your hand, Pauline Archange, or I'll break my neck on that hill!"

"If you hadn't put on ten sweaters, one on top of the other, like a little nun, you wouldn't be so heavy to pull."

Her face hidden behind her woollen scarf, she struggled up the slope in her heavy ski boots, gasping all the way; but when we reached the summit of the last hill, she exclaimed with joy over "the low-lying sky . . . the clouds resting on our heads," for what she sought at the end of her climb was "space, the limit-less horizon," and like an eagle returning to its nest on a mountain peak, she did not budge for hours from the branch of the oak tree where she had temporarily made her home and from which she contemplated the sunset after her long, arduous day on the slopes. "Come and light the stove in the cabin," called Louisette Denis, but quietly poised between earth and sky, Marthe Dubos no longer heard us.

We had inherited from the scouts, in the ruins of a house that stood open to the night and the stars, a little old stove which smoked but about which we huddled in the evening to read by candlelight. Only Marthe Dubos continued to prowl about her cabin, her crunching footsteps the only sounds to break the vast white silence which surrounded us. She appeared suddenly in the doorway, her shadow stretching grotesquely before her, waving her arms:

"I don't want to bother you, but I hear voices . . . maybe it's the scouts on a moonlight hike."

When two students who had lost their way timidly approached the cabin on snowshoes, Elisa Moutonnet stepped boldly up to them, and shining her flashlight in their faces, greeted them in a voice which I did not at once recognize, its tone much softer and dreamier than the one she used with us. The elder of the two boys abruptly ducked his head, but his brother, who was not so shy, looked at us with his shining eyes, though he too remained silent.

"A good thing you came along," said Elisa, smiling. "You can light our stove for us. We were just about to knock down the door for firewood . . . We'll be safer here tonight with you two in the cabin, don't you agree girls?"

But hearing only the sighs of Louisette Denis, who was climbing sullenly into her sleeping bag, she added with a coquettish air: "As you can see, exams are approaching and we're studying like fools!"

The indignation of Louisette Denis was only augmented when she arose at dawn to discover Elisa Moutonnet and François Lepique curled up in the same sleeping bag.

"I don't believe it," she said, shocked at this shameless spectacle. "Elisa Moutonnet hasn't even begun to have her period yet! Say something, Marthe Dubos, and stop gaping at them like that! Oh God, it isn't possible!"

"So much the better if she hasn't had her period!" said Marthe Dubos calmly. "She's lucky!" And she turned and walked toward the door, shrugging her shoulders . . .

The return trip was a very gloomy one: while Marthe Dubos and I repeated our Latin declensions to each other, we cast stealthy glances in the direction of Elisa Moutonnet and François Lepique, who were furtively holding hands, scarcely daring to look at each other, our vigilance paralyzing their every movement.

Pressing her face against the window of the train, Louisette Denis seemed very upset; for one who had always professed an almost chivalrous attitude toward friendship (she read Maritain ardently), a sentiment which even surpassed love in her heart, it seemed to her that Elisa Moutonnet had betrayed the affection which held us together by inviting Louis and François Lepique into our midst. "It is in the spirit that friendship is rooted," she contended, "but when people became stupid lovers like Elisa Moutonnet and François Lepique, when the became infatuated with just anyone, they lose their heads, it's that simple." She could tolerate the idea of love on the part of an older person, like Germaine Léonard, sensuality allied with intelligence seeming to her an almost mystical thing, and she retained such a clear memory of that day when, from our hiding place in the bushes, we had witnessed the surrender of Germaine Léonard to the overtures of a suitor, that she could not meet her in the street now without revealing her admiration for this imperturbable woman with clumsy greetings and awkward gestures; but if Germaine Léonard received our respect as if it were something she considered her due, she was annoyed by the excessive veneration of Louisette Denis and replied to her exuberant greetings: "Good morning, Mademoiselle Léonard, and how are you this morning?" with only a quick toss of her head and a curt reply: "Very well, thank you," before turning and hurrying on her way. When we went skating together on Saturdays, the spectacle of our lively group passing beneath the windows of the hospital must also have irritated her, for her only response to our boisterous greetings was a haughty look levelled upon us from beneath half-closed lids.

"She's locked up in her principles, like a woman in an iron corset!" declared Elisa Moutonnet, who could not understand the admiration of Louisette Denis for "such a straight-laced person," a woman who seemed to love no one and who was loved by no one in return.

This coolness which Germaine Léonard manifested toward others was at least partly the result of her desire to be seen as an honest and virtuous woman, and if she exhibited with such pride the insensitive side of her nature, in which there seemed to be no trace of love or compassion ("but that concerns only me"), it was because she wanted, above all, to conceal from the world "an insane affair" into which she had allowed herself to be drawn with a colleague at the hospital. "Married and the father of two children," she would say to herself, severely berating herself, though it was in vain that she dreamed this time of a separation, for they were colleagues in the same research project and collaborators on the *Journal of Scientific Investigation*, and even if she repeated to herself each morning, "I must speak to him tonight, things cannot go on like this . . .", her resolution forsook her when, following an exhausting day with her patients, she closed herself up with Pierre Olivier in their temple of study, the laboratory, where, bent over a microscope, she was too absorbed in the life which she saw in the cells before her even to think of her companion as a lover. Suddenly, in that peaceful setting, the relationship seemed less threatening than it had appeared earlier in the day, redeemed perhaps by the intellectual exaltation and zeal which she ostensibly shared with Pierre Olivier. Even there, however, she continued to question the humanitarian designs of her colleague, sensing at times beneath the impassive beauty of that face and that body which she loved so dearly and which, in moments of intimacy, she compared with those of a god (asking herself at the same time if Pierre's phlegmatic expression could possibly be considered divine), an obscure resistance, a deliberate aloofness, which was vindicated perhaps by the man's youth but which filled her nonetheless with uncertainty, as if she had suddenly discovered in that body which seemed at times to mechanically possess her with no trace whatever of tenderness, a brain without a soul.

Germaine Léonard had acquired the habit of dominating those whom she loved (convinced that she was admired for her strength, she often displayed nothing but the awkward and impotent side of her character), but in this latest relationship, she accused Pierre Olivier of unconsciously wanting to dominate *her*, for everything which she failed to understand in others she classified as "a lack of consciousness, a state of unfortunate blindness," shortcomings which were clearly her own but of which she absolved herself by projecting them onto others. Presumptuous and rigid in her judgments, she was quick to condemn the intellectual pretentiousness and morose pride of Pierre Olivier, without recognizing these same faults in herself, for she was incapable of admitting Pierre's spiritual superiority, and in spite of the flashes of modesty which periodically pervaded her heart, she did not even dare to think, "We are equals" (an admission which would have been a fatal blow to her pride), thinking instead: "His superiority is nothing but an illusion!"

Thus, she spoke rarely of Pierre's scientific achievements. He had published at a very early age, *Studies in Proteins*, a work which had gained him more enemies than admirers amongst his elders in the scientific community, and Germaine Léonard, like the others, preferred to ignore the virile determination and courage which prompted this young man to defend his work against the accusations of obscurity which were repeatedly levelled against it. In this fight against ignorance, he repelled pitilessly "every religious shadow which still hangs over our medical texts and infiltrates our operating rooms! What stupidity, for example, for a fine surgeon like Dugal to raise his eyes to the crucifix and to invoke God's intervention during an operation! That sort of thing embarrasses me to the point of disgust!"

"You're too free in your judgments of your superiors," replied Germaine Léonard. "I have a great deal of respect for Antoine Dugal. He is a fine surgeon."

"Unfortunately, his Catholic practices poison his skills. Piety of this sort is not worthy of him! You told me yourself the other day that 'a breath of fresh air always enrages those conservative spirits who want only to protect their privileges.' And now, though you admit that you have no faith yourself, you defend those very privileges, the morbid presence of God in our operating rooms."

"I never said that," replied Germaine Léonard sharply.

Germaine Léonard was offended by the audacity of Pierre Olivier when he indirectly criticized "such respectable professional," for she saw his attack as being ironically directed against herself. "In spite of his noble allure he is nothing but a proletarian," she thought angrily. What could he possibly understand of "the refinements of the elite," amongst whom she included herself, along with the other doctors, lawyers and judges who represented the nucleus of "privileged families," though in her articles she continued to condemn their "pale, uncharitable Catholicism." But when Pierre Olivier attacked her for the same privileges, she immediately turned to the defence of her class with a vindictive ardour, pleading the cause of those eminent people "whose images should not be so indiscriminately sullied," while simultaneously continuing to attack the reputation of poor Benjamin Robert, who had long been the helpless victim of her voracious condemnation.

"In fact, you appreciate only those individuals who resemble you," Pierre Olivier told her, "those whom you consider to be worthy of your moral esteem . . ."

Germaine Léonard firmly denied such accusations, but if the following day Pierre Olivier showed too much enthusiasm for the *Prison Chronicles* of Philippe l'Heureux, the very sound of that author's name caused her to shudder, and forgetting for the moment her vehement protestations of the previous day, she passionately took the offensive:

"I don't like the way Philippe l'Heureux imposes himself upon the reader, abusing his patience and offending his ear. A writer ought to be more discreet in respect to what he says in his work, if he has anything to say at all, that is. Otherwise, he just becomes a bore, he succeeds only in irritating and exasperating his reader. This young man is too delirious, his characters aren't at all realistic, you know as well as I do that such conditions do not exist in our prisons! He invented those defective, disgusting characters, and I wonder what you see in him and in the troubled sensuality of his book, I though you knew something about life . . ."

"But a writer communicates his own vision of life, that's all. Healthy or unhealthy, it is *his* vision of life!"

"I know, I know, but you must admit that there is a limit to the morbidity which a reader can be expected to tolerate in a work, and the characters in this book exceed that limit. Indeed, they are quite repugnant. More than once, I have heard people describe the characters and events in poor Philippe l'Heureux's books as 'nauseating.' Well, that's what comes of trying to build stories around characters who are in an advanced state of deterioration. There is a positive sort of deterioration, evil though it may be, but that isn't what I'm talking about, what I'm talking about is a deterioration of the spirit, an internal disintegration of the soul, resulting in a total absence of good and evil. We mustn't forget that this poor boy wrote his book while he was lying in a hospital bed, suffering from cancer, and that sickness and the fear of death run like a curse through the entire work."

"No matter, you know as well as I do that we are all steeped in the heavy airs of putrefaction that rise from each of our crimes. If Philippe l'Heureux seems farther gone than most of us, it is simply because we lack his gift for expression, for exposing this poison in painful print! Our sickness is a secret one, but it is there, nonetheless!"

"I don't know what you're talking about. Nor do I understand this obsession of yours with affliction — in literature, I mean, for in life I haven't noticed that the suffering of your patients greatly moves you." Without giving him the opportunity to reply to this pernicious remark, Germaine Léonard continued in a less assured tone: "What is the meaning of all this masochism, this antiquated guilt, in a practical man like yourself? Misery exists, it is universal, it is profound, but we must rise above it, you know that as well as I do. Otherwise, how will we ever accomplish anything in this life? To wallow in it, like that fanatic Benjamin Robert (forgive me, but what a wicked priest!), leaves one as useless to oneself as to others. The work of Philippe l'Heureux is nothing but a mad, incoherent cry, one that rises from the entrails, not from the head or the heart! It's sad, really, for the strength and the skill which he seems to command could so easily have been transformed into something positive, a great sea of inspiring prose . . ." Carried away by the lyricism of her words, Germaine Léonard's voice suddenly seemed softer and more dream-like: ". . . a cool body of fresh water in which the reader might quench his thirst . . ."

Often, having crushed a young writer with insults (an artist whose very youth constituted a threat to her), Germaine Léonard would linger emotionally over "the noble shadow of the works of the past," and when she dined with Pierre Olivier at the Doctor's Club (a place which she always chose in order to preserve the fragile neutrality of their meetings), she yielded to a sort of rapture when speaking of "the idyllic seasons in Russian literature . . . yes, in Chekhov, the lovely pastoral seasons in Chekhov . . . practically nothing, only a line or two in a play . . . yet they touch one with a familiar spark of recognition . . ."

Smiling, Pierre Olivier listened to her, but the moment their eyes met, the smile disappeared from his face and he absently refilled her glass. "Go on . . . go on . . ." he said dryly, for he did not want her to see the resentment he felt as she spoke for the third time in a year of "the springtimes in Chekhov," words which awoke in him, not only a certain tenderness towards this woman, but also a violent feeling of impotence, her unconscious repetition throwing him into a state of profound melancholy, the melody of those few words, "the springtimes in Chekhov," reminding him painfully of the passage of time and of the senseless flight of their lives. "The seasons which pass, the springtimes which will never return," a voice seemed to say within him, softly insinuating itself into his innermost being, throwing a shadow over all his joys; but he suddenly stifled the voice and said indignantly:

"I was right then, to believe that your preference is for writers who are dead rather than for the living. And why not, haven't they taken with them to the grave all the secrets which inspired the beauty of their works? We have only the works themselves, purified by death . . . Yes, a pale bouquet of passions distilled by time!"

"Lower your voice please . . . people can hear us . . ."

While she covered her face with the back of her hand, beseeching him in a humble, frightened voice to be silent, he thought with a rush of amorous pity, "Though she will never change, there are moments, in spite of everything, when she seems more lovable to me than anyone I know." But gazing at him with eyes that were clouded with wine and fatigue,

Germaine Léonard could see only his hostile attitude toward her, reading beneath the surface of his gaze thoughts of contempt which were not even there.

"You're talking nonsense," she said, her throat constricted. "Sometimes, I wonder if you have any feelings at all for others . . ."

It was only at night, when they found themselves alone, that Germaine Léonard forsook her patronizing tone for a more submissive one. Pierre Olivier had already waited for an hour in a nearby café before climbing to her room, but even then she was not ready to receive him. Prone to sleepiness and occasional migraines, he looked desperately at her as she sat on the bed, busying herself with papers and books that were spread all about her.

Finally, picking up his coat, he said gloomily, "I'll take a shower and come back."

If, at the beginning of their relationship, he feared doing her some harm through his bold advances, Pierre was quick to discover that the Germaine Léonard he met by night was not at all the same person he knew by day. Then, for a few fleeting hours, they would shed their rivalry and their rancour to lie with one another in the accord of sensual passion, no longer divided and argumentative but serenely united in their mutual bliss; and even if, at times, Germaine Léonard feebly erected a final principle in some remote part of her mind ("There are thresholds which must not be crossed"), she floated, as in a dream, over this obstacle which she had erected in her conscience, and as tyrannical as she could be in the daytime, she found herself suddenly with no control whatever over the flowing streams of her passion (prompting acts which she would normally have classified as "permitted" or "forbidden"), which ran their smooth course now, far from her designing mind, as freely as the waters of a stream. Their relationship seemed so perfect then that it even caused her at times a little fear: if night could so completely close the gap, the gulf of misunderstanding which separated them during the daytime, would either of them ever find the courage to terminate the relationship? She wanted to wipe the love she felt for Pierre Olivier from her heart, but she knew that her attraction for him was much too strong for that, and that beneath the aura of disapproval and bruised indifference which she exhibited in her daily relationships with him, her passion was steadily growing. Even when she said to herself, lashing herself for all those pleasures which she come now to anticipate. "Of course, he's kind, and he makes love well, but he only wants to dominate me" (the conflicting attitudes of ironic gratification and cruel debasement of which she silently accused him), such pitiful defences provided her with very little protection against such a deep-rooted and ineradicable attachment. When she shifted suddenly and inexplicably from tenderness to cruelty, saying in a cutting tone, "You must leave now, Pierre, I have to be up at six in the morning . . ." he did not dare to approach that proud back which moved slowly about in the shadows and said simply to her in a distant voice, disguising those true emotions which he felt for her at the moment and which she could not, or would not, grasp: "Yes, you're right, it's time for sleep."

Standing in the doorway, he silently waited for her to come and embrace him before he disappeared into the night. They stood for a long while, clinging to each other, postponing the moment of separation with promises of future encounters: "Sunday . . . Sunday," said Pierre, holding her in his arms. "We'll have the whole day to ourselves . . ." But she protested in a low voice, "It's not like us to behave in this way, no . . . we must stop seeing each other . . . the whole situation has become quite insane . . ." When, finally, she consented to spend Sunday with

Pierre at his house in the country, it was with a great deal of reticence, promising herself to put an end to the whole thing at the end of the day.

Such thoughts of separation assailed her during the entire trip, and sitting apart from him in the front seat of the car, she pulled her hat over her eyes, as if to avoid having to look at him, and when she spoke to him, it was only to remark unkindly, "What an idiotic way to drive on an icy road!"

They continued in silence toward the little green house that sat beneath the trees at the end of a long road lined with apple trees, the orchard concealing for a time the blue contours of the river, then as suddenly opening out to reveal the river again, which was no longer blue but an almost dingy brown beneath the leaden sky. When Pierre opened the door to the cottage, pushing Germaine gently into the icy room, saying, "There is wood in the basement . . . wait here, you'll be warm in no time," she was suddenly afflicted with remorse and regrets, and rubbing her hands together to remove the cold, she thought, "It's not reasonable, my God, no!" But with the first flames that rose in the chimney, a sort of self-indulgence took hold of her, warming her, and though she said severely to Pierre, "What a mistake this is, what madness, my dear!" she did not shake off the hand which rested lightly on her shoulder, the dormant sensuality which always lay between them reconciling them for those few fleeting hours in the country. While they made love before the fire, their passion all but effaced the nature of their daily relationships in the hospital, driving out with the exaltation of the senses all traces of their former selves, banishing anxiety and impatience, and allowing them to become for those few hours two individuals who saw themselves only through their caresses and their mutual happiness. In a dream which occasionally tormented her, Germaine Léonard came upon the Pierre Olivier whom she held now in her arms before the fire, but a shadow always threatened this dream of living joy: it was the silhouette of another Pierre who haunted this voluptuous landscape, a man in a white doctor's coat who accused Germaine Léonard of having lost an important document which they needed in their research, a strange individual who always seemed to exercise a mysterious control over her. Even as she emerged from this dream to find Pierre sleeping peacefully at her side, she was so baffled by the images of the dream that she found herself once again overflowing with animosity for her lover. The dream seemed to her almost prophetic when, during their afternoon stroll, confiding to Pierre her great hopes for the future, she observed how insolently he opposed all her ideas, his hair blowing in the wind, his hands thrust in his pockets, timing his words to the quick lithe movements of his feet. Walking behind him, weary and irritated, she trembled as she heard him say:

"You say, 'We're working on a cure for cancer for the benefit of future generations, for the children of tomorrow,' but what troubles me is this: will my children even survive to see that world? The thirst for destruction that hangs over our world is slowly consuming all our efforts, all our hopes, and in the end, I'm convinced of it, our love of life will be crushed!"

"You're neurotic, Pierre. It isn't healthy to be so obsessed with death."

"And what about your obsession with Utopias?"

"Well, I think that's fine, to be sufficiently concerned about mankind to contemplate the possibility of a Utopia, based upon some humanitarian and scientific ideal. One day, there will be hundreds of people like myself to bring such a Utopia to pass. The children we see dying today, we may be able to save tomorrow. Don't you ever think of that? Your pessimism is very irritating, I must say, even morbid at times . . ."

He listened to her with an outraged expression on his face. Once again, he thought bitterly, their characters were clashing, and even if Germaine occasionally displayed a little tenderness toward him, while simultaneously crushing it with her censure, he scorned this need of hers "to rehabilitate others" at the expense of her own inner stability. Beneath the veil of reason, she was reducing, even suppressing, the natural strength which he sensed within her in order to embrace all the risks which she faced in her daily existence, and what she referred to as his "mindless pessimism" was no more to him than the manifestation of "a rational fury," the course of which one could not easily divert toward the shores of wisdom or insipid sobriety. Such a lack of imagination offended him, and avoiding her gaze as she anxiously sought out his eyes, he walked along the beach, taking long strides and fixing his eyes on a patch of light which hung on the horizon at the far end of the quay.

He thought, then, of other moments in his life when he had been misunderstood, of the sterile grip of all those who, professing a desire to participate in the incubation of his natural aptitudes, were in fact only interested in smothering his audacity, his temerity, his errors; and this, to his way of thinking, only succeeded in confounding the inventiveness of an agile and curious mind.

He had always emerged from his conversations with Antoine Dugal, a man of science whom he deeply respected, angry and indignant, for this former professor of his had persisted in seeing in him nothing but a simple student, resorting to the false authority of spiritual remarks when their misunderstanding was already so profound. However, Pierre Olivier was almost moved today as he recalled the hours he has spent with Antoine Dugal: walking along the strand, he called to mind the ascetic features of that old man who had held him by the arm, almost as if he were his own son, and pleaded with him to turn his eyes toward God . . . He heard again that deep, troubled voice murmuring in his ear: "It is not possible for me to separate God from science. I served at mass for thirty years of my life, I fled all the mundane pleasures and achievements of life, finding my simple joy before God's holy altar. How could I live otherwise, tell me? Without the help of God, I would lose touch with the souls of all those mutilated bodies I treat. But the breed of spiritually-minded doctors to which I belong is gradually disappearing, my friend, and it is being replaced by people like yourself, with all your profane fervour. But, for you, what is life, what is a crippled existence awaiting deliverance? You will no longer serve the Lord . . . indeed, you have already forgotten him . . ." And when, in the naïve belief that he was rendering homage to his friend, Pierre Olivier wrote in one of his articles of "the prodigious achievements of this master of orthopaedic surgery in the field of bone structure," he was astonished to learn that Dugal preferred, as a testimonial to his medical achievements, the modest stammerings of a semi-literate nun who had worked in his shadow for so many years at the clinic, and who expressed her veneration in words like these: "He is a great doctor, a benefactor of the people, a saint who receives the sacrament every morning on his patients' behalf and whose visits to his patients are always preceded by moments of reflection before the Holy Sacrament. Operating only in the divine reflection of the holy tabernacle, this is a man who exercises his art like a sacred minister, a sort of priest . . ." Moved to tears by such tributes, Dugal repelled with a good-natured smile the gratuitous esteem which Pierre Olivier attempted to heap upon him, as if to say, "For the true Christian, there is no earthly reward."

"What is more insulting to science," thought Pierre Olivier as he walked along the beach, "than the humility of a great man who renounces all earthly honours to satisfy an invisible Master? I'll never understand him. He may have risen above professional vanity, but to what avail, when he has simply replaced it with another, worse sort of vanity, the vanity of self-sacrifice, the pride of the martyr?" He was convinced that "the puerile spirituality" of his friend hid from him the other, more engaging, more passionate side of the man's character, and thinking of Germaine, with whom he earnestly engaged in lively discussions about the heroes in the novels they had read (so vivacious, both of them, their quick imaginations transporting them far from the incurable patients they could no longer help, far from the methodical concentration of their work in the laboratory, sometimes passing an entire Sunday reading in bed, the divergence of their opinions setting them occasionally at odds when Germaine Léonard claimed that what she was seeking in literature was "strength and natural order"), thinking of those hours they had spent reading together beneath the warm sheets, Pierre would have liked to hear Germaine speak to him of Antoine Dugal as if he were a character in a book. But coming back to himself suddenly and turning to her, he was astonished to observe that she was already far from him, moving in the opposite direction. She looked so frail and awkward as she shuffled along the sand, her head bent beneath the weight of her unhappy thoughts, that he forgot for a moment why he had been so stung by her earlier words and ran toward her, leaping child-like over the sand. The sky had cleared now, and the air was milder than it had been earlier in the day, and he thought elatedly, "I must tell her that she was right about Chekhov." But rebuffed by the morose gaze which she levelled upon him when he rushed up to her, he said nothing.

Though she subdued the initial sense of excitement she had felt when she saw him running toward her (feeling dizzy at the contact of his rough cheek against her forehead, his strong arm encircling her waist), a proud irritation brought Germaine Léonard to a dead halt there on the beach, and she thought, articulating every syllable of her words with quick little movements of her head: "Once again, he has bungled everything with his appetite for destruction! How tiresome he is!" Other more comforting thoughts conflicted with these censorious remarks in her head, however, and Pierre observed imperceptibly the transformation of her face as she thought: "He is not even sensitive to the beauty of carnal love, to the tender submission to the loved one, to the reconciliation of oneself with the universe, to the acquisition of a certain worldly grace . . . he does not seem to realize that such things even exist in this world . . . but they do, they do . . ."

Finally she said in an authoritative tone, "It is sometimes our duty to be happy."

"I want to be happy, very happy, but don't ever speak to me of duty."

He drew her into his arms, then, and for several moments their reconciliation enveloped them in a deep sense of bliss.

They returned to the city in almost jovial spirits. Eased of remorse, Germaine Léonard thought of their responsibilities, their mutual dedication to the work which, she believed, raised them above "the tumult of the senses," and no longer apprehensive about yielding to her desires, she lay a hand from time to time on Pierre's knee as he drove the car steadily through the night. "Oh, if only we could always be like this," she thought, "in the warm glow of a peaceful harmony!" But when Pierre provoked her suddenly by launching into a medical explanation of the epilepsy of Prince Mychkine, that character from literature whom she prided herself on understanding so well but whom, he added with an ironic smile, she would have systematically rejected in life, she immediately resorted to her earlier bitter attitude (though in her sensual distraction she forgot her hand resting on his knee) and replied angrily:

"The illness of the Idiot was primarily an allegorical malady. The poor man was consumed with pity, and like Christ, he came into this world to bear witness to an impossible love and charity. There was something disquieting about his pity, to be sure, but I'm convinced that Dostoevski saw his characters only through a strong and critical eye. I doubt that he ever wallowed in their misfortunes. And nothing is more beautiful than the noble, detached examination of a conscientious writer. Why do you laugh? I'm serious. You can't tell me that the Idiot resembles these deranged young people we see all about us today, these spineless creatures with their empty hearts, these dishevelled wrecks . . ."

"I laugh because the doctor in you seems to be seeking, even in literature, a magical cure for the diseases of the soul. You dissect these passionate emotions and violent instincts as if they were corpses."

"Oh, hold your tongue please!"

"If the prince were suddenly to appear before you, looking just as he did on the train following his long illness and his exile in Switzerland, you would be repelled by him, for you don't approve of vulnerability and there is no doubt that he was very vulnerable on that day. If he were to fix you with his strange glassy eyes, you would recognize at once the grave illness from which he was suffering, and like the cold, dispassionate observer you are, you would find yourself thinking: 'What a hopelessly deranged man!'"

"That's not true!"

"Look at him, rushing up the staircase of that old house. Somewhere above him, Rogojine awaits him in the shadows. Suddenly, he sees those eyes gazing silently down upon him, but a strange sensation of recklessness propels him on, straight in the direction of his assassin. It is that hour at which he normally experiences the exquisite rending of the soul which makes him so happy, but the critical moment approaches, and in an instant of painful semi-consciousness, he hears the wild animal cry that escapes his lips, terrifying his assassin, who crouches in the shadows above him. Tell me, seeing that twisted body and those convulsive features, can you deny the force, the irrational violence which must have seized the writer when he probed the mind of that man? Could Christ himself have been as compassionate as that sickly angel who, in an inexplicable moment of tenderness, wept on the shoulder of Rogojine, caressing his hair and his cheeks? And you say that Dostoevski 'never wallowed in the misfortunes of his characters.' Well, it seems to me that he saw himself at once as Rogojine at the moment of his crime and as the stupefied prince who felt such an intense pity for him."

Germaine Léonard suddenly felt very dejected. In his intuitive flight into regions into which she could not follow, Pierre had left her shuffling alone in the fog behind him, and reproaching herself once again for her heavy sluggish spirit, she resented his eloquence, as if it were a personal affront, taking offence at the poetic vigour which he dispersed so selfishly in their discussions, while she herself became more and more stolid, less and less lyrical. Once again, she left him in a state of jealous exasperation, and even as he caressed her cheek, saying, "I'll see you tomorrow, my dear . . ." she knew that he had already left her, that he was once again back in the security of his own private world. To restrain the tears which she felt rising to her eyes, she thought bitterly, "I must finish my article tonight, I've already wasted too much time . . ." and without so much as a glance in her lover's direction, she fled into the night.

When we returned to the city, the sun was already setting. We walked toward the station, gazing over our shoulders at the string of empty cars that sat on the smoking rails. It was hard to think of returning home when so many routes, lying pink and purple in the twilight, invited us to depart, routes which others would follow in their own stead: a crowd of passengers was impatiently stamping its feet on the farther side of the track . . .

Elisa Moutonnet left us, murmuring wearily, "Good night girls, I'll see you tomorrow at the exam. And don't worry, I'll pass you the answers," still clinging negligently to the arm of François Lepique. In the grip of a nostalgic resignation, we watched them withdraw together, staring rudely after them until they reached the corner of the street, where, laughing, their heads tucked into their shoulders, they were swallowed up in the darkness.

"Well, we'll just have to go to the Café de la Prune alone. Walk in front of me, Marthe Dubos, you're treading on my feet."

"No mistake about it," said Marthe Dubos, "Times are changing."

"And how! You wouldn't have caught my mother in a sleeping bag with François Lepique. In her day, when they went to the mountains, it was for the mountains, not for men."

"You're right, Louisette Denis."

But in the Café, Marthe Dubos and Louisette Denis chain-smoked cigarettes in order to gain the attention of a group of boisterous male students who sat on the farther side of the room, sipping beer and ignoring us, pounding their fists animatedly on the table and exclaiming: "Jesus Christ, that's no argument to prove the existence of God!"

They seemed so strong, so intelligent, each of their gestures filling us with admiration and humility, though amongst themselves they merely mocked us: "Schoolgirls get out from under their mothers' skirts too damned fast these days, if you ask me! I'd yank the cigarettes out of their mouths and give them a good spanking, that's what I'd do!"

Finally, Louisette Denis rose with a sigh. "For the love of heaven, let's get out of here! Some people have no manners at all!"

Even though we chewed great wads of mint gum to remove the odour of tobacco from our mouths, my mother glared at me when I opened the door to the house.

"I could smell you a mile away," she said. "Smoking at your age! You're going to end up in the gutter, just like Huguette Poire!"

"I wasn't smoking."

"I have a nose. Don't lie to me."

I wanted to read alone in my room, but my mother followed me into the bedroom, an expression of concern on her face which troubled me. She seemed to want to open herself to me, inviting confidences which I was not at that moment prepared to grant. Seated on the edge of the bed, I raised my eyes to the ceiling, which seemed suddenly incredibly vast, for while my mother spoke to me, all the things in my room, the chair, the ugly dresser with its mirror, all those too familiar objects, worn and faded with time, closed in upon me as if to imprison me there and hold me in their iron grip. I tried to break the spell by lowering my eyes and bringing them to rest upon a small lighted space in the kitchen, where my sister Geneviève sat, eating her supper and playing with a glass, studying the shape of the glass between her plump fingers (I hoped that the glass would fall to the floor but it didn't), but in vain did I try to escape that room and the hard dry hand of my mother which rested lightly on mine.

"Are you listening to me, Pauline Archange?"

"Yes, yes."

"You're grown up now. Have you noticed anything unusual?"

"No, nothing."

"All the same, you're not abnormal, I hope. Do you have pains sometimes?"

"No, of course not."

"Don't hiss at me like an angry cat when I speak to you. Life is not an easy business. The nuns must tell you about these things. Do you understand what I'm talking about?"

"They told us about the stamens, they told us the whole story, I already know all that."

"There are some things you don't know."

"I know everything I need to know. You don't have to tell me anything."

"It's a mother's duty to speak to her daughter. It's all very well that the sisters tell you these things, but when you think of it, they don't have children, do they? They're women like the rest of us, it's true, but what does that mean when they don't have children? One more sacrifice for God! You don't have stomach aches, or cramps?"

"If I did, I wouldn't talk about it."

"There are things I must tell you. Stop twitching as if you had worms."

"Leave me alone."

"You're going to hear me through. It's a big mystery, it seems, in God's plan, we're inferior creatures, we came out of

Adam's side and we have to beget children in sorrow and grief, just as the Good Book says. Sometimes I wonder if it's worth it, though. But what can you do, the Good Lord was never a woman, he doesn't understand the sort of things we have to go through. He had enough to do creating the world in seven days. But when you think of it, losing your blood every month for the better part of your life, it's like a prison sentence. I suppose we deserve it because of Eve, who was disobedient in the garden. Even so, she wasn't one to think much of others. Well, I'm not going to beat about the bush, I see I'm going to have to tell you straight out what this is all about: it's all this misery known as mens-trua-tion!"

"Yes, yes."

"What do you mean, yes, yes? Do you think you're like the Blessed Virgin, that it won't happen to you one day, too? You must tell me when it starts, I'll give you some rags and you can wash them in a pail. I don't want you to leave them lying around the house where your brothers and sisters can see them. They're not old enough yet to know about the mysteries of life, do you understand? I remember when I was your age, there was a poor girl at the convent who was so afraid of the nuns she hid all her rags every month in her desk. Oh, it was a terrible thing when the sister who was on duty opened her desk and found them! How humiliating for that poor little girl when she was driven out of the room by the nun with her ruler!"

Suddenly, Jean came running into the room, and without removing his coat, broke into a breathless account of the film he had see that afternoon in the parish hall:

"Saint Narcissus should have stayed with his friends playing with flags in the street but he went down into the catacombs in his white dress like a girl and there were jealous people there who stoned him to death but it was his own fault because he didn't defend himself he just let them hit him like a frog he wasn't even brave . . ."

"Stop wriggling like that and go to the toilet. The films they show on Sunday afternoon! They're always filled with murderers and martyrs. Sometimes, I wonder who's responsible for showing you things like that."

"The crows."

"How many times have I told you not to speak of the Brothers of Christian Training like that? You repeat everything you hear, don't you?"

But stamping his foot, Jean merely repeated: "*The crows, the crows, the crows!*"

"Shameless child, get out of here! Your father will hear about this!"

My mother did not resist Jean, however, for already in her eyes he represented that obscure masculine authority before which she must obediently submit herself, as she had done long ago with my father. Even when she scolded her son, her severity was always tempered with mildness and her reproaches were gentle:

"Doctor Léonard was mistaken when she called you a dull little boy with no brains. The brother says that if you would only make a little effort, you could be the first in your class. But you're lazy, all you think about is reading books about birds. I swear I don't understand you."

But Jean was already moving toward the kitchen door. Running after him, my mother overtook him.

"You're going to do your lessons!" she said. "No more games in the street! You're not going to slip through my fingers this time!"

Standing against the wall, I saw the desolate look which she turned upon me then, a look which seemed to be filled with comprehension and concealed humour, as if she wished to say to me in my solitude:

"I didn't want to talk about you, no, for just once I wanted to talk a little about myself. But you wouldn't listen, would you?"

❧ Chapter Three ❧

*I should very much like to see you again, my
dear Pauline. Meet me on Thursday at four
o'clock in front of the church of Saint-Thomas-
des-Rois. It is there that I instruct my disciples
every week, in the manner of Plato . . .*

I crumpled Julien Laforêt's note in my hand, troubled by the
prospects of this meeting after a whole year of silence, during
which the metamorphosis which I prayed for daily had not yet
come to pass. Selling stockings with Louisette Denis at Gagnon
et Frères (behind a green counter which resembled a prison wall,
piled high with nylon stockings which we sold at fifty cents a
pair), I feared Julien's rediscovery of my shameful ignorance and
of my inability to master that shortcoming.

"Something must be done, Pauline Archange! We have to
sell four pairs every minute to make any money at all! Why
shouldn't we slip a pair or two into our pockets? After all, we
earn them with all the overtime hours we put in . . ."

"I'm afraid of the boss."

"Elisa Moutonnet 'found' a ten-dollar sweater the other day.
The boss didn't see it. He was so busy admiring her breasts, he
didn't even notice the sweater. She thinks she's a star, that one,
since she met her François Lepique!"

The moment the store closed, I hastened to meet Julien
Laforêt, who was waiting for me at the far end of the city, but
when I jumped off the bus, he scarcely noticed me. Standing on

the church steps, he was gazing intently at a group of students who stood at his feet, proclaiming louder and louder his praise of Plato:

"Is man a free animal? Yes, my friends, it is even conceivable that he is too free, as Plato says. Have you ever contemplated this statement by the famous philosopher: 'Only he is free who has established a divine order within himself?'"

His disciples did not reply, but merely dispersed quietly into the night, carrying beneath their arms their copies of the theological text, *The Beauty of Catholic Dogma.*

Turning to a frail-looking student who walked at his side, Julien Laforêt said gravely, "You see, Chevreux, philosophers, like poets, are misunderstood. Of course, poets, in their celebrated love of freedom often exaggerate their cause, even Baudelaire, whom you admire so greatly, yes, even he went too far in his blasphemous attempts to enhance evil and to redeem the sinner. And I'm not sure that I approve of that."

"You're wrong, Laforêt," said André Chevreux timidly but resolutely, raising his strange, almost ugly face toward Julian, who was taller than he, his expression suggesting a certain intelligence and goodwill. "You're wrong, there is no blasphemy in the work of Baudelaire, a certain pride perhaps, but a pride that is the result of suffering . . ."

"Oh, you unhappy Christians!" exclaimed Julien Laforêt, shaking his finger at his friend. "You're always so sensitive to suffering, you men of God!"

When André Chevreux caught sight of me waiting for Julien on the farther side of the street, he disappeared quickly in the direction of a group of students who stood a little farther off.

"What a wild animal!" said Julien Laforêt, shaking my hand, the tone of his voice still reproachful. "Can you imagine a timid Napoleon, Pauline, or a frightened Hercules? No, of course you can't for timidity is the shortcoming of little men, whereas arrogance is the strength of giants." He paused for a moment, then went on in the same fervent tone: "Chevreux exasperates me, he has always been my friend, but there is nothing more boring than a person without faults. It's an anomaly, even in a Christian. Come, Pauline, it's a lovely evening, let's go to the *Terrasse des Braves*. Aristotle tells us that 'perfect friendship is rooted in goodness, a bond which exists between two individuals who resemble each other in their respective virtues. Only this friendship endures,' he says. Alas, as far as virtue goes, I could never resemble Chevreux. I am a gourmand, while he fasts every Friday. I am miserly with my possessions, while he possesses nothing and is prepared to give even his shoes to the first person who is in need of them. I am proud, as vain as a bishop, while he is so humble that he won't even tell me where he lives. The only thing I know about him is that he thinks of nothing but the injustice which exists in the world . . . Yes, my dear Pauline, what is friendship without understanding?" He looked at me coldly, allowing his gaze to pass slowly over me, and then added, "I see that you haven't changed, you're still as poorly dressed as ever, you're still earning your own living, I see, and you still chew gum." When Romaine Petit-Page sees you tonight at the airport, she may well exclaim:

> *"My dear Pauline, O my*
> *poor sweet soul,*
> *My dove, you are not*
> *yet dead then?"*

"Yes, she's returning! Still dripping juice and honey, and no longer alone, no, they have a daughter now. 'A child as soft and lovely as a cloud,' as she told me in one of her letters. Another picture for their album! It's fashionable these days for people to produce children in their own image, but let's not fall into that trap, Pauline, we might succeed only in bringing into the world creatures inferior to ourselves. And that would be very humiliating, indeed! Oh, if only Aristotle had seen fit to people the earth with his own superb sons, we would be so much less miserable today!"

Romaine Petit-Page greeted us with joy which seemed quite sincere for all its overt affectation: crushed against each other in her arms, assailed with noisy kisses, Julien Laforêt and I did not dare to move. But if she embraced us so indulgently, it was not to bring us any closer to each other, but only to bind us more tightly to "her sublime poet's heart." In a sudden rush of envy, she separated us and exclaimed:

"My poor little Julien, I'm afraid you've not always been faithful to me! You wrote to me so seldom while I was in Paris! Oh, my dear lion, you haven't changed! And you, my little Pauline, you look a little pale, you're working too hard in that store. But I'm back, and I'll never leave you again, my dear friends, you need my protection, you need a mother's guiding hand, my dear orphans! Here, Louis is coming with the baggage. See how slim and handsome he is, still so young, with his long flowing hair! His book is going to be published in Paris, you know. Isn't that right, my love? My God, the baby, our darling child, where is she, I've lost her . . ."

"She's here," said her husband impatiently, appearing before us as graceful and lethargic as ever. "She's right here, behind the suitcases."

"My poor love, I'm not helping you, I know, but it's not good for my figure. But how charming you look beneath the weight of all those suitcases! He resembles Sisyphus, don't you think, Julien? Oh, you haven't met our little girl!" She took the child in her arms and pressed her warmly to her breast. "She's adorable, don't you think? A little flushed, but that's because of the measles, she suffered so, the poor little fairy! Say hello to our friends, Julien and Pauline, say hello, my angel . . ."

"What's her name?" asked Julien. "She must have a name, like everyone else."

"Yvonne," said Romaine Petit-Page, a little abashed. "Yvonne de Galais."

The child looked at us sharply with her small, quick eyes that resembled the eyes of a nun.

"She has a very disagreeable expression," said Julien in an undertone, but Romaine Petit-Page did not hear him, so engrossed was she in her display of maternal affection.

"Yes," she said, "Yvonne de Galais, as in *Le Grand Meaulnes*, the book which gave us such comfort and pleasure in our youth, and which still does today, isn't that right, Louis? Yvonne de Galais, her château, her visions, the paradisal world of our lingering illusions! What a blessing it is to be the mother of such a lovely, gifted child! What daily enchantment I find in her presence! Smile, my angel, come, show us your starry smile . . ."

"*Ma-man! Ma-man!*" cried Yvonne de Galais, weeping on her mother's shoulder. "*Waaah, Ma-man!*"

"She speaks already! And sings like a bird!" Turning to her husband, she added in an authoritative tone, "Come and take her, my love. You can see she's tired."

"I can't. The suitcases . . ,"

"Do as I say, my love. Do you hear me?"

Bent beneath the weight of the suitcases, his daughter clinging to his neck, Louis seemed to sense that he had lost forever "the silken raiment" of Grand Meaulnes for the iron fetters of marriage, and that even if he continued to play the seductive role which Romaine Petit-Page exacted of him, the cloak of fantasy hung more and more heavily upon his shoulders, like armour. How far he seemed to have retreated from that world when, in love with Romaine Petit-Page and at peace with himself, he had written to Julien:

Romaine and I live in the miraculous glow of a golden summer, and we cherish our happiness as if it were a buried treasure, enriched as we are with such a wealth of hope and expectation . . . Let us always keep our eyes open to the beautiful things in life . . . I am writing this letter on a lovely summer afternoon, while Romaine dozes at my side, the pages of her manuscript lying on her breast, like the poet who writes even in her sleep. Contemplating her, I sense that the happy moments in life are as secret and surprising as snowdrops. What a quiet, flower-strewn road we travel down . . . You'll understand one day, my dear Julien, that it is only in suffering that one finds these oases in the desert of life, you'll understand that all that is needed is a sudden stirring of the soul to make it possible for one to pin the star of courage to the map of the old enchanted night, yes, the soul with its limitless dimensions, where the gods who await one speak a strange language through which they teach one the secret of piercing the mirror of the infinite . . .

"The mirror of the infinite," thought Julien. "But how he exaggerates!"

Forgive me, Julien, I don't know what I'm saying, but perhaps you can sense beneath the elaborate garment of my words the true meaning of my thought. My poor letter is swimming in words because, for several days now, I have felt rather poorly. I

*know that my novel is not good enough for publication, and I
have returned to my sorrow as to a rosary, in the hope that it
might restore a certain vitality to my soul . . . The presence of
Romaine troubles me, moreover, and I have become very nervous. It's ghastly, even criminal, to be the enemy of a universe
which one has created oneself . . . Yes, what a sad day, my heart
bends itself toward the three children I see in the garden below
me, gathering chestnuts in the autumn sunlight. I seek happiness by turning into myself, moving as it were through a swamp
. . . but my soul still exudes the odour of a small, sweet orange
. . . I can even taste it . . . I leave you now in this blue garden,
my friend . . .*

But now, taking his handkerchief from his pocket and wiping the tears from his daughter's face, Louis seemed to be thinking: "Oh, Yvonne, the days of first love are over, and when you
cry at night, who comes to console you? It is I, always I! And in
the morning, when I wash you, your mother lies in bed writing
until noon . . . She is writing the story of our love, a novel full
of sweetness and light . . ."

"*Pa-pa! Pa-pa!*"

"Oh, be still!"

"You must speak to her gently, my dear," said Romaine,
"she's such a sensitive and precocious child! You're irresistible,
Louis, even when you're angry. You look so much like Augustin,
holding his daughter wrapped in his coat, as he carried her
toward new adventures. Oh, my darling adventurer!" she cried,
caressing her husband's arm. "How sweet it is always to be in
love!"

But Louis turned his head away without replying, his heart
heavy with dreams and adventures that he would never know,
for the tepidity of his love for Romaine was slowly corrupting

him, and almost in spite of himself, he found himself moving in a dull, ethereal stupor . . .

"We learned the art of mime in Paris," said Romaine to Julien, "and one of these evenings we must perform for you, my dear forsaken children. But what is wrong, Julien? Why are you suddenly so sullen? I can see very well that you have retained your purity. You're at the awkward age, I know, it isn't easy. But am I not in a sense your elder sister? You're just a little boy in the difficult process of growing up, you must confide in me. And you, too, Pauline. Yes, Julien, you used to speak to me so brilliantly of Corneille, Sophocles, Racine, Socrates . . . and now you've become so morose. Is this the influence of your friend, André Chevreux, the intellectual? There was a time when I welcomed your opinions, when I was moved by the growing depth of your thought . . . As for you, my dear Pauline, you have become so rebellious that you have lost me. So much anarchy is alarming. You have lost your faith, you say. But how can you say such a thing at such a tender age? Why did you say in your letters that it was impossible for me to understand you and Julien, when I love you both with an unremitting fervour that is born of my deep concern for the temporal, the inaccessible, the incomprehensible . . ."

Several days later, we witnessed the performance which Romaine ·Petit-Page had promised us. Their bodies ensconced in black tights, Romaine and Louis strode triumphantly about the improvised stage, dragging behind them a cloud of moths, danced by the ballerinas Clémence, Gyslaine and Gabrielle Laforêt in their white tutus. The graceful insects soon tired, however, of whirling about Romaine Petit-Page and fluttered toward Julien, who drew them like a flame, and who, irritated by the mocking caresses of his sisters, drove them off with a loud cry: "They're nothing but little cats, they're always trying to touch me . . ." They hopped out of his reach, then impudently returned in his direction, skipping and laughing about him in an almost demented fashion.

"Louis!" exclaimed Romaine Petit-Page suddenly, allowing her lovely velvet eyes to pass slowly over her husband's body. "Oh . . . Louis, how could you have the nerve to dance like that, without your athletic support?"

"What athletic support?" asked Louis, his pride momentarily stung. "What's the purpose of a dance if it isn't to reveal the perfection of the human form, the shapeliness of the body?"

"Oh my darling, but you must be mad! A young man does not dance *à l'état pur,* so to speak, no, not in loose tights that reveal the sort of thing that one doesn't necessarily want to see at all hours of the day. Quick, your athletic support!" she declared, exasperated.

"No athletic support! No athletic support!" cried Julien's sisters.

"My sisters are right," said Julien Laforêt gravely. "After all, we're amongst men here."

"And what about me?" asked Romaine. "Am I not a woman? And poor little Pauline? I must say, Julien, you shock me!" And in a burst of hysterical sobs, she threw herself into Louis' arms, a terrible cry of desire and triumph escaping her lips: "Oh, my darling, don't you understand that your sex is a sacred thing to me, that your entire body is like the host which I gently place on my tongue?"

Louis replied to this appeal with a feeble grimace that Romaine interpreted as a smile, so bewildered was she at that moment by her passion.

Reconciled, they completed their performance in a series of syncopated leaps and swoops, a manifestation of the affection they felt for each other, "that love made exceptional by its purity," as Romaine Petit-Page described it. And doubtless she truly believed that, through the precious liturgy of her movements and words, she was giving expression to the spiritual side of her marital life; whereas, in fact, her exaggeration of even the simplest gestures merely accentuated their voluptuousness and impiety. Her performance greatly pleased Louis, who was bored with trying to seduce a woman so inordinately infatuated with virtue, ceaselessly masking her desires with subtle and provocative pieties, for he found momentarily in her impersonations those very qualities which he had occasionally loved in other women, the charming prostitutes with whom he had betrayed his fiancée in Paris (no longer able to await a reward so often promised and as often withdrawn by the Catholic Romaine). Never having yielded to the erotic fantasies in which her husband swam, Romaine Petit-Page now unwittingly gave way to her capricious imagination, and performing acts which she ostensibly attributed to the sincerity of her artistic performance, totally abandoned herself to those very things which she would normally have referred to disdainfully as "the fury of the instincts, the indulgence of the senses!" Little by little, they progressed from an imitation of birds and their mating ceremonies to the sly contortions of two serpents confronting each other, and their faces touching, their arms and legs coiled inextricably together, they stood finally, gazing deeply into each other's eyes, gasping faintly.

"Bravo! Bravo!" cried Julien Laforêt, taking a deep breath. "A very impressive show! And not the shadow of a scruple!" Then grabbing one of his sisters by the hair, he said, "You girls should be home in bed."

"Julien!" exclaimed Romaine Petit-Page, still a little faint from her performance. "You seem not to have understood that our 'show', as you call it, was a marriage in pantomime of two souls, as in Lamartine. What sort of thoughts are going through that head of yours, my angel? Oh, my child, I no longer recognize you. Not only have you become anti-clerical during my absence, but you and Pauline seem to have become secret accomplices, constantly whispering to each other behind my back. And you used to be so kind, so gentle! Yes, I recall, Julien, when you were twelve years old, I used to sing you to sleep in the evening, and you told me things that were so deliciously fresh . . . I didn't think I'd ever escape the spell which fell over me when you uttered that superb phrase of *Tacitus: Non solum . . . sed etiam . . .* And now, how cruelly you slam that precious door in my face! Is it because time has begun to harden your eyes, your hands, your heart? And yet, how often I dreamed of you in Paris, beseeching God in all his fullness to protect you! For what is friendship but that?"

But with me, she adopted a much harsher tone:

"Is it you who have done this to him, Pauline? Are you trying to take my little Julien away from me?"

"Pauline's feelings for me are purely platonic," said Julien Laforêt before I could reply. "'Friendship,' says Aristotle, 'is the innate sentiment in the heart of the creator for his creation and in the heart of the creation for its creator.' It is in this sense that I wish to make Pauline my student, the creation of my spirit."

"And where do I fit into all this? Am I not the solitary sister and friend of your youth? Have you forgotten the day I left you on the train and I couldn't stop crying? Yes, I held you closely, you looked so pale behind the bouquet of red carnations you had brought me! And your sisters, too, with their tight little pigtails, yes, they were crying too, the dear children! Was that then the end of the cycle of our friendship, since you think now only of betraying me? The poet must forgive, I know, but the scars of the whip are long to heal!" In a rush of confidence, she took Julien's hand, brushing it lightly with her fingertips. "I know that our summer will never end, that you will always be my dear friend, my dear little boy. Tell me that nothing will destroy the pure, loving fraternity which exists between us."

"No, nothing, no one," said Julien Laforêt, shrugging his shoulders, and unaware of the irony in his reply, Romaine Petit-Page immediately recovered her playful spirits. Proud of the forgiveness which she had just bestowed upon us, she enveloped us in her long supple arms, exclaiming: "My darlings, don't leave us again, we shall be so happy together!" But her cry of joy was followed by a long uncomfortable silence . . .

On Mondays, which were examination days, Mother Sainte-Alfréda would seize our papers "on the wing." Disliking the exams every bit as much as we did, she avoided boredom by sitting at her desk, staring at a little black watch which lay on the desk before her and reaching out automatically to snatch our papers from our hands.

After the exam, Elisa Moutonnet and Marthe Dubos could usually be seen lounging about the corridors, eating oranges, or sitting near the window, watching the boys pass to and fro in the seminary yard below. But on this particular day, Louisette Denis sat huddled in a chair in the corner of the room, sobbing loudly, and Elisa and Marthe were so irritated by the sounds of her weeping that, finally, Marthe gave in and asked her what was wrong.

"Why are you sitting there all by yourself, bawling like a calf?"

Louisette refused to reply.

"You failed the geometry test!"

"No."

"Then it can only be one thing," declared Elisa Moutonnet. "You're pregnant."

"No. But I've lost my reputation anyway," said Louisette Denis, weeping. "The boss caught me! It's the end! I'm a thief!"

"You didn't steal anything, it was only a misunderstanding."

"Open my book bag, Elisa Moutonnet, and tell me I didn't steal anything."

Elisa opened Louisette's bag and removed several pieces of clothing, which she held up to the light and examined with delight.

"Oh, how pretty! Leather gloves! And a woollen skirt! But listen to me, Louisette, you didn't steal them, you bought them on credit. I'll speak to the boss myself, don't worry. Come, girls, we're going to straighten this thing out . . . you have to know how to deal with men!"

"I'm not a real thief," thought Louisette Denis, struck by the injustice of the accusation which had been levelled against her. If she had "stolen" some things from Eloi Gagnon et Frères, it was out of "necessity," not dishonesty, for she knew that otherwise she would never be able to afford those clothes which she needed so badly; and because she was confronted daily with objects which she deeply coveted, she was no longer able to separate in her mind her dreams of possession and the dangerous implications of the realization of those dreams. To acquire the things she desired, she assumed the gestures and the attitudes of the sleepwalker, clearing an inculpable path for herself in the night; but when the hand of Eloi Gagnon came down upon her shoulder, the dream suddenly became a nightmare, one from which she could not so easily escape, for the burglary committed in reality did not carry with it the merciful absolution of her dreams, and the accuser who tore aside the terrible curtain, crying, "Thief! Thief!" was no longer a phantom from another world but a creature of reality, a reality whose terrible laws Louisette was to painfully discover as she emerged from her sleep. What was the point of repeating, "I'm not a thief, it's not true!" when a more powerful voice, that of Eloi Gagnon, crushed her pitiful resistance, the voice of authority permanently tainting the image which Louisette held of herself and of her own inner integrity? Moreover, she thought, think of all the people who stole and killed every day, disguising their illicit behaviour beneath the comfortable mask of dreams and customs! It was easy enough to admit your guilt when the monster in your dream seized you by the throat and cried, "See what you've done, you've killed a man, you've robbed your brother!" But in real life, those who wielded such power, like Eloi Gagnon, both justice and judge before his employees, were often the greater criminals, for they were able to realize their most pernicious dreams in the most unscrupulous ways, and unlike Louisette Denis, they never had to confront the judgment of reality and its stark terrors.

Even when we pleaded with our employer in his office to excuse Louisette Denis' error, Eloi Gagnon did not for one moment renounce this terrible power which he wielded over us. Though it was only through the efforts of individuals like ourselves that he had been able to accumulate his great fortune, "paying unjust salaries, exploiting little salesgirls," as Elisa Moutonnet said, trying to soften him a little, the indignation in her voice not devoid of a certain vanity, a seductive provocation to which her bozos remained completely unmoved, no appeal would touch this master swindler who had long ago quit "the bottom of the ladder," as he put it adding pompously:

"Look at me. I began as a clerk at five dollars a week, and see where I am now!"

It seemed that those early years of Eloi Gagnon's life, that impoverished existence in which twenty years later we too found ourselves trapped, was no more to him now than a vague and distant memory, and I thought that, for this reason, the injustice which he represented would continue for a long while yet in the world.

"I'm a good Catholic, I'm not going to call the police, but I don't want your friend Louisette Denis to set her thieving feet in my store again. I will have only honest people about me!"

"All right, if that's how you want it!" declared Elisa Moutonnet, moving toward the door, swinging her hips. "Come on, girls, we've had enough of working for men with less heart than a stone! We prefer to be unemployed . . ."

During our afternoon poetry class, Louisette Denis began to sniffle again, but more quietly this time, keeping her grief to herself. What hurt her more than the fear of punishment was the shame that had been inflicted upon her that morning, and she thought that if the world was made up of "executioners" and "victims," she ought perhaps to feel as much compassion for the one as for the other, for at the same time that she had been deeply humiliated by her experience, she had also understood how vain it was to condemn men for their obscure treachery and their lack of forbearance, because, after all, was it in their power to change? And wasn't she herself one of that group over whom the winds of fate and circumstance blew their thin dust?

But this thought was so painful that she found herself once again brushing the tears from her eyes. She looked up at Mother Sainte-Alfrèda, and forgetting for the moment the nun whose black habit she had always abhorred, she seemed to understand for the first time that this woman was probably also deserving of pity, for she too seemed to suffer great humiliation at the experience of reciting poems to students who only mocked her and laughed at her behind her back. Through her passionate readings, Mother Sainte-Alfrèda was simply attempting to shake off her heavy chains – just as we were attempting to rid ourselves of our own – though we persisted in looking upon her as a woman who gave herself up to emotions which she had no right to experience:

> *Gay, I am gay! Inexpressible May evening!*
> *Ridiculously gay, can it be that I've –*
> *Not drunk either – that I'm happy to be alive?*
> *Has it at last been healed, my old wound of living?*
>
> *The bells cease, and the evening scents follow after*
> *As the breeze takes them, and the wine rustles and throbs.*
> *I am more than gay, hear my resonant laughter!*
> *So gay, so gay! I am breaking into sobs.*

We looked upon these verses as a miser looks upon his hoarded wealth, for to us they were nothing less than a celebration of youth and beauty; though Mother Sainte-Alfrèda continued to claim them austerely for herself, twisting the folds of her mourning skirt into a gesture of revolt, revealing the despair of her vanquished flesh and her parched soul! The passionate cry which escaped her lips caused her breast to heave, while the students laughed. In vain did she try to reach us, for if she found no consolation amongst her inferior colleagues who spent their days embroidering or praying to God, the intellectual appreciation and esteem which she sought from us were equally rare in forthcoming, and when she saw all those indolent bodies lounging in their desks before her, all those faces with their mischievous eyes constantly spying upon her, she lowered her head and stared at her watch, or worse, began to count all those feet which she so passionately abhorred, those innumerable feet which reminded her "of the feet of tomorrow's students, of all the feet of the future," the dark fatality of her vision filling her with a deep and ineffable sadness. There remained to her, she was convinced, nothing but the vicarious stimulation of the emotions of others, and contemplating the voracious madness in the poetry of Nelligan, she compared her exile in the convent with the isolation of the poet in the asylum. She devoted her spare hours to the editing of a Greek grammar for her students, but in vain, for we had no interest in Greek. As for her remarkable gifts in the field of mathematics, she was given very little opportunity to exercise these either, for our talents in these subjects were all but negligible. She concluded that we were incapable of appreciating beauty and that we deserved "the bland teachings of the bad Catholic authors" whom the other teachers imposed on their students in the neighbouring classrooms. It was always with disgust that she listened to those nasal voices reciting stanzas from *Our Best Authors* to their students:

> *I am my only love. I am great. I am fine.*
> *A more perfect creature would be proof of divinity.*
> *Being one of the chosen I am marked by a sign.*
> *Shining at night in the sky's blue infinity.*

> *But such vanities fade: all expires, all passes,*
> *The star in its brightness, the world in its strength;*
> *And man, who fills space with his clamour and clashes,*
> *Will measure his greatness in a casket's length.*

She was constrained too, by an excessive religious zeal, as revealed in the following discourse, in which she denied any trace of racism:

"The language is the guardian of the faith. Fundamentally cerebral, created for the thinking man, our noble language is capable of communicating the deepest sentiments of the human heart, though to realize its full potential the speaker must subjugate all rushes of passion to the control of reason illuminated by faith. Espoused for centuries by the greatest geniuses of our race, speaking in the service of the Catholic faith, Catholic morality, Catholic order. Catholic tradition; adopted by the governments of the world as the language of international diplomacy; embraced by the superior minds of all races and creeds as the ideal channel of communication between peoples of different nations who wish to reach some sort of understanding in the highest spheres of human thought . . . it has become the single living Catholic language, which is to say universal, in every sense of the word. Moreover, it has produced, and continues to produce, the greatest number of works which extol the truth of Catholic dogma, the necessity of Catholic order, the superiority of Catholic morality, inspiring all men to admire Catholic enterprises and traditions and to love God and the Church."

Even when Mother Sainte-Alfrèda spoke to the Superior of her disapproval of mediocre Catholic writers, she met with no more than a stubborn indifference, for the Mother Superior read nothing but prayer books and the lives of the saints and spurned all such discussions with a quick flip of her long black sleeve. To fully understand Mother Sainte-Alfrèda, we would have had to admit that she was no more selfish in her own stilted way than we were in ours, but our own selfishness was such a blind and ferocious thing that it was impossible for us at that point even to recognize the sufferings of others. Each strange will which attempted to impose itself upon us became for us just one more obstacle to overcome, just one more garden to plunder, and on that day when she had been so cruelly accused of theft, Louisette Denis was perhaps the only one of us to understand that this mysterious woman whom she observed and studied was not quite as bad as she seemed to be, that those people who exercised their authority over us were not all bad weeds to be trampled underfoot in our rebellious efforts to reach those sunny spaces we so passionately dreamed of, that some of them were creatures she could occasionally compare with herself, at least during those moments when she had suffered an injustice, as had been the case that day, contemplating her lost job and the anticipated confrontation with her father that evening. But even if Marthe Dubos and I shared her uneasiness, we could not comprehend her sympathy for Mother Sainte-Alfrèda, for we continued to see in our teacher nothing but a woman who enjoyed the privilege of "free room and board" and whose parents did not demand from her a payment for rent already two weeks overdue, and thus we were filled with jealousy and bitterness . . .

I already knew what my father would say to me that evening; "In September, you're leaving school, is that understood?" And although he had uttered those very words on numerous occasions in the past, it seemed to me on that day that my fate was finally sealed.

"Yes, you'll have to get moving and find yourself something to do. Otherwise, I'm taking away your typewriter. Your mother and I have worn ourselves out to give you an education, so you could get a job as a clerk in an office or a cashier in a bank, and what do you do? You spend your time daydreaming and dragging yourself around the house like a prisoner in chains. Well, let me tell you, if your rent is not paid in three days, your typewriter is going . . ."

I forgot my friends, then, and thought of nothing but that typewriter: it was an old, grey, metal machine, ugly and battered, but I loved it as if it were a person. As dilapidated as it was, that instrument was a perpetual source of inspiration to me: in its company, I never felt alone, and the moment I touched its shaky keys, my thoughts became mysteriously clear. Nothing in the world seemed more precious to me than that strong, yet strangely fragile, companion – strong, for I often awoke at night, dreaming that it could actually write in my place, such a degree of clairvoyance and precision did it seem to possess in its iron brain; fragile, for my parents never ceased talking of separating us. And when I left in the morning for the convent, I thought I ought at least to have hidden it under the bed, for I spent the entire day in the paralyzing fear that it would no longer be there when I returned home that night. All these fears were driven out, however, by the sublime peace which settled over me the moment I closed the door of my room and sat down before the machine, facing the window. The cries of Jean and Geneviève who were "bowling" on the freshly waxed floor, and the voice of my mother who was calling me to come and wash the dishes, no longer penetrated the quiet world of my meditation; and even if I did nothing but type out long rows of words, without at all comprehending their significance, forsaking all form as I arranged them on the page for my own pleasure, each word glittered beneath my eyes like a blazing comet and my intoxication was complete.

On Sunday after mass, I carried the radio into my room though my mother, who continued to accuse me of walking the streets like Huguette Poire, said in the same irritated tone, "You spend too much time in the house, it's not natural for a girl of your age to be cooped up all the time, you should get out more, get some fresh air. And besides, it isn't normal music you listen to in there, it sounds more like a funeral march! *Boom!* . . . *boom!* . . . *boom!* . . . What on earth is the orchestra doing, burying hordes of dead people?"

"It's Mozart."

"You can Mozart all you want, Pauline Archange, but let me tell you, your father is becoming very discouraged with your idleness, he's had just about all he can take of your typewriter and your operas on the radio!"

In their awkward resonance, the words I wrote were no more than an anthology of meaningless sounds, but the music of Mozart seemed to throw a certain light and texture upon my discordant composition, and it was sweet no longer to be the victim of my stammering outbursts, to be able to transcend them momentarily and to enter a world from which ignorance had been suddenly and inexplicable banished. I had not written a single note of the symphony that was playing on the radio, but the music momentarily lent me a power that was not my own, carrying me into a world of sublime enchantment – which was dashed to pieces, alas, each time the announcer broke in with his rude announcements:

"Olive Blue, ladies and gentlemen, Olive Blue is the scented soap for your bath . . . Remember, Olive, Olive Blue . . . And now for Mozart at his most sublime!"

This gross interruption was suddenly effaced by the fleet incantation of a flute: like a proud, agile dancer who uses his body, not so much to dance as to sing, the notes of the music were at once crystalline and ponderous, like the voices of angel flutes. This graceful, energetic exaltation lifted me toward a summit of pride and hope, where I silently exclaimed: "Nothing is impossible! If I want something badly enough, I'll find a way to achieve it . . ." but I was brought back as abruptly to my sordid surroundings as my mother opened the door and said:

"I've called you four times, Pauline Archange. Now, take this dish towel and dry the dishes. Sometimes, I wonder who you think you are!"

Standing beside my mother (who wore her indispensable spotted apron), drying the dishes, my thoughts were already less elevated and the future seemed suddenly to hold no further promise for me. How often had I heard it said that genius was "a miracle from heaven," but it seemed to me at that moment that it was more in the nature of a malediction. Elisa Moutonnet had often remarked with a lofty air that, "It's just as easy to be Mozart if you're born Mozart as it is to be Elisa Moutonnet if you're born Elisa Moutonnet," but her words never failed to irritate me; it seemed to me that we were always too quick to respect stupidity and too slow to honour intelligence. Only Mother Sainte-Alfrèda had had the courage to scorn this inherited reverence for ignorance, though her audacity amused us. She had bought for our classroom a reproduction of a Dürer print, and though it had never serious caught my attention, the details of that magnificent *Melancholia* came rising slowly to the surface of my mind as I stood there beside my mother, drying the dishes: the sullen, unruly angel, lost in contemplation, his big fist pressed against his cheek, his hair crowned with flowers that resembled thorns. Was this not the work of a creative spirit of a truly exceptional order? When a simple-minded nun said, "Genius verges on madness," I sensed that all human intellect was expected to bow beneath the weight of her trenchant observation. It was in the face of such misunderstanding that the Spirit of Dürer seemed to me so sad, so vulnerable. Endowed with an unearthly vigour, the angel was nevertheless tied to the earth: seated on the rough ancient earth, his wings were open but he did not fly, as if he were so discontented with himself at that moment that it was more than he could bring himself to do to leave his heavy, muscular body, which was dressed in a tunic, the folds of which fluttered loosely in the wind. In him, all was violent and passionate meditation, but this was a violence that would be appeased only in labour. In his right hand, he held the tool of his mysterious trade, but his eyes were distant now, they worked no more. The objects which surrounded him were simple and modest, symbolizing the efforts and endeavours of his daily labour. An empty ladder stood near him, and beyond it, the dawn rose over the sea, though the angel was not looking in that direction. His gaze spoke of uncompromising and practical thoughts, and indeed, his appearance bore a closer resemblance to that of a solitary labourer than an angel. The place in which he meditated, moreover, was not a peaceful or a restful one; it was a humble workshop where the entire fervour of his immense genius would shortly awaken. But awaiting that moment, he brooded alone, his only companion a dog whose bones could be seen through its mangy coat and who seemed to share the anxious thoughts of its master, though it feigned sleep. At the angel's feet lay a hammer and saw. Several nails glittered in the shadows.

The evocation of this powerful angel, who was at once the symbol of strength and impotence (perhaps because he saw in the distance those very things which I myself so deplored in my misery: cupidity, the blindness of men, a horizon veiled in blood – a future in which shame inhabited all his thoughts, yes, was it not the dark side of the world toward which his gaze was turned as he sat there, the destruction of beauty and dissolution of innocence which he would soon depict in his work, though in his innermost heart he desired nothing but the happiness of men and the ability to contemplate them without hated?) – this profound evocation attacked my courage, while inflaming my faith in a superior life, which had always been mine, though only in the guise of a confession or a book. But, unlike this prodigious angel, if I possessed the will and the energy to create, I lacked the gifts to express all that I felt. During those days of waiting, I stared at my typewriter without daring to break the silence that lay between us. I loved no one else (even the memories of Jacob and Séraphine were slowly fading from my mind), but the thought of Dürer's angel filled my heart with an immense longing, for which there was as yet no outlet, and I spent long hours sitting motionless in my chair, imagining the presence of a loved one at my side (an illusion of which my mother was clearly ignorant when she said: "I know you inside out, Pauline Archange!"), someone whom I had personally chosen, though as yet I did not know who he was, a creature born of my own imagination, so real and so ready to respond to my every need that whenever I asked him to sit by my side or to place his head on my shoulder he immediately did so, though the ties which bound us were so fragile that I had to hold my breath (recalling that my mother had told me that I breathed too much through my mouth, sounding like "a train passing through hell!"). When my brother suddenly threw his football against the door, my imaginary lover fled in fear, vanishing as abruptly as he had appeared, and I thought with a rush of nostalgia, "Oh! if only it were true!" It seemed to me that he would not escape very far, however, since he was my lover. But even more astonishing than that was the fact that, henceforth, whenever I bullied Jean or my mother, as I was in the habit of doing in moments of irritation or impatience, the lover whom I had created in my imagination seemed to have transformed them in my eyes, and I began to look upon them a little differently, thinking at times, "Perhaps, after all, I love them, too . . ."

ᴥ Chapter Four ᴥ

In the morning, at the hour when I left for my work at the *Banque du Roi* (a building which was sumptuous only in name, a great morgue-like structure located near the harbour, in the quarter where Huguette Poire and her sisters "plucked men by the sleeve," as my mother put it), I occasionally encountered Elisa Moutonnet, Marthe Dubos and Louisette Denis walking arm in arm toward the convent, where they continued their studies, while I was performing what my father frankly called "the good respectable job of a cashier in a bank." Too miserable to join them, I usually managed to avoid them by stepping into an alley, still bathed in shadows in those cool early morning hours before the September sun rose to warm the city; and as I withdrew from them, I thought that I would be too tired by evening to join them in the café, too tired even to read the books with which I had filled my pockets before leaving the house. Philosophical volumes lay open before me the whole day long, while I played distractedly with the dirty green bills and counted money like a blind man, though I understood none of the words I read. At times, I would gaze endlessly at a single sentence, but I could not echo Julien Laforêt's proud words: "I read Aristotle as easily as I breathe." I no longer dreamed of improving my mind, for too many things about me seemed to contribute to its abasement. There was, above all, my hunger, an incessant hunger which, like an attack of dizziness, prevented me from reading or thinking clearly, opening great holes in the fog of my mind. I had time only to drink the bowl of coffee which my mother set before me in the morning, and because the other employees made it clear that they did not enjoy my company at lunch hour, I did not eat again until evening.

"If you didn't have your nose buried in a book all the time, you wouldn't be such a snob and you'd do your work as well as everyone else. Look at her, girls, she's still a little bit of a thing and she thinks she's the cat's miaou!"

"Leave me alone."

"You don't even know how to count, Pauline Archange. What did they teach you at that convent? If the manager catches you, you'll hear about it, I can tell you. You were fifty dollars short yesterday, and all because you don't know how to count. And she thinks she's so smart because she studied at the convent. The rest of us didn't study at any convent, but we know our catechism, and we know how to count, too!"

This wall of hostility which was raised by the other cashiers, most of whom were scarcely older than myself, and against which I incessantly beat my head, resulted from their belief that I had deliberately set myself above them, and perhaps in a sense they were right, for even when friendship more than hunger drew me toward the communal table where they at their lunch, talking loudly and boisterously together, I sensed their resentment at my presence. "When a person goes out of her way to be different, is it any wonder she's disliked?" my mother said, and this thought plagued me in the evening as I sat alone at the back of the bus. Sometimes, however, I preferred my solitude, as leaning against the window, I watched the students from l'Ecole des Arts returning from the harbour, where they had spent the day painting. What could be more excruciating, I thought, than this spectacle of a capricious liberty which always lay just out of reach? And how did one silence that nagging inner voice which demanded the freedom of a carefree existence? But then another voice, a much harsher and drier one, the voice of the manager who suddenly placed a hand of my shoulder, brought me abruptly back to my senses:

"Listen, mademoiselle, it's all very well to stand staring out the window, but because of you I'm losing as much as fifty dollars a day. This isn't a rest home, you know, it's a bank. If things don't change, I'm afraid I'll have to let you go . . . A cashier must have some feeling for money. A cashier who doesn't like money is a woman without a future."

But in my case, "correcting an error," as the manager put it, was simply an invitation to commit several others.

"Don't set your feet in this place again!" he exclaimed, irritated almost beyond words at my performance. "How do you ever expect to find a husband if you don't even know how to balance an expense account?"

"I don't want a husband."

"Oh, so that's how it is! Well, you have a lot of cheek, I must say, you don't like money, you don't want a husband, and what is more important in life, may I ask, than money and a husband? Ask the other cashiers, they always have their eyes open for a man, especially a rich one, yes, they've learned their lesson, they know what they want in life and they go after it, they'll get themselves settled down, as the saying goes. But with you it's another story, you've made a bad beginning. Oh, I can see you now, spending the rest of your life lining up at the Unemployment Office, and alone at that!"

The manager was right, I often had to present myself at the Unemployment Office, mingling with people who were even poorer than myself (for it was there that I seemed to encounter the most destitute individuals in the city), and I fell very low in the hierarchy of human labour. Employed as a "cookie wrapper" in a bakery or an "envelope folder" in a business office, all aspirations to an intellectual life quickly deserted me in the humiliation of my daily work. I understood then why those repetitive acts which are performed in the pursuit of earning a living and which invariably leave one with a feeling of absolute uselessness, are so often referred to as "degrading."

Then I remembered my cousin, Cécile, a nurse at Notre-Dame-des-Fous, working for ten dollars a week plus room and board . . . and I went to implore the Superior of that hospital for work, any work she might be able to give me, my gesture acquiring in my eyes the appearance of a redemptive act. Oh yes, I would do anything, I would even wash the patients . . .

"But, my child, that is no vocation!" replied the Superior categorically, ensconced behind her desk. And then, in a more anxious voice, she added, "Our patients are dangerous. They are not ordinary madmen, you understand, they are raving lunatics. Sometimes, when they go too far, we have to take the hoses and spray them a little, even roughly at times, yes, just as if we were putting out a fire. They play all sorts of tricks on us. We do everything we can to keep them calm, but in vain, for madness is a pagan disease, you understand, that's the most important lesson I have learned during my stay here. We give them shock treatments, we pour water on them as if they were live coals, we clean out their heads just as you clean the entrails from a chicken, and what do they do? They start in all over again! They're pagans, my child, and there is no end to what they will do just to satisfy their lust. But you're too young to witness such a spectacle of flourishing vice, I'll send you to assist the Mother Treasurer with her accounts, there you will learn the art of economy, for in this house, you know, we have the reputation of never throwing anything out, not a pin, not even a stamp. That will be a better education for you than watching the debauchery of our Blessed Ones in the Kingdom!"

I had to leave home before dawn, while the sky was still dark and the streets were deserted, and exalted by this silence which lay all about me, I walked in the direction of the hospital, which stood illuminated against the pale horizon, but there was such a rawness to the light of those electric bulbs that shone behind the metal bars, that it seemed to me at times that the structure which stood there on the hillside was not a hospital at all but a prison, totally cut off from the world. Before passing through those gates, behind which gigantic demons bent beneath heavy yokes were transported by madness to ethereal heights – as inspired as saints, but lacking the saint's franchise to indulge in their cruel ecstasies – before penetrating that iron gate where reason (dressed in the habit of a nun) punished instinct and held it cowering beneath her iron fist, it was necessary for me to pass fields that were still brown in the shadows of the dying night, meadows where the patients played in the daytime when the weather was fine; though, in my eyes, this singular landscape, these swamps, these leafy roads, bore a closer resemblance to those other swamps, those ghostly fields in which there rode on horseback, alone and unbridled, the majestic inflamed brains of whom the Superior said simply:

"When a fire gets too hot, it must be extinguished. Two thousand nervous souls swarming about you day in and day out, it's too much even for a woman of my stability. In twenty years, I have not known one moment's silence. Those savage voices hum incessantly in my ears. And they say that in paradise, silence is also rare, so it seems we must accustom ourselves to everything!"

Back there, behind the forbidden doors, where all the most audacious fantasies and dreams were played out (and where the bodies of so many tormented creatures were imprisoned by day and released at night as mere wrecks), it was in vain that one attempted to contain, like a swarm of fish in a net, the fury of all those desolate dreamers, and even when the Superior said authoritatively, "What do you expect, when madness becomes not only treacherous but criminal, and thirsts for vengeance, there remains no recourse but the straitjacket or the ice bath! Common sense must rule. And common sense, in my opinion, is the only thing left to unimaginative people like myself." – even then, I sensed that madness would never lose its boldness nor the strength of its inspiration. The Superior might subdue the frenzy of those she called her "disobedient children" when they yielded to their bestial desires or their peculiar fear of invisible enemies, she perhaps had no choice but to cry, "Quick, the straitjacket!", to bring a little calm into her "purgatory", but she seemed to know, even as she acted, that it was not in her power to soothe those pale martyrs' brows, those faces lacerated with beauty and vice; even as she heard them wailing like beasts, she seemed to understand that she would never be able to reach her unfortunate charges not to appease their vague sufferings, that she lacked the strength and the imagination to raise herself to the level of their primitive complaints, and that she did not possess the key to the secret of an anguished life delivered at last of its suffering. "Even as disfigured with pain as they are," she said, "they tell us nothing that we do not already know, though we may be unwilling to admit it: that man is capable of anything when he is not guided by the love of God; and even more scandalous than that, my child, that the goodness, the virtue, which we arrogantly believe to be a part of man's natural make-up, is far from being natural, that we all arrive on this earth more or less rejected, like little dogs in the gutter, entering this world in a state of loud fury and, I fear, ready to indulge in just about any sort of wickedness!"

I followed her through the corridors, stumbling along in the wake of her bold gestures and her eloquent words, fascinated by the accounts she gave of her varied experiences, but she often repulsed me by saying:

"The Mother Treasurer needs you, go to her, she'll be working on her accounts now. I have several 'escapees' to round up. I don't know why we bothered to put bars in this place, it was a waste of time putting locks on the doors and filling the house with warning alarms, they just slip through our fingers, I don't know how, but they're sly, you know, they could slip through the eye of a needle! And then, of course, they're fearless, and that in itself is enough to render them invisible!"

Even if I quit the world every morning to follow the dark paths of the jungle (which, closed to society and its laws, was the battleground of the gods of delirium, a world ruled by fever and enchantment), moving amongst those crying voices, I often imagined that they were actually coming from myself, and unlike the Superior, I did not possess "the gift of reason" nor the ill-natured benevolence to rid that jungle of all its dark and sinuous shadows. Prisoner of the haunted landscape through which I moved, I was unable to echo her courageous words: "I'm too accustomed to their tricks and their lies, they're just as clear to me as spring water, and even in the midst of the storm, I remain on my rock of tranquility!" Immersed in self-pity, ensconced behind the same ivy-covered walls, I felt at times as stricken, as delirious, as the sickest of those patients. The Superior locked me into the Treasurer's office, but the strident wail which reached my ears one day as I was passing a barred courtyard (where hundreds of invisible bodies and faces rushed about like beastly figures in a swamp) followed me through the corridors and into the silent office, where sitting beside the Treasurer, I arranged stamps and gave myself up to those simple tasks which she exacted of the more feeble of her patients. Seated about her, their knees touching her own big knee (thus, she explained, were they "attached" to her), they wagged their heads and sewed on buttons, or merely stared at the floor, drooling onto their striped cotton gowns, those gowns of submission. For the Treasurer, who lived at all times in their presence, these creatures had become "as tame as sheep," but she forgot that they possessed something more than sheep, a dignity, a candour, which was revealed in their suffering and which I had once observed in the look of Emile, the essence of a supernatural tranquility floating in their eyes and irradiating their almost translucent white skin.

At that time, I was also exploring those same forgotten regions of the universe in my reading, particularly in Philippe l'Heureux's *Prison Chronicles*, the book which Elisa Moutonnet had loaned me, saying: "You'll like it, it's an immoral book, but when a book is well written it's always immoral!" though it seemed to me that, skimming too quickly and frivolously through its pages, she had quite misunderstood the work. As for Germaine Léonard, whom I still saw from time to time, she expressed nothing but a cruel contempt for "that impure, disorganized, barbarous book." But the confessions which Philippe l'Heureux had gleaned from his prison companions, revealing as they did a subdued violence whose strength had been entirely misjudged, reminded me of those other places of penitence, those asylums, where, if men were not chastised for their actions, they were rudely reprimanded for their dreams, where the crime committed in thought (the perpetual dream of so many of the madmen I encountered) was as rigorously expiated by confinement as was the actual murder to which others, like Philippe l'Heureux, consented in their newly-awakened awareness. There was, in both cases, an absolute fervour for life, which resulted invariably in social oppression. Philippe l'Heureux wrote that "the condemned occasionally heard the bells of ringing on the distant deserted plain," but he wondered whether this symbolic deliverance was not, in fact, a mere chimera? Nothing seemed more dismal to him than the walls of his cell, but as he sought his *raisons de vivre* in the interior world of his captivity, was it not necessary for him to exalt courage even crime, in the only human community he had come to know? Like the choir of madmen when their dreams expired, he felt intensely the burden of his oppression and the humiliation of his almost animal existence in that prison. What troubled him most (and what troubled me, too) was "the boundless energy" of imprisoned men, "the monstrous sacrifice of their lives," as he expressed it, even going so far as to wonder if the true community of assassins was not that class "which legislated the laws of expiation and sacrifice," returning to the very act which he had wanted to accomplish with his first murder, the trial of his father, "a just man, a good man, who was nonetheless responsible for the execution of a fellow man." According to him: "All judges live in a very fragile citadel, where they wrongly imagine themselves to be protected from the hordes of criminals whose energies and desires they have confined, but who are already prowling as restlessly as wild beasts about their shaky dwelling, awaiting the hour of Justice . . ."

I recall that, as I sat one evening at home, reading those very words, I heard the announcer on the radio say in a hushed voice, "A man was hanged tonight," his words scarcely penetrating my hazy consciousness.

My father was angry. "Hanging a man is worse that cutting the throat of a bull!"

But my mother disagreed. "You forget, Jos, that this man chopped his wife up into little pieces before they strung him up!"

Like myself, my father had to resign himself to an injustice which he lacked the power to denounce, even if he deplored all such barbarous behaviour.

"To hang a man is like death pulled right down over him, from his head to his feet. It's worse than the death of a beast."

But my mother only repeated stubbornly: "And do you think that poor woman enjoyed being chopped up into little pieces?"

Those who, like my cousin Cécile, were besieged on all sides by criminal fantasies and who spent their days displaying a saintly courage, washing the worst of the maniacs, patients who very often pulled their hair or pinched them, did not have the time to consider the true nature of such crimes or their moral implications, which were at any rate far too complex for their simple and humble minds to grasp. On the contrary, they rejoiced when they were allowed to bestow "the mercy of shock treatment," as the Superior called it: "Yes, my daughter, it's the only thing which brings us back to earth!" My cousin had witnessed so many convulsions that all those distorted bodies had come to seem quite natural to her, the powerful shock which shook those heads and rattled those bones being no more to her than "a current of cold air running along their bones," as she put it, adding with the same candour:

"My God, Pauline Archange, what do you want us to do, let all the lunatics loose in the morning to run free in the streets? Where's your common sense, that's what I'd like to know? But you never did have any, did you? Have you thought of what would happen to good Catholics like us who never hurt a fly if all the devils were let loose in our neighbourhoods? You don't do anything but sniff the air in the madhouse – Oh, I've seen you, tripping along behind the skirts of the Superior, like someone on vacation! – but cleaning up their filth is another matter, let me tell you, and catching their lice isn't so funny either, and straining your nerves and being scratched and beaten for ten dollars a week, oh, sometimes I wonder why I put up with it! You don't know what it's like, there's a dark tunnel down there, and every morning when I pass through that hole, I shake like a leaf, there's a big maniac who sits in a corner, he's harmless, I know, he just sits there, but when he sees me coming, he reaches inside his pants and pulls out his thing, yes, right there in the broad daylight, and he just sits there and looks at me and waits. What would you do about that, eh? Oh, what's the use, the shock treatments don't clean out their brains, they just start in all over again!"

It always astonished me to see my cousin emerge from one of her shock-treatment sessions, nonchalantly pushing before her a little trolley upon which there lay a child more assassinated than dead or asleep, the pale brow with its bright stigmata showing through the sweat-soaked hair, looking as if it had been scorched by a candle flame . . . If I ran toward her to ask, "What did he do to deserve that?" the concern in my voice only irritated her and she went on her way, chewing her gum and muttering:

"What are you doing in here with your long face? We didn't punish him, poor little thing, we just gave him his medicine. He looks like a statue, but that's because he's asleep. Yesterday, he tried to kill his mother with a knife, and when they went for him in the ambulance, he was as wild as a wolf."

"Look at how he's shaking . . ."

"They always shake afterwards, what an idiot you are!"

And pushing her trolley before her, she moved in the direction of those dark corridors which filled her with such apprehension but which she nonetheless braved.

One day, when I was trailing again in the Superior's wake, she said good-naturedly to me:

"I don't want to see you going through my instruments again, my child, you're much too curious for your own good, you know. And not only that, I see you every morning slipping into the hysterical ward, and I've told you so many times to stay away from there. Your job is to help the Mother Treasurer. I found you a safe position in the hospital, otherwise I knew it would be only a matter of time before I awake one morning and found myself with yet another lunatic on my hands. I'm going to send you to the Monastère de l'Allégresse, to visit the Capucin Fathers, you'll run errands for them, that will help you to forget all the horrors you've seen in this place. Oh! how I'd like to visit our good Capuchin friends myself, they sing and babble all the day long, and as you'll discover, they work very little, may God bless that seraphic race of dreamers, they have found peace here on this earth! How I envy them! In their company, you'll read the lives of the saints, which will be much more edifying for you than hearing the sacrileges of our blasphemers always whistling in your ears. But, you know, God gets used to them, and in the end I believe He does as we do, He pretends not to hear, He forgives. Ring the bell at the Monastery at eight o'clock tomorrow morning, and a little waltzing father will let you in, his name is Father Plumeau, he's a very nervous, unsteady little man and he flies very high, near the Lord. He even pays us a visit here from time to time, happily for me, otherwise I'd be quite alone in this world. I look after him when he comes, I give him a room near the garden, and I listen to his marvellous tales of things that could happen only in paradise, for his soul is as light as a butterfly, you know, and if he is guilty of a sin, it is the sin of innocence, yes, at the age of fifty he is still as simple-minded as a child. He even imagines that Jesus speaks to him in the chapel during his meditations. And, who knows, perhaps He does. But why doesn't He speak to me? Ah well, it may be better to float in the golden clouds than to wallow in the mud, but here we have both, yes, we have everything here. The Capuchins are my friends. Sometimes, the good Father Eugène also pays us a visit, he's the one who looks after the books in the Monastery – but how absent-mindedly, that Monastery will go bankrupt one of these days, I swear – yes, Father Eugène comes here for his annual rest-cure, but he's a grumbler, that one, look out for him, when he comes here he refuses to speak to me, he just sulks all alone in his cell, and God does not like sullen people, you know. But you will enjoy working for those men, they're so charming with their long beards and their sandaled feet – reasonably clean too, I must admit – but then, why is cleanliness so important when we love God? Remember to ask for your salary, otherwise Father Eugène will forget to pay you, those men have so little concern for the practical affairs of life, it's a barrier which they hurdle too easily. They're like those frisky little calves you see sometimes running in the fields, jumping over pickets. I knew enough of those in my youth, I had to drive them home with a stick, though without offending them, of course. But Father Eugène has one serious fault: there is no order in his life. Most of the priests are too orderly, but not that one, oh no, and to think that he is their accountant, it's enough to give a person nightmares! His office is in a little garret, where he surrounds himself with all the old maids in the parish who help him with his accounts, though in my opinion those 'vestry bugs' are a bad influence on him, they simply spoil him, and then, they're too devout for him, not whimsical enough for this man who is whimsy itself, even if his appearance suggests the opposite, for he has a belly which you will notice even before you see his face, big feet, too – but we mustn't judge people by their appearance, the

Good Lord didn't see fit to give us all the sort of looks we might like to have. You'll see that this man is literally 'running over with grace,' if I may say so. But in his office, what disorganization! Even his cat can't see its way clear through the place: things all thrown together, old bottles he has found, I don't know where, old chairs, everything he comes across, and behind that thick curtain of trash and dust, he entertains those 'vestry bugs!' Imagine! They claim they're suffering from tuberculosis, that they're too sickly to work at ordinary jobs, and so he looks after them, as if they were his own daughters, with a slightly absent air, to be sure, for he's always somewhere else (if we only knew where, but it can't be a very pleasant place, for he's so sullen most of the time), yes, those poor old maids stick to him like fleas and he has only to say, 'A glass of water, Justine,' for them all to come running with full decanters. To tell the truth, he's incurably lazy, but God bless him, for after all, we can't overcome all the vices in the world, can we? And then, you'll also have the pleasure of meeting Father Allaire, who is culture itself and who has written several theological texts, though I haven't read them, for I can't understand them. It seems to me that he too is a little lost, flying somewhere in the mystical regions, too high for me, always somewhere above reason and common sense. But we can't have everything, can we? If Father Allaire had to live with my lunatics day in and day out, 'the spaces of pure delight,' as he calls his heaven, would very quickly become a stifling abyss. But what do you expect: those men, for all their culture and their refinements, imagine that heaven is like a refrigerator, inhabited only by men like themselves; whereas, for me, heaven is just like this place here, except that God is there to instill a little order in things, of course. Father Allaire sits all day in his heaven, watching the words flow from his pen, gazing at the stars that shine all about him, but then I'm not so sure that those stars shine very brightly. Those men have inspiration, but I have only my common sense."

When I arrived at the Monastère de l'Allégresse, Father Plumeau opened the door and gathered me in, dancing a little jig. I walked behind him, trying to follow in the steps of his choreography (it seemed to me that anyone who attempted to walk in the wake of this little man must automatically begin to dance), and watching the folds of his brown robe as they swirled about his little child-like legs, I thought that this elf disguised as a monk, who opened to me that medieval door which led into that medieval kingdom (though one which was strangely bathed in joy), was inviting me to probe the secrets of another congregation of madmen, one which, like the company of the elect in their celestial sphere, revelled in what the Superior had called "not the pleasures of the strong but the joys of the weak," adding that in their company I would have nothing to fear.

"This way," said Father Plumeau in his shrill little voice. "I'm so happy to have a little girl in our house, though Father Eugène will make a scene when he sees you. He's a very harsh man, you know, the only person he loves is Sainte-Catherine. He's generous, but he has a mania for old useless things, and he imagines, because we're always being deprived of our electricity or our heat, that the government is persecuting us, whereas the government is actually very fond of us. The moment we lose our electricity or our heat, he summons everyone to his office for a conference. Father Allaire, too, becomes quite alarmed at such moments . . . he says he can't write in the dark, and he complains of cold feet. But I call that a whim. We're too attached to our material comforts, if you ask me. Why do we need electricity when we have God to guide us in the darkness?"

From the undergrowth of miscellaneous objects and papers where he sat with an enormous cat in his lap that resembled a feather pillow, Father Eugène made a sign to Father Allaire to be rid of me, but standing beside him, absorbed in a difficult account with which his companion showed little inclination to assist him, Father Allaire said sadly, without looking up at me:

"Listen, Father Eugène, we must find that bill."

"I never saw a theologian so frightened of the cold," said Father Eugène, clearly irritated.

"Winter is fast approaching, Father Eugène, and we cannot live without heat."

"Of course, of course . . ." Then, turning to the old maids who sat huddled in the ferns at the farther end of the desk, he cried, "Come, my daughters, my secretaries, make yourselves useful. Quick, find the bills. As you can see, Father Allaire is upset again, as if it were my fault that the government keeps cutting off our electricity!"

"Well, you're the accountant of the house," said Father Allaire gently.

"There are accountants and there are accountants. My vocation in this world is not to pay the government's debts. What ideas you have, Father Allaire! Be patient, I'll look after it. Everything is taken care of here, sooner or later . . . Look, here it is, the bill!" he exclaimed triumphantly, lifting his big grey cat from a pile of papers on his desk. "Monseigneur was sleeping on it. He too dislikes bills."

"Permit me to remind you once again, Father Eugène, that Monseigneur is of the female sex and the mother of an inordinately large family. I found her kittens yesterday morning on the pages of my manuscript. How are we going to feed all those mouths, Father Eugène?"

"The mile of God is rich and abundant," replied Father Eugène, gazing admiringly at Monseigneur, for he had a particular reverence for this striped prelate which he had found one day in the garden. "When God gives us a gift, it is that it might bear fruit. Did He not say, 'Go forth and multiply?' So, here is your bill, now leave me in peace. What have you got there, Father Plumeau?"

"Someone to run your errands, Father. She comes straight to us from Notre-Dame-des-Fous, from the very hands of your friend, the Superior."

"It's just like her to send me another mouth to feed. Send her back. You know that we're poor, simple men and that the government doesn't support us!"

"She will be a faithful companion to you, Father Eugène. What is the point of our being so preoccupied with the material world in which we find ourselves always crying and groaning?" asked Father Plumeau, wringing his hands. "Doesn't God feed all his little flies and his flowers and his birds?"

"I'm not so certain about that," said Father Eugène, caressing his cat, which sat purring on the desk. "And besides, it's your fault, Father Allaire, if we have nothing to crack our teeth on! Your books don't sell. You write a great deal, to be sure, but why, I ask myself, when you don't sell ten copies in a year? Even the nuns, who love boring books, don't read your works. It seems that the government doesn't like you very much either. At least, make an effort, Father Allaire, try to be a little less boring, talk about the beauties of Christian marriage or the virtues of celibacy, something like that, who wants to read a book with the title, *Astral Voyage of a Religious Soul*? Even a monk on retreat wouldn't want to have such a book on his bedside table. You bore people to death, it's as simple as that! You're as boring as Saint Thomas Aquinas . . ."

"Stop insulting that great man, Father Eugène, I beg of you. You may find yourself one day seated at his side in paradise."

"Never. In that case, no paradise . . ."

"Well, Father Eugène, you can't be expected to comprehend the mysteries of accounting and the mysteries of heaven at the same time!"

"Of course . . . of course . . ."

Whenever it became too cold for me in Father Plumeau's quarters, in his library which he had consecrated to the saints and in which little Thérèse of the Child Jesus was accorded first place, I visited Father Allaire, a priest whose Roman profile seemed to speak more of earthly delights than celestial splendours, but whose virile, almost ethereal energy had been delicately polished by self-discipline. This man understood the desire I expressed to become a writer, but sitting with his feet on his foot-warmer and his hands hidden in the sleeves of his robe, he often spoke to me of the dangers of a profession which he had chosen himself, as he said, for its nobility.

"Come now," he said to me one day, "one cannot appreciate Rimbaud without certain reservations, his work is powerful, to be sure, but isn't the sweet flavour of that work a little tainted? That young man did not lead a very exemplary life, I fear. Nor did Monsieur Verlaine, his friend. Do you ever consider that? We mustn't judge, I know. As for Monsieur de Lautréamont, whom you so greatly admire, he wasn't an angel either, especially in his private life. That has nothing to do with the tragic greatness of his work, I admit, but mustn't we first seek a certain harmony between the work and the man, a certain moral accord? There are several authors who have succeeded in controlling the propensities of their instincts. Monsieur Mauriac, for example. Now, there is a man whom you can admire without reservation, and the admiration is deserved, for it is directed toward a man who lives and writes like a saint. So, what will you write about in your books? Who are your muses, what are your ideals? In order to write, you must have an ideal. Like the priest who consecrates the bread to God, you must learn to consecrate even the basest things, so that only the finest incense will rise toward the reader's nostrils . . ."

"I don't have an ideal yet."

"Oh, but you must acquire one, my child. Is it not true that the pulse, the nervous centre of all our works, is the heart of God, the sacred driving force, the redemptive source of all things? Of course, you will not be obliged to name God everywhere in your work, too many religious writers fall into that indiscretion, their approach lacks subtlety, their love for the Creator is much too naïve, but we can speak of God in a thousand different ways, of the beauty of His works . . ."

"What works?"

"But surely you are familiar with the magnificent works of our Creator. Nature, for example, the fish, the quiet forests, the majestic mountains. You must have run through brooks. Oh! the fresh water of brooks, what could be more delightful! And the singing of birds, don't you sometimes listen to that?"

"No."

"You must awaken all your senses to nature, to the divine things of this world, and not only to the suffering of men, because there is too much suffering and we cannot assume it all, our shoulders are too frail for the weight of the cross. And then, you must remember that Jesus sacrificed His life for us. Open your heart to His love, you will see, your inspiration will soar. Life is no longer a nightmare when we have love in our hearts. Yes, as Monsieur Mauriac says, a life without love is a desert. What a subtle, sensitive mind! There is also Monsieur Claudel, whom you can admire without reservation, though I would say that the flesh is a little too present in the works of that poet who sang so eloquently his praises of God. But what passion – too much passion perhaps, sensual passion, I mean – but how good to hear a Catholic poet singing of the perfect consummation of carnal desire transfigured by divine love . . ."

Father Eugène greeted me in his habitual misanthropic fashion:

"Oh, it's you . . . again! What do you want? Why don't you stay with Father Allaire? He loves to talk, and he lives somewhere amongst the stars, whereas I am just a sullen old man."

"I've come for my salary, Father Eugène."

"What salary? I don't owe you anything."

"Father Allaire said you have a cheque for me."

"It's just like him to rob me of what I don't even have. Come back next week, my secretaries need time to organize my finances . . . it takes time to prepare a cheque, you know, give me at least a few days . . ."

The weeks passed, and still they did not pay me. "It's nothing," said Father Plumeau, "don't trouble yourself about it, doesn't God look after all His little worms and His little green snakes in the fields? Let us imitate those patient, gentle creatures! But since you are so resolved to have a salary, my child, I shall organize a pilgrimage to Lourdes, sometimes that helps us to get our heads above water, so to speak. I have a friend, a holy man (there are so many holy men in this world), who often goes on pilgrimages, he's a recent immigrant who leapt one day from his boat, I don't know where he came from, but isn't it true that all those who come to us from afar are gifts from heaven? Let us open our arms to those migrating birds in search of paradise on our shores, let us not be miserly, let us open our doors to everyone! Albert and I have organized several pilgrimages to Lourdes, and our hearts are still there, in exile, at the feet of the Virgin of Miraculous Cures. This generous man, almost like a priest without a habit, opens his heart to all sinful souls, he confronts evil everywhere and he meets it head-on, though it does seem to me that he goes a little far at times in search of it. He says that during the course of his many voyages, he passed through 'all the houses of lust in Europe,' always to lead the lost sheep back to the fold, of course, and I expect that is a risk which a saint who lives in the world can safely take, whereas for priests like us who have taken vows of chastity and obedience, it seems more prudent to offer grace to the more modest souls of our acquaintance. Yes, we shall organize a pilgrimage to the Virgin who has left me with such tender memories! The crippled of our parishes never used to travel, you understand, and all those Sainte-Catherines for whom Father Eugène has such an abiding affection were becoming a little mouldy, sitting there behind the ferns in his office. How generous it is of him now to fly off for a month, two months, and to pray while the airplane carries us from one continent to another! Oh! heaven lies so close to us as we recite the *Ave* . . . To travel, my child, what a joy, to fly over this world which God created for His greater glory and ours!"

But the sanctity of Father Plumeau's friend seemed a little suspect the day he came to visit the Monastery. The moment Father Plumeau disappeared in the direction of the elevator (this movement of levitation seeming so natural to him that I almost imagined him rising without even touching the elevator button), Albert drew his chair closer to mine, and placing his feet on my desk, began to lecture me:

"If you'll permit me, mademoiselle, I feel closer to you in this way. I like to be close to people, to look into their eyes, to read their thoughts. Don't lower your eyes: if your thoughts are pure, you have nothing to conceal. I know women very well, I have travelled a great deal and I have frequented, I believe, all the places of sin in this world. But in my presence, prostitutes never yield to temptation, no, I draw from their lips the most savoury prayers, even at times, I must confess, through their insults. Sanctity shocks these creatures who are immersed in the iniquity of their sins, but caressing them a little, as I might caress a child, I draw from them tears of repentance. 'Pray, pray!' I say to them. 'Let us pray together, let us kneel beside the bed and pray.' Thus, little by little, they become my friends, my faithful companions, and embracing them with recognition, I even weep a few tears myself. What can be more touching I ask you, than these poor women who humbly prostrate themselves and beg for forgiveness? Oh, if I were God, I would love only sin!"

Little by little, Father Plumeau discovered that, even with the help of Albert "and all the other saints in the world," who assisted him in filling the Monastery's bread box, we were headed toward a state of fatal but dignified privation, not unlike that of Saint Francis.

"Yes, we are on the verge of collapse, my child, it's unfortunate that we cannot keep you here any longer. I'm sorry to lose you, for it's the first time we've had someone of your age here, and the moment he sees you turning the corner of the street, Father Eugène will profit from your absence, the sly creature, by opening his doors to yet another of those flowers from the sanatorium whose fragrance he so enjoys. He cannot live without being served and surrounded by old maids, and worse than that, he likes them ugly and sullen, which makes things even more depressing! They feed on the crumbs that fall from his table, he says. Well, go and say goodbye to him, perhaps he'll have some crumbs for you, too. It will be time, too, for a person cannot live on God's benevolence alone, still less on wit and vanity!"

"Come in," said Father Eugène, "what are you frightened of, I won't eat you. I'm not like the government, which spends its time devouring people. It's because of you that we are facing bankruptcy, you've taken our last pennies. Here, take this cheque, and be sure to cash it today, for tomorrow we'll be bone dry. Why do you need money, anyway? For frivolous things, I daresay!" He caressed the head of his cat, which was sleeping on his knees. "Oh, Monseigneur, we've seen some unhappy times, you and I! We've licked some empty milk bowls, haven't we? And then, it isn't every day that we've found mice in the garden. At least with us, our Mother of the Holy Church hasn't got fat, oh no, that we have prevented at least! And you, Monseigneur, as agile as you are, you will pass through the straight gate to paradise . . ." Then, abruptly changing his tone, he added, "So you want to write books like Father Allaire? I can't imagine why. There are already enough boring books in the world. In your place, I would get married quickly, marriage is the answer to everything. For us, too, marriage would be the answer, at least we would eat better. Oh, when you think of it, for thirty years the nuns have been doing our cooking, it's enough to turn your stomach! Onions! They're full of attention for us, it's true, they wash us, they iron us, but sometimes a person has enough of eating out of the hands of religion, sleeping in the sheets of religion. Go and get married, that will change your mind . . ."

With Father Allaire, the farewells were a little more subtle, though the theologian was so cold that his teeth chattered:

"Winter is almost upon us, you're leaving at an opportune moment. And I had just begun to become accustomed to your presence here. Do you recall the Little Prince at the moment he took leave of his rose? What a beautiful friendship! It is important in this life to be like him, to cultivate the most exquisite roses of friendship. Do you have a confessor, Pauline, a friend capable of guiding you away from the impure paths of existence?"

"No."

"But adolescence is a perilous age when it does not have this vigilant shadow to watch over it. You will find someone, Pauline, yes. And while you are waiting, you have your friends, your books. Of course, there are dangerous books just as there are dangerous people, but perhaps we must discover the one just as we discover the other. I recall, in my own adolescence, which burned like a solitary flame, God was still very distant from me, my proud spirit drank of other sources . . . but, suddenly, like Saint Paul struck by lightning and toppled from his horse, the grace of God fell upon me and I wept. Yes, I wept. So, goodbye, my child, whenever you find yourself alone, come and see me. For I too am alone, you see, and there is no one here to read to me."

All trace of tenderness seemed to vanish from my life as Father Plumeau shut the gate of the garden behind me. Winter was settling upon the city, the first snow already covered the streets, and at the Unemployment Office where there were several lines of waiting people, their eyes betraying that same sense of apprehension which I felt so strongly myself, someone said to me:

"Come back later, you're not the only one in the world, you know, we take the heads of households first . . ."

Recalling that Germaine Léonard had once said to me, "I don't feel very much affection for you, Pauline Archange, but if one day you need assistance, come and see me, I'll do what I can," I decided to visit her in her office at the hospital. But in my clumsiness, I only provoked her anger.

"One day, it's that fanatic, Benjamin Robert, who comes to solicit aid for his alcoholics and his delinquents. The next day, it's you. I can't help you. At any rate, there's no work for you here."

"But it's urgent. My father will sell my typewriter if I don't pay my rent."

"What an impatient lot of people you are, there's no end to the irritation you cause! You never change, do you?"

She levelled upon me a gaze that was not completely lacking in goodwill, but in her fatigue and bitterness, she could not conceal her ill-tempered disappointment at seeing me again, always the same in her eyes, "the defective child playing in the gutter with Jacquou," and even if I tried to tell her that I had changed a great deal since those days, that what she saw before her now as no more than a pale reflection of my former self, she could only speak condescendingly of my new life and what she called my "little experiences in the working world."

"A person has to be demented to go and work in a lunatic asylum."

"I don't regret it. It was an experience."

"Of course, you never regret anything. Like that Philippe l'Heureux, whose works you so admire, you cultivate your delirium. Well, it's very deceitful of you, under the pretext of needing work, to come and seek what you call your 'experience' here in the hospital where I work. As if I felt enough affection for you to tolerate you at my side all day long. When my life is already so crowded with people . . ."

"I'm not deceitful."

"That just goes to show how little you know yourself. For your deceit is hidden even from yourself, it's instinctive, it's unconscious, it's an impulse that rises from the dark side of your soul, it's an irrepressible deceit because it's blind even to itself. Have you thought of visiting a psychoanalyst? I know a few excellent doctors who might be able to help you. Not only you, but also that Philippe l'Heureux of yours, that pitiful, decadent criminal . . . They could help you from behaving so stupidly at times. I won't say that this sort of deceit works against the person it inhabits and that one day you will suffer a great deal from it: after all, that is none of my business, I have no time to lose on a person like you. In all the years I've known you, you haven't made a single effort to change. Look at you: you're as poorly dressed as ever. And that's surely a sign of apathy!"

As I rose to leave Germaine Léonard's office, not wanting her to see my tears, she said to me in a more gentle tone:

"Here, take this money, it might come in useful . . . And consider what I've told you, I didn't speak out of ill will, you know . . ."

But this gesture did not wipe out the memory of that other gesture, that singular gift which this woman had seen fit to bestow upon me that day: the gift of her irrepressible scorn . . .

But if Germaine Léonard was not perceptive enough to discover who I was beneath the dull appearance which I presented to the world, perhaps I was not any more able to discover who she was. In her determined efforts to protect her secrets from the scrutiny of others, she had found it necessary to effect a complete transformation of her character, and because she was afraid to let it be known that she passionately loved a man, the constraint which she placed upon her emotions manifested itself as a sort of avarice of the heart, a dryness of the soul which sprang from the same source as that love which she was never able to conquer. Though she still spent her entire day in the company of Pierre Olivier, continuing their research in the laboratory, she had destroyed "the ties that bind," as she called them, and it was always with an aggressive, painful tone that she proudly repeated:

"I told you, it's all over between us!"

For suffering as she was, she nonetheless resented the necessity of hurting him and of seeing him suffer with her. But if he dared to meet her vehemence calmly, saying simply, "How you enjoyed punishing yourself!", she became even more furious and exclaimed in a tone which he no longer recognized:

"I despise your sympathy!"

After having uttered these words, which were not at all a reflection of her innermost feelings, she became suddenly calm and did not insult him again for several days. Pierre Olivier was saddened to see that this love, which had once been so joyful and creative and which had brought such a delightful harmony into their lives, was now the cause of so much conflict and torment, seriously threatening their work. Germaine Léonard's irrational conduct bewildered him. He had been shattered to discover that this desire to terminate the relationship was the result not only of what she so often referred to as her "moral beliefs" and her "love of integrity," but of a more secret fear, the fear of losing him, and that she preferred, therefore, to sever those ties which (as in other earlier relationships in her life, less happy perhaps and less beautiful, but which she continued to use as models) risked being terminated in humiliation and sterility. But it was not the fear of humiliation alone which prompted Germaine Léonard to so abruptly sever her relationship with Pierre; it was her fear of the very violence of her love for him. To submit to this love, which she secretly considered "a sickness," to invade his thoughts and his life, to disturb his work habits, as she had been doing, was to her, "a lapse of conscience," resulting in a spiritual disorder which resembled drunkenness more than love. At the same time, she did not succeed in riding herself of Pierre, for she had to admit that she needed him, and though in the days before she had met him she had always cherished her solitude and her independence, she could no longer tolerate the thought of living a single day without him. It was with a great deal of courage, therefore, that she constructed this fortress of denial and resistance about herself; though just when she was convinced that the task was completed, saying to herself, as if in reassurance, "At last, I'm free of this affair," suddenly, she didn't know how, with a simple gesture against which she did not know how to protect herself, in a moment of unexpected tenderness which she could not resist (as if all at once she had suddenly forgotten all her principles), Pierre Olivier brought the walls of the fortress she had so patiently erected tumbling down. The moment he took her in his arms, though she struggled a little, saying, "Leave me alone, I hate you . . . I hate you . . ." a mad hope inflated her heart, and from the savage creature who had just exclaimed, "I hate you!", she heard a rending cry of joy split the air, a declaration which she would later deny, though to no avail ("for in spite of everything," she thought, "we always return to the source"), and it was with a deep anguish that she heard that voice rising in her to betray all her secrets, that other voice which she could no longer control and which declared to Pierre Olivier: "How I wish I didn't love you as I do!"

I presented myself each morning at the Unemployment Office, where I was told repeatedly:

"You again! Come back later, young people are taken last!"

My father became so irritated at seeing me prowling about the streets in my ragged coat, that he said to me one day:

"Come to the store, I'm going to buy you a new frock. I'm tired of seeing you dressed like that."

"It's my coat."

I couldn't bear to part with that garment which had been with me for so long, and I rejected my father's generous gesture, which was the fruit as much of his embittered pride (nothing offended this hard-working man quite so much as the appearance of poverty) as of his love, which was in any case more maternal than paternal, for hadn't he also said to me that I made him look pitiful? Yes, it was this more than anything else which he deplored, for, as he said, it was the first time that he had undertaken to sacrifice everything for one of his children.

"Too bad for you then, go about in your old rags if you want to be so ungrateful!"

The storm which my father had described in such vivid terms (and which had prompted my mother to say, "It's coming down in great drifts, like the storm on that New Year's Day before you were born!") now held the entire city in its imprisoning grip. Crossing the city in search of work, I feared that I would be lifted from my feet by the howling winds, for it was no ordinary blizzard which I fought my way through but an ocean of fury, and recalling that complaint which had terminated my father's soliloquy, "Oh! I'm so tired, it seems as if my heart had stopped beating at the end of its cord!", I already felt the exhaustion of this winter which seemed so long but which, in fact, had scarcely begun.

But one evening, as I was passing before a lighted butcher shop, I looked in, and there, in a white coat spotted with blood, standing beside a man who must have been his father and with whom he was carving a side of beef, I saw André Chevreux, the student of whom Julien Laforêt had said, "See how he disappears every day after class, I wonder where he goes, he refuses to tell me." And I thought that if André Chevreux had said nothing to his friend about his nocturnal occupation, it must have been because of a certain fastidiousness on his part, prompted by that sentiment of shame which I too had so often experienced in the face of privilege. He approached the frosty window and smiled at me. And there was in his smile such an affection, such a gentle valour, that I suddenly sensed my courage being reborn within me, and carrying that precious image with me through the storm, I broke into a run, exclaiming joyfully: "It's him . . . Dürer's angel, I've seen him, I've see him at last!"

Related Reading

Gilbert, Paula Ruth. *Violence and the Female Imagination: Quebec's Women Writers Re-Frame Gender in North American Cultures.*
Montreal: McGill-Queen's University Press, 2006.

Green, Mary Jean. *Postcolonial Subjects: Francophone Women Writers.*
Minneapolis: University of Minnesota Press, 1996.

Kristeva, Julia. *Revolution in Poetic Language.*
New York: Columbia University Press, 1984.

Laurent, Francoise. *L'Oeuvre Romanesque de Marie-Claire Blais.*
Montreal: Collection Approches: Fides, 1986.

Lewis, Paula Gilbert, ed. *Traditionalism, Nationalism, and Feminism: Women Writers in Québec.*
Westport: Greenwood Press 1985.

Marks, Elaine, ed. *New French Feminisms.*
New York: Pantheon, 1987.

Mitchell, Juliet. *Women: The Longest Revolution: Essays on Feminism, Literature and Psychoanalysis.*
New York: Oxford, 1984.

Roberts, Joan I., ed. *Beyond Intellectual Sexism: A New Woman, A New Reality.*
New York: Longman, 1976.

Sellers, Susan. *The Helene Cixous Reader.*
New York: Routledge, 1994.

Questions

1. Father Robert is the spokesman in the novel for what he calls "the disgrace of unreasonable charity." It is a disgrace that the hero of *The Idiot*, and Christ Himself, carry on their backs, too. What is meant by "unreasonable charity" and how can it be a "disgrace"?

2. Mother Saint-Alfredo is said, socially speaking, to have had the "courage to scorn this inherited reverence for ignorance," an inheritance too quick to respect stupidity and too slow to honour intelligence. Discuss the validity of such an assertion in our time.

3. *The Manuscripts of Pauline Archange* is a novel that operates in a long tradition, the *roman à clef*, wherein the novelist creates a central character in his or her own image. Find two other such novels and discuss the techniques the three novelists use to tell their own stories as writers.

Of Interest on the Web

http://www.thecanadianencyclopedia.com/index.cfm?PgNm=TCE
&Params=A1ARTA0000810

http://www.collectionscanada.gc.ca/writers/027005-1000-e.html

http://www.athabascau.ca/writers/mcblais.html

http://www.britannica.com/eb/article-9015578/Marie-Claire-Blais

http://www.movingimages.ca/catalogue/Art/marieclaireblais.html

Exile Online Resource

www.ExileEditions.com has a section for the Exile Classics Series, with further resources for all the books in the series.

Exile Classics by Marie-Claire Blais

Coltman, Derek (trans). *A Season in the Life of Emmanuel.*
Toronto: Exile Editions Classics Series, 2008. [Originally
published in French in 1965.]

Dunlop, Carol (trans). *Deaf to the City.*
Toronto: Exile Editions Classics Series, 2006. [Originally
published in French in 1979.]

Ellenwood, Ray (trans). *Nights in the Underground.*
Toronto: Exile Editions Classics Series, 2006. [Originally
published in French in 1978.]

Fischman, Sheila (trans). *Anna's World.*
Toronto: Exile Editions Classics Series, 2009. [Originally
published in French in 1982.]

Fischman, Sheila (trans). *The Wolf.*
Toronto: Exile Editions Classics Series, 2008. [Originally
published in French in 1970.]